IN THE
ORBIT OF
SIRENS

T. A. BRUNO

Cover design by Daniel Schmelling
Interior artwork by Jason Michael Hall

First edition: 2020
In the Orbit of Sirens by T. A. Bruno

Soft Cover: 978-1-7346470-0-6

Hard Cover: 978-1-7346470-1-3

E-Book (MOBI): 978-1-7346470-2-0

E-Book (EPUB): 978-1-7346470-3-7

Audiobook: 978-1-7346470-3-7

To my parents, who hum lullabies.
To my wife, who harmonizes perfectly.
And to our sons, who whistle the tunes we pass on to them.

PART 1
VOID and VESSEL

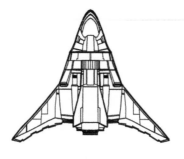

ONE

PRESENT DAY

"FOLLOW ME," ELIANA VESTON said, taking measured breaths as she walked through the forest. "It's just through here." She wiped dew away from the soothreader device on her wrist, watching the satellite image display their location in the space above her gloved hand. The air hissed inside the helmet of her atmospheric suit as she breathed in the purified oxygen.

Eliana was twenty-six years old, with dark skin and deep-hazel eyes that she kept behind a pair of rectangular glasses with burgundy rims. She'd always thought glasses were "cool," because her father wore them, and she'd decided to stick with them even though contacts and corrective eye surgery were readily available. Her short ebony hair was pulled over the right side of her face in twisted locks that rested comfortably under her helmet.

"We must be getting close," her father, John, said over the communication channel that linked their helmets. "I remember some of these trees." He patted the white trunk of a tree that had curving branches terminating in crimson leaves. Blue veins of light pulsed up through the bark, waves of gently flowing energy pulled straight from the interior of the planet itself.

John didn't wear his black-rimmed glasses because he thought they were stylish; he wore them because corrective eye surgery scared the Hells out of him. He had a hard-edged face and short black hair, the wrinkles on his brow gained from years as the lead engineer on the Telemachus Project.

"Let's hope they have what we need," George Tanaka said, then huffed. "I'm getting too old for this stuff. If we've hiked this far for nothing, I think I'll just lie down and let nature take me."

George laughed and leaned against a tree for a moment. He was of Japanese descent, although he, like the others, had never actually been to Earth. His hair was completely gray now, but it had been less so before the long journey to this planet.

"Do you need me to carry you?" Captain Roelin Raike asked, masked by the reflective visor of his combat suit. He was taller than the others, and the suit made him even more so. It was covered in thrusters, referred to as a "jump-jet," that allowed him to move around a battlefield at a faster speed. He had a particle rifle strapped to his back, and a collider pistol hung at his hip. Roelin had been a war hero back in the Sol System, but today he was escorting a group of scouts.

"Would you actually do it if I said yes?" George asked.

Roelin shrugged.

"There!" Eliana scurried over some boulders ahead.

"Elly, wait!" John said over the comm channel, but it fell on deaf ears as his daughter vanished from view behind the rocks.

Eliana stood at the edge of a clearing bursting with glowing blue flowers. The petals glistened in the fading sunlight, becoming more incandescent as the sun sank further behind the horizon line of crimson trees. As she stepped into the field, small alien creatures wriggled their way into the cover of the forest.

"Let's see what you're made of," Eliana whispered to the flowers as she brought her bioscope into her hand and thumbed the button on the side. No light emitted from the cylindrical object, but she could feel soft vibrations on her palm through her glove. After a moment, the vibrating stopped, and a green light flickered on at the back end of the scope. "Give me some good news!" Eliana urged the device.

She didn't turn to see John, George, and Roelin scrambling into the clearing, focused entirely on the readout the bioscope had transmitted to her wrist-mounted soothreader. Her excitement faded when the soothreader stated, *Failed Synthesis*, then rattled off the other potential uses for the flowers, such as in allergy medicine.

"Does us no good if we can't breathe the air without dying." Eliana sighed. "Thanks anyway, Homer," she told the artificial intelligence that lived inside all their technology.

Homer was brought to life by the Telemachus Project, an endeavor led by John Veston. It was almost like a step-brother to Eliana. Homer was designed to help humanity find a new home in the stars, compiling all the known information and star data people had gathered throughout history and taking its best guess. Homer worked—this moment was proof of that.

"It was a long shot anyway," Eliana said into the comm channel as she put the bioscope away. "I just thought we'd get lucky—these flowers haven't bloomed for us until now. Sorry to drag you out here for nothing." She looked toward the others.

They were frozen still, save for Roelin, who was slowly lifting his particle rifle toward Eliana. For a moment, she thought he was aiming at her, but then she followed the invisible path his rifle was tracing over her shoulder.

At the other end of the clearing, behind Eliana, stood a figure. The creature had the features of a large bird but stood like a man. It had red and white feathers and a sharp black beak with ice-blue eyes. Long ears protruded from the sides of its head and twitched as they listened for any sudden movements. The bird-man was adorned in colorful sashes lined with glistening gemstones that rattled and twinkled in the setting sun. Two wings spread outward from its shoulder blades, making the bird-man look even more imposing. In one claw, it clenched the limp body of a small, monkey-like creature. In its other hand, it held a long staff topped with a sharp metal hook.

Eliana found herself paralyzed. Her muscles insisted she run, and she could almost feel her body dashing toward her father, but they remained stones under her skin. Sweat began to bead on her forehead, enough so that her helmet detected it and quickly wiped the moisture away with a small sponge.

"Don't. Move," Roelin said in a measured tone into the comm channel.

The bird-man dropped the limp creature it was holding, the dead weight shaking the bright flowers as it thudded to the dirt below. It was clear the bird-man wasn't some wild animal. It was clothed and carrying a tool or weapon, and it showed signs of intelligence.

"No ..." the bird-man said with a grunt, and there was a reflexive gasp from the colonist observers, "shoot ..."

Dumbfounded, Eliana mustered up her courage and asked, "You ... speak our language?" She shook her head, trying to understand. "*How* is that possible?"

The bird-man let out a low caw and turned its open palm toward Eliana, keeping it flat. She took this as a sign of peace, but she couldn't be entirely sure. She thought to herself, *If it would drop its weapon, I'd feel safer.*

The bird-man dropped its hooked staff into the flowers.

Can he read my thoughts? Eliana found herself wondering. She noticed something in the creature's eyes that told her it might be possible.

Eliana almost jumped out of her atmospheric suit as her father approached from the side and asked, "You have been watching us. Haven't you?"

The bird-man cooed.

Is that a yes? Eliana wondered

"Do you know what we are, where we come from?" John asked.

The bird-man took a moment to respond, possibly trying to

understand the words John was saying. *Or perhaps,* Eliana thought, *trying to understand the thoughts he was thinking.* She decided to try something.

"We are humans," Eliana said, and brought a hand to her chest. The bird-man seemed to light up at this. It straightened itself and brought a hand to its chest in return.

"Auk'nai," it said.

"Great work, Elly," John whispered with a smile. Eliana felt like she was getting the hang of this.

"Mag'Ro," it said, and spread its hand outward. Eliana thought the bird-man was saying something about peace or, *It's sure nice to meet you,* and was about to respond when the auk'nai shook its beaked head and reiterated, "Auk'nai," then brought its hand back toward its chest and said, "Mag'Ro."

"I'm not sure I—" John began.

"It's his name." Eliana nodded, then put her hand on her chest again and said, "My name is Eliana."

Mag'Ro cooed, and his feathers rustled on his neck.

"I think you got it there," John said, and then put a hand on his chest and introduced himself. Mag'Ro pattered his feet and cooed again as each of the humans presented their names. He let out a loud birdcall, collected his hook and his kill, knelt down, then sprang into the air, pulling up glowing flower petals into the sky as he vanished into the sunset.

"That was amazing!" John said. "We need to get back to the colony and tell everyone about this." He patted Eliana on the shoulder. "First contact with the natives."

"They're beautiful," Eliana said, still looking toward the sky.

George let out a loud laugh. "We found it!"

Eliana and John turned toward George and Roelin to see the words *Partial Synthesis Success* floating above George's soothreader.

"What? How?" John asked.

"The minerals on Mag'Ro's sashes," George said. "While you two were chatting, I scanned him up and down with my bioscope.

It's not a complete synthesis, but if we can figure out where they got those gems, we might be able to develop a cure for lung-lock."

"Do you think they will tell us?" John asked.

"We'll have to convince them," Roelin said as he silently scanned the perimeter for any more surprises in the trees.

"Either way, this is fantastic news," Eliana said. The three scientists celebrated and congratulated each other as Roelin looked at the setting sun.

"Alright, time to head back. We don't want to be out here after dark," Roelin said, slinging his particle rifle back over his shoulder. The others agreed, and they began to hike back toward the colony.

This was Eliana's life now. Exploring the planet Kamaria for the betterment of Odysseus Colony. Kamaria orbited a star similar to Sol, in a Goldilocks Zone, with all the essential elements humans needed to survive. It was Earth-like, but different from Earth in a lot of ways. The mountains had arches that laced outward like the rib cage of a dead giant. The grass was wavy and amber colored, hiding creatures that were waiting to be named and categorized by the human invaders. The rivers flickered with a full spectrum of color as if God had spilled his whole collection of paints into them.

Kamaria was heaven—if it weren't for the airborne bacteria that caused human lungs to immediately cease functioning.

They had named the affliction "lung-lock." More colonists fell victim to the deadly bacteria the longer they remained on the planet. The previous week, a family of four had perished to lung-lock, slipping away in their sleep as the bacteria crept into their rooms through a faulty window seal. The journey to Kamaria took three hundred years of space travel; while the humans on board were preserved in stasis beds, time had worn down some of the equipment they'd brought with them.

Lung-lock would need to be solved, and that was what made the Scout Program so vital. The chemists back at the colony had gotten as far as current human science would allow, but the final pieces of the puzzle had to be somewhere out in the alien wilderness.

"Always a welcome sight," George said with a sigh. They had hiked back through the crimson forest and could now see Odysseus Colony in the valley ahead.

Two hundred and fifty people lived there. The interstellar spacecraft that was also the colony's namesake stood like a skyscraper at the edge of the territory. Glass domes pocked a once-grassy meadow, with tube walkways connecting each in a honeycomb pattern. These domed areas were used for research, meetings, construction, agriculture, and recreation. Some of the taller, more rectangular buildings housed the colonists, and there was extra empty space for more to fill as the colony grew and more buildings were constructed. A refinery sat atop a hill and spewed smoke into the otherwise clear night sky. A water-reclamation plant greedily sucked in water from the rainbow-hued river.

Eight starships rested in the shipyard, mostly unused except for exploration. In the past, these ships had fought wars in space and traveled to all the worlds of the Sol System, as they were not equipped to fly to distant stars like the unique engines of the interstellar vessels the *Odysseus* and the *Telemachus*.

"Five years left," John stated. "Let's hope it's enough time."

The *Telemachus* was already in transit; it had departed half a decade after the *Odysseus* had begun its journey. It was bringing with it ten thousand more colonists, people who needed to breathe air and live in purified homes. Lung-lock had to be cured before they arrived, or else the casualties were going to start rising.

"We can do it," Eliana said. "We have to."

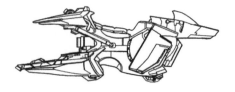

TWO

THREE HUNDRED YEARS AGO

DENTON CASTUS WAS DOING his best to ignore the apocalypse, but it was getting harder every day. There was a constant bombardment of news feed images of the Undriel, the nightmarish machines that were taking over the Sol System one planet at a time. Soon they would be on Ganymede, Jupiter's largest moon, and Denton's front door.

In his efforts to remain blissfully unaware of the End of Days, Denton focused on what he did best: manual labor. For months, he accepted any job, big or small, that came into his family's shop. His parents were proud, and his brothers were excited to have less work, but Denton didn't feel anything toward the jobs. Working was all he knew how to do, and when he stopped doing it for any amount of time, he started wondering about things, which felt much worse.

This day was like the others; there was work to be done. Denton thumbed a button on his atmospheric suit's forearm, and a small sponge wiped his brow inside his dusty helmet. The broken antenna Denton was repairing was almost finished, and probably would have been completed already if his brothers shared the same anxious energy he was venting out. Ignoring work, Jason and Tyler chose to take turns racing their rushcycle instead.

The surface of Ganymede was made up of rocky crags and icy lakes, mostly gray except where Jupiter's immense red-orange glow was reflected. During the thirty Earth Standard years of Denton's life, he had never felt the cold on his bare skin—anyone who did was dead within seconds. He had never sniffed the fresh air, because there was none to sniff. He had never felt the ground with the soles of his feet because his work boots were always tightly fastened. Even with the barrier between Denton and his homeworld, it was *his home* all the same. He grimaced at the thought of what the Undriel might do to it.

There was a plan to escape, but only a few knew the details, and Denton wasn't in that group. The average citizen remaining in the Sol System only knew that there was an interstellar starship named the *Telemachus* and that it was going to be their life raft. No one knew where the ship was hiding or where it was going to take them; the secrets were maintained to protect the *Telemachus* from the Undriel. When the time came to leave, each colony would get a call from the *Telemachus* with coordinates, and then it was up to the colonists to rendezvous with the ship before it made its escape. If they missed the boat, the Undriel would be happy to absorb them instead.

In Denton's mind, the call was coming any day now.

In reality, the call had come an hour ago. And he'd missed it.

"Almost done here," Denton said to his brothers through his helmet's communication channel. He stood up and stretched his back, twisting his right arm in a circular motion. Denton's work site was on top of a large rock outcropping over the ice lake. Below him, on the frozen surface of the lake, his brothers Jason and Tyler took turns revving the rushcycle and taking a lap around the perimeter of the work area. A beat-up old hover truck was parked at the base of the work site, full of extra equipment should Denton need it.

"I'm sure the haulers will be glad to hear that," Jason said as he mounted the hovering motorcycle and got comfortable. The ice haulers refused to work without the antenna functioning, concerned they would miss the rendezvous call from the *Telemachus*. Denton shared the same concern, but being a Castus meant you didn't get to worry about things like that when something needed repair.

The Castus Machine Shop was popular in the Arrow of Hope Colony. Denton lived above the shop with his brothers, his parents, and the memories of his grandparents, which reminded him of the family legacy that existed in the dust on the shelves and the scrapes on the workbenches.

Jason revved the rushcycle and zipped off across the ice, kicking up a string of jagged ice chunks. Tyler watched his wrist-mounted soothreader, eyeing the time it took his brother to complete the lap. Denton shook his head and bent down to finish welding the last piece of the antenna in place.

"You just had to do it, didn't ya?" Tyler said as Jason chuckled into the comm channel. "You couldn't let me keep the record for fastest time."

"Face it, the bike just loves me more," Jason said, spreading his arms out to his sides as the rushcycle drifted to a stop.

"Well, Mom and Dad love me more," Tyler said as he lifted himself onto the flatbed of the hover truck. He waved Jason forward. "Go ahead, do another lap, show me what I gotta beat."

With a tilt of his helmet, Jason zipped off again, ice chunks drifting in the low gravity of his wake. Denton finished his weld and activated the antenna. There was a low hum as the machinery warmed up, and the data screen at its base displayed a loading icon. Denton clapped his gloves together and turned toward Jupiter. The layers of gas swirled on the planet's surface, like oil and water. It was easy to get lost in the red-orange spectacle, especially when Jupiter encompassed the entire horizon.

Denton could see his home colony from his perch on the rock outcrop. The Arrow of Hope was the only colony on Ganymede, and it looked like a pimple on an otherwise desolate landscape. The Arrow was the broken promise of bigger things for Ganymede. The Sol Terra Program had cut funding to the moon in favor of more profitable prospects such as Callisto, Io, and Europa.

Colonists of the Arrow lived together in large dwellings, some of which housed up to three generations of hopeful citizens. The Castus family lived on the upper floor of their own shop, which some would have considered a luxury for its slightly larger size when compared to a normal dwelling, but Denton never thought of it that way. It felt like he was sharing a sleeping bag with his whole family.

A trail of light sailed upward into the stars from the Arrow, followed by another, then another. Denton activated the binoculars on his helmet and watched as starships exited the colony en masse. Flashes of light indicated they were entering ultra-thrust.

"You guys seeing this?" Denton asked his brothers.

"Yeah, sure," Tyler said, looking toward Jason as he finished another lap on the rushcycle. "Wasn't better than the last run, though."

"Not that," Denton spat the words out. "Over there!"

Denton pointed toward the Arrow, and his brothers snapped their attention in that direction. They all flinched as an explosion blinked in the area near the fleeing starships. More explosions followed, creating an unusual glimmering effect in the stars.

"You don't think—" Jason was interrupted as the communication antenna finished warming up and blinked green. Denton's soothreader pinged with several notifications, followed quickly by Jason and Tyler's soothreaders adding to the symphony of alerts.

"Time to go!" Denton shouted, and slid down the rocks toward his brothers. Jason revved the rushcycle again as Denton jumped into the driver's seat of the hover truck. Tyler held on tightly to the truck bed. The brothers raced toward the Arrow.

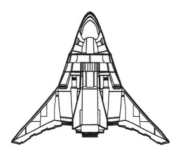

THREE

PRESENT DAY

WINTER CAME TO ODYSSEUS Colony, covering the amber grass with ivory snow. Eliana stood in the graveyard once again, surrounded by fellow colonists. They each wore their civilian atmospheric suits with a black sash over the left shoulder pad. They looked like statues of astronauts, standing still as snowflakes drifted over them while they bowed their heads over four freshly covered graves.

The holographic tombstones were the footnote to another family that had fallen victim to lung-lock. This was not the first time they had gathered in this forest clearing; it was happening often enough to feel routine.

Funerals reminded Eliana of her mother. Amaryllis Veston had succumbed to a malignant astrocytoma in her brain when Eliana was very young. She often thought of her mother as she was falling asleep, looping the only memory she retained of her.

"Follow the wind, that blows the dust ..." Amaryllis sang a Martian lullaby. Eliana remembered the slow movements of the rocking chair, the creak it made as it ended one sway to begin another.

"To a place I found, just for us ... " Her mother's breath tickled at her curly black hair, but she didn't mind. She just felt relaxed the way a four-year-old could. There were no worries, no obligations to see to, no appointments to make. Just the sway of the chair, back and forth.

"So far away, yet also near ... " She remembered her mother's face, so beautiful, so young. Her dark-brown skin was soft and warm. The gentle caress of her hand eased her into sleep.

"You'll know it then, 'cuz I'll be here ... " And then the memory ended as Eliana drifted off to sleep.

With this memory, Eliana carried her mother's spirit with her across the stars.

Eliana, John, George, and the lead chemist of Odysseus Colony, Marie Viray, stood motionless as the crowd in the graveyard dissipated. Marie was an older Filipina woman with short gray hair and wrinkles obtained from a life of love and laughter. On this day, she faced the tombs solemnly, their existence an accusation.

Eliana looked over to the chemist. The Madani Cure, as it was to be named after the first family to have perished from lung-lock, still eluded Marie's team. Over forty people had died since then, and more lives were at risk every day. It was a heavy weight for her team, and it was only getting heavier. Eliana sniffled, wishing she could wipe her nose through her helmet.

Marie stared down at the fresh dirt that sat on the bodies of the victims. George placed his hand on her shoulder, only to have her shake him off. She held her arms weakly together, hugging herself.

Eliana said, "It's not your fault."

"I failed these people." Marie spoke in broken sentences, as if her lungs were struggling to push the words through her lips. "Every day that goes by with no cure is my failure."

The scout team had been like a surrogate family for Eliana ever since the early days of the Telemachus Project on Mars. She had seen these people accomplish feats that made all of human history blush in their majesty. But right now, Eliana was seeing the team's spirits at their lowest.

A silence that the dead could appreciate hung over the graveyard. Snow slowly drifted from the Kamarian sky, evaporating against the heated atmospheric suits of the mourning colonists.

"This isn't right. That's not the Marie I know." George broke the silence and stepped in front of her, the visor of his atmospheric helmet pressed against hers. "This is the planet's challenge to you. Kamaria's angry because we came here uninvited. We defied physics and the cosmos itself to trample her rosebushes and walk through her house with our boots on. She isn't going to give us what we need. But the Marie I know doesn't let that stop her. The Marie I know doesn't give up."

"George, it's just—" Marie was interrupted when George put his hands on her shoulders as if he were going to shake some sense into her.

"It's a challenge, and a worthy one. If you give up now, that will be your only failure."

Marie closed her lips and nodded as she blinked a tear back into her eye. She removed George's gloved hands from her shoulders.

"You're right," Marie said, mustering all her strength. "I knew I kept you around for a reason."

George laughed. "There she is. We've been waiting for you."

Marie looked each of them the eye, then led them out of the graveyard.

The graveyard was a short ride away from colony central on a flat, hovering platform called a ground sail. Access to outside the colony walls was only granted in specific circumstances, such as for scouting business, sample retrieval, and cemetery visitation.

The group made it back into the domes of the colony and removed their atmospheric suits. Eliana stuffed her helmet and suit into a container on the wall, where Homer vacuum-sealed it and pulled it into a storage area. Her equipment would be ready for her no matter which exit she used, thanks to a transportation system built into the inner workings of the domes and tunnels themselves.

Eliana stepped out of the prep room and into the dome, which was known as Central Park. It was a place for recreation and had been designed to soothe the homesick feeling of leaving Sol behind. The grass was green, along with the leaves on the artificial trees that dotted the hilly area. The glass dome above her was wet with moisture from the slowly falling Kamarian snow, which was unable to make purchase due to the residual heat of the glass.

Although the dome was filled with breathable air, some concerned citizens insisted on wearing atmospheric suits at all times, scared that a room's purifier would malfunction, and lung-lock would take them. Eliana held the same concerns in the back of her mind, but she refused to live in constant fear. Seeing children playing inside the domes in complete atmospheric suits motivated her to keep searching for the cure.

"Let's take the scenic route," Eliana suggested to the others. "Maybe it will give us some inspiration."

They agreed, and Marie led the group through the botanical garden of the park dome. Earth flowers were intricately on display, with some hanging from the ceilings in spiral casings. It was an explosion of blues, purples, magentas, and yellows, with green interlacing the entire show.

Eliana found herself thinking of the auk'nai they had met months ago. Mag'Ro's vibrant feathers would blend right in with the botanical garden that surrounded her. Since that day, they had not seen any sign of him. The colonists' hope that Mag'Ro would lead them to the minerals that contained the cure for lung-lock was beginning to wane. Perhaps the auk'nai did not deem humanity worthy of speaking to, figuring that if they waited long enough, there wouldn't be any humans left to talk to.

Eliana followed the others into the dome dedicated to the Scout Program. It was located near the shipyard for easy access to a quarantine laboratory that sat five kilometers outside the colony walls. It was a temporary setup, as construction was underway on an actual scout pavilion near the quarantine lab, but it was functional.

A rectangular holographic table rested against the back wall of the room, with a data screen directly above to display anything they needed. Stations designated to chemistry, biology, botanical research, and geology lined the perimeter of the room.

A woman with tanned skin, short black hair, and exotic yellow eyes approached Eliana from the geology station. "Hey, guys," she addressed the team as they entered. "Come check out this satellite image. It's got some interesting things going on."

"Interesting bad or interesting good?" Eliana asked.

Faye Raike, lead geologist of the Scout Program and wife to Captain Roelin Raike, had not always been a scientist. In the past, she had fought the Undriel in space from the cockpit of a Matador-class starfighter, a combat ship shaped like an old Earth jet known for its high maneuverability. She had met her husband during the war, but where Roelin remained the strong, silent type, Faye had never let the vocation dictate her sense of humor.

"Hey, you're the smart ones. You tell me," Faye said. She joined them near the holographic table as the other scouts observed the data.

John spoke to the one entity who was not personally in the room: "Homer, what exactly is this?"

The satellite data displayed a top-down view of an area shrouded in dead trees. The twisted branches obscured a lot of the picture, but what was visible through the decay was the strange part.

They appeared to be large circular platforms, each about the size of a colony dome, with odd-looking structures stacked on top.

"An auk'nai city?" Eliana asked.

"It is likely," the gentle robotic voice of Homer said through a speaker in the table, "but I am not detecting any vital signatures in the area."

"You think maybe it's been abandoned?" George asked.

"Possibly. I am also detecting an anomalous bacteria," Homer said. "It matches no records from Sol history. I can't be sure if a full synthesis is possible at this time."

"Is there a chance the bacteria is messing with the life reading?" Marie asked.

"I am unsure. There was no movement detected, which aids the readings."

"No movement at all?" George asked. "Not even minor creatures, like a mouse or a blue jay?"

"Nothing."

"See," Faye whispered to Eliana, "I said interesting, didn't I?"

Eliana nodded, then said, "Maybe the area is toxic. Or maybe even something like a nuclear meltdown occurred there."

"Our suits would protect us from anything like that," Captain Roelin Raike said. Eliana had not seen him come in. Roelin stood next to Faye, a few heads taller than her. He had a short, military-style haircut and deep-brown eyes. He was muscular from years of combat and training.

"This is it! Don't you see?" George said, his face lighting up. "We don't need to wait for Mag'Ro to return. If this is an abandoned auk'nai city, I'm sure we can find some of the minerals we need to complete the synthesis for the lung-lock cure."

"We'll have to be extra careful with this bacteria," John said, his hand on his chin as he weighed all the variables. "If it's radioactive, we'll have to keep any samples we get in the quarantine lab."

"It's worth the risk," Marie said. "We have to try."

Everyone in the room nodded in silent agreement.

"Then it's settled," John said. "I'll inform the council. We'll leave tomorrow morning."

Eliana looked at the satellite image once more. Something about the tangled dead branches and the silent city below them made her skin crawl.

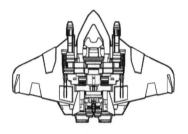

FOUR

THREE HUNDRED YEARS AGO

THE CASTUS BROTHERS SPED across the ice lakes of Ganymede toward the Arrow of Hope Colony. With the Undriel in high orbit above Ganymede, the colonists were forced to scramble. Hundreds of ships were breaking into orbit, abandoning the Arrow and making their way to the *Telemachus* rendezvous point. Many were caught in the crossfire between human defense forces and Undriel battlecraft. The bright flashes overhead grew more extensive and more violent, reflecting off the ice as the brothers closed the distance to their home.

"They are going to leave without us!" Tyler shouted.

The gateway to the colony was just ahead. It was open, leaving only the glossy, transparent encasement barrier between the colony and the harshness of Ganymede's atmosphere. The heat that filled the colony and made it livable blasted the brothers on the way through the barrier, melting any stray ice particles that came in with their suits.

The streets of the Arrow were empty except for the loose litter that rattled around on the roadway as they sped past. A dome surrounded the entirety of the district their family shop was located in, and lights danced on the glass, reflected from the battle in the stars. It was much like Christmas lights flickering in an abandoned mall. The dull booms of ships entering ultra-thrust echoed off the walls of the dome.

"Please be there, please be there," Tyler worriedly muttered into their comm channel as they turned the last corner to get to the family shop.

The shop was twice the size of the standard buildings in this district, with a large garage taking up half of the floor plan. Their family apartment was on the upper floor, as it had been for generations. A balcony their grandfather had constructed protruded from the front, serving as an excellent place to watch Jupiter swirl while having a beer. A sign hung from the front of the balcony that read, "Castus Machine Shop, circa 2280." The interior shop lights were still on, beckoning those with repair needs to stop in and allow the family to help—for credits, of course.

They came to a screeching stop in front of the shop's garage as the battle above cast multicolored lights onto the small colony town. Jason pinged the garage open with his soothreader, and the large door rose slowly, revealing their father, Michael Castus. He was in his mid-fifties, with a grizzled brown beard and short messy hair peppered with areas of gray from years of hard work. Michael had his atmospheric suit on and was lifting his helmet toward his head when he noticed them.

"About time!" Michael shouted. He pointed at their family ship, the *Lelantos*. "Get yer asses on board! I was about to go out there to get you idiots." His classic Ganymede accent always surfaced when he was angry.

The *Lelantos* was a prototype that his grandfather had hoped to use to lure in clients, but none had ever taken the bait. It was shaped like a midnight-blue manta ray, with large, flat wings on each side that widened where they met in the middle.

To ward off pirates, the *Lelantos* was equipped with a turret-mounted magnetic repeater, a gun that used magnetic material as ammo to pierce enemy hulls. It had never been fired. Two large-barreled mining lasers at the base of each wing represented the drilling capabilities of the *Lelantos*, and in a pinch, might be used for defense.

Denton and Tyler left the truck on the street and ran inside as Jason piloted the rushcycle up the ramp and into the cargo hold of the *Lelantos*. The inside was cluttered with workbenches and crates of items they were bringing to the *Telemachus*: tools, materials, food, and clothing. The brothers removed their helmets.

Denton, the youngest of the three brothers at thirty Earth Standard years old, had light-brown hair, pale skin, and green eyes like his mother. His hair was never tidy, always tussled about in a mess. Jason, the oldest, was hairless except for his eyebrows and a tuft of beard that jutted out from his chin. Tyler, the middle brother, had the longest hair of the three, which he kept tied up in a bun under his helmet.

"Get in your seats, we're leavin' now!" Michael shouted, and stepped up the ramp, closing it behind him with his soothreader. He and the boys entered the bridge of the *Lelantos*, where their mother, Brynn Castus, stood facing them.

Her brow was squeezed upward in the middle of her forehead, and a long sigh escaped her as her sons entered. She was just past fifty, her chestnut-colored hair cut just above her shoulders. The atmospheric suit she was wearing had its history pocked on its exterior in scrapes and old stains.

"Boys!" Brynn grabbed her sons and gave them a big squeeze, followed by a slap on the back of each of their heads. "That damn rushcycle again, at a time like this? We called a thousand times!" Before Jason could say anything, he was interrupted by the sound of their neighbor's family spaceship blasting off.

"Looks like Bill Herman's hightailing it!" Tyler said, watching the ship slip past the upper dome encasement barrier.

"Strap in!" ordered Michael. "I'll be damned if the Hermans make it to the *Telemachus* and we don't." Michael and Brynn took their places up front, going through the remainder of the preflight checklist as quickly as possible. Denton and his brothers took the seats behind them. The engines of the *Lelantos* roared to life, knocking over anything that had been discarded behind the ship during the rush.

"We're ready!" Brynn said. Michael held his hand on the throttle and grimaced.

Denton knew what was going through his father's mind, because it was going through his as well. They looked back at the shop one last time.

The inside was scrambled, but then again, it had never been very orderly. The Castus family had brought everything they could fit onto the ship, leaving most of the shelves bare. Permanent workstations, unlike their hover mules, would remain here, bolted to the floor. Denton remembered his grandfather fixing various mechanical doodads and gizmos on the station in the back of the garage. He thought he could even see him now, watching them prepare to leave, wondering how they could go when there was still work to be done.

"Hey! *Dad!* Did you forget something?" Jason asked. "Like, maybe the damn apocalypse outside?"

Michael inhaled sharply. "Sorry. Let's get out of here!" He slammed the throttle forward as the rear hangar door of the garage opened. The engines boomed, and they rocketed through.

Denton felt his whole body jerk backward into his seat as the ship launched. The *Lelantos* rapidly ascended toward the upper dome. He looked out the window to see that the colony still had the lights on.

In his mind, Denton said goodbye to the Arrow. He thought of his grandfather, his childhood friends, ex-girlfriends, ditching school to race rushcycles, and the trials of his teenage years. He was rocketing away from it all, but he was leaving part of his heart there on the rocky ice moon.

The ever-changing lights of the space battle explosions dancing over the site gave it an eerie glow. They jolted in their seats as Michael swerved out of the way of spaceship wreckage.

"Get ready for the boom!" Michael shouted, and punched the ultra-thrust. The *Lelantos* rattled violently as it entered its hyper-cruise speed. After a few moments adjusting to ultra-thrust, the rattling stopped.

"We should be safe now," Brynn said. She gripped Michael's hand in hers and squeezed. "We just have to make it to the *Telemachus*. They will take care of us."

"Hey, did anything fall off?" Tyler asked.

"Fall off? Why would anything fall off?" Brynn asked, her question laced with suspicion.

"Last time we—" Tyler began.

"No reason." Denton punched Tyler's arm and mouthed the words, *"Shut up!"*

"Coming out of ultra-thrust in *Telemachus*'s proximity," Michael said, then looked back over his shoulder at his sons before hitting the button. "Fully *in-tact*. With nothing missin'. Or so help me *God*."

Tyler laughed nervously in his seat. Michael pressed the button, and the *Lelantos* faded back into standard thrust.

"Oh no, here too?" Denton said.

The Undriel were everywhere, not just in Ganymede's orbit. Explosions sent debris rattling against the hull. Denton assumed the Undriel were also battling near Callisto, Io, and Europa. The actual size of the Undriel force was unknown, but the picture this reality painted was horrifying.

"Telemachus Proper, this is *Lelantos*, ready for rendezvous," Michael said as formally as he could. Denton found it unsettling.

"*Lelantos*, this is Telemachus Proper. Follow these coordinates to the rendezvous point," a gruff voice responded over the communication channel with the signature *T-Proper* displaying on the windscreen HUD in front of Michael.

"Ah shit," Michael said, watching his holographic display take their route straight through the thick of the battle before them.

Michael looked at Brynn, his brow pushed upward, a slight dampness beginning to form there. She responded with a curt nod and looked back at their sons.

"We need a marksman," Brynn said. Her brow furrowed as she looked each of the brothers in the eye.

"Got it!" Jason said.

"Will do!" Tyler shouted.

"Yep," Denton said.

They each clicked a command button on their armrest in unison, resulting in a red error light flashing.

"We got *one* damn gun! Pick one of you, and get to it," Michael commanded.

"Rock, paper, scissors?" Tyler suggested.

"Best three out of five," Jason said, and readied his hands. Tyler followed suit. They waited for Denton to bring his hands forward to begin the countdown, but instead, he thumbed the button on his seat. A joystick rotated toward him from behind his chair, and a visor popped its way out of the headrest.

"Dirty trick!" Tyler said.

"You want to make it there alive, don't you?" Denton said as he put the visor over his head. It gave him a view from the perspective of the magnetic repeater turret on the top of the ship, and the joystick allowed him to rotate the gun and shoot.

"Here we go!" Michael said, and throttled forward into the fray.

They entered the battle as if walking into the ocean and being hit with a powerful wave. Debris from ally and Undriel craft drifted and spiraled in the void, and lasers lanced through space, sending deadly splashes of light across the hulls of the combatants' ships. The headless body of a man who had been ejected from his spacecraft during the fight drifted by Denton's turret-gun view. He didn't have time to think about the man; he needed to stay alert or his family would end up joining him.

Denton's holographic display labeled friendly combatants, taking the guesswork out of who to shoot. It didn't take long for the

Undriel to notice the *Lelantos*—two battlecraft split off from their formation to head off the Castus family.

"Here they come!" Denton warned.

Denton had never seen an Undriel battlecraft up close. It was a nightmare of machinery. A hulking mass of metal in an impossible shape. When the Undriel absorbed a victim, they replaced all non-essential parts with mechanical elements. The result was usually a rotting human head encased in a robotic, spider-like frame, or at least that was what any autopsies on fallen Undriel foot soldiers had yielded. In this case, the absorbed human had been converted into a spaceship, forced to watch their own body work against them as a weapon of genocide. It moved unnaturally, seeming to defy physics.

Michael rolled the *Lelantos* to the left, narrowly dodging the body of the battlecraft. They were pushed into the backs of their seats with the force of the spin.

"Too close!" Michael huffed, and steadied the ship in time to see an allied vessel plummet past their bow. He quickly jerked the *Lelantos* out of the way to avoid a collision with the ship, watching through a rearview display as the Undriel battlecraft smashed its way through it, sending fire and debris sailing into space.

"They aren't even trying to shoot! They can just ram us," Jason said.

Denton had a better vantage point through his holographic visor, but he could see two pieces fall off the battlecraft and become their own small ships with arms and tendrils. These small ships hurriedly searched the wrecked ship and plucked a person from its mess. Denton's face went ghost white as he watched the Undriel searchers clip the heads from the space suits and scurry away.

They were collecting their heads, not even bothering with the non-essential, meaty appendages.

Denton had seen enough. He squeezed the trigger on the joystick and sent a round of supercharged magnetic bullets into the battlecraft that chased the *Lelantos*. The front of the Undriel ship splintered and burst with electrical violence, but it did not halt its pursuit.

"Get under it," Denton urged.

"Roger that," Michael said. He pushed his flight stick forward and cut the thrust. The *Lelantos* dropped speed fast enough that the Undriel had no time to react. As the battlecraft passed over the top of the *Lelantos*, Denton unloaded a full clip into its underside. Pocks of small explosions and metal boiled off the ship. The family watched as the Undriel sailed over them and began to turn around.

The battlecraft made it halfway into its turn before the front end burst. More explosions followed as a chain reaction was set off inside the ship. The family whooped and hollered.

"Good shoot'n, Denny," Brynn said.

"You know she's required to say that as our mom," Jason said, looking over his shoulder at Denton.

Another Undriel craft began shooting at the *Lelantos* from the front. Michael pitched the ship sideways but wasn't fast enough to escape a few blasts.

"*Ah crap.* Impact!" Michael shouted. The family shook in their seats as the hull of the *Lelantos* took a glancing hit.

"I need a reload," Denton said.

"On it," replied Jason.

"Wait, you don't want to rock, paper, scissors for it?" Tyler jested as he groaned nervously. His face was a shade greener than usual.

Jason ignored him and unlatched himself from his seat. He floated toward a station on the starboard side of the ship, unhinged the latch, and grabbed a large roll of ammo. The compartment on the wall opened, and he slammed the cylindrical roll inside. Denton's visor informed him the gun had been reloaded.

It was an outdated process. Many early battles with the Undriel had gone on for so long that they were lost when the human defenses ran out of ammunition. After the fall of Earth, scientists had reverse-engineered Undriel particle-collider technology. With collider tech, reloading was unnecessary, as the collider cylinders could pull particles from the surrounding area and smash them together to create ammunition instantaneously.

The Castus family had collider pistols that the Telemachus Project handed out, but they'd never updated the turret on the *Lelantos*. They fought a high-tech enemy with low-tech weapons, a club in a gunfight.

"Bring it!" Denton shouted as he squeezed the trigger. The Undriel battlecraft rushed toward the *Lelantos*. It was a game of chicken that the battlecraft was designed to win.

"Rolling!" Michael shouted, and jerked the flight stick to the left. The Undriel scraped the bottom of the *Lelantos* as it passed by. They felt the ship bounce from the impact. Denton saw sparks fly as the battlecraft rocketed past; some debris from the *Lelantos*'s undercarriage followed.

Denton waited for the barrel roll to end, then tracked the battlecraft with the turret. He let out more magnetic ammo as the Undriel pivoted to chase them once more. Instead of attempting to ram the *Lelantos* again, the pursuing craft began to shoot.

"This guy behind us won't die!" Jason shook his head in frustration.

"He's tryin' to clip our wings," Denton alerted Michael. Lasers whipped passed the windscreen as Michael used all his tricks to keep his family safe.

"Everyone get ready for a somersault!" yelled Michael, and then pulled back on his flight stick. The whole ship pitched into a 180-degree flip. The Undriel attempted to track the *Lelantos* but couldn't get a shot on target.

Denton targeted the areas where the lasers were coming from with his turret, sending magnetic bullets smashing into the battlecraft. The enemy ship shook violently, rotating as one explosion rocked it one way, then rolling again as another sent it spiraling to death in space.

"That's right!" Michael whooped and laughed.

"Need another reload!" Denton said as he high-fived Tyler.

"Too bad!" Jason shouted.

"What?" Denton asked.

"We ain't got any more ammo."

There was a short silence.

"Well, *shit*," said Tyler.

"Three! Portside," Brynn warned.

"Oh, just perfect," Michael said, pitching the *Lelantos* to the starboard side.

The three oncoming enemy ships began returning fire. Lasers cracked on the outer hull, rocking the interior. Sensing the advantage, one of the vessels began to thrust toward them at ramming speed.

"*Lelantos*, heads-up," a gruff male voice called over the comm channel with the signature *K. Steadman* on the HUD windscreen as a massive Undertaker-class warfighter came into view. The hulking warship looked like a charging rhino with cannons strapped to its head. The heavy turret gun atop the ship looked ready to fight the Hells themselves. It was designed specifically to fight the Undriel in space. It launched an assault against all three Undriel ships at once.

The blasts from the Undertaker's massive particle cannons not only destroyed each Undriel ship, but also punched them sideways with tremendous force. A Matador starfighter joined the Undertaker.

"I got them!" a voice with the signature *E. Murphy* spoke over the comm. He launched a missile into another Undriel craft and dodged the resulting explosion with grace.

Michael whooped and hollered with his family. "Thanks! You guys just saved our asses!"

"*Lelantos*, stick tight with me," E. Murphy said. "I'll get you back safe." His Matador split off from the Undertaker and moved toward Jupiter.

"Roger that!" Michael said into the comm.

He piloted the ship to follow E. Murphy's Matador starfighter. Denton noticed something coming over the horizon of Jupiter. He couldn't make out the shape at first, but as it approached at rapid speed, he realized what it must be.

"Oh no," Denton muttered.

The Undriel's masterclass ship, the *Devourer*, loomed ahead. The vessel was legendary, known for turning entire colonies to dust. The flagship had taken Earth and Mars, and was the largest mechanical structure in the known system, at four times the size of the Arrow of Hope colony on Ganymede.

"*Devourer* ahead," E. Murphy said over the comm.

"Got it in my sights," K. Steadman replied.

K. Steadman's Undertaker broke formation and rocketed toward the nightmare ship that threatened the *Telemachus*. There was silence over the comm line as they watched the warship shrink into the distance, looking ant-like next to the giant boot of the Undriel.

"Alright, let's get you folks home safe," E. Murphy said.

The *Devourer* lanced out a massive particle beam that slammed into one of the defending human warships. It crumbled apart like a discarded piece of trash, sending large chunks of white-hot metal and fire bursting into the void around it. The Castus family shielded their eyes from the explosion and electrical shock waves. Denton turned his attention toward movement in the surface clouds of Jupiter.

"Look at *that*!" Denton shouted.

The *Telemachus* breached the outer cloud layer of Jupiter, shedding its pressure-deflection barrier and pulling gaseous orange and red streamers with it as it ascended into orbit. Its engines fired at full throttle, a hot trail of blue light in its wake. The ship was shaped much like an aircraft carrier from old Earth, but one hundred times the size.

"Oh no!" Brynn shouted, her eyes darting back and forth between the massive ships.

The *Devourer* was heading straight for the *Telemachus*.

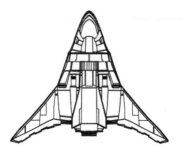

FIVE

PRESENT DAY

"WE HAVE ARRIVED AT the Anomalous Zone, everyone. I'll be here when you need me," said Rocco Gainax, the pilot of the *Rogers*. Pilgrim-class explorer ships like the *Rogers* were the mobile bases for the scout teams. They were arrow-shaped with a white and black hull and equipped with scanners, a quarantine bay, and enough cargo space for all the ground equipment the scouts needed.

Captain Roelin Raike was the first to walk down the ramp of the *Rogers*. He stepped out into the alien wilderness, followed closely by Lance Corporal Allen Jensons—who preferred to be called AJ. Each of the combat marines scanned the perimeter for threats, particle rifles aimed, and slowly drifting along the tree line.

They emerged into an eerily quiet alien forest. The twisting branches of the dead trees reached toward the sky like a witch's twisted, knobby finger. Sunlight entered through the canopy in rays from high up the redwood-size tree trunks. The only sound was a light breeze ruffling through the otherwise dead place.

"All clear," Roelin spoke into the comm channel. The team began piling out of the ship, including the scout captain, John

Veston; the geologist, Faye Raike; the chemist, Marie Viray; the biologist, George Tanaka; and the doctor, Eliana Veston.

"It's a little creepy, right?" Eliana said.

"It is strange. I wonder if the toxicity killed these trees," George said, pulling out his bioscope and scanning the area.

"I've been a lot of places," AJ said, keeping his eyes open and his head on a swivel, "but this place feels wrong. I can't explain it."

"The structure we saw from the satellite imaging should be straight that way," John said, pointing forward through the dead forest. With final preparations completed, the team began their hike.

Eliana noticed the silence that followed. Their footsteps sounded like fireworks compared to the nothing that enveloped the strange place. A lack of small animals and insects made the forest feel more like outer space. They hiked until they came upon the peculiar shapes they'd seen in the satellite imagery.

The structures were made from some sort of metal or plastic; Eliana couldn't tell at first glance. Each was circular with a rounded bottom, hovered six meters above the ground, and was as large as a colony dome. Some were tethered together with small bridges. They did not fluctuate in space like human hover tech. Instead, they remained completely motionless, even as the light breeze ruffled dead branches on the surrounding trees. From the scouts' vantage point, it wasn't possible to see what lay on the upper surface of the structures.

The team stood in awe for a moment, dumbstruck by the incredible technology. John walked forward and spun as he tried to take in the entire structure. "This is amazing," he said. "Leagues beyond anything we could create back in Sol. Whatever is keeping these things up isn't emitting any sort of energy fluctuation. It has to be exhausting energy somehow, or else this is impossible."

"I think I see it, look here," George said as he pointed toward the trees growing between the structures. "Those sorts of trees typically have energy flowing upward into the leaves. But if you look very closely, you can see the energy is flowing back down into the roots."

"I see what you mean. Is that causing the anomalous energy signatures?" Eliana asked. She noticed the structures continued all the way to the forest tree line. "There are so many of them."

"We should start mapping—maybe it will help us figure it out," John said. "Keep an eye out for a way up." John pulled a cartographer's orb from his suit's shoulder harness and tossed it into the air. The small mechanical object caught itself as it began to drop, then began to float around, scanning what it could and building a map that appeared on the team's soothreader displays.

Faye and Marie walked through the dead leaves, observing the bottoms of the platforms. They could almost reach up and touch the smooth, rounded bases. The forest underneath was shrouded in shadow.

"No ladders or stairs, that's for sure. Wait, here's something," Marie said, kneeling to observe a fungus that was growing in the darkness beneath a platform. It sprouted from the ground on a thin blue stalk. The top flowered out into a spiraling red spaghetti-like display, a black ooze seeping from its small spindles.

"Gross," Faye said, averting her eyes from the ugly fungus.

"Hey, not everything in botany is roses," Marie said as she scanned the fungus with her bioscope. "You never know where we'll find our last element for synthesis."

Faye noticed a shape in the shadow of the adjacent platform, something on the ground. She zoomed in with her helmet's binoculars and discovered what appeared to be a corpse. She gestured to the rest of the team. "Hey, guys, come take a look at this."

They approached the corpse slowly, as if they were trying not to awaken it from a deep slumber. It was a deceased auk'nai with black feathers and brown sashes. The team was quick to notice the dead creature had none of the gems they sought.

"What do you think happened to it?" Eliana asked.

"See here." George pointed at the horrible angle of the auk'nai's neck. "Looks like he might have broken his neck." George looked up. "Maybe he fell from between the platforms up there."

"Do you think he was a traveler?" John asked. "Maybe the auk'nai that live here haven't noticed him yet."

Roelin and AJ continued to look for a way to ascend, also scanning for any threats that might be waiting to ambush from above. The scientists focused on the specimen.

"We should ask Mag'Ro next time we see him." George grunted. "*If* we see him." He scanned the body with his bioscope, and jolted at the results. "That's *impossible*. Damn thing must be broken," George said as he whacked the side of the device. "It says the body has been here for almost three hundred years."

"I got some weird readings over here too," Marie said through their comm channel. "I don't think our scopes are broken."

"How could that be? Wouldn't bacteria have broken the body down long ago?" Eliana asked.

"Yeah. Hold on, let me try this," George said, and adjusted his bioscope to scan at a microscopic level around the body. "There is no decomposer bacterium in the area. Hells, there are almost no common bacteria in the area."

"What does that mean?" Eliana asked.

"Well, from our other observations, Kamaria has a lot of similar bacteria to those on Earth. Obviously, there are unique characteristics here, but for the most part, they serve the same functions. So, normal would be: a thing dies, it decomposes as bacteria eats it, and so on and so forth," George said. "But here, I see a bacterium that preserves things in a sort of stasis. The cells of this body could technically still be considered alive, where the consciousness itself has passed on."

"I thought we didn't get any life readings from the satellites?" Eliana asked.

John said, "Our satellites wouldn't pick up life readings on such a microscopic scale. It can see things as small as a mouse, but nothing like this." He looked up and waved his hand, gesturing to their surroundings. "Let's collect some samples. How many autopsy coffins do we have on the *Rogers*?" he asked, referring to the pods they used to transport deceased Kamarian creatures back to the quarantine lab at the colony, where they could further examine them.

"Four," George said. "I'll have Rocco send them over, just in case we find more we want to take back with us." He made a gesture over his soothreader and summoned the coffins from the ship. They would arrive in a few minutes, drifting silently over the dead leaves and unknown bacteria like ghosts.

George shifted his head back and forth and said, "Well, I was going to say whatever killed this auk'nai did it three hundred years ago, but stranger things have happened. We could potentially have a three-hundred-year-old bogeyman running around in the woods here."

"Comforting," Faye said, and nudged her husband. Roelin didn't react in any way, keeping his focus on the perimeter.

"Roelin, can we get up there?" John asked, pointing at the floating platform above them.

Roelin assessed the situation, then said, "Yes."

The captain removed a combat knife from its sheath on his chest and sprinted forward. He activated the jump-jet on his back and propelled himself upward onto a tree and slammed the knife into the trunk. Roelin pivoted and jump-jetted again toward the platform, where he vanished from sight after clearing the lip of the structure. A rope flung down from the platform. Roelin said over the comm channel, "It's secure, come on up."

"Everyone ready?" John asked.

"Yeah, let's see what's up top," George said.

"If we find any of those gems, take them," Marie said as she readied herself for the climb. She was very limber for her age, and Eliana was convinced Marie could beat her to the top.

They climbed up one at a time. When Eliana neared the top, Roelin's hand was waiting to help lift her up.

"Oh my ..." she whispered, looking ahead. The surface of the platform was covered in oddly shaped buildings, each pocked with holes like a piece of Swiss cheese, with access points all along the exterior walls. Auk'nai could potentially enter the building from any of these openings; their ability to fly made ground access points more cumbersome. Each building had a small dome shape on top with a bridge tethering it to the adjacent building. The structures on the platform were in complete disarray, as if the place had been ripped apart by a massive battle.

It wasn't the state of the buildings that horrified Eliana, it was the corpses. The auk'nai bodies appeared to be fresh, as if this event had just occurred an hour before the *Rogers* had landed. Some of the bodies were connected to each other in death grips, with talons forever locked into throats and sharp beaks embedded in the chests of their neighbors. Auk'nai hook staffs littered the ground like tombstones.

"Scope's still saying these bodies are three hundred years old too," George said, shaking the device, still not convinced it was working correctly.

"What the Hells happened here?" Eliana asked.

"Let's see if we can find out," John said.

Roelin and AJ cleared the area, door to door. Roelin approached a dwelling and swung himself inside, checking all the corners of the dimly lit interior. Strange objects had been knocked around during whatever struggle there had been. Roelin winced when he found a family of auk'nai ripped apart in the back of the dwelling. The tallest of the corpses sat against the wall with its head removed. The blood was still fresh here thanks to the bacteria, and the roof prevented rain from washing it away.

Roelin stumbled out of the dwelling and looked up into the sky.

"Roe, you okay?" Faye's voice sounded muffled to him as he tried to blink away the images of carnage. She touched his shoulder. "Roe."

"Don't go in there," Roelin said, calm again. He moved forward to clear more dwellings.

Eliana approached Faye and watched Roelin move around the dead city. Faye turned to Eliana and said, "This place is horrible."

"I've never seen anything like it," Eliana said.

"We have," Faye looked away from Eliana. "During the war. The last days of Mars. The day Roelin's brother died in combat with the Undriel."

"I didn't know Roelin had a brother," Eliana said.

"It happened before you got to know him," Faye said. "One of the Undriel's greatest tricks was spreading misinformation. We answered a distress call from an outpost near Olympus Mons Square." Roelin came out of another dwelling slowly and shook his head. He moved forward.

"It was a trap, wasn't it?" Eliana asked.

"Yeah. There wasn't anyone left alive in that damn building. You can tell when the Undriel had been around for a long time if there were a bunch of the spider bots crawling around," Faye said. The spider bots were the head casings the Undriel used for human brain absorption, with legs to help them move back to their collection site. "If you saw those, you knew that a lot of the big Undriel soldiers had already broken down their own bodies enough times to absorb more people."

"That's awful."

"The worst part is the Reaper," Faye said. "You ever see that thing? Most people don't survive it. Hells, for all I know, we might be the only ones who did."

"What is it?"

"It's the machine that protects the spider bots, like a shepherd. We call it the Reaper because if you see it, you know the Undriel are done absorbing people. It's designed only to kill." She looked down as they walked through bodies of slain auk'nai. "That place was like this. The Reaper had gone through anyone who didn't get absorbed. It was so fast. We only made it out thanks to Talfryn."

"Talfryn was Roelin's brother?"

"Yes," Faye said with a sigh. "Roelin still has nightmares. Sometimes shouting his name. I wish I could make all the bad memories go away. I'm only thankful he wasn't absorbed. Roelin wouldn't be able to stand it if his own brother became one of them and liked it."

Very little was understood about Undriel absorption, but what had been gleaned over the years was that each Undriel unit was connected to a vast network of shared data, yet they still retained their sense of self. Based on some of the things newly absorbed victims would say just before turning on their fellow humans, whatever was left of the person inside the machine seemed to enjoy the experience. The euphoria of being absorbed was so grand, the victim felt compelled to share the experience with more people, and that was how the Undriel spread across the Sol System.

Eliana put a hand on Faye's back and rubbed it reassuringly. She said nothing as they continued into the City of the Dead.

As they moved forward, they witnessed more carnage but found no answers. The gore was everywhere. It was a battle that the entirety of the village had participated in—old, young, mothers, fathers, children, it didn't matter. They'd all fought, and they'd all died.

"No gems," Marie said. "I was hoping that we'd at least find gems in this awful place. Have something good come of this."

"Maybe Mag'Ro is the only one with gems like that," John said. "He could be some sort of miner or trader—"

George interrupted. "I don't understand, why would the auk'nai do this?"

"There's a lot we still don't know about them," Eliana said.

"We don't know what we are looking at yet," John said. "Maybe a virus broke out that caused some sort of madness. We'll know more after an autopsy."

"I can't imagine a species that would kill each other off like this would survive long on this world. My gut says this was some sort of freak event," Eliana said.

Roelin said, "These could just be the victims of conquest. They might war with each other, just like humans."

There was a silence among the group. They all thought it at once. If the auk'nai had done this to themselves, they could do it again to Odysseus Colony. John continued forward toward the lip of the platform to think, and the rest followed.

As they reached the edge, Roelin could see something outside of the city in the distance, past the tree line. He toggled the side of his helmet to give him an optical zoom.

In the valley beyond the trees, there was a scattering of rock formations that looked like skeletal structures. The statues surrounded a cave opening in the middle of the valley that looked like some sort of natural elevator shaft. Fog drifted out from the entrance and reached in tendrils over the grass between the rock formations. It was a gateway to the Hells.

"I would like to get closer to that," Faye, the resident geologist, said.

George swiped through data on his soothreader. "I have taken plenty of scan data. With the specimen we gathered before and the bacteria to analyze, I'm satisfied with leaving this awful place too."

"Yeah, let's get moving," John said.

Eliana looked out at the strange cave a little longer as the others began to leave. She heard a crunch and turned to see Roelin shift his boot. He'd stepped in bone fragments. A thin slime caked the bones in a purple mess. It was unlike the carnage they had seen everywhere else. The fragments had no visible source, like a pot that had been broken and partially swept up. Roelin continued toward the rest of the group. Eliana felt a chill run up her spine.

Somehow, she thought, going into that cave was going to be worse than staying in the City of the Dead.

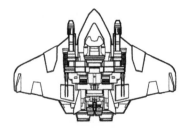

SIX

THREE HUNDRED YEARS AGO

THE *LELANTOS* FOLLOWED E. Murphy's Matador into the large
hangar of the *Telemachus*. Even with the threat of the *Devourer*, the
hangar was still less dangerous than being out in open space with the
battle raging on. Denton only hoped the human defense was
sufficient to stall the Undriel long enough to allow an escape.

"Have you ever seen anything like this?" Jason asked, his wide
eyes scanning the interior of the *Telemachus*'s hangar.

"Not in my days. This has to be the biggest engineering project
in the history of engineering!" Michael said, his mouth hanging
open.

The hangar was a long rectangular hallway filled with a variety
of colonist spaceships. It stretched so far back that the wall on the
other side of the bay appeared no larger than a football to an observer
standing at the entrance. The walls were mostly brown, gray, and
black, with orange highlights. Trams moved back and forth rapidly,
helping people get from one end to the other without having to walk.
Open hatches lined the sides of the hangar, with encasement barriers
keeping everything from venting out into space.

When the *Lelantos* had entered through the barrier, Denton felt the weight of artificial gravity pushing down on them: reverse-engineered technology gained from the Undriel during the war. It made Denton feel queasy as he adjusted to the tugging sensation in his guts.

"Just follow your HUD vectors and land where it tells you to, *Lelantos*," E. Murphy said into the comm.

"Roger that, thanks!" Michael said.

"Stay safe," E. Murphy added followed by a click that announced the comm link had been severed. His Matador landed near a squadron of other parked Matadors. The pilots scrambled from their ships, and those injured during the fighting were escorted to the medical bay.

"*All colony ships accounted for, Admiral,*" a static-filled voice sounded inside the *Lelantos*.

"What in the Hells?" Michael asked, searching the mechanisms and double-checking his comm settings.

"*Tell them to buckle up!*" a second static-filled voice said.

"I have a confession," Brynn said weakly.

"Oh yeah?" Michael said as he landed the *Lelantos*, listening to the chatter through the static.

"When Beth Herman kept talking about their wave transmitter, I had her get me one too, and I installed it on the *Lelantos*."

"*Devourer bearing in. Undertaker line is heading it off,*" the static said.

"No way!" Tyler laughed. "So this is illegal comm hacking, right?"

"Hey! It's not illegal," Brynn said.

"It's not totally legal either, Brynn." Michael sighed. "That being said, who wants the transmission sent to their soothreaders?"

The brothers raised their hands in unison almost before Michael had finished asking.

———◆———

"Tell them to buckle up!" Admiral Hugo Marin said, bracing himself as another blast rocked the command bridge of the *Telemachus*.

Before the admiral sat an array of technicians and analysts, each at their own station, monitoring multiple signatures of the *Telemachus* and the battle around them. The massive windscreen was all they needed to see the *Devourer* barreling toward them. It punched through any spacecraft unlucky enough to stray into its path. It looked like a rabid dog rushing toward a child with its fangs out.

"*Devourer* bearing in. Undertaker line is heading it off," Second Officer Kenji Nakamura reported.

"Prep the LPC!" Admiral Marin snapped.

"Ten seconds to full power, but we won't be able to cascade warp for another fifteen minutes after firing," Nakamura stated.

"That's going to have to do. What is the status of the hull?"

"Holding, but we can't take too many more direct hits. Any further damage, and there's no certainty the ship will hold during warp."

"It will hold." Marin looked upward as if speaking to God. "Isn't that right, Homer?"

Homer's soothing computerized voice responded from speakers on the command bridge. "All parameters are within acceptable status currently, Admiral. But as Officer Nakamura stated, we need to be careful."

The *Devourer* began firing its front particle cannons. Three Undertaker-class warships readied to meet the beast. They lined up in formation and powered their weapons for a heavy assault.

"Target its weaponry. Launch the hadron missiles," Commander Kenard Steadman ordered. He toggled the commands to rain the Hells onto the *Devourer*. The Undertaker-class warfighter launched all eight of its large hadron fighter missiles toward exterior particle cannons on the *Devourer*, striking the eight targets directly. Explosions boiled on the surface of the nightmare ship, but it refused to slow down.

The other Undertakers followed the same tactic of unloading their ordinance of hadron fighter missiles. Each missile struck the array of particle cannons. The smoke cleared, revealing the guns had been reduced to scrap metal.

"Direct hits! Weapon capabilities of the *Devourer* are—" Kenard stopped himself when he noticed the Undriel's sleight of hand.

The *Devourer* ejected the broken weapons into space. New particle cannons rolled into position from inside, replacing the ship's entire arsenal instantaneously. It unleashed a volley of lasers.

"Evade!" Kenard shouted. The barrage destroyed the Undertaker to Kenard's port side. The light from the explosion blotted out the left side of his windscreen. Lasers struck the ship on Kenard's starboard side.

"We lost movement capability!" the captain of the injured warship reported through bursts of explosions.

The *Devourer* came rushing toward them at breakneck speed, unnatural for something so massive. Kenard rolled his ship out of the way, but the other Undertaker was rammed head-on, leaving behind only dust and smoke. Kenard fired all weapons into the hull of the *Devourer* as it careened wildly toward the *Telemachus*.

"If you're going to do something, *do it quick!*" Kenard shouted to the *Telemachus* over the comm line.

Admiral Marin grabbed the railing in front of him and squeezed.

"Fifteen seconds to impact!" Nakamura shouted.

"Fire the LPC!" Marin snapped.

The weapons officer opened a hatch in his counsel and slammed a button. There was a shudder through the *Telemachus* as the large particle cannon roared to life on the ship's bow. Energy began to build around the titanic weapon.

A beam of white-hot light unleashed from the front of the ship and sustained itself for a solid thirty seconds. The beam bashed directly into the *Devourer*, causing it to slowly lose speed and then melt. Several explosions happened inside of the Undriel ship, and it sheared into pieces like a bullet shot into an iron wall. It ripped in half and dissolved into the lance of light.

In the end, only fragments of the Undriel masterclass ship remained.

Then there was silence. Then, human forces began to cheer. Their hopes were dashed as they watched another giant ship rocket over Jupiter's horizon from behind the *Telemachus*.

"All remaining essential fighters return to *Telemachus* immediately," Admiral Marin commanded. The power started to cycle for cascade warp.

"Admiral," Kenard said over the open comm, "there are still too many in the area. We'll keep them busy. Make it count."

Admiral Marin heard Kenard and hesitated to respond. He was right. Too many Undriel were in the area for the *Telemachus* to safely escape. He ground his teeth together, then nodded. "Affirmative, Commander Steadman. Humanity thanks you."

"It's an honor, sir," Kenard said, and clicked off the comm.

———◆———

"How in the Hells is that possible?" Michael Castus said. The Castus family stood with many of the civilian colonists in the crowded hangar bay of the *Telemachus*. Colonist ships lined the large room, with more of the essential military craft coming through the encasement barrier as the battle raged on outside.

Everyone stood elbow to elbow, mumbling their worries as the battle developed.

"No, that's not even fair, is it?" Tyler asked in a whisper, listening as the wave transmitter gave them confidential information.

"Oh, *fairness*! That's right! The Undriel just forgot the rules," Jason hissed back.

"Did command know they had two *Devourers* this whole time?" Denton asked quietly.

The *Telemachus* was being pursued by another masterclass ship, identical to the *Devourer* that had just been obliterated by the LPC.

A person stood atop the second masterclass ship, the infamous Tibor Undriel himself, the creator of the machines that were taking over the Sol System. His frame resembled a man's, but that was where the similarities ended.

The Undriel took inspiration from insects, combining the most effective elements of every bug ever squished by a human to create the most ruthless enemy humans would ever face. Tibor's head resembled that of a spider, with an array of glowing white eyes lining his skull and blotting out any blind spots. In an emergency, Undriel had been known to eject their spider heads and scurry away to rebuild their bodies before rejoining the fight. The Undriel were very hard to sneak up on.

Tibor's carapace was made of jet-black metal, camouflage in a space combat arena. A cloak shrouded each Undriel, made of a unique material that blotted out sensors and glitched targeting computers. It gave the Undriel a grim reaper-esque appearance, and their effectiveness on the battlefield supported that metaphor. They were very hard to see.

Tibor's appendages could take on a multitude of tasks. If an Undriel needed to leap over an obstacle, its legs would morph into the form of a locust's for extra jump height. If it needed to sprint, an Undriel's legs could split into an array of legs like a centipede, allowing it to race effortlessly over any obstacles in its path. If it needed to climb, its legs would shift into those of a spider; it could even hang upside down from most ceilings. An Undriel's arms worked the same way, morphing between a particle rifle for long range, a retractable claw for medium range, and a mantis-shaped scythe for short range. The Undriel were very hard to evade.

Tibor shared this appearance with most Undriel foot soldiers, except he stood a meter taller and withheld from shapeshifting. He was the looming figurehead of the nightmare, and his human silhouette reminded his enemies of his origins.

No one fully understood the Undriel's motivation for the war, but everyone knew Tibor was at the center of it. Some theorized that the Undriel had suffered a glitch in the early days of their engineering when they were just part of an artificial intelligence experiment that was being designed to help humanity explore the stars. Others suggested Tibor created them out of spite, having been beaten by the

Telemachus Project in the race to develop true AI. Only those absorbed by the Undriel knew the truth, and they weren't willing to give up that information for free.

Tibor rode aboard the second masterclass ship as it chased the *Telemachus* over Jupiter's cyclone.

Red alert sirens went off in the hangar of the *Telemachus*. The civilians began to shout and scurry.

Bill Herman was sweating and frantically tugging at his son's arm. Denton looked over to him and could tell the Herman family were listening to the transmissions on their own wave transmitter.

"Beth, get Tony back into the ship, we're not sticking around for this!" Bill said, shepherding his wife toward their ship. He was stopped by a voice on the hangar intercom.

"Listen, everyone," the smooth robotic voice of Homer said, "please get back in your ships and await further instructions. Strap in and do not, under any circumstances, attempt to leave the *Telemachus*. We are preparing for cascade warp."

As the crowd began to hurry into their various spacecraft, cries of panic echoing in the hangar, Denton approached the Hermans.

"Hey, Mr. Herman," Denton said to Bill, noticing the terror on the man's face and worrying he might do something stupid. "It's going to be alright. You can stay with us if you want. We'll take care of each—"

"Not now, Dent!" Bill said as he called up a display on his soothreader. Denton recognized he was starting a flight pre-check. The exterior lights of the Herman family ship confirmed his assessment.

"Mr. Herman!" Denton grabbed his arm. Bill shoved Denton hard, forcing him backward. "Think of Tony. You'll all die!" Denton said, moving closer to Bill again.

"Shut the Hells up, *Castus*!" Bill was done talking, and pulled out his collider pistol, aiming it directly at Denton's head. Tony Herman began to cry. The pistol's collider cylinder began to whirl rapidly as it gathered up particles from the space around them, smashing them together into a volatile bullet that it could unleash at near light speed.

Denton put his hands up.

"You point your *fuckin'* gun somewhere else, Bill!" Michael Castus shouted as he rushed over, pulling his own pistol out and aiming it at Bill's head. For a moment, there were only the sounds of whirring guns and Tony crying.

"You all back off! We're getting off this damn death boat," Bill said. He kept his pistol trained on Denton as he pulled Beth and Tony toward their ship. Michael kept his gun on Bill until the outer hatch of their ship had closed.

"Damn it!" Denton shouted, clenching his fists. Michael slung his pistol back into its holster on his hip.

"That moron made his choice. You did all you could, Denny," Michael said. "Come on, let's get into the *Lelantos*."

The Herman's spacecraft lifted off and sped through the encasement barrier just before the metal hatches of the hangar sealed completely.

Denton couldn't help but wonder if Bill Herman had made the right choice.

"Prepare for cascade warp in five …" Homer alerted the hangar. The hangar was now a ghost town, everyone hidden back inside their ships. Denton unclenched his fists and hurried to the *Lelantos*.

"Four …"

They sealed the access ramp and made their way onto the bridge.

"Three …"

Denton and his brothers buckled in. Tyler was white-knuckling the armrest, and Jason was muttering a prayer he was improvising on the spot. Denton closed his eyes and breathed heavily through his nostrils.

"Two …"

Michael and Brynn buckled in and held hands. They looked into each other's eyes, unsure if this was the last time they would be able to do so.

"*One.*"

Bill Herman thought he had saved his family. Surely, the second *Devourer* would destroy the *Telemachus*, but they wouldn't be on it. Those poor idiots on board thought they could outrun the Undriel. He was sad the Castus family hadn't seen reason in time to escape certain annihilation.

No one could beat the Undriel.

There was a bright light. Bill, Beth, and Tony shielded their eyes. There it went—the *Telemachus* disappeared in a fiery explosion, and with it, all of humanity, a doomed race in a doomed star system.

"Daddy, look!" Tony said. He tugged on his father's shirt sleeve. Bill and Beth looked toward where they assumed they would see the massive debris of the *Telemachus*. Instead, they saw nothing. Where there had once been humanity's most massive spacecraft, there was now only empty space.

The *Devourer* began to slow down.

Over the wave transmitter, Bill could hear Commander Kenard Steadman's voice. "We did it. Mission accomplished."

At first, there was silence.

"Oh God." Bill Herman trembled as he realized his mistake. His eyes bulged, and sweat began to drip as the immensity of the repercussions became apparent. He regretted not trusting the *Telemachus*, but also felt a sense of vast loneliness, a bottomless pit of despair unfamiliar to humans before the Undriel had taken the system.

Bill hugged his wife and son as their family's ship was pulled apart by the robotic limbs of an Undriel battlecraft seeking to bring new victims into its network.

———— ◦ ————

Kenard and his squadron fought with all their might, but in time, they too succumbed to the Undriel.

Commander Kenard Steadman was the last man alive in the Sol System. His Undertaker-class warship had been rammed, forcing him and his crew to eject. The Undriel were quick to dispatch his crewmen, but they waited to finish off Kenard. For a few minutes, he floated in space, weightless, helpless. He looked toward his home star, Sol.

Kenard thought about Earth, about all the people who had lived there. All the people he had lost.

It was as if he were looking into the bottom of the ocean. Everything in front of him was now devoid of humanity. What the Undriel had done to the ruins of human civilization was their own secret.

Tibor Undriel's mechanical insectoid figure loomed into Kenard's view as the masterclass ship drifted toward him, blotting out the light of Sol. His cloak floated gracefully in the vacuum as if these two were meeting underwater.

"Sol is yours now. But you can't have *us*," Kenard said into a comm filled with ghosts, unsure if Tibor could even hear him. He looked into the leader of the Undriel's false white eyes. Tibor's face was expressionless, as all Undriel faces were, but Kenard sensed a moroseness in those robotic, spiderlike eyes.

An obsolete human staring at his successor. Tibor's metal hand reached forward, clasped around Kenard's neck guard, and brought him closer.

"Hells to you!" Kenard ripped his air hose out of his suit, causing rapid decompression. The visor of his atmospheric helmet splattered with blood. The last words of the last human in the Sol System.

Tibor watched as Commander Kenard Steadman died in his hands. He released the human's body and allowed the corpse to drift off into space.

The Undriel had finally won the war. Humans had abandoned their cities, homes, technological advancements, playgrounds, schools, movie theaters, malls, farms, everything. They had left their roots behind in order to begin anew elsewhere, far away from their failures and accomplishments. What remained was a silence unlike any that had come before.

Humanity was gone.

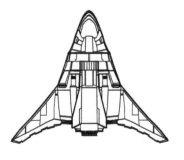

SEVEN

PRESENT DAY

ELIANA FOLLOWED THE OTHERS into the lush valley beyond the City of the Dead. In the middle of the valley stood a tall rock formation with a gaping hole sliced from the ground to its center. Fog spilled from the darkness within.

It looked like a doorway.

Eliana felt cold looking at it—that fear children get when they don't want to step into a dark basement. The primal fear of the unknown in a world filled with unknowns.

The cave opening was surrounded by carved rock statues covered in plant life, like forgotten ancient ruins that nature had reclaimed. The sculptures took on various configurations of arms, legs, torsos, and alien heads, each more haunting than the last. The only consistency between them was the cyclopean eye socket present in the center of each stone skull.

Directly in front of the cave, a taller statue stood guarding the entrance like an eternal sentry. Its body resembled a centaur, with four hooved legs and two long arms that hung close to the ground. Twisted stone talons sprouted from the ends of each finger. The head resembled a hollowed-out bull's skull, with one cyclopean eye hole in its center. The skull was attached to the torso by four stone tentacles.

"These are amazing," Faye whispered as she gently caressed one of the statues.

"Amazing is one word for it," Eliana said, keeping her distance and moving toward the cave entrance.

"The bacterial layer is thicker here. The source may be close," George said.

Eliana approached the mouth of the cave and peered in. She heard a crackling of stone and turned quickly to her left to face the giant sentry. It had not moved.

Or had it? Eliana wondered.

She could have sworn the head was now positioned differently among the stone tentacles it sat upon. Eliana attributed it to nerves.

Faye said, "These statues are so intricate. Someone put a lot of care into their design. Surface readings tell us these were crafted over four hundred years ago."

"So, one hundred years before the massacre in the city," George said.

"There's some unique plant life on these statues," Marie said. "I'm going to spend some time collecting them for research."

"Anything that could lead to a cure?" John asked.

"I won't know until I get it back to the lab and really dig in. But you never know, maybe," Marie said, palming a collection scalpel.

John touched the face of one of the statues and whispered, "I wonder what statues we left behind in the Sol System for some unknown future traveler to find." He paused and removed his hand from the statue. "And what they might think of our legacy."

"Should we make our way inside?" Roelin asked.

"Do we have to?" Eliana replied.

"If it means we might find those minerals for full synthesis, then yes," George said.

"Come on, it'll be fun," Faye said. She pulled out her collider pistol and activated it. "Just stick close to Roe and me."

Roelin turned to AJ. "Keep watch out here."

"Got it. We don't know if there's some sort of space bear coming home to hibernate," AJ said with a laugh. No one joined him, and he sighed. "I'll keep watch," he reiterated. Roelin nodded to him and walked to the front of the group.

"Be safe in there," Marie said. "I'm going to take some samples up here. If you find something, just holler."

"Scaredy-cat," George winked at her. Marie waved him away with a swipe of her gloved hand.

Roelin, John, George, Faye, and Eliana entered the cave with their headlamps on. Marie and AJ watched them disappear into the fog.

The cave's floor was thick with mist. The team was extra careful with each step, doing their best not to slip on the ramp that led into the darkness. With each step, Eliana's feet would sink as if she were walking on wet pillows.

George waved his bioscope in front of him like a metal detector and said, "There's a faint amount of electricity running through the slime on the floor here."

"That checks out," Faye said, pointing ahead at the glowing rocks scattered around the interior of the cave. "See the laser stones on the pillars? I bet they pulse energy into whatever this slime is."

Eliana stayed close to Roelin. The fog rolled around them, distorting the light from their headlamps. At one point, Eliana thought she saw a man standing near the back of the cave watching them. She turned toward the shape only to see a wisp of vapor.

Roelin had seen something too; he jerked his rifle to the right and held it firm for a moment. Eliana strained her eyes to see what was there, but only fog drifted by. Roelin continued farther into the cave.

The cave had a low ceiling, with only a meter of space between the top of Roelin's helmet and the slimy roof. Pillars of stone angled their way through the cave, connecting the ceiling to the floor like slimy tethers. Laser stones dotted the room with faint lights of pulsing energy. Traces of electrical current licked over Eliana's boots as she moved.

"There's something over here," John said, waving to the rest to join him. He stood in front of a large pile of skulls, many made of stone like the sentry outside. John looked down into the fog and gasped.

At his feet was a corpse. It was a creature unlike any they had seen on Kamaria. Its skull resembled a bird's, with a sharp horn at the base of the beak. Two hauntingly large eye holes stared up at the explorers. The back of the skull looked as though it had been smashed in, perhaps causing the creature's death long ago. Its head was tethered to its torso by four long, tentacle-like connectors.

Its chest and shoulders were all one solid piece of bone, with gnarled spikes thrusting outward in every direction. Its arms and legs looked like purple worm skin, each terminating in sharp talons. Under each shoulder blade was a long tentacle that ended in a barbed hook.

"Incredible," George said, kneeling over the body. He scanned it and gestured to the head. "These large openings have a slimy interior, a lot like the walls of this cave. This is just my theory here, but this slime inside the eye sockets might actually have been the creature's way of sensing the world around it."

"What do you mean?" John asked.

"Well, look at the head—it looks like a skull with no skin. But the unique thing about this area is that everything is preserved. So, we can safely assume that the skin didn't rot off the skull; it just never existed on this creature." George pointed out where the jawbone should have been. "And see here, the skull is smooth, with no evidence that we are missing a jawbone of any sort. So, these openings might act as an all-in-one receiver of the world around it." He looked at the body as if he had found buried treasure. "I wonder if this specimen was a water-dwelling animal. Maybe this cave was submerged at one point?" George looked up from the body toward the ceiling.

"This isn't a cave," Eliana said. "It's a crypt."

"I think you're right," John said, eyeing the pile of skulls. "Maybe an ancient auk'nai burial ground?"

"Does *that* look like an auk'nai to you?" George asked rhetorically.

Eliana shuddered. This was an old place. It felt like she was being watched by all the history that had occurred here before. The shadows, the walls, the mist—they were all observing the new things that trespassed. They had seen the birth of the planet and had been waiting here ever since.

Eliana turned to Roelin. He had moved away from the group with his rifle up, investigating something. He held his hand up to his helmet as if he had been stung by an insect.

"Hey, Roe," Eliana said. She wanted to approach him, but her muscles refused to walk farther into the dark place alone. "Everything okay over there?"

He grunted and shook his head. "It's so *loud*."

"What?" Eliana asked. She thought she saw something out of the corner of her eye, and jerked her head. The man made of mist was just playing his tricks once more, fading away into tendrils of fog as soon as she looked.

Eliana hated this place.

Roelin put his hand up in front of his face and stumbled backward as if pushed by something. He fell to one knee and coughed raggedly. Eliana was done being frightened of the dark, and ran to him.

"*Hey!* Look at me," she said, and snapped her gloved fingers in front of his visor. "Are you hurt?"

Roelin's eyes darted around the cave, looking for his attacker.

"What is it?" Faye asked. She moved toward Eliana and Roelin with her collider pistol scanning the fog for anything hostile.

Roelin grunted again and winced, recoiling into himself. "Thought I saw something. Must be the fog playing tricks on me." He stood up and shook his head, then held his hand against his helmet. "This damn headache."

"Here, let me help you," Eliana said. She opened a patch on the shoulder of Roelin's suit and plugged her medical kit directly into the socket inside.

"It's just a migraine. I'll be fine," Roelin said.

"I'm sure you will be, tough guy," Eliana said, "but I have a job to do." She checked her medical kit's data readout, noting nothing abnormal. Roelin was correct; he was suffering from a migraine. Eliana tapped a few buttons on the med kit. "You're right, you'll live. Vital signs look normal for the most part. I'm going to get some mild pain relievers in you, they'll clear up that ache no problem."

"Thanks." Roelin shook his head again.

"Don't scare me like that." Faye slung her pistol back into her holster.

"Back to it, Martian." Eliana smiled. They moved back toward the group. Eliana thought she heard her name being whispered in the darkness, like something was calling to her. It was as if the fog were desperately trying to tell her something, reaching out to her with curling tendrils. Her spine tingled with pinpricks of fear, and she rushed toward the rest of the group.

An hour later, the scout team had finished their exploration of the cave and had loaded the mysterious birdlike corpse into an autopsy coffin. As Eliana walked up to the ramp to the *Rogers*, she noticed Roelin was staring out toward the cave, motionless.

"You feeling alright, Roelin?" she asked.

"I'm fine." Roelin shook his head again as if breaking a trance. He looked around for a moment before meeting Eliana's eyes, appearing as if he'd just walked into a room but had forgotten why. He grunted and moved up the ramp. "Let's just get the Hells out of this place."

"Don't have to ask me twice!" Eliana said.

The *Rogers* lifted away from the valley and rocketed toward Odysseus Colony.

The stone sentry guarding the crypt stirred.

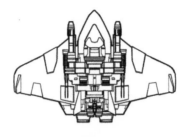

EIGHT

THREE HUNDRED YEARS AGO

SILENCE.

The void between the Sol System and humanity's next destination was an empty place. There were no stars here, no planets, no asteroids—here, it was raw nothing.

Then, something.

The *Telemachus* burst into existence, falling out of cascade warp into the null place. The vessel reflected the damage from the last Undriel attack on its skin with pocks of small explosions, many ruptured from the violence of the warp. Electrical torrents flowed around the ship's exterior.

As time passed, the ship stabilized. Homer had brought the damaged systems back to fair condition. The external wounds would be a problem solved later. Humanity had leaped from the skillet and landed on the chopping board.

It was time to regroup.

"Are we dead?" Denton Castus groaned as he pushed a crate away from himself and stood up inside the *Lelantos*, which was now pitched at a 45-degree angle on its port side. Brynn was helping Tyler with a cut he'd received during the chaos of the warp, while Jason and Michael were busy moving debris away from the door to the ramp.

"I have been asking you boys for weeks. I says, 'Hey, did you fix the port landing leg on the *Lelantos*?' I must'a asked a thousand times!" Michael was chastising his sons. "But, 'Oh yeah, Dad, we'll get to it today.'" He mocked their voices in a nasally high pitch.

"We're lucky we made it here in one piece," Brynn said. "Let's be thankful for that."

Denton heard glass bottles rolling around near his feet and reached down. He smiled when he discovered six bottles of Ganymede ale in a small case. He lifted the six-pack up and was thrilled to see it wasn't damaged.

"Hey, Dad!" Denton said, and tossed his father a bottle.

Michael caught it and smiled mischievously, then pointed to Denton. "Favorite son right there."

Denton tossed bottles to each of his family members. Michael lifted his, still unopened. "Boys, Brynn"—he made eye contact with each of them—"I am damn proud of every one of you. Regardless of this leg still not bein' fixed." He smiled, and in unison, everyone cracked open their beers. Foam launched all over in a fizzy mess.

"Not sure why I didn't see that comin'," Denton said, wiping the foam from his face and slapping it onto the ground. He took a small swig, then walked over to help Jason and Michael open the hatch.

Denton was the first out of the *Lelantos*, followed closely by the rest of his family. The ship's landing leg had indeed failed, causing the whole thing to tilt wildly after the shock from the cascade warp.

He could see for the first time how much damage the *Lelantos* had taken during its approach to the *Telemachus*. There were deep cuts on the underside, with metal fragments sticking out like thorns on a rosebush. The wings had sustained particle blasts, leaving behind areas of exterior wall damage. If those pilots, Steadman and Murphy, hadn't come by and saved them when they had, the whole ship could have combusted.

"Yeah, we have some work ahead of us," Denton said with a sigh.

"Whatever," Jason said as he pushed past Denton. He began to walk away from the ship.

"Where are you going?" Brynn asked.

"Going to see what's left. Is that a problem?" Jason asked, not slowing down.

"Hey, we should stick together!" Michael shouted. Jason waved a hand in the air, brushing off his father's suggestion.

"I ought'a slap that kid," Michael said, clenching his hands into fists.

"He gets like this sometimes," Denton said, watching his oldest brother leave them behind. "After what we just went through, probably better to let him deal with it the way he wants to."

"I'd still like to see you slap him, though," Tyler said. Michael sighed in defeat. He shook his head and looked back at the *Lelantos*.

"So, this is it," Michael said, "the last piece of the Castus legacy." He glanced down at his feet and brought a hand to his brow. Brynn put her arm around his shoulders.

"We're the legacy. Not the shop. It's us," she said.

Denton and Tyler watched their father struggle to hold back his tears. That shop was their lives, and they knew their parents had been happy with it. Denton was surprised that he didn't miss the shop. But there was so much to absorb, he wasn't sure what he was feeling. He wanted to walk away and figure himself out like Jason had, but felt obligated to stay with his family.

Michael huffed, "I need a drink. Something less foamy." He smiled through his sadness, but his eyes betrayed his humor.

"I'll see what we got," Tyler said. "I know where Jay stashed all the good stuff."

"Hey, he ain't here to stop you," Denton said. "Get the best you can find."

"Roger that."

Denton looked around the *Telemachus*'s hangar. Families had exited their spaceships and were standing quietly, recovering from the shock of the battle. Some wept openly, some searched frantically for friends and neighbors, and some even cheered and cracked open champagne bottles.

"Hello, everyone," came the voice of Fleet Admiral Hugo Marin over the hangar intercom. "We have escaped the Undriel. The warp was a success."

There was some clapping, but it was awkwardly quiet, like sympathy applause for a bad joke at a comedy club. The admiral continued.

"I want to take a moment to acknowledge what we have lost. A lot of good men and women fought bravely today, and many gave the ultimate sacrifice to defend our escape. It is because of them that we are here now, away from the threat of the Undriel. Because of them, we have a second chance, a chance to be better than we were before. I want to take a moment of silence for those we have lost. Let us bow our heads in respect and think of them."

Denton bowed his head. The silence hung in the air for what seemed like an hour, as each survivor reflected on what had been lost in the war.

"Thank you," the admiral said. "Over the next few days, those in leadership roles will be briefed on our plans moving forward. We have a lot of work to do, but for now, find peace. We have escaped our pursuers. What we do next will affect the legacy of humanity in the universe."

"Escaped," Denton whispered to himself. For almost half his life, the Undriel had been pushing their way across the Sol System and conquering planets. He had forgotten what life had been like before the machines, the carefree days of his childhood. The idea that they were free once more gave him a rush of excitement.

"Here we go!" Tyler said, coming out of the *Lelantos*'s cargo hold. "Arrow whiskey."

"Perfect," Michael said. Tyler handed out shot glasses to the family, and they all stood silently as he poured them each a shot of the brown liquid.

"I'm—" Michael started. "I don't—" He choked on his words.

"To Ganymede." Denton locked his eyes with his father. "To the Arrow. To the shop."

"To the shop," Michael repeated, as he nodded at Denton. They all tipped their heads back and downed the shots.

"I'll get us some chairs," Tyler said.

"Good thinking," Michael said. "We're gonna be here awhile."

———◆———

Denton rubbed his face as he woke up. The lights were on again in the hangar. For a moment, he thought the sunrise was peeking through the window next to his bunk on the *Lelantos*.

The ship still had a hefty tilt, which made sleeping complicated, and the Arrow whiskey from the night before certainly hadn't helped. He looked over to see his brothers still passed out. How he managed to sleep through Jason's snoring, he did not know, but he was glad to see him back with the family. Denton swung his wrist close to his face to check the time on his soothreader, surprised it was already afternoon—at least, afternoon on Ganymede.

Denton sat up and thought about what had happened. The Undriel attack, leaving the Arrow, the cascade warp into the empty void between what was home and what would be their new home.

Have I changed?

In some ways, yes, his mind was wandering more. His day used to revolve around work, play, and sleep. Now he was beginning to think he could change that. He didn't have to follow Ganymede's rules anymore. Who would he become in a new world?

Who is Denton Castus now?

He gently tried to get down from his bunk and stumbled sideways along with the tilt of the ship. Tyler stirred but didn't fully awaken. Denton decided it was time to do something about the slope in the *Lelantos*, and maybe afterward he could figure out who he wanted to be. Work never failed to distract Denton.

He got dressed, then exited the crooked ship with a hover mule, a hovering device that acted as both a work bench and a storage unit.

He inspected the damage the *Lelantos* had taken when the Undriel scraped underneath it.

"Damn, that sucker got closer than I thought," Denton said to himself, and whistled as he ran his hand next to the gash. He gripped a piece of fragmented metal and yanked hard, releasing it. It was part of the Undriel ship that had grazed them. The metal looked wrong to him, perverted in some way by an engineer that wasn't entirely human but wasn't fully machine either. "I need a harness to get you upright," Denton whispered to the *Lelantos* as he inspected the Undriel metal.

"I didn't hear that. Could you repeat the request?" a gentle synthetic voice asked. Denton was startled and slipped his hand across the sharp metal, cutting his hand open.

"Ah *shit!*" He winced in pain. Holding the wound on his hand, Denton whirled around to locate the source of the voice. A panel on the floor opened, and a console rose from within it. It had a flat top that looked much like his wrist-mounted soothreader and stood on a thin rod that terminated waist high.

"What the …?" Denton asked the air around him.

"I believe you asked for a harness. Is that correct?" The console emitted a holographic blue orb that blinked through data readouts and options.

"Uh, yeah. You got one?" Denton walked up to the console, grabbing a loose cloth from a drawer on the hover mule along the way to wrap his bleeding hand.

"I will request one to come over shortly. Is there anything else you will need?" the voice said.

"Nah, I'm good. Thank you, uh …" Denton finished wrapping his hand and realized he didn't know who he was thanking.

"No need to thank me. I am Homer. I am here to help. If there is anything else you need, please do not hesitate to ask, Mr. Castus." Upon completing the request, the console retracted back into the floor panel. Shortly, a robotic harness attached to the ceiling on a track system made its way over. A terminal on one of the long arms of the harness was ready for Denton to use.

"Now that's what I call service!" He smiled and input the commands on the harness's terminal to get it in place around the *Lelantos*. Within minutes, Denton had the harness in position and chained to the ship.

The *Lelantos* groaned as the chains pulled the ship even. Denton laughed as he imagined his brothers rolling around inside as the ship balanced itself. He went pale as he remembered his parents were also inside. Once it was completely level, he waited a few moments in silence, but no one emerged to yell at him for rolling them around inside.

Good whiskey. Time to work.

Denton pulled the hover mule over to his work area, and unlatched the hood. He activated the replicator, and a box-shaped appendage rose from the top of the mule. With this tool, he input the specifications for a hydraulic cylinder for the landing leg. The replicator box asked for rods of material to be inserted.

Denton dragged a supply box off the *Lelantos* and pulled out a few refined metal rods. He slammed them into the hover mule with the casual skill of a professional. The replicator box gave him an estimated build time of about fifteen minutes.

He didn't wait for the build to finish; Denton went right to work repairing the exterior hull damage. He grabbed a welding torch, mask, mechanic's gauntlet, and toolbox, and climbed deftly up the side of the *Lelantos*.

Time raced by as Denton mended the wounds of his family's ship. When he finished, the scars were patched with shiny silver metal and the vessel no longer leaned to the side. Denton removed the robotic harness and watched it slide back across the hangar.

He checked the wrapped cloth on his hand and noticed that the cut he'd sustained from the Undriel metal hadn't stopped bleeding. In fact, it looked as fresh as the moment he'd sliced himself.

"Shit, might need stitches," Denton grumbled to himself.

"I'm sorry," the robotic voice of Homer said, "I didn't catch that. Do you need medical assistance?"

"No," Denton said, then watched a torrent of blood exit his palm. "Well, maybe."

"Allow me to be of service," Homer said. An orb with a red cross on the side floated out of an opening on the floor. It hovered toward Denton and asked, "What seems to be the problem?"

Denton lifted his wounded hand and removed the bandage. Blood began to spill out freely; the wound was becoming worse over time.

"Was this laceration caused by an Undriel metal fragment?" Homer asked. Denton nodded, and Homer continued, "It contains a chemical that causes localized hemophilia. Allow me to treat this wound, or it will continue to bleed at an increasing rate."

"Go right ahead," Denton said. Arms projected outward from the orb, one with a syringe filled with a clear liquid, the other with a spout.

"You will feel a mild numbing sensation," Homer said. The spout spat a foam over Denton's wound, washing it and numbing the pain. Denton held his hand still as Homer then injected his hand with the syringe. The spout arm rotated, and a metal hand grabbed Denton's wrist and gave it a good shake.

"This will help the medicine circulate," Homer said as the smiley face reappeared. The spout rotated back into position and spat more foamy substance onto Denton's hand. It tickled for a moment, then Homer wiped it away. The wound was sealed shut, leaving behind only a jagged pale line in his palm.

"Thanks, Doc," Denton said.

"No need to thank me. I am Homer. I am here to—"

"Yeah, yeah. I know, I heard you before," Denton said. "So what's going to happen now?"

"The wound will fully heal within—"

"No, I mean to us," Denton interrupted.

"After repairs have been made to the *Telemachus*, you will all be assigned a stasis bed for the journey. The voyage to the Delta

Octantis system will take three hundred years, Earth Standard Time."

Denton raised his eyebrows. "Three hundred years as a *slushie?*"

"Correct. The interstellar spacecraft the *Odysseus* began its journey five years ago, Earth Standard Time. They will arrive five years before the *Telemachus* and begin to build the foundation of a new colony."

"Y'all have known the war was going to go so badly for five years and didn't bother to tell us?" Denton thought about smacking the robotic orb but knew it would hurt his recently healed hand more than Homer.

"No. That is not true, Mr. Castus," Homer said. A sad face appeared on the orb.

"Well, how could the Odysseus folks know how many people to prepare for?" Denton asked.

"They are not aware that we are bringing twenty thousand more colonists than anticipated. Leadership is assessing the situation."

Denton's heart dropped. They were building a colony for only one-third of the passengers on the *Telemachus*. He was going to travel for three hundred years just to become homeless. Denton thumbed his chin, then said, "Well, you got to tell them."

"Mr. Castus, I am only a partition. The other Homer partition in the Odysseus Colony is too far to reconnect with at this time. Once we get within the Delta Octantis system, I will be able to make a connection with the Odysseus Homer partition and assess the situation more accurately."

"So for now, I just got to trust you."

"Affirmative!" Homer said, and a smiley face appeared once more on the orb's screen.

"Wow." Denton sighed, nodded, then said, "Well, thanks anyway."

"No need to thank me. I am—"

"Yeah. Got it," Denton said. The robotic orb drifted into the floor and sealed itself away. Denton looked around the hangar filled with newfound knowledge of the fate in store for them. He had seen what fights over resources look like—the Arrow had had its fair share of them. Those fights would spread out over twenty thousand desperate humans trying to survive on an unknown planet. There was nothing he could do except trust that Homer would do everything right.

"It's gonna be a long ride," Denton said, and then looked for more work to do.

———— ◆ ————

Within two days' ship time, the *Telemachus* had summoned each of its thirty thousand colonists to the stasis bedchamber. Each of the survivors was placed into a bed and sealed away.

Denton lowered himself into his stasis bed and looked around the room. He had already said good night to his family as if this were just a camping trip. The lid slid shut over him, and the bed began plugging tubes into dozens of tiny outlets on the outside of his sleeping suit. The tubes rapidly filled with various colored liquids, and Denton began to feel woozy.

"Ready or not, here we come," Denton whispered as he drifted off to sleep. The bed completed its job and sealed him away for the journey.

The *Telemachus* cycled its engines, then shot off into the stars.

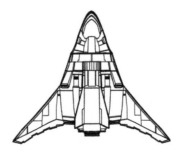

NINE

PRESENT DAY

ELIANA COULDN'T SLEEP.

Somewhere between the thoughts of never seeing Mag'Ro again and the fears of the lung-lock creeping into her room, she couldn't find her dreams. She sat at the edge of her bed and pinched the bridge of her nose. Her soothreader claimed it was 1 a.m., Kamarian Standard Time.

Time for a walk.

This was not the first night Eliana had found herself restless. Ever since they'd landed on the planet over a year prior, she had found it challenging to get comfortable. Maybe it was her body remembering the three-hundred-year journey in a stasis bed, or perhaps it was just the weight of the human lives that rested on finding the cure.

Eliana slipped her shoes on and left her room. The residential building she lived in was arranged much like an old Earth hotel, with long hallways filled with doors that led to single bedrooms, each with a small shower. Across the hall from her door was her father's room, and surrounding her were the rooms of the other long-time Telemachus Project members.

It was quiet, as it always was at night when there was less than a movie theater's worth of civilians living on a planet. Eliana didn't mind the quiet; it helped her think. She traveled her usual route on nights like this, toward the central park dome.

The synthetic crickets chirped, and the artificial breeze gently blew across the artificial turf of the park. Eliana had never been to a place like what this dome was simulating. She'd been fifteen when the Undriel had first approached Mars. Her father and the others had been moved from the terraformed planet to space stations orbiting Jupiter. She'd spent most of her formative years living at the academy on Remus Orbital.

Still, the park dome was pleasant. It was okay to pretend this triggered old memories of Earth. Eliana found a spot near the glass dome exterior to sit and watch the stars.

For a moment, she thought nothing of the figure standing beyond the glass wall, her mind tricking her into thinking it was some blurry fragment of her reflection. But before she could plunk down onto the grass, it moved.

It was a tall shape, nearly hidden in the darkness outside except for the glistening gemstones adorning its sashes.

"Mag'Ro," Eliana whispered, not believing it. As the auk'nai stepped closer to the glass, the light from inside the dome illuminated his feathers. The auk'nai they had been waiting months for was right here, just beyond the wall.

The dome was soundproof, but Mag'Ro's body language was clear. He held his grand hooked staff in one hand, and in the other was a bag. Mag'Ro stabbed the staff into the ground, where it stood rigidly upright, and opened the bag to Eliana, revealing more gems twinkling in the starlight.

"How did you know we need those?" Eliana asked, then thought to herself, *Where have you been?*

Eliana held a finger up in an attempt to stall Mag'Ro. There was a gateway nearby that would allow her to get outside. She scrambled toward it and entered the preparation area. There wasn't any time to wait for the others to wake up and join her; she'd have to convince Mag'Ro to give her the gems by herself. She scanned her soothreader against the locker terminal, and Homer summoned her equipment.

Within a matter of minutes, Eliana was in her atmospheric suit and equipped with her medical kit, some suit-repair tools, a bioscope, and a collider pistol that she prayed she wouldn't have to use. She used her scout access pass to exit the air lock and head into the night.

Mag'Ro waited for her not far from the air lock. The light from inside the dome bled outward onto the Kamarian grass.

When Eliana approached, Mag'Ro held the bag of gems at his side, still clutching his hooked staff in his other hand. Eliana held an open palm forward but kept her other hand low near her collider pistol, just in case.

"Have you brought those for us?" Eliana asked. She was still unsure how this creature could speak Sol Common, but she knew that he understood her somehow.

Mag'Ro cooed.

"Where have you been?" Eliana asked. "We waited for you."

Mag'Ro stood still for a moment, and at first, Eliana thought he didn't understand the question. Then he broke the silence. "Ve'trenn … fears human."

"Ve'trenn?" Eliana asked. "I don't understand."

"Ve'trenn." Mag'Ro puffed out his chest and emitted a rolling chirp, then said, "Old one."

Eliana thought she understood. "It's a name. Your leader? He's scared of us? We have never seen this Ve'trenn, though."

"Mag'Ro watch human. Speak of human to Ve'trenn."

"So you *have* been watching us," Eliana said, realizing her father's theory was right.

Mag'Ro cooed.

"But if Ve'trenn is scared of us, why give us the gems?" Eliana asked. Mag'Ro's long ears flopped downward reflexively, and Eliana eased up when she saw this moment of vulnerability. "Ve'trenn doesn't know you're giving these to us."

Mag'Ro cooed again.

"I can't tell you how much we need these. This will save lives," Eliana said as she reached for the bag.

Mag'Ro retracted the bag closer to his chest and said, "That."

Eliana traced the auk'nai's gaze to her collider pistol.

"I promise I won't hurt you. Do you want me to drop—"

"Give," Mag'Ro said.

Eliana froze. "You want me to give you this weapon?"

Mag'Ro cooed.

Eliana remembered the City of the Dead, the auk'nai citizens locked in a gory massacre. If she gave Mag'Ro the gun, she couldn't guarantee he wouldn't kill her with it.

Mag'Ro seemed to sense this thought. He plunked his staff into the dirt once more and rotated his open palm outward. It wasn't a good enough gesture to sooth Eliana's worries this time.

"Can you read my thoughts?" Eliana asked him flatly. At first, Mag'Ro said nothing, processing the question with an ear twitch.

"Auk'nai hears the tune of the unsung," Mag'Ro said, keeping his posture rigid. "Voice behind voice. Do humans not?"

"No, I'm afraid we can't." She couldn't take her mind away from the City of the Dead. "Before I give you this weapon, tell me …" Eliana queued up an image of the dead city onto her soothreader and displayed it to Mag'Ro. "Do you know this place? Are you from there?"

Mag'Ro's eyes went wide. His pupils rapidly pulsed, he let out a rolling birdcall, and his feathers fluttered.

"Ahn'ah'rahn'eem!" Mag'Ro shouted. Eliana pulled her soothreader away and put both her hands up to try and calm him down.

"Sorry! Sorry!" Mag'Ro's feathers slowly began to settle. Eliana winced. She wished her father were here to guide her; she felt like she might be triggering a war between a handful of sick humans and an unknown amount of alien bird people. It was like walking a linguistic tightrope. Eliana was making a secret trade with a strange creature she couldn't be sure wouldn't kill her and hide her body in the Kamarian wilderness. The risk was worth it.

"Auk'nai no go to Ahn'ah'rahn'eem," Mag'Ro grunted out, interrupting Eliana's self-doubt. "The unsung loud. The voice behind voice makes auk'nai lose self"—Mag'Ro shuddered as he searched for the right human word—"evil place."

A place that drove the auk'nai insane. Suddenly the intense feeling of dread Eliana had felt while exploring the place had weight to it. Fear was viral to mentally sensitive creatures like the auk'nai.

Eliana clutched the grip of the collider pistol at her hip and eyed the bag of gems as she weighed her options. She could keep the gun, but Mag'Ro would leave with the last element needed for the cure to save her people. She could shoot Mag'Ro, but if the auk'nai leadership was already untrusting of humans, then that would give them good reason to remain that way, and her people would never find more gems to cure lung-lock. She could hand him the weapon, take the jewels, and save her people, but that could potentially arm a hostile alien life-form. She could only wonder what the auk'nai could reverse engineer from the collider technology, and what violent things Mag'Ro might do.

There was only one correct choice.

Eliana pulled the pistol from her hip with measured speed, keeping it close to her abdomen as she held it on top of both her palms to not seem threatening.

Mag'Ro cooed, and his eyes pulsed.

Eliana held her breath. She wished the others were here to back her decision, to validate that this choice was the correct one. Eliana had to go with her gut instinct alone, which might sacrifice the only advantage humanity had over the auk'nai should they turn out to be a violent race of conquerors like Roelin had theorized.

But it was the only play she could make to cure lung-lock.

Eliana extended the collider pistol toward Mag'Ro, and he held out the bag of gems. They exchanged the items and investigated the authenticity of their prizes. Eliana waved her bioscope over the bag and confirmed the *Partial Synthesis Success* reading.

Mag'Ro activated the collider cylinder on the pistol and pointed it at the floor. He already understood how to set the weapon to fire, and the rotating cylinder on the outside of the gun made Eliana's guts drop.

She was unarmed, and Mag'Ro had not only the activated pistol, but his hooked staff could easily be used to slice her in half. Eliana was at the auk'nai's mercy, and for a moment, she couldn't move.

Mag'Ro deactivated the pistol and tucked it into the sash near his hip, mimicking human behavior. Eliana sighed loudly into her helmet as Mag'Ro grabbed the hooked staff he had jammed in the ground and bunched up the wings on his shoulders, preparing to fly away.

"Wait," Eliana said. "Where can we find you? We may need you again, and I don't want luck to dictate that."

Mag'Ro cooed and said, "First place."

"The flower grove over in the hills?" Eliana clarified.

Mag'Ro cooed, then fished out a device from a sash near his shoulder. It looked like a small whistle but with an alien bird-man flair about it. The mouthpiece was made of gemstone. Mag'Ro waved the object, and as air passed through it, it emitted a birdcall that resembled that of an old Earth eagle. He twirled it in his clawed hand and presented it to Eliana in one deft movement.

"Use it. It is for old ones who lost the heard-voice. Mag'Ro hear it, Mag'Ro find human," Mag'Ro said. Eliana took the whistle and tucked it into a pouch on her upper thigh. Before she could thank him, he pushed himself away from the ground and sailed off into the sky.

Eliana watched as he vanished into the starry night and almost forgot that she now had the answer to all of humanity's problems on Kamaria.

She was shaking, unsure if it was from the encounter with the alien life-form or because she was holding the objects they had been searching for so long. Thoughts about what she had given up to obtain the gems faded into the background as Eliana shouted in excitement.

"I need to tell the others!" she said to herself, then quickly scurried into the air lock and passed through the purification process. With her equipment packed away, she walked back into the park dome.

"Homer," Eliana said into the soothreader on her wrist, "I need you to wake the team and tell them to meet me in the scout dome. Tell them it's a top priority."

"Alert sent," Homer said. "Shall I prepare the helmet camera footage as well?"

"Good idea, there's a lot we need to go over."

Eliana rushed through the botanical gardens to the scout dome. She opened the door, and the lights flicked on. The rectangular meeting table in the center of the room hummed as it cycled its power, and each research station lined against the walls became illuminated.

Eliana almost dropped the bag when the light revealed Captain Roelin Raike standing near the biology station. He was looking upward at nothing in particular, equipped in his combat suit, his helmet resting between his elbow and torso.

"Hells, Roe. You scared the ghost out of me," Eliana said.

Roelin didn't turn to face her. He kept staring toward a corner in the ceiling. She realized there was no way Roelin could have responded so quickly to the alert Homer had just put out. He must have already been standing still enough so that the motion sensors decided no one was there.

"What are you doing here?" Eliana asked. She didn't move closer to him; in fact, she felt like backing out of the dome slowly. Something seemed wrong with his eyes, but she couldn't figure out what it was.

Faye had mentioned that Roelin was prone to night terrors. *Was sleepwalking also part of that?*

There was no way for Eliana to get Roelin back to his bed safely. Residential housing was a few domes away, and the man was built like a walking jetfighter, and he was even more bulky in his combat suit. So she had no choice but to wake him.

Eliana clapped her hands once.

Roelin's head snapped in her direction, unnaturally fast for someone walking around unconsciously. There was a strange glint in his eyes, and Eliana noticed she had not seen him blink since she'd entered. Something changed in his face then, as if he had been wearing some sort of mask and had just taken it off.

Roelin blinked a few times, then looked around the room and said, "Elly? How did I ..." He looked toward her and shook his head once more, pointed at the bag in her hand and asked, "What's that?"

"I'll show you!" Eliana said with glee. "The others have been alerted and are on the way."

Almost on cue, John Veston entered the room, his brow wrinkled, and he approached Eliana so quickly he didn't seem to notice Roelin was there. "What's wrong, Elly? Are you hurt? Did someone's purifier malfunction? Did something—"

Eliana opened the bag of gems and spilled some onto the table. John's brow eased as a smile spread across his face. "How did you—"

"I'll tell you all about it, Dad," Eliana interrupted him. "But first we need to help Marie get these synthesized."

"You're damn right," Marie Viray said from the doorway. She glided across the room and embraced Eliana tightly, then held her at arm's length. "I don't know how you did it. But you just saved humanity."

Marie grabbed the bag and held it high. "Alright, everyone, we have work to do. But most importantly ..." Marie said, turning to Roelin. "Captain, could you brew us some coffee?"

Roelin smiled and nodded, although Eliana could tell he was having a hard time figuring out how he'd gotten there.

Work on the cure to lung-lock began immediately.

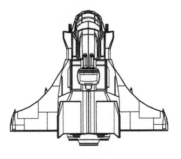

TEN

ROELIN RAIKE AWAKENED TO the sounds of a scream. His mind failed to register that something was wrong. The world he had woken up to felt normal, but a fully conscious Roelin would be terrified to see his windows open and a soft breeze gently blowing through the curtains.

He sat straight up in his old bed on Mars. This used to be home before the Undriel had forced them out. Roelin searched with his left hand for Faye, but she was missing. More screams echoed down the hall, just outside their bedroom door.

Faye was screaming.

He ran through the bedroom door.

It opened into the valley of statues outside the cave. The sky was pitch black, with an awful purple star boiling above. Time was shifting impossibly fast. Grass would grow and die, snow would fall and melt, alien flowers would bloom and decay. Everything was rapidly changing except the cave. The cave remained the same no matter how fast time moved. It was haunting.

Another scream told Roelin he had no time to stop and figure it out. It came from the mouth of the cave, as if the fog-filled maw was calling out for help. Roelin rushed inside and lost his footing on the slime that lined the floor. He tumbled through the fog into the abyss.

Roelin landed facedown in the muck. He pushed himself up, stopping halfway when he heard a gurgling noise. Something was on him, more than a dream—this thing was touching his mind. Needles dragged through his brain matter. His eyes felt as though they would burst from their sockets. Something was pushing against the back of his skull. He coughed, and blood came out of his nose and mouth.

Roelin stood and turned to see his captor.

Standing three meters tall, it was the corpse they had found during the expedition into the cave, although it was no longer a corpse. Standing before him was a towering monster. Its horned, birdlike skull was fully intact, and its deep-set eye sockets seeped a black tar. Roelin felt a sting in his shoulder and saw one of its barbed tentacles protruding from his skin. This brought Roelin back down to his knees, his eyes wide and bloodshot. The monster held its arms to its sides, fully extending the talons on its long fingers.

Roelin's scream was cut short as the claws clapped together on his skull.

———◆———

Roelin awakened, gasping for air. The windows were sealed plastic panels, no deadly breeze wafting into the room threatening to force him into lung-lock. He was sweating profusely and was about to wipe the moisture from his brow when he noticed the blood that was trickling onto his wrist from his nose. Roelin held his palm to his nostrils and walked to the bathroom. He staunched the blood flow from his nose, cracked open the medicine cabinet, and gulped down another dose of pain relievers. Roelin had been taking them regularly since the last scout excursion, but they weren't working.

Roelin shut the medicine cabinet and looked at himself in the mirror. He had been neglecting his regular morning routines, and a beard was beginning to grow. His hair was becoming ragged and uneven. It had been a week of constant nightmares, and these goddamned headaches.

"Suck it up," Roelin told himself, and then splashed some water on his face. He exited the bathroom and saw that Faye was still sleeping peacefully.

———— ◆ ————

Roelin awakened, this time in an atmospheric suit in front of the *Astraeus*, his old Undertaker-class warship. He had fought the Undriel for years in the pilot's seat of this metallic beast. Signs of hard-won battles still showed on its skin, even after extensive repairs, and the memories never faded. It had a large turret gun positioned on top and multiple guns lining its sides.

What am I doing in the shipyard, though?

Roelin didn't remember walking all the way across the colony to the shipyard. AJ approached him and said, "Good morning, Captain. Can I help you?"

"Just checking in on her," Roelin said, confused but not wanting to cause concern. "I have to go now."

"Roger that," AJ said, waving and carrying on with his business. Roelin shook his head and tapped the visor of his helmet.

———— ◆ ————

"Are you feeling alright, Roelin?" John Veston asked.

Roelin awakened and found himself sitting in the suit-donning room.

What the Hells? Are we on a scout mission?

The last thing Roelin remembered was standing in front of the *Astraeus* and talking to AJ.

"Roelin?" John asked again. Roelin noticed John wasn't wearing a suit, and no one else was around. "Faye was worried about you—she said you didn't come home last night."

"I didn't ... *what?*" Roelin mumbled to himself.

"Why don't you take some time off, get some rest. Sergeant Foster can escort us for a little bit," John said, and clapped his hand on Roelin's shoulder. Sergeant Clint Foster stood behind John. He was a tall, pale, gaunt man with sunken eyes. He gave Roelin a smile.

"Where is the body?" Roelin asked. *Why the Hells did I ask that? What body?* He didn't care about a damn body; he cared about these headaches! He wanted to invite John to help him, but couldn't.

He was being blocked by something.

"The body?" John asked. "Which body, Roe?"

Roelin stopped himself from almost saying, *My body.* Instead, he stood up and looked around. They were not on a scout mission. Roelin must have been in here by himself until John and Clint found him. How long had he been in here?

"You're right. I'm going to go get some rest," Roelin said.

"Take as much time as you need."

———◆———

"Are you listening to me, Roe?" Faye said.

Roelin awakened.

He was sitting at the edge of his bed with his back to Faye. She couldn't see that his eyes and nose were bleeding profusely. Roelin didn't respond. Instead, he stood and walked to the bathroom to clean up the blood.

He looked in the mirror and didn't see himself. He saw a husk of who he was—his hair had grown long and his beard was covered in blood. He felt like his brain had been pulverized.

Is this even real? What is real?

In his nightmares, he had felt himself being torn apart by his fellow colonists. John had cut deep into his chest cavity with a bone saw. Roelin checked himself for a wound but didn't find one.

He could hear constant screaming in his head.

It is so loud …

———◆———

"Ahn'ah'rahn'eem," Eliana said. She sounded far away, as if muffled by a wall.

Roelin awakened.

He was in the quarantine bay near the scout pavilion, looking into an empty autopsy room.

"Ahn'ah'rahn'eem?" John said. The two were discussing something in the adjacent room. *Do they know I'm here? Am I hiding?* Roelin wondered. "He got really agitated when you showed him the images," John continued.

"I think that's what they call the City of the Dead," Eliana said. "Mag'Ro used it as a noun."

Roelin turned his head, and blood trickled from his tear duct and splashed onto the floor in small droplets. He could hear the audio of video footage being played through a speaker. Eliana and John were studying the footage.

"He said the place was evil," Eliana said. "What do you think that means?"

———— ◆ ————

"Captain? What the Hells are you doing out here?" AJ asked.

Roelin awakened.

He was in his combat suit, walking in the middle of the night. *Where am I?*

After gathering himself, he saw the quarantine lab behind AJ. Had he really walked four kilometers in the middle of the night? Most colonists would have taken the ground sail.

"Sir! That's *dangerous*!" AJ shouted at his superior. "You haven't been right for weeks now! What's going on with you?"

Weeks? Weeks! To Roelin, these disjointed moments seemed to occur one after another. *Have I really been so off for weeks?* He began to sob in frustration.

"I don't know what's going on," Roelin said.

AJ looked him over. "Captain, I'll take you back to the colony and keep this quiet. But you have to promise me you'll get medical help in the morning. Can you do that?" AJ asked.

"Yes, I need help," Roelin grunted as AJ pulled the ground sail over. They boarded for the trip back. Roelin watched AJ navigate the night terrain. The lance corporal was saying something, but Roelin couldn't hear him. There was a high-pitched ringing in his ears that filled his world.

Roelin began to hyperventilate. Then he saw red.

———•———

Faye Raike awakened, alone again.

Damn it, I'm going to do something about this. She got herself dressed and called John Veston on her soothreader.

"Faye? Is everything alright?" John asked, checking his soothreader for the time. It was the twenty-fifth hour of a Kamarian day. "It's Roelin again, isn't it?"

"Yes, I'm worried about him. These night terrors and sleepwalking excursions are getting out of hand. I'm worried he'll hurt himself or get lung-locked somewhere, and we won't find him until—" She cut herself off to inhale. "He hides from me. I can't help him if he keeps evading me."

"Faye, it will be alright. I will make him my top priority. Do you know where he is now?" John asked.

"No. He shut his locator off," Faye said.

"Okay, I'll find him and bring him back to you. Try and get some rest. We'll get him the help he needs. I promise," John said. "What happened to AJ won't happen to Roelin, you hear me?" John said firmly.

Lance Corporal Allen Jensons had gone missing a few nights before during his security detail. The ground sail he had been operating had been found in the nearby woods with blood on it. The theory was that he'd been attacked by some predator during transit back to the colony. The colonists had been afraid of the surrounding forest ever since.

"Thank you," Faye said. She ended the call and sank to the floor. She waited for a moment, sitting and thinking of various ways Roelin could have accidentally killed himself sleepwalking around the colony, then plunged her face into her arms and wept.

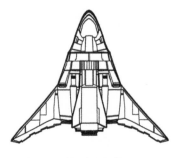

ELEVEN

JOHN VESTON DONNED HIS atmospheric suit to venture out into the night and find Roelin Raike. He pinged Homer on his soothreader and heard the calm robotic voice answer, "Good evening, John. What can I help you with?"

"Homer, I need help locating Captain Raike. He turned off his locator. I need to know if we can trace him from his home."

"No need, John," Homer said. "I have already located him. He was last seen entering the autopsy bay of the quarantine lab."

"What the Hells?" John said to himself. "We would have been notified if a ground sail had been transferred from the colony to the lab, though."

"No ground sail has been activated since earlier in the evening. Captain Raike has not exited the autopsy bay in approximately three hours."

"He walked there?" John asked rhetorically. Then: "What is he doing?"

"I am unsure. Roelin didn't turn on the power to the autopsy bay upon entering. I am blind to his actions inside. Before he went out of sight, I noticed he was armed in his combat suit."

John trusted Roelin with his life; they had been friends since their days on Mars. So why did Roelin's current whereabouts give John chills?

"Thank you, Homer. I'll be heading there now," John said, slinging a collider pistol into his hip holster, hoping he wouldn't have to use it.

"Should I alert General Raughts?" Homer asked. John thought that might be a good idea, but ultimately decided against it.

"That will be unnecessary, Homer. Roelin is a friend, and I intend to treat him as such."

As John walked across the open field to the ground sail station, he received a call from Eliana. "Hey, Dad, everything okay? I just got a call from Faye. She's worried about Roelin."

"Everything's okay. I'm heading to fetch him now. He's in the quarantine lab. I'll make sure he gets home safe." John took a breath, then added, "Please tell Faye it will be alright."

"What do you think this is? It's pretty severe for just sleepwalking."

"I'm not sure—he may need therapy. Maybe something in the City of the Dead dragged up old memories of the Undriel War that he needs help shaking. I wish I'd seen the signs sooner. I hate seeing a friend in pain."

"He hid it well from us. Whatever he's dealing with, he is trying to do it privately. But enough is enough. You're right, he needs help. And especially after what happened to AJ—" She cut herself off, superstitious that saying it out loud would cause it to happen to her father, then added, "Just be careful out there."

"I will. I'll let you know when I'm on my way back. Just keep Faye company in the meantime, alright?"

"I will," Eliana said, and they ended the call.

John started the engine on the ground sail and took off toward the lab. He kept one hand on his pistol and the other on the steering wheel. The ride was smooth, but his senses were heightened. John couldn't tell which unnerved him more: the thought of whatever happened to AJ possibly happening to himself or of Roelin doing something dangerous.

Would Roelin hurt me? John thought. He reminded himself that Roelin was a friend. A friend who needed his help.

He arrived at the lab, and as Homer had said, the lights were off. John entered the room slowly, keeping one hand on the grip of his holstered pistol. The lab was split into two rooms, the observation room and the autopsy chamber.

"Roe, you in here?" he asked the darkness, but it didn't respond. The quarantine bay was disconnected from the colony, and as such ran on different reserves of power. Soothreader access wasn't implemented yet, so old-fashioned switches and buttons were used to operate various functions of the lab.

John made it to the light switch and flipped it. The lights came on for a moment, then shuddered and gave out. The room returned to darkness.

In the brief flicker of light, John thought he had seen two figures in the autopsy chamber, but the moment had passed so quickly he wasn't sure exactly what he'd seen. He jerked out his pistol and kept it in his hand near his hip, pointed at the floor.

With a loud thud, the backup generator jolted to life, and the room became lit by the secondary emergency lights. John removed his helmet and placed it on the table. In the dim illumination, he could see Roelin sitting in the corner of the autopsy chamber by himself.

He was wearing full combat gear, with a machete on his shoulder, three hand grenades harnessed to his belt, a combat knife in its sheath, and his particle rifle leaning against the wall next to him. His helmet lay on the autopsy table.

John was shocked to see that Roelin had blood dripping from his mouth and nose. He placed his collider pistol on the observation room table as he rushed to Roelin's side.

"Roelin!" John shouted as he entered the autopsy chamber. "What the Hells, man! Are you hurt?"

Roelin lifted his head. His eyes rolled back into their normal position, and he asked, "Where did you move the body?"

John hesitated. Roelin's voice was wrong—it sounded like it was coming from far away. He wasn't sure what Roelin was asking.

"The *body?*" John asked with a mixture of worry and confusion. He turned his head toward the autopsy table. Did he mean the corpse they'd found in the crypt?

"The Siren?" he asked, referring to the name George had given it.

"Siii … rennn …" Roelin stretched it out, making it sound more like a guttural growl than a word.

"We did an autopsy and stored it away. What is happening to you?" John asked as he placed his hands on Roelin's shoulders and shook him, trying to break his trance. Roelin's eyes widened, and he looked at John's hands as if he had just been slapped.

John backed off a few steps. This was more than some post-traumatic stress episode. It was clear to him that Roelin had become infected with something, but how it could have happened, he was unsure. They had taken every precaution on their scout missions, wearing full atmospheric suits and taking biometric scans of every area, yet something had found a way to infect Roelin. Something beyond human comprehension and defense.

Roelin squinted, and tears began welling in his eyes. "Something's wrong." He lifted his hands to his head. The combat knife was now in his right hand, pressed against his head as he bobbed in pain. "*It hurts so much.* I felt everything. I felt the *autopsy.*"

John took another step backward, realizing that Roelin, with his combat equipment, could do great harm not only to himself but to others. He looked over his shoulder through the observation glass into the other room. His collider pistol lay uselessly on the table. He felt stupid, then considered his other options. He could take a few more steps toward the wall and hit the *Emergency Quarantine Lockdown* button, sealing them both in the chamber until someone unlocked it from the outside. He would just need to reach the button.

"Don't worry, Roe. I'm your friend, I'm here to help. We're going to fix you." John took a quick glance at the lockdown button on the wall and stretched his hand out toward it.

John was pulled back so quickly, the whiplash almost made him black out. Roelin slammed him onto the autopsy table with a loud bang, and the knife immediately followed. John cried out as the blade twisted into his shoulder. He begged through broken breaths, "Roe … *Please …*"

"I'm. Not. Roelin." Roelin's voice vibrated with the sound of another speaker behind it. The pupils of his eyes were vibrating, undulating in place like gelatin, and blood seethed from between his teeth. Roelin pulled the knife upward and brought it down again, this time into John's chest.

John struggled to breathe as the air was ripped out of him from the impact. He couldn't scream as the knife came down on him over and over again.

———— ◆ ————

"Marie thinks we'll have a full synthesis any day now," Eliana said. She was sitting with Faye in her residential unit. Eliana felt like she was talking to a wall, but it was the only way she could think to put Faye at ease. She continued, "We've been trained in how to use the temporary cure; we have enough for medical staff at least. We need to convince Mag'Ro to get us more gems to make enough to put in every home—"

"I'm done waiting," Faye interrupted.

The air purifier hummed quietly, reassuring everyone that they would not fall victim to lung-lock while the soft buzz continued. Eliana sat on a couch, bouncing her foot.

"I'm sure they are okay," Eliana tried to convince herself, then sighed and said, "I'll go with you."

Within twenty minutes, Eliana was piloting the ground sail as Faye kept her eyes on the tree line. She shined her helmet's flashlight into the forest beyond the meadow, hoping not to find a downed ground sail and two more victims to whatever beast had claimed AJ. Eliana was relieved to see the other ground sail parked at the quarantine lab. They hopped off and entered the lab through the air lock.

They found the lab dimly lit by the emergency backup lights. Eliana noticed John's helmet and a pistol on the table. The autopsy room's lights had flickered off when they'd entered, shrouding the room in darkness.

"Dad? Roe? You in here? We saw the …" Eliana trailed off when the light flicked on again.

Faye screamed at the top of her lungs.

Roelin was repeatedly bringing the knife down on John's body. The autopsy table shook with each impact, and wild arcs of blood splattered onto the observation window with every outward pull. John's corpse took the stabbings without protest; his life had drained away completely.

Eliana couldn't say anything. Her eyes were wide, her lips trembled, and she was frozen in place. Her breaths were shallow and automatic. She watched the violence of her father's murder and couldn't move a muscle to stop it.

Faye pulled out her collider pistol and aimed it forward, her hands shaking. She said nothing, only grit her teeth and tried to keep her eyes clear of tears as she focused her gun on her husband.

Roelin stopped his relentless assault, holding the knife upward. Blood dripped from the blade. He turned his head toward them, his face hidden by his blood-splattered helmet. He snatched his rifle so fast neither of them saw his hand move toward it.

Eliana managed to duck in time as Roelin shot three particle blasts through the observation window. A shot hit Faye in the arm and knocked her back against the wall, then smashed holes in the wall behind her. Dangerous Kamarian air began to leak rapidly into the room.

Eliana and Faye went lung-locked within moments. Faye writhed around on the floor, hopelessly gasping. Eliana desperately attempted to reach for her helmet but couldn't grasp it. She blacked out as Roelin stepped over them and exited the lab.

General Martin Raughts was awakened by an alarm. He was an old war vet, happy to be done with the Undriel. He had dark-brown skin and short black hair, with a scar on his chin from a close encounter with an Undriel soldier.

Homer announced, "We have an emergency. There has been a hull breach in the quarantine laboratory. The emergency staff has been deployed."

"I'll make my way there now. Alert essential staff," Martin said, and he hurried around his room.

The emergency medical staff arrived at the scene within moments. The ambulance craft landed near the ground sails, and the ramp lowered. Dr. Cassandra Wynter was the first off the ship, a medical kit in hand. She was a young woman with long blonde hair she kept contained in her atmospheric helmet. Her assistant, Fergus Reid, was a pilot from the colonial makeshift military back in the Sol System. He had recently signed on to the medical team as a part-timer.

Roelin exited the quarantine lab and trudged toward them. In the darkness, neither of the medical staff could see the blood on his combat suit or the rifle in his hands.

Dr. Wynter saw him first and said, "Roelin! Can you help here? I need—"

She was cut short as a particle blast from Roelin's rifle smashed through her helmet's visor and burst her skull open. There was nothing left but blood and brain matter inside her helmet. Her body dropped to the ground like a sack of meat. Fergus Reid saw Dr. Wynter go down and looked in horror at Roelin.

"Shit!" he shouted as Roelin brought his rifle up once more. Fergus pushed himself against the side of the access hatch of the ambulance craft as shots sliced through the interior of the ship. He slammed his hand against the door lock, and the hatch instantly sealed.

"General Raughts!" Fergus shouted into his soothreader on the private channel.

"Yes, what is the situation?" the general responded, rushing to don his atmospheric suit and round up more people to help.

"Ah Hells! One of the security officers just shot Dr. Wynter! She's dead, sir!" Fergus shouted. General Raughts turned to his left to see George Tanaka also donning his gear. The general gave him a stern look.

"Holy Hells, do you think it's *Roelin?*" George asked.

Outside of the quarantine lab, Roelin boarded a ground sail and took off at full speed toward the colony. Fergus watched him leave, then remembered the lung-locked victims inside the quarantine lab. He ran over to Dr. Wynter's body and grabbed the medical kit she'd been carrying, then sprinted into the lab. He found Eliana and Faye twitching on the floor in the late stages of lung-lock.

"Ah *shit!*" Fergus fumbled around in the medical kit for two syringes of the temporary lung-lock antidote. He knelt in front of them and slammed the needles into each of their chests. They inhaled sharply, but they still needed purified air while the cure worked. Fergus grabbed their helmets and placed them back on their heads, hoping he had made it in time.

Roelin pivoted the ground sail.

He was now heading toward the outer wall of the colony shipyard. Homer was active on the ground sail. "Captain Raike, please stop this." Roelin looked down at the device Homer spoke through and bashed it with his armored fist.

He dove from the ground sail as it smashed into the exterior wall of the shipyard. There was a loud crash as the vehicle made it halfway through the wall on impact. Roelin got to his feet and unhooked a grenade from his belt.

A platoon of Tvashtar marines waited inside the shipyard. These soldiers had been trained on Jupiter's moon Io. They were considered some of the best soldiers humanity had to offer.

The crash alerted them, and at once, all of their guns were trained on the impact zone in the wall. George and General Raughts entered just as a grenade exploded.

Roelin burst through the flames and immediately threw his remaining two grenades toward the marines. George watched as one of them bounced near General Raughts.

"Watch out!" George shouted, and tackled the general to the side, both narrowly missing the full blast of the grenade. A few marines were caught in the explosion, their blood splashing onto George's visor as he watched the chaos unfold in horror.

The marines returned fire with a barrage of particle blasts. Roelin was one step ahead of them, each shot missing by fractions of a millimeter. The jump-jet on his suit propelled him across the yard at an incredible speed.

"Run for your lives!" Roelin shouted, his voice amplified by the external megaphone on his helmet. George was confused into utter silence as he watched Roelin move through the shipyard, urging his victims to get away from him.

"Save yourselves!" Roelin shouted, then began picking off marines with precision shots made during a full sprint, making it look easy. George watched as a marine near him was struck in the chest, his blood plastering the spacecraft behind him.

Roelin approached the *Astraeus* and saw Sergeant Clint Foster defending it. Clint let loose a volley of shots that almost seemed to pass through Roelin, but tiny movements allowed him to dodge each blast with inhuman speed. Roelin covered the distance and propelled his knee into Clint's chest, knocking the sergeant backward.

Clint slid on his heels and used his own jump-jet to counteract the momentum. The maneuvers Roelin was pulling off with the jump-jet were unheard of, and the sergeant couldn't keep up. Roelin whipped his collider pistol upward from his hip and shot Clint directly in the collarbone, expelling blood and venting purified air. Clint flew back once more from the impact, this time tumbling across the shipyard as he began to go lung-lock from the suit puncture.

Roelin boarded the *Astraeus* as the access ramp closed behind him.

"Roelin, I will not allow you to take command of this warship," Homer said over the intercom.

Roelin said nothing in return.

"Roelin, surrender. I will not—" Homer urged, but was silenced as Roelin shot the control panel on the main bridge. The *Astraeus* would now be hidden from Homer's always-watching eye. Roelin sat in the pilot's chair and began the preflight sequence, accessing manual overrides with every step. The ship remained unaware that its captain had been hijacked and allowed him to proceed with his unlawful escape.

The *Astraeus* roared to life, a titan demon awakening from its slumber. Marines approached the exterior of the Undertaker-class warship as it began to lift off from the ground.

"Open fire!" General Raughts shouted. The marines unleashed a torrent of particle blasts into the warship, but their rifles were no match for the reinforced hull of the *Astraeus*. General Raughts could do nothing to stop Roelin from taking flight. The shipyard was an open area, unlike the gated hangar of the *Telemachus*. "Get some pilots down here, now!"

Pilots scrambled to get their atmospheric suits on in time. The *Astraeus* lifted straight upward and cleared the top of the shipyard wall. Instead of blasting off, it pivoted toward the marines.

General Raughts heard the familiar sound of a turret spinning its collider cylinder and shouted, "Get down!" to everyone in sight.

The turret whirled and launched a barrage of lasers into the surrounding ships. Some pilots still attempting to get into their Matador starfighters were vaporized. Blood and gore filled the yard, ships exploded, and those who tried to shoot back were met quickly with a deadly bolt from the *Astraeus*'s turret.

When enough carnage had been dealt, the *Astraeus* spun around and blasted off at full speed, leaving behind the dead, the wounded, and the crackling of fire.

George and General Raughts got to their feet and watched the warship shrink into the distance. They looked at each other with wide eyes. George attempted to pull up data on the *Astraeus* and discovered it was offline; he knew right away that Roelin had covered his tracks.

"He's gone ..." George whispered as he watched the chaos in the shipyard. Fires crackled, smoke billowed, people rushed around him.

Outside the quarantine lab, Eliana and Faye were in stable condition. Faye remained unconscious as Fergus monitored her life signs.

Eliana was trembling from the nightmare she'd just witnessed. Her father was dead, murdered by a man she considered family. She looked above her as the *Astraeus* roared past them into the night. Across the valley, she could see the fire in the shipyard from Roelin's violent exodus.

Eliana wanted to go to her father—he'd make it all better. She looked over her shoulder at the paramedics exiting the lab with a concealed body on a stretcher.

She cried into her helmet. She was all on her own now.

Kamaria had lost its innocence.

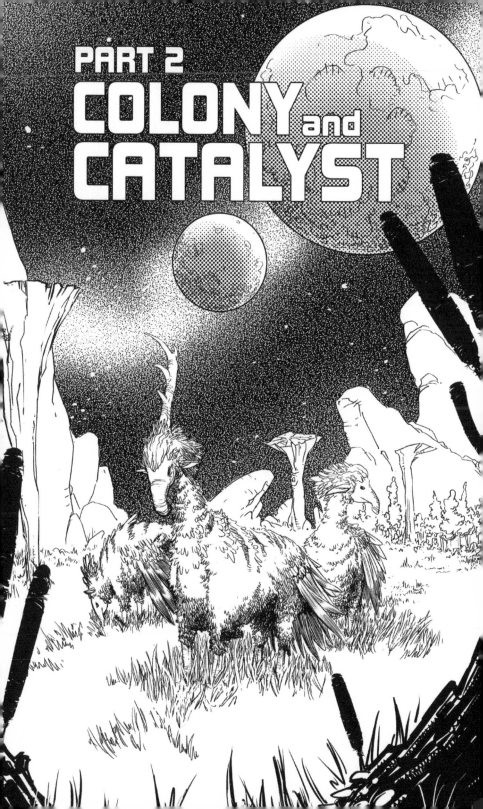

PART 2
COLONY and CATALYST

TWELVE

RAIN RUSHED AGAINST THE windscreen of the Undertaker-class warship known as the *Astraeus*. The onslaught of the downpour couldn't wash away the horror it had left behind in the colony. The bridge of the warship hummed with energy, loose items clacking together as they reacted to every twist and turn the pilot enacted.

Captain Roelin Raike breathed heavily under his combat helmet. His hands gripped the controls as if they were fused to them. He was the heart of the *Astraeus*.

Roelin's breathing stuttered sharply, then calmed. After what seemed like eons, he loosened his grip on the controls and inched his shaking hands to his helmet latches. The seal hissed as he unclicked the fasteners, and he pulled his helmet over his head slowly.

He coughed violently, allowing dark mucus to escape his throat and spray the console before him. Roelin wretched, thinking he would pass out from the strain of his vomiting, then he coiled into himself, holding his head in the palms of his blood-soaked gloves, his elbows resting against his blood-stained kneepads.

Roelin let out a long, strained scream until he almost felt the clutches of unconsciousness grab him. He screamed until the darkness clouded his vision and he could scream no more. When his screams ceased, he slammed his fists against the armrests of the pilot's seat, denting one of them. Then he grabbed his face in a futile attempt to rip his own head off, but failing, he slumped out of the seat and fell to the floor on his hands and knees.

He had seen it all. The Other that had blinded him had forced him to watch.

"Faye," he cried out weakly, allowing the drool of sadness to spill from his nose and lips onto the floor. "Faye, oh God. What have I done?"

Roelin had been awake inside his body when his arms had reached for John and stabbed him. He'd been awake when Faye and Eliana had entered the room and he'd shot at them, leaving them to die of lung-lock on the floor of the quarantine bay. He'd been awake when he'd shot Dr. Cassandra Wynter in the face, blowing her head off her shoulders in a spray of blood and gore. He'd been awake when he'd killed the Tvashtar marines in the shipyard. Worst of all, he'd been awake when he'd turned the large cannons of the *Astraeus* on his fellow colonists.

Roelin was unsure of exactly how many had been killed that night, but he knew they had died because of him. His hands vibrated.

Awake, yes, but in control, no. Roelin's functions were not his own, but that of this Other. Roelin was the handgun but not the trigger finger. He pressed his gloved hands against his face once more, hoping his tears would drown him and make it all go away.

The madness of the moment gave him an idea. He could go back to Odysseus Colony and turn himself in. It was the right thing to do; he needed to face punishment for his crimes. Maybe he could explain what had taken control of his body and the scientists could do something about it.

Roelin stood and threw himself back into the pilot's seat. He kept nodding as waves of optimism rolled through him. This was the right play, the correct call, and it would fix all of this. He took the controls in his hands once more ...

Roelin awoke still in the pilot's chair of the *Astraeus*. He checked his vectors and found that he had not corrected his course. The *Astraeus* was heading south; he would have to turn completely around to make it back to the colony. Roelin grabbed the controls …

He awoke again in the pilot's chair, heading south. *What is happening?* "This is ridiculous!" Roelin shouted in anger. "No! We're going back! Enough of this!" He grabbed the controls …

Pilot seat, heading south. There was no stopping it. Roelin slammed his fists against the armrests in a hopeless tantrum. He felt a sharp pain in his arm and looked down and saw that the right forearm of his combat EVA suit had been punctured. He squinted, confused. He searched the bridge for the answer and found something written on the wall in blood.

NO TURNING BACK.

Roelin's eyes widened in fear. He stood from the pilot's seat and backed away. "No, not possible."

Another idea came to Roelin, and he looked upward and shouted, "Homer! Take us back to Odysseus Colony and ignore further orders from me!"

Roelin smiled—this would do it. He waited for the kind robotic voice of Homer to soothe his worries and fix everything, but there was only silence.

"Homer! Homer, I command you!"

His heart dropped a few inches inside his chest as he realized he was no longer connected to Homer. He thought back to earlier that night and remembered blasting the Homer mainframe with his sidearm as he'd entered the *Astraeus*. The Other had somehow known that severing the ship from Homer would make it impossible for Odysseus Colony to track the *Astraeus*.

What the Hells is this thing?

One last idea. Roelin went back to the pilot's seat and sat down. He reached for his sidearm, unclasped it from its holster, and pushed the barrel under his chin. He closed his eyes.

Roelin awoke to see his gun on the floor across the room. The pain from his right arm had increased. He blinked weakly and saw a new message written on the wall, his blood the ink once more.

WE ARE GOING TO SYMPHA.

Roelin blinked again, confused. Where was Sympha? Hells, *what* was Sympha? He held his forearm to stop the blood flow. He checked the holographic displays to see where the Other was taking him. Still south, toward a Kamarian jungle at the base of a hook-shaped mountain. He was farther from the colony than any of the colonists had ever been before.

The rain continued to batter the windscreen of the *Astraeus* as Roelin looked out over the jungle canopy. A flash of lightning revealed the silhouette of an enormous shape in the distance. He squinted and waited for another flash.

Roelin let out a silent shriek as he felt pain lance through his skull. He choked out agonized breaths and thought he could hear people talking.

No, not talking—screaming.

"TURN BACK, NHYMN!" the voice, angelically fierce, boomed through his mind. Pain behind his eyeballs felt like his face was going to tear away from his skull.

What is a Nhymn?

Roelin wanted nothing more than to obey and turn back, but his body began to move again on its own. He stood like a puppet on strings and sat back down in his pilot's chair. His fingers performed a dance they had done many times before, but the movements were not of his design. The large turret of the *Astraeus* activated and rotated into a forward position. Roelin could only watch his body betraying his mind.

"TURN BACK!" the voice shot through him once more. Roelin's hands punched the throttle forward, full speed ahead. He looked through the large windscreen into a mess of storm clouds and jungle trees whipping around in the intense winds. Through a flash of lightning, Roelin could see something immense moving in the distance, closer now.

It was a monster.

It looked like the Siren body they had found in the crypt near the City of the Dead, but its skull was shaped like a child's drawing of a human heart. It was taller than the most significant buildings Roelin had seen in the Sol System, looming hauntingly above the jungle canopy inside of a cyclone.

There was another lightning blast. Roelin noticed this time that the lightning was not coming from the swirling storm clouds above, but instead from the jungle floor below. The whole world was wrong. Roelin was panicking on the inside, but on the outside, his body was ready for war.

"*NHYMN!*" the voice boomed again. He winced and pushed the *Astraeus* forward. The turret began to fire, lighting up the night. The monster ahead moved its massive arms to cover its skull from the impacts of the laser blasts.

Huge tentacles flailed outward, uncoiling through the sky like whips the size of mountains. The *Astraeus* dodged them and let out another round of punishment. A roar shook the planet. A dozen unknown sources on the jungle floor launched green electrical bolts of light at the *Astraeus*.

The Other was not fast enough to dodge this volley, and the *Astraeus* took the full impact of the bolts across its hull. Roelin felt the electricity pass through him as it waved through the ship. His teeth wanted to eject from his mouth like ivory bullets. His eyes threatened to engorge, then burst. Roelin's vision turned solid green, and he thought his death wish might be granted after all.

Roelin fell sideways from the pilot's seat. As he blinked away the residual pain of the electrical bolt, he looked to his right and saw the phantom figure of the Other inside the ship with him.

It was the Siren they had found in the cave, the specter that haunted his nightmares. The two monsters resembled each other enough to clearly be the same species, but their sizes were vastly different. The Other inside the ship stood a few heads taller than Roelin; the one outside dwarfed the mountains around it.

The Other was not looking back at him. Instead, it was focused on the monster outside in the rain. The *Astraeus* began to tilt, slamming Roelin against the wall. He watched the cliffside sail toward the windscreen, and he started screaming at the top of his lungs.

Then there was darkness.

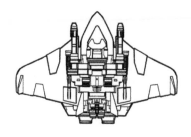

THIRTEEN

PRESENT DAY

FOUR YEARS AFTER THE MASSACRE

HIGH ABOVE ODYSSEUS COLONY, beyond the clouds in the Kamarian sky, past the outer atmosphere and away from the planet, the void waited with endless patience. For now, it was an unremarkable spot of emptiness. Particles danced their microscopic waltz in an uninterrupted evening. The universe moved undisturbed, as it had for time eternal.

The *Telemachus* burst into existence in the Delta Octantis system. The spacecraft had been propelled at near light speed during its three-hundred-year journey from the Sol System. It began the deceleration process on approach to Kamarian orbit.

Homer slowly began awakening some of its sleeping travelers, nursing them back to consciousness like newborn babies.

————— ◆ —————

"There we go, looking good," a kind female voice said. It was the first thing Denton Castus's ears had heard in three centuries. It only felt like one night had passed since he and his family had been put into their stasis beds.

In time, the woman before him came into focus. She was wearing a tight-fitting atmospheric suit with her helmet removed. She had dark skin, and her short ebony hair was combed to hang over the right side of her face in twisted locks. Her brown eyes looked big behind her thick, burgundy-rimmed glasses. Her name tag read, "E. Veston."

"Can you tell me your name?" E. Veston asked.

Denton was still gathering himself. He needed to vomit, and his head felt loose on his neck.

"D-Denton." He paused and crushed his eyelids together, frowning, holding back the urge to throw up, then powered through it. "Denton Castus."

"Good, good," she said, checking his health readings on her soothreader. "Your brothers and parents are all doing well. We're just here aiding in the awakening process. We've added a component that …" She stopped herself as she looked up at Denton, who was still trying very hard not to throw up in front of her. "Mr. Castus, please allow yourself to vomit." E. Veston pushed the receptacle toward him and tapped its rim.

"Nah, I'm good. What's the new component?" He was turning green.

"No shame in it, Mr. Castus." She ignored his attempt to change the subject. "Go ahead, use the pan."

Denton held his cool for a moment longer, maintaining eye contact but screwing up his face in the process. E. Veston stifled a laugh at the display.

"I'm—" Denton started, then grabbed the receptacle and hurled his guts into it.

"There you go, tough guy," E. Veston said, smiling. She let him finish and then handed him a wet wipe.

"Sorry 'bout that," Denton said, dabbing his lips with the wet wipe.

She smiled and handed him a pouch of water. "There's nothing wrong with throwing up. Vomiting means your body is adjusting correctly. If you didn't do it, we'd have a problem. Just like your red skin color." She waved her tablet pen over his entire body.

Denton looked down at himself for the first time. He was wearing the sleeping suit designed to connect with the stasis bed, but his skin underneath felt hot. He looked at his hands and noticed the bright-red color they reflected.

"Woah, *this is normal?*" he asked.

"Completely normal, Mr. Castus," E. Veston said with a reassuring smile. "Now, if you were purple or blue, that would be a dif—"

"You can call me Denny, Doc," Denton interrupted her. She smiled and flicked her soothreader. His alias changed from *Mr. Denton Castus* to *Denny*.

"Alright, Denny," she said. "You can call me Elly."

"Sounds good." He flexed his hands, trying to cool them off. He wanted to jump in a bathtub of ice. "It's as hot as Hells in here. How long does this last?"

"Your body is reacquainting itself with your blood again after using a synthetic solution as a lubricant during the trip. Your actual blood was kept in its own stasis chamber inside of your bed to keep it from coagulating. If you had any blood diseases, which"—Elly thumbed through Denton's information—"you did not, by the way, the bed would have cleaned out any abnormalities."

"Pretty freaky stuff." Denton coughed.

"What? *Freaky?*" She chuckled. "It's just your blood not being inside your lubed-up body for three hundred years, what's so freaky about that?" She laced her words with sarcasm. Denton grinned and nodded.

"You mentioned you added a component?" he asked.

"Yes. On Kamaria, there is an airborne bacterium that causes human lungs to go into paralysis. We called the symptom lung-lock. It took us years to develop a cure, but we eventually solved the issue. We call it the Madani Cure, after the first family to succumb to the affliction. You will be able to breathe Kamarian air reliably. As a bonus, the cure will be passed to any children you have in the future."

"Amazing. Must have been rough before the cure," Denton said. Elly looked away from him and down at her soothreader. She had pain behind her eyes. Denton felt like he'd stung her somehow.

"You know, you're lucky," Elly said without looking back up at Denton.

"Is that right?" Denton spat again into the receptacle.

"Your skill set as a mechanic, as well as those of the rest of your family, has given you a priority awakening schedule. We were only expecting ten thousand travelers. Imagine our surprise when thirty thousand of you showed up."

"Surprise." Denton waved his hands in mock enthusiasm.

"We have to synthesize more of the Madani Cure before we can wake everyone up. But until then, there's plenty to do."

"Of course there is." Denton deflated. There was a silence as Elly input a few commands into the holographic display of her soothreader.

"So, the war really …" Elly began to ask but couldn't seem to find the words.

"We lost," Denton said. Elly said nothing, and her eyes darted toward the floor. Denton felt like he'd slapped her. He fumbled for something to say and landed on, "But we have a second chance, thanks to you."

Elly blushed. She looked him in the eyes and winced out a curt smile. "Well, Denny, everything looks good here. You will get further instructions shortly. Homer will be monitoring your vitals, and we'll rush right in if there are any issues."

"Thank you, Elly," he said.

"See you planetside," Eliana said. She bobbed her head, then left the room.

———— ◆ ————

After three days of physical testing and vital checks, the Castus family was finally allowed to return to their spaceship. Michael and Brynn sat in the pilot seats. Denton, Jason, and Tyler sat in three chairs behind them. Everyone had their atmospheric suits on for the trip, as mandated by Telemachus Command.

"Alright, old gal. Don't fail me now," Michael said, and activated the ship. Old lights flickered and chugged for a second, then everything shut off. Michael punched the terminal above him, and the interior ship lights reactivated and hummed smoothly. Dust shot out of vents, and the scrubbers kicked in and cleaned the air. "There we go," Michael said with a big grin on his face.

"Everyone ready?" Brynn asked.

"Yeah, Ma," Jason said.

"All set," Denton said.

"Are we there yet?" Tyler teased. Denton reached out and whacked him in the chest while Jason laughed.

"*Lelantos*, this is Telemachus Command. You are cleared to launch. Please proceed out through the encasement barrier. Follow your in-flight coordinates to Odysseus Colony," an official-sounding flight controller informed them.

"Thanks, Command. We enjoyed your hospitality. Over and out," Michael said, and grabbed his controls. The *Lelantos* roared to life. "Like old times, eh, gal?" Michael said to his ship. He pushed forward on the throttle, and the ship moved through the hangar bay and slipped through the barrier, and the family watched as the *Telemachus* shrank into the distance. Denton noticed the *Telemachus* begin to rotate.

"Show-off." Brynn smiled and playfully pushed her husband's shoulder for barrel-rolling the *Lelantos*.

"The old lady wants to dance—who am I to say no?" Michael said, and began more flight tricks, rolling the ship in different ways, bobbing and weaving around, creating an engine trail that looked like a doctor's handwriting.

"*Lelantos*, please follow your flight coordinates," the Telemachus Command controller said with a stern voice.

"Yes, sir!" Michael said, and aligned the ship with the

holographic display on his windscreen.

"Oh, you're in trouble!" Jason said with a hearty laugh.

The *Lelantos* entered Kamarian atmosphere.

Denton was relieved and yet also a little surprised that nothing flew off the ship during reentry. Brynn and Michael removed their helmets and nodded to Jason, Tyler, and Denton, who did the same.

There was a thick layer of clouds resting in the sunlight of the alien star. Denton had never been to a place with clouds before. They were fluffy and gray, inviting weary travelers to rest on their pillow-like bodies. The ship bumped as they drew closer to the clouds, the violence of the turbulence contradicting the gentle invitation.

A score of other colonist ships joined the *Lelantos* in their flight path to the colony. Denton felt good about traveling to a rendezvous without being chased to it by the Undriel. Out the window, other ships ducked in and out of the clouds, creating trails of fluff. The vessels dropped altitude, and moisture built up on the front window. Once clear of the clouds, Denton was finally able to view the alien horizon.

It was early spring on Kamaria. The grass was a deep purple, with explosions of orange and yellow flowers. Large swaths of light shined through the patches of clouds into valleys below.

"What the Hells are those?" Jason asked, amazed at the creatures he saw roaming among the flowers. They were quadrupeds with hard crimson carapaces and mustard-colored fur, like a buffalo crossed with a giant beetle.

"We are not on Ganymede anymore, boys," Michael said with wonder in his voice.

"*Lelantos*, this is Odysseus Local," a new voice said over their communication channel.

"Go ahead," Michael said.

"There's a daunoren heading in your direction. Please raise altitude to allow it to pass," the flight controller said, and a prompt popped up on Michael's display, indicating his current altitude and the target they wanted him to achieve.

"Affirmative, Odysseus Local," Michael said, and pulled back on his flight stick until his display was green, indicating he had completed the request. Underneath, the family could see the daunoren the controller had mentioned.

It was an enormous bird of various wild colors. Denton guessed that, with its wings fully spread out, it was double the size of the *Lelantos*. The alien bird had long tail feathers that chased it across the sky. It was like a battleship cutting through the clouds.

"All clear, thanks, *Lelantos*. Continue approach," Odysseus Local said.

"Roger that," Michael said, and exchanged glances with Brynn.

The colony finally came into view. The Odysseus team had accomplished a great deal in the six Kamarian years between the first landing day and the arrival of the *Telemachus*. There were no longer domed habitats interconnected by glass hallways but, instead, a walled-off village full of traditional homes that did not need to be sealed off from the dangerous Kamarian air. People walked through open areas without atmospheric suits on.

Construction was underway on an entirely new section of the colony, with more homes being built, as well as apartment complexes to accommodate multiple family units. The shipyard was extended and filling up with the arriving colonist spacecrafts. Families were off-loading equipment and luggage from their long journey. Denton remembered what the doctor had told him: this influx of colonists was only a portion of those needing to be revived from cryosleep. The still-sleeping colonists aboard the *Telemachus* were going to need Madani Cures and homes. Denton imagined the pristine landscape covered in buildings and wondered if humanity had earned the right to molest this perfect place.

There was a tower of scaffolding in the center of the colony. This construction was going to be the expanded Kamarian council building, which would house meeting rooms and feature more representation for the influx of colonists arriving from the *Telemachus* that day.

Two kilometers outside the colony wall, Denton could see the *Odysseus*, standing tall where it had touched down when the first colonists arrived. It looked like a relic, a symbol of victory over the challenges of space exploration. It was the foundation ship that people like Elly had traveled on to Kamaria years ago.

"Prep for landing," Michael said, clicking a few toggle switches on the console above his head.

"Landing gear deployed," Brynn said as she flipped a switch. Michael throttled back and let the *Lelantos* drift gently to the ground of the large shipyard area. The ship vibrated with the gentle impact of landing, and the legs held this time.

"Landing successful," Michael said, grabbing Brynn's hand and giving her a toothy smile. Denton unlatched his seatbelt, stood up, and stripped off the rest of his atmospheric suit. Jason began to do the same, then turned to see that Tyler had fallen asleep during the ride.

"Seriously?" Jason said as he waved his arm toward Tyler. "Like three hundred years wasn't a long enough catnap?" He slapped his glove against Tyler's leg. Tyler jolted upright in his seat.

"What's up?" Tyler said groggily, then looked out the window and saw they had landed. "Oh Hells! Why didn'tcha wake me?"

"I just did, dumbass!" Jason said.

Denton lowered the access ramp, and a rush of fresh air hit the family. Enough sunlight peeked through the dissipating clouds to dance on Denton's exposed hand. The sun warmed his skin without the filter of a glass dome; it tickled in a strange, warm way. He turned his palm upward, catching the sunlight.

Above him, the sky seemed to go on forever. For a moment, Denton felt a sort of reverse vertigo. Without the roof of a dome, he felt like he'd float away from the planet and drift back out into space. His legs felt wobbly. Denton closed his eyes and took a few deep breaths. When he opened them, he noticed each of his family members had taken a moment to adjust to the roofless sky as well.

He took another deep breath and allowed the fresh air to enter him. The light faded, and a slow drizzle of rain began, bringing with it more brand-new sensations. They shared a moment of elated silence as the gentle rain soothed them.

"Hey, is that what I think it is?" Tyler said, looking to the nearest building.

"You got to be kidding me," Jason said. He dropped his arms to his sides and cocked his head.

Less than a kilometer from where the *Lelantos* had been ordered to land stood a medium-size machine shop. It looked empty, waiting for something. A new hover truck pulled up, Tvashtar design, and a gaunt man got out of it wearing a military uniform.

"Welcome, Castus family," the marine said. He had a voice synthesizer in his throat, adding a robotic rattle to his words. The man had a visible scar peeking out from the collar of his uniform. The family waved to him, and he said, "I'm Sergeant Clint Foster. I'm here to assist you with anything you need."

"Thanks, Sergeant Foster. But I have my boys here to help," Michael said.

"Great," Clint said. "If you wouldn't mind coming with me, sir, we have a special arrangement for you and your family we'd like to discuss. Feel free to off-load your belongings into the machine shop over there." Clint thumbed through data on his soothreader and passed the information to the readers of each family member by flicking his hand toward them.

"Is that …" Michael said, and his jaw dropped. "Is that for us?" He pointed to the empty machine shop.

"Yes, Mr. Castus," Clint said. "It appears your colony leader, Councilman Trever Blaise, said you had the best machine shop on Ganymede."

"The only machine shop on Ganymede," Jason muttered. Denton nudged him discreetly.

"Councilman Blaise requested to have you represent the Arrow of Hope's worth in the new colony." The sergeant swiped his hand across his soothreader. Denton looked down at his own soothreader and noticed he had been granted access to the new Tvashtar hover truck Clint had arrived in. Denton looked up, and the sergeant smiled and added, "The truck is yours as well."

"Hells yeah," Jason said. He walked past the marine toward the truck.

"Sounds like I should have voted for Blaise in the last colony election," Michael muttered.

"I did," Brynn said. Michael raised his eyebrows. Brynn shrugged at him.

"You will find the shop should be a little larger than your original one on Ganymede. There are living quarters on the second floor with room for your whole family," Clint added.

"This is too kind," Brynn said.

"Don't thank me. Thank your councilman," the sergeant said, then turned to Michael. "But, please, if you two would come with me, we'll get all the official business out of the way."

"Alright, lead the way," Michael said.

"You guys all right unpacking? Don't go getting us kicked off the planet," Brynn said, and waggled a thumb toward Tyler and Jason.

"No promises," Denton said, and smiled. He watched his parents walk away down the road toward the center of the colony.

Denton looked at the shop. It was bigger, that was certain. The Castus family would be able to pick up right where they'd left off on Ganymede. He could see how excited his father was about the opportunity to forge their legacy anew. Denton hadn't known what sort of life awaited him on Kamaria, but he had hoped for something different than the life he'd left behind.

This boon of resources felt like a cage.

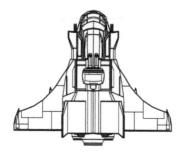

FOURTEEN

FOUR YEARS AGO

DAY 2 OF ROELIN'S EXODUS

ROELIN RAIKE FELT THE familiar puffs of cold air mixed with blasts of heat. The sky above him contained only a bright-purple sun that peered down like a cyclopean eyeball. He stood before the cave of the Siren, a place he had been many times in his mind since that scout mission.

He was having another nightmare. No matter how many times this vision repeated, he felt the need to run from the approaching shadow. It was racing toward him with its talons stretched out and its long horn thrust forward from its birdlike skull.

The Siren was coming for him. Every night, he ran, and every night, she engulfed him.

Roelin inhaled sharply as he awoke.

He lay against the wall in the bridge of the downed *Astraeus*. He patted his right hand on his chest and face to make sure he wasn't missing anything. His left arm was immobile.

The combat suit he wore absorbed most of the impact of the crash from the night before. The battle of the sirens had not claimed his life, and the fact he was breathing meant the bridge had stayed intact during the wreck. Otherwise, he would have been lung-locked already.

Roelin stood, his body protesting as he straightened himself out. The harsh sunlight shined through the windscreen and forced him to shield his eyes.

Is it dawn or sunset?

Roelin forced himself back into the pilot seat and queued up the holographic display. There was no power, but the *Astraeus* had contingency plans in place for this situation. He bumped his fist against a panel on the side of his seat, and it slid outward, revealing a crank.

Roelin pushed the crank in a circular motion, generating just enough power to jump-start the system. Once he could hear the humming of the air purifiers, he shoved the panel back into its compartment. He was thankful the purifiers worked, a small victory.

The holographic display flicked to life. There were blank spots due to the damage, but overall, it was still mostly legible. It illustrated the level of damage to the ship and calculated his new limitations. He would be able to walk around the ship without a helmet, luckily, but the *Astraeus* was not going to fly again without extensive work. Roelin coughed and felt the sting of a thousand needles against his arm.

Roelin shuffled over to the medical bay. There was equipment tossed around the room, making it appear as if there had been looters in the night. Roelin would have welcomed looters. Hells, he would have welcomed assassins.

Roelin opened a field kit and grabbed a medical scope to scan himself. Lacerations lined his arm, and his left shoulder was dislocated. He sighed, knowing how to fix himself but not looking forward to the extended pain. He took a strap off his suit and wrapped it around his shoulder and elbow. Once secure, he grabbed the loose part of the strap and gave it a rough yank, hearing a crunch as his bones clicked back in place. He grunted through the pain, then let out an elongated groan.

Taking long, deep breaths, Roelin calmed himself. He could now flex his arm enough to remove his suit. He unbuckled the armor plating, allowing it to drop loudly to the floor with metallic clangs, then he pulled the undersuit away from his upper half slowly, still feeling the pain of the shoulder fix.

Roelin winced as the sticky blood from his forearm that the Other had used as an inkwell clung dryly to the interior of the sleeve. One more pull, and his upper half was free of the suit, but his arm still bled. He reached for the suture foam in the field kit and squeezed it onto the wound.

The bleeding stopped instantaneously. The foam expanded and then slowly began to shrink, pulling the skin surrounding the wound together and sealing it. Roelin grabbed some painkillers from a locked cabinet and swallowed a few, then sat in the recovery couch for some time, allowing himself to heal.

Hours later, Roelin felt the need to assess the exterior of the ship. He equipped a scout suit that had been left in the locker room. Having never worn a civilian space suit before, he felt like he had been sucked into a big marshmallow.

The air-lock door sealed behind him as he stepped into the threshold between the ship and open air. Then nothing happened. His heart sank when he thought he might be trapped in this claustrophobic space, left to die of starvation whether the Other intended for it to happen or not. He banged his hand against a panel on the wall, and a misty spray blasted out over him. He sighed with relief. Once the decontamination spray finished its work, the outer door opened, and Roelin stepped out.

He dropped down to the jungle floor, stumbling to his knees. A strange clicking and honking noise bleated out from the trees around him. He looked up to see a very odd creature laughing at his misfortune. The creature stood a meter tall and had a tubular snout with a fuzzy back and a tail like a beaver's paddle. Roelin's first thought went to George and John. Those two would have had their bioscopes ready. Roelin remained on his knee as he thought back on the night of horror.

"John," Roelin whispered as he shook his head, "I'm so sorry. For everything." He stood up and ignored the creature's laughs and took in the perimeter of the ship.

There was a small pond that received a waterfall from a cliff ledge above and cascaded to another shelf below. This was good; he could create a water purifier and sustain himself. The trees nearby had ebony trunks and crimson leaves, giving the clearing a macabre feel.

He turned around and saw an overhanging rock ledge that thrust its way from the side of the mountain, casting a dark shadow over the *Astraeus*. Beyond the ridge, Roelin could see the oddly shaped mountain peak, like a sharp knife pointing toward the sky. He was surprised to see there wasn't a broken row of trees from the crash. It took him a moment to discover the *Astraeus* must have smashed, top first, into the cliffside under the overhang, then dropped into position in the clearing below. If it hadn't been a warship, the hull would have crumpled like an old soda can, but the *Astraeus* was built to withstand devastation.

Roelin walked around the ship, noting what would need to be repaired on the outer hull. The *Astraeus* was right side up, although tilted slightly. It was resting on its belly, without the use of landing gear. Smoke billowed from the top of the ship where it had collided with the cliff wall. Two windows on the starboard side were blown out; those rooms would need to be vented and purified before he could go inside them without a helmet. The *Astraeus* needed a lot of work, and Roelin wasn't sure if he had the skills to perform the required repairs.

He made his way back inside and checked the food supplies. He opened a few cabinet panels and discovered he had enough rations from the *Telemachus* to live comfortably for a few months, longer if he split his portions.

What is there to wait for? Possibly the scouts would stumble upon him, or maybe a search party looking for him would come this way?

Whatever it was, he was sure the Other inside him would force him to stay alive until something happened.

Roelin dug a little deeper into the cabinet and found a bottle of Arcas wine, which he'd been saving for a special occasion but had completely forgotten about. He popped the cork and sat against the wall of the hallway as he swigged straight from the bottle.

Roelin thought of having a glass of wine with his wife, Faye. They'd enjoyed a few romantic dinners under the domes of the colony habitats after landing on Kamaria. He especially remembered how happy everyone was after the first scouting mission. He wanted to go on more scouting missions with his wife and friends.

His friends. He paused at the thought. John Veston was dead. Had he killed Faye as well? He had no idea who was still alive after that night. Roelin took another swig of the wine and then began to sob uncontrollably. He covered his face and shrank into the corner, wishing he could just slip away into the shadow.

He caught his breath when he thought he saw something at the other end of the dark corridor. It was the Other—he could feel it scratching in the corners of his mind, but he could not see it. *What does it want? Why did it take me?*

Why did this happen?

———◦———

PRESENT DAY

The first few weeks on Kamaria were filled with adjustments for Denton Castus. The job was familiar, but the clients were different. On Ganymede, in the Arrow Colony, everyone had known the Castus family and had relied on them for their repair needs. On Kamaria, their name held little weight. Even with a more extensive shop and new equipment, they found it difficult to compete against the previously established Tvashtar machine shop on the other side of the colony.

Historically, it had always been like this. Denton's grandfather had competed with the Tvashtar engineers for colonial contracts, and had lost every time. It was worse now, having only kilometers between shops instead of the space between Io and Ganymede. There were many afternoons where there wasn't enough work to do in the shop, and the brothers would help with the construction of colonial housing.

Denton felt like he was living each day on repeat. He would wake up and work in the shop on scraps the Tvashtar guys didn't have time for, repairing whatever broken thing came his way until midafternoon. Then he would help with the construction of colony houses until early evening. After these jobs were completed, he would finally go home and pass out, only to repeat the process the next day.

Denton sat against part of the scaffold of the home they were constructing, looking at the sandwich wrap he was about to eat for lunch. His brothers chewed their food quietly. Jason slammed his sandwich back into his lunch box.

"Okay," Tyler said. "What's wrong?"

"They set us up to fail," Jason said.

"What makes you think that?" Denton asked.

"Just look at the Tvashtar shop over there!" Jason thrust his hand out beyond the scaffolding at the machine shop down the road. There was a line of trucks waiting to get serviced, and workers moving around performing various tasks with the garage door open.

"They sure look busy," Tyler said, and took another bite of his sandwich.

"Yeah, exactly," Jason said. "And Councilman Blaise gave us this pretty shop and these pretty things, but how could we compete with that?"

"We just need time to establish a name for ourselves," Denton said.

"No, screw that." Jason stood up and began pacing. "It was a political power move. Blaise just wanted some Arrow representation here on Kamaria. But it ain't doing us any good! He's just locking us into a job."

"Don't you want to help Mom and Dad?" Tyler asked.

Jason slammed his fist against the scaffold, and Tyler jolted in his seat. Jason took a deep breath and said, "I never asked to work in the shop. I never wanted it."

Denton looked down at the floor. Tyler winced, then said, "What are you saying? You just want to quit?"

Jason said nothing. He kept staring at the wall. Tyler jerked his head over to Denton. "Denny, you believe this?"

Denton sighed and looked out over the horizon. He said, "I was hoping for a different life too."

Tyler stood up. "You both gotta be kiddin' me! What about grandpa's legacy?"

"That's *his* legacy, not ours," Jason said.

"I'm not going to abandon Mom and Dad," Denton said, keeping his eyes on the horizon and away from his brothers. He felt deflated.

"I'm not planning on sticking around forever," Jason said. "As soon as the colony gets built up more, I'm finding my own way. We can do that now; we have room to move out. We don't have to live cooped up like we did in the Arrow."

"Screw this," Tyler said. He picked up his tools and moved to another spot of the project to work. Jason and Denton watched him get into position and begin hammering away on some framework.

"How about you, Denny?" Jason asked, not turning to face him. "You stickin' around the shop forever like him?"

Denton looked at Tyler. He worked away, putting a piece of framework in position and hammering it into place, then brushed some tears from his eyes and continued the job. Denton stood up and grimaced. "I don't know what else I'd do."

———◆———

Before noon one day, a man wearing a unique jacket walked into the Castus Machine Shop. He was tall, with a grizzled face covered in a white beard. He looked to be in his sixties but was built strong like an ox.

Denton had seen people wearing similar jackets before. He'd watched them loading equipment into the Pilgrim-class explorer vessels in the shipyard and flying off into the Kamarian wilderness. Colonists usually didn't have privileged access to leave the colony walls, but people wearing these jackets did.

"Good morning," the man said with a thick pre-Sol Common Russian accent. "Is this where I can drop off tool for repair?" He gestured to a particle saw, a tool that could cut through spaceship hulls, or in this case, trees for lumber.

"Yeah, let me take a look." Denton wiped his hands with a dirty rag as he walked over to assist the man. He took the saw and noticed chunks of some unknown material caught in part of the particle emitter. "Looks like it might have a jam. What were you cutting with this thing?"

"Oh." The man chuckled. "Collecting samples out in field. Some of the trees are hard as rock. Is like cutting into mountain. No good for saw."

"Out in the field?" Denton was curious. He pulled the saw over to his workbench and began removing the junk from the emitters. "What is it you do for the colony, Mr. ..."

"Volkov. Pavel Volkov," he said. "I-yam Beta Team scout captain."

"Scouting sounds interesting," Denton said as he plucked another chunk of rock-hard bark away from an emitter. "I'm Denton, by the way."

"Nice shop, Denton," Pavel said, looking around at all the small projects being repaired in the back of the garage. "Normally, I use Tvashtar shop, but is so far from shipyard. Pain in ass."

Denton winced at the mention of the Tvashtar shop but grinned it off. "I'll tell my dad you like the shop. He runs the place." Denton turned to his workbench and had the replicator create a few replacement pieces while he continued to pluck tree bits away. "I couldn't help but notice your accent. Where are you from originally?"

"*Da*, grew up Martian. Descended from old cosmonaut colonist family," Pavel said with a pride Denton could sense.

"Never met a Martian before. I'm from Ganymede, descended from ..." He paused, thinking for a moment, unsure of his ancestry beyond his great-grandpa. "Descended from more Ganymede folk, I suppose."

"At least you didn't get pulled into war," Pavel said, looking around the shop. "Was very bad. I was a major, commanded Argonaut Tank Brigade. They still have my tank on *Telemachus*, I hear." He pointed upward. Denton thought back to when his family was sucked into the war briefly during the last battle, but he knew the old major had fought the Undriel much longer than the Castuses had. Martians were a rarity because of the war; most of them had been absorbed or killed in the fighting.

"Major! Should I have saluted?" Denton said. Pavel shook his head and smiled.

"*Nyet*. Not unless we are driving Argonaut tank into battle on Martian soil." He looked around the workshop as Denton continued to repair the saw. "I prefer scouting to war. I hope to never command tank again."

Denton fastened in the new replicated pieces and stood up. He held the particle saw at waist height. "Let's see what we got!"

He pushed a button and pulled a cord. The saw roared to life. The sound it made vibrated the countertop near him, shaking loose bolts. The saw felt like it was trying to fly away from him with the power it was revving out. Denton nodded, satisfied with his work.

"Ho-ho! There we have it!" Pavel shouted above the roar of the saw. "Didn't think you would get it done so quickly, comrade."

"No problem." Denton put the saw on the counter for Pavel. "This one is on the house. Just tell your scout buddies where to come if they need good work done quick, ya hear?"

"I'll be sure to. *Do svidaniya*, Denton." Pavel grabbed the saw and left the shop, giving Denton a casual salute as he exited. Denton wondered what it would be like to join the scouts. His view of

Kamaria was limited, and being forced to work inside the colony walls wasn't allowing it to expand. He had seen many wonders on their descent into the colony, but the idea of seeing such things up close was tantalizing.

Three hours later, Denton wrapped up work on a faulty ground sail. He consulted his daily task list on his soothreader, checking off what he had already accomplished. To some, it might have felt great to remove tasks from the list, but Denton knew there would be more to replace them tomorrow.

"So, this is where they got you holed up?" It was the friendly voice of Eliana Veston. Denton quickly tried to wipe some grease from his face with the dirty rag, only adding to the problem. He noticed she was wearing the same jacket as Pavel.

"Oh, hey, Doc!" Denton said with a smile. "I just had Pavel Volkov in here not long ago, and he was wearing the same jacket."

"He's the one who recommended your shop to me, actually," Eliana said, walking into the lobby with a box in her hands.

"What's that you got there?"

She brought forward a small plastic box and opened the lid and retrieved a metallic orb. "This. It was acting all batty in the field— think you can fix it?"

"Give it here," Denton said, and she handed him the orb. He inspected it for a moment, noticing it had a few buttons and indentations on its nearly perfect outer shell, but he wasn't sure what the object was.

"What does this thing do?" Denton asked.

"It's a cartographer's orb. The Tvashtar guys invented it awhile back."

"Well, there's your problem." He winked at her, and she flashed her teeth with a smile. He continued, "So you can make maps with this?"

"That's the idea, but the only thing it makes right now is garbage."

"Well, let's look and see what we could do. You got anywhere you need to be?"

"I got some time." Eliana smiled. They walked over to Denton's workbench, where he ran a diagnostic on the cartographer's orb. He could see a small piece inside had been moved from a track it was meant to stay on. Eliana noticed the problem over Denton's shoulder.

"Yeah, I had a feeling something like that had happened," she said. Denton held the orb in his palm and pushed a button on its surface. It opened like a treasure chest, and Denton could see the slipped track.

"Okay, not too bad," Denton said. He pulled out his tools and got to work. "So, how did this happen? You guys play soccer with it or something?"

"Turns out lemurbats like to throw rocks at things they see in the sky. We're not sure if they hunt that way or if they are just resourceful little jerks."

"Lemur … bats?"

"I didn't name them. You can thank George Tanaka for that. It's a common little animal around these parts. I'm sure you'll see one sometime," Eliana said.

"Not so sure I'll get to see anything stuck in here," Denton said. He pushed the last piece into place, turned the orb, and clicked a switch on the side, and the sphere jumped out of his hand and hovered in front of them.

"There we go! Look at that!" Eliana said, clapping her hands together in excitement.

"Glad I could help. Feel free to bring anything that needs fixing here, I like a challenge." Denton smiled. He liked seeing her happy— her whole face lit up, and that pain Denton sensed behind her eyes seemed to vanish briefly.

"Sounds like a plan, Denny. Thanks again," Eliana said, and hugged Denton. He hugged her back, making sure to avoid getting black grease on her scout jacket.

"See you around!" she said. Eliana flicked a gesture over her soothreader to pay for the service, then she gathered her box and left the shop.

Denton fiddled with a socket wrench as he watched her go. He really enjoyed her company, and he hoped to hear more adventures from scouts in the future. His soothreader pinged, alerting him to the next task he had to perform.

"Back to the cycle." Denton sighed.

———◆———

Another long day down, and another one to begin again in the morning. Denton showered the grime from the workday off, and for a moment, he contemplated his role in the colony. He knew he had to help with construction, and fixing broken tools and vehicles was an important job, but it left him unfulfilled.

Denton toweled off and was about to head to bed when he looked out the window of his room. Kamaria's twin moons were both fully lit, creating large spheres of light in the starry sky. The valley beyond the perimeter wall was awash in the soft glow of twilight. He could see glowing shapes dancing there.

"Screw it," Denton said, and decided to break his cycle. He put on a hoodie and pants to go for a walk. On his way out, he grabbed his sketchpad device and stylus.

He quickly realized this was his first time exploring the colony at night. Rock paths would glow a variety of colors, making a beautiful walking path for him to follow. He saw little alien gnat creatures hovering above the purple grass, going about their business as if humans had always been there.

Denton made his way up the stairs to the parapet of the perimeter wall. From there, he could see the forest tree line beyond a peaceful valley. Denton loved the smell of fresh air that rolled from the nearby mountains. He let himself enjoy the moment. Then, he noticed there was a soft glow coming from behind his family's machine shop.

It begged him to investigate.

The glow intensified as he approached. What he had seen from the perimeter rampart was just the indirect lighting bouncing off the wall from the source. He walked down the cluttered alley between the shop and the nearby apartment and found a fence. Beyond the fence was a slope, and beyond the slope was the mysterious glow.

He scaled the fence with ease, dropping down on the other side. Close to the wall, shrouded by Kamarian trees, he found the light source.

It was a small field of incredible glowing flowers. Tiny insects danced about the flowers, gathering all the pollen they could carry and buzzing away. It was a place that seemed forgotten since the construction of the wall.

Denton decided this was a great place to call his own. He sat on a boulder, turned on his sketchpad, and began to draw one of the flowers.

He let time slide by as he sketched, free from interruption.

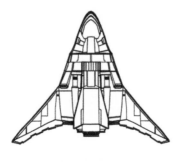

FIFTEEN

FOUR YEARS AGO

DAY 3 OF ROELIN'S EXODUS

ROELIN AWAKENED FROM ANOTHER nightmare, the relentless chase of the Siren on his mind. His hangover from the bottle of wine he'd drunk the night before didn't help his mood, but he decided he would rather get on with the repairs than sit and die in the ship. If death were even an option.

Roelin returned to the bridge to organize his thoughts. He pulled out a printed blueprint of the *Astraeus* and marked off known problems. After making a long list, he sank back into the pilot's chair and thought of his restrictions outside the ship. With no cure for lung-lock available to him, he would need to build his life around the problem instead of solving it directly. If his math was correct, he only had a range of about sixteen kilometers outside of the ship to work with before he would need to come back and replace his air purifiers with freshly cleansed units.

He looked at the walls of the bridge. Splattered on them were the words *NO TURNING BACK* and *WE ARE GOING TO SYMPHA*. Roelin thought to himself that he could at least scratch one job from his list right now. He grabbed a towel and a chemical cleanser from a cabinet panel nearby and wiped away *WE ARE GOING TO SYMPHA* first.

As he reached upward to erase *NO TURNING BACK*, he hesitated. The statement was true. Even if he fixed the ship, the Other would not let him return to the colony. Also, if he did return, he couldn't guarantee that the Other wouldn't force him to kill more people. He frowned.

Sighing, he rubbed the bloody message away. He felt like he had already begun the long process of fixing the *Astraeus*. One job down, only a billion other things to fix.

———— ◆ ————

PRESENT DAY

"So far away, yet also near ..." Eliana Veston's dream began, but she was no longer the child in it. She watched, a formless observer in the nursery of her mind, as her mother rocked a baby to sleep, singing softly.

"With you my love, we'll soar like birds ..." Eliana turned to her left and saw her father, his eyes focused on Amaryllis and his little girl.

"O'er bright stars, across new worlds ..." Amaryllis continued to sing. John walked over to her and placed a hand on her shoulder. His eyes grew warmer, his smile tight and filled with sadness. Tears welled up and dripped down his cheeks as the door to the nursery opened.

"So far away, yet also near ..." Amaryllis didn't see who had walked in. John looked up at the intruder as if this visit had been planned. He huffed weakly as the man stepped into the room.

Smoke trailed behind him, and blood covered his combat suit and dripped from the blade he carried in his hand, staining the carpet crimson. His face was concealed by a helmet. There was a flash of lightning, and Eliana closed her eyes.

———— ✦ ————

Eliana woke up in her one-bedroom apartment in Odysseus Colony. She pressed her hand against her face and felt the cold sweat that had formed there. She let her arm drop to the bed as she sat with her thoughts. The details of the nightmare faded as her heartbeat evened out, but the pain stung like an angry wasp.

It had been a little over four years since the day her father was murdered by Captain Roelin Raike. Eliana was an orphan, armed only with the knowledge her parents had given her before they'd left this mortal plane. There were times she wanted nothing more than to hug them, say nothing, and just hold the embrace. Her eyes grew wet when she thought of how nice that would be, and her face felt the pressure of emotion like a hand pushing on her skull. She sniffled, then snatched her burgundy-rimmed glasses off her side table and put them on.

They were her armor against reality.

After a shower, Eliana got dressed and made herself a coffee. She held the cup in both hands, enjoying the warmth beneath her fingers as she softly blew against the heat. She kept her focus on the coffee as she asked the air around her, "Homer, what's on the agenda for today?"

"Good morning, Dr. Veston," Homer said. Whenever she was acknowledged that way, she thought of her father. "You have the day off. There are no scheduled plans for the Alpha Scout Team. The Beta Team will be collecting samples in the area known as the Rib Cage to the west."

"A day off," Eliana said to herself. She hated these, as she felt like she had nothing to do and no one to talk to, which forced her to live with herself and her thoughts. She'd rather spend the day with someone, but ever since the massacre, the team had grown apart. Being with her family of scouts just reminded her of that day. They treated her kindly, but it was different between them now. "I think

I'll go for a walk," she said, taking a sip of coffee.

Outside, it felt more comfortable. She carried a backpack containing an emergency medical kit and a change of clothes, unsure of what the day held for her. The warm spring air caressed her skin, and the smell of wildflowers surrounded her. She took the main road, walking deliberately yet without an objective.

"Good morning, Eliana," Pavel Volkov said as he approached from her right side. She turned and gave him a smile. She liked the old major; he was always kind to her and never treated her like a victim. Pavel wore his scout jacket and carried a particle saw over his shoulder.

"I have the day off," Eliana said, watching her feet as they moseyed.

"*Da*, I hear," Pavel said, mixing in his ancient Russian accent. He focused on the path they were taking. "I always hated free times. Nothing to do makes jitter."

"Me too."

"You know, you could always join Beta Team for day. More hands, more done."

"I'll consider that," Eliana said as they neared the shipyard. She saw other scouts boarding the *Henson*, a pilgrim-class explorer. She thought about joining them until she spotted the Castus Machine Shop.

The garage door was open, and the *Rogers* spacecraft was parked inside. She saw the family readying a robotic harness around the ship; a large truck with a sign that read, "Pastor Paints and Supplies: Finest on Ganymede!" on its side was connected to it by a series of long hoses.

"It's good shop. Denton repair saw," Pavel said, noticing where she had focused her gaze.

"Yeah, he fixed my cartographer's orb in no time. Thanks for recommending them to me." She kept her eyes on Denton.

"Go on, say hi. You have day off, remember?" Pavel said, and winked. Eliana smiled and nodded to the old major. He walked toward the shipyard to join the Beta Team on the *Henson*. Eliana approached the machine shop with nothing to fix but her troubled thoughts.

"Hey, Elly!" Denton said when he saw her.

Eliana looked past him at the *Rogers* and said, "I saw our ship in your garage and was wondering how you managed to steal it."

"You guys handed us the keys, and we all thought, Hells, it's ours now!" Denton said. They shared a laugh. Denton turned toward the ship and said, "We've had it here all morning doing some maintenance. I guess you scout folk like our business. We appreciate it!"

"Keep up the good work, and you got us." She smiled.

He pointed toward the paint truck. "Hey, I don't know if you're busy or anything—"

"I'm not," Eliana said quickly. Denton's smile got a little bigger.

"Well, we were just about to paint the ship, if you wanted to watch."

"Watch paint dry …" She looked at the *Rogers*. "I don't know about watching, but if you need an extra hand, I'm ready to help."

"Of course! Here, I'll show you how it works."

Eliana followed Denton over to the paint truck, where a man waited, leaning against the passenger-side door. He was a middle-aged man with tanned skin and black hair that poked out from beneath a baseball cap. The cap read, "Ganymede Bow Notchers," in a swirly font. Eliana couldn't tell if it represented a sports team or a strip club. He perked up when he saw them. Denton greeted him and gestured over his soothreader.

"Hey, Mateo, thanks for bringing it so fast. Here's your cut." Denton flicked his hand toward Mateo, and the man nodded.

"No problem, Dent," Mateo said in a gravelly voice. "Anytime you do a job like this, you know who to call. It'd be great to work together with you Castus folk like we did back on the Arrow. Keep the old team going."

"That's the plan." Denton winked. He gestured for Eliana to

follow him, and they walked over to the robotic harness that surrounded the *Rogers*. Two men stood on platforms on the harness wearing plastic suits with re-breathers strapped to their faces. They had backpacks filled with paint from the truck, each with a hose that flanked their side and was fastened to a long spray gun.

"Hey, Denny, who ya got there with you?" Jason asked.

"This is Elly," Denton said while gathering supplies. "She's gonna help us paint the ship."

"Is that right?" Michael Castus said. "I can't pay ya, miss."

"That's alright. I'm just here to kill some time and learn something," Eliana said.

"You ain't from that damn Tvashtar shop, are you?" Michael eyed her suspiciously. "Trying to figure out our secrets now that we're stealing your business?"

"No, I'm a scout, actually." Eliana raised her chin.

"Well, *shit!*" Michael said, and slapped his knee. "You guys are great! It's your ship anyway, so feel free to help as much as ya like!"

Eliana laughed and nodded. Denton grabbed a couple plastic suits to protect their clothes, rebreathers to keep paint out of their lungs, and two paint sprayers. Denton and Eliana slipped the equipment on and boarded adjacent platforms. The visors on the rebreather masks lit up with HUD displays.

"Okay, so how does this all work? Do we just spray and pray?" Eliana asked, waving her spray wand around like an action hero mowing down enemies with a machine gun.

Denton chuckled and jerked a thumb toward the robotic harness. "You see that? It does most of the work. We're just here to cover the spots it misses. It will do a pass, spraying the ship with a coat, then we go in and get the small stuff that got passed up. Your HUD will tell you what setting to use on the sprayer there, and where to spray it."

"Sounds easy," Eliana said, and looked at her spray wand.

"It is. This is the fun part, we already did all the tedious maintenance," Denton said.

They watched as the truck pumped paint into the robotic harness and fed it into tubes. The paint then misted outward from nozzles in the harness onto the ship.

"Where did he get the paint from?" Eliana asked as the first coat was applied.

"Mateo?" Denton shrugged toward the truck. "He's an old friend of the family. The Pastors and the Castuses go way back. He managed to get a few truckloads onto their ship before the call came from the *Telemachus*. But they need to make more paint somehow, and that's impossible if they can't get past the colony wall."

Eliana thought to herself about the importance of making new paint. Up until the *Telemachus* arrived, most of the colony had been a combination of white-colored metal and plastic. New houses were built but left unpainted until there were enough for everyone. Paint could make the colony look more like a living city than a shantytown.

"On our scouts, we can find ingredients to make new paints. Maybe we can get a lesson on what to look for from your friend Mateo," Eliana said.

"You can do that? That would be great!" Denton said.

"I'll submit the idea to the team. I'm sure there's a way we can help."

The robotic harness stopped. The *Rogers* was now coated in a burnt-orange hue, much more vibrant than the solid white it had been before. It was time to fill in the gaps. Eliana's and Denton's platforms rose to the top of the *Rogers*. Her visor's HUD gave her all the information she needed to do the job right. She began spraying and covered the area, then stepped back and smiled. She said, "Pretty satisfying!"

"Yeah," Denton said. "I've always enjoyed this process. I'm sort of an artist—not professionally or anything." He gestured to a few murals he had painted on the walls of the shop. They had a unique graffiti style to them. Above each station in the garage was a tattoo-like design that detailed the workstation's abilities. It gave the shop an attitude Eliana had not seen anywhere else in the colony.

"You did those?"

"Yeah. Before you guys came along with some steady work, we had a lot of downtime in the mornings here. I took it upon myself to give the shop our own personal touch." Denton stood up straighter.

"I think it's great," she said. They finished their part of the job, their platforms lowered, and the robotic harness began another pass. They watched it go for a moment; this time, it sprayed thin blue lines on top of the orange.

"What do you like to do to unwind?" Denton asked.

"Oh, me? Well, I …" Eliana had to think about it. She didn't unwind much these days; her thoughts kept her strung up. She thought of where she felt the most comfortable: the Kamarian Archive. It was a place that collected all the knowledge the scouts discovered and made it accessible to the colonists. She turned to Denton and said, "Well, I like to study."

"You *enjoy* studying?" Denton said with mock disgust.

Eliana laughed. "Yeah. I like learning new things." She pointed to the spray wand in her hand. "Like this, for example. This is new to me."

"Well, we have all sorts of new stuff around here. If you ever get bored, just come by."

"I'm going to hold you to that."

Denton smiled. Eliana liked the warmth in it. This man didn't know her past, and he didn't treat her like some delicate little flower that couldn't face the world after what had happened. He treated her like a human. She was beginning to like Denton Castus a lot.

They chatted and painted for a few hours until the job was completed and the *Rogers* rested under a heating device. Its hull was now a burnt orange with blue and white stripes, with a black underbelly.

Rain began to fall outside, but under the roof of the machine shop garage, it was warm and comfortable. Brynn made dinner, and everyone grabbed a plate. Jason, Tyler, and Mateo hung out with their plates near the rushcycle that the brothers were trying to get race ready. Brynn and Michael went over the day's invoices on a console in the office. Denton and Eliana watched the rain fall outside as they leaned against a workstation and chewed their food.

"Your mom grills nurn like a pro!" Eliana said, stuffing her mouth with the soft meat.

"Which one is a nurn?" Denton asked.

"It's the deerlike one with the trunk for a nose and the feathers."

"My mom can grill anything. Funnily enough, I don't think she's ever seen a nurn alive—I know I haven't. She probably got the details from one of our clients, maybe even one of you scouts," Denton said.

"That's a shame, there's so much to see out there. Have you had a chance to make it over to the archives?"

"Not going to lie, I didn't even know about them."

"If you get a chance, go look. It's got everything we know about Kamaria in there. My dad came up with the idea for the building." Eliana pushed the food on her plate around with her fork as she thought about her father. "He always said it was important for the people to know everything. He wanted to be completely transparent."

"Smart man!" Denton said. "I can respect that."

"Yeah, he was," Eliana whispered as her smile faded.

"Tell me more about scouting. Do you like it?" Denton asked while munching steak off his fork.

"Oh, immensely." She lit back up again. "I can't see myself doing anything else. I'm the Alpha Team doctor. I was actually part of the very first scout to take place on Kamaria, back when I was training." Eliana felt taller as she said it.

"I keep forgetting there was a six-year delay between the *Odysseus* and the *Telemachus*. You have so many more years of experience here than me."

"That makes me sound old. I'm pretty sure we're the same age now," she said, and chuckled. "Hey, we should head down to the archive tonight!"

"That could be fun. We're all done here for today anyway," Denton said, and the two shared a warm smile.

"Okay, we'll finish up dinner and head on—" An alert on her soothreader cut her off.

"What's that?" Denton asked.

A rock dropped in Eliana's chest as she read the alert. Her eyes darted around, looking for something but not sure what.

"Medical staff needed for a distress call from the *Henson*. It went down on approach to the colony. I need to get there fast," Eliana said, and grabbed her backpack. "Hells, I need to summon a ride."

"I'll take you," Denton said. He put his plate down and walked over to the Tvashtar truck they'd been given. He opened the door. "Where are we going?"

"Not far—I'll get you access through the gate. I have all my gear in my backpack. We can beat the field ambulance craft if we hurry," she said. Eliana got into the truck and checked her soothreader. The truck roared to life, lifting a meter off the ground. Denton crunched the pedal down, and the truck sped down the street toward the colony gateway, leaving the rest of the Castus family and Mateo scratching their heads.

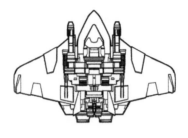

SIXTEEN

DENTON HAD ADMIRED THE meadow from the colony wall parapet a few times, but he had never been beyond the gateway. He drove his truck up to the gate at full speed.

"Don't stop," Eliana said, waving her hand over her soothreader. The light on the reader flicked from blue to green, and the colony gateway opened. Denton saw a marine on the wall pointing out over the distance.

The truck reached the end of the road and began hovering over the tall grass of the meadow beyond. The rain came down harder now, shrouding the field in darkness. They passed over a hill and saw the *Henson*, a bright spot of fire on an ocean of dark-purple grass.

"Oh God." Eliana gasped. They drove the truck right up to the wreck and parked. Denton reached into the glove box and grabbed a collider pistol. Eliana nodded and said, "Good thinking, we don't know what brought it down."

"I was worried about predators in the field," Denton said. "But now I have two worries."

They left the truck and walked out into the rain. Eliana approached the *Henson*, thumbing her soothreader. "This is Eliana Veston, I am on the scene. The *Henson* looks completely totaled; we'll need emergency evac for the entire Beta Team."

Denton thought he heard someone inside the ship, but the

sound of the roaring fire obscured it. Eliana finished her soothreader call and turned to Denton.

"Help is coming, they'll be here soon," Eliana said. There was another shriek, and this time, they heard it clearly. A woman was screaming from inside the wreck; they couldn't wait for backup.

"So, what's the protocol here?" Denton asked.

"Follow me." Eliana approached the outer hull hatch and input a code. It opened limply, crunching metal against metal, and they could hear the woman screaming louder.

"We're here to help!" Eliana shouted. "Can you make it to us?"

The woman continued screaming, but it was hard to find her in the smoke. Denton thought he heard a loud buzzing noise, but couldn't discern the source. He moved forward and pushed aside some heavy machinery that had fallen over during the crash, revealing an injured man under the mess.

"I got someone here!" Denton shouted. Eliana dashed over to them.

"He's alive, but he's suffering from some sort of paralysis. Help me pull him out," she said, and they grabbed the man under both of his armpits to drag him out the door. Denton thought the buzzing sounds were growing louder as they pulled him free.

They laid the injured man on his back outside of the wreck in the wet grass. Eliana got a better look at him and noticed that he was bruised from the debris that had fallen but also had a deep puncture wound on his left shoulder.

"What is this?" Eliana asked as she began to treat the wound.

Another scream came from the interior of the ship.

"I'm going back in!" Denton shouted as he rushed toward the *Henson*.

"Wait!" Eliana shouted back, but it was too late. Denton had already made it back through the hatch. The injured man began to cough, and she switched her focus to aiding him. She reached for her medical supplies in her backpack and whispered, "Be careful in there, Denny."

Denton flicked a switch on the side of his pistol, and a flashlight activated under the barrel. Another scream led him toward the source, where he found a woman trapped under heavy metal rods. A shape moved in the debris, something alien.

Hulking over the mess was an insect-shaped creature much like an old Earth wasp but the size of a large hound dog. The wasp had two long arms, each with two fingers and a thumb. It had four insectoid legs that ended in knifelike blades and an array of eyes that were glowing fiercely green in the dark, hazy room. Its wings emitted the buzzing sound Denton had heard before as it tried to push its way through the debris to get to the trapped woman. Three large, barbed stingers protruding from the wasp's tail were getting close to the woman's abdomen. The woman and the wasp turned their attention to Denton when his flashlight lit up their area.

"Don't let the mactabilis wasp sting you!" the woman shouted. "It paralyzes its victims!"

"Well, *shit*," was Denton's knee-jerk response. The wasp flicked its large body toward him. It moved erratically, buzzing forward in increments followed by pauses. It reminded him of the unnatural way the Undriel ship had moved during that final fight on approach to the *Telemachus*.

Denton aimed his pistol but didn't fire. He was afraid that if he shot the wasp, he might hit the woman behind it. Thinking fast, he snatched up a metal pipe from the mangled debris to his left.

The glowing green eyes rushed toward him. The buzzing escalated into a shriek as the wasp closed the distance. Denton swung the pipe and smashed it into the wasp, flinging it sideways. The wasp slammed against the nearby wall and caught fire, but it didn't stop. It launched toward Denton again with even more ferocity, its shriek deafening.

Denton pulled his pistol quickly and let out three shots. The first shot clipped a wing, the second took off a quarter of the wasp's face, and the third struck dead center on the remainder of the wasp's head, exploding it into a burst of wet insect blood.

The wasp was dead, but its momentum propelled its body forward and it collided with Denton. He fell backward onto a burning pile of debris with the massive insect corpse on top of him.

Denton could feel his vest catching fire and a sharp pain in his arm as jagged metal cut him. He held the wasp away from his torso and watched as the three stingers desperately tried to avenge their own fallen body. Denton pushed the twitching body off of him and stood up.

"I'm going to get you out of here!" Denton shouted to the woman as he pulled hard against the debris pinning her down. He lifted it high enough to allow her to scramble out.

"Thank you! Oh God, thank you!" she said with tears in her eyes.

"Get outside, there's a doctor out there!" Denton shouted, and dropped the heavy debris back down. The woman wasted no time and exited the *Henson* the way Denton had come in.

Denton scanned the hazy interior, coughing as smoke continued to fill the room. The locker room staging area door was open. Denton investigated and found a room in complete disarray. Atmospheric suits had been flung around during the crash, and workbenches lay at weird angles on the floor with their contents scattered about haphazardly.

A ragged voice reached him through the mess. "Denton, is that you, comrade?" Denton recognized it as Major Pavel Volkov's.

"I'm here, Major! Where are you?" Denton called out.

"Stuck over here," Pavel said weakly. Denton made his way around a row of lockers and found the old major on the floor.

Pavel's leg was pinned to the ground, pierced by a metal pipe that had burst. The contents of the pipe, some sort of liquid, covered him. It wasn't clear if the fluid was flammable or not. The particle saw that Denton had repaired for the major the day before was just out of the man's reach.

"Are you stung?" Denton asked, checking Pavel over and reaching into his belt for his roll of duct tape.

"*Nyet*, they were busy with Hank. I could do nothing," Pavel said, helpless tears welling up in his eyes. Denton followed Pavel's line of sight to a man hanging upside down from the ceiling. He was covered in some sort of viscous organic matter. Denton noticed the body wasn't struggling.

"We're going to get you out of here. We have help on the way," Denton reassured Pavel. His heart skipped a beat when he heard more buzzing in the room, louder this time. Denton looked up toward the ceiling to see three more giant wasps leering at him with glowing green eyes.

They were climbing over pipes and tanks, moving in his direction. Denton knew it wouldn't be good to shoot up the pipes on a burning ship, especially with Pavel covered in what could be a flammable liquid. Denton grabbed the handle of the particle saw.

He stood, thumbed the button, and then pulled the cord, roaring the saw to life. The blade's rim emitted a bright-white light. The wasps buzzed fiercely, leaning backward for a moment and twitching their heads about as they assessed the situation, then they launched forward.

Denton swung the saw in an arc, cutting entirely through one wasp and cutting through the flank of another. They screeched in pain, their awful shrieking mixing with the loud whirring of the particle saw. Denton managed to barely sidestep the last wasp as it came toward him. He kicked out with his leg, knocking the wasp away from Pavel and himself, then spun and thrust the saw forward into the last wasp's face.

The rest of the wasp's body moved independently, crunching itself into a stinging position and pushing its lancelike stingers outward toward Denton. It thrust so hard that the bottom half of the wasp detached from its head, its stingers flailing wildly in the air.

"*Cyka blyat!*" Pavel shouted as the bottom end of the wasp jerked its way toward him on the floor. As the stinger was clear of the pipes and tanks on the ceiling, Denton pulled the pistol out once more and obliterated the independent bottom end of the wasp with a few particle blasts.

The wasp with the damaged flank regained its posture and crouched dangerously in the dark corner. A purple glow surged through the wasp. Denton attempted to rev the particle saw, but it sputtered out. The wasp pushed itself backward in preparation for another lunge. Denton slammed his hand against the particle saw, desperately trying to reactivate it.

The wasp sprang forward with a horrifying shriek. Denton had no other choice but to slam the end of the inactivated saw into the oncoming wasp. The wasp shrieked as the blunt end pushed into its thorax. Denton felt something shift inside the saw and reached for the pull cord.

He grabbed the cord and yanked back, narrowly missing a bite from the wasp's maw. The saw activated inside the wasp, slicing through the insect. Denton pulled upward and cut the wasp in half vertically, spraying the room with insect blood. The two halves flailed for a moment, then settled in death.

Chills ran up Denton's back as he heard more buzzing coming from above. He revved the particle saw again, preparing for another wave of wasp attacks. He wasn't sure how long he would be able to keep this up.

An electrical bolt lanced through the air and struck an incoming wasp. It shook wildly as surges of energy passed through it. Its eyes exploded, and it fell to the floor, twitching. Denton looked past the other wasps to see Eliana enter the locker room, flanked by Tvashtar marines. Their rifles were set to electrocute their targets with deadly bolts of white-hot lightning. The marines made quick work of the remaining wasps in the room.

"I need help over here!" Denton shouted, dropping the saw to the ground. Eliana ran over and saw Pavel pinned under debris. The old major had passed out.

"Smoke inhalation. We need to get him out of here," Eliana said. She quickly scanned the area and discovered the particle saw. She grabbed it and turned it on, slicing through the pipe that held Pavel's leg in place.

"Help me with him," Eliana requested.

Once outside, Denton saw that a whole team of medical officers was now on site. The field ambulance craft was ready to lift patients back to the colony hospital. The normally empty alien meadow was now bursting with human activity.

Denton and Eliana brought Pavel to the ambulance craft and loaded him on. They watched as the craft took off with a full load of patients, then Eliana hugged Denton.

"I have work to do. Excellent job in there, Denny." She kissed him on the cheek. "Hells of a first date, though." She winked at him and rushed off to help with the remaining victims. Another doctor approached Denton and threw a blanket over his shoulder and put an air mask on his face. Denton sat down in the bed of his truck.

"First date?" Denton whispered to himself with a smile. He didn't hear anything the doctor was saying because he was still blindsided by Eliana's kiss. He came back to reality when the doctor began stitching the wound on his shoulder.

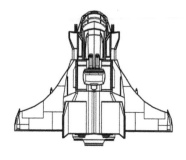

SEVENTEEN

FOUR YEARS AGO

DAY 15 OF ROELIN'S EXODUS

EACH NIGHT, THERE WAS the nightmare, and each morning, cold sweats. Roelin maintained a routine, planning his repairs in the morning, fixing what he could, then working on building tools to help him continue to survive in the jungle.

The *Astraeus* had enough full kits for a squad of marines. He set up a perimeter trap, trip wires attached to grenades. He tied several around the radius of trees, marking each with yellow spray paint on the bark facing the *Astraeus*. If anything felt like sneaking up on him, it would be sorry it tried.

Roelin created a water purifier and a fishing pole, along with a smoker to keep his fish fresh longer. He used natural resources, cutting down nearby trees.

Has it really only been fifteen days? The nightmares distorted his gauge of time, stretching hours into eons.

Roelin failed to catch any fish, and returned to the ship. As he moved down the hall, he passed doors with large red *X*'s sprayed on with paint. These rooms were off-limits to Roelin, deemed unsafe by hull ruptures that allowed the deadly Kamarian bacteria in. Roelin's limited world was confined to the bridge, his bunk, and the galley. He shuffled into the galley, took a small portion of military rations, already half-eaten from a previous day of fruitless fishing, and returned to the command bridge.

Roelin plunked down into his pilot seat and watched the sunlight drain away from the sky, neglecting to crank power into the room and instead allowing the darkness to engulf him. The last of the mist burned away from the jungle trees, creating their own weather as clouds began to form and pour rain onto the greedy roots below.

Memories of Faye wandered into his mind. He pictured her with him, watching the sunset. She would turn and smile at him, and he'd smile back. The war with the Undriel was over. This place was supposed to be their fresh start in more ways than one. Marriage had been a harsh adjustment for Roelin Raike. To Faye, it had come naturally. She had passion in her heart for peaceful things. Once the battles had ended, Roelin wasn't sure what his role in the colony would be. Escorting the scouts was an important job; he felt the most himself when protecting others. But war had come naturally to Roelin, and without it, he felt like a stranger in a strange land.

A bite of agony lanced through Roelin's head, and blood spilled from his nostrils. He felt like his teeth were being forcibly removed with a wrench, and he choked out grunts of pain before blacking out entirely.

Roelin came back to consciousness, heaving air through his lungs. The Other had only visited him in his nightmares for the past couple weeks, and he'd been almost convinced it had left him entirely. The pain stung in his arm once more. Roelin lifted his head high enough to see a new message written on the wall in blood, illuminated by the moonlight.

WE NEED TO LEAVE.

Roelin coughed. "No shit." He spat more blood onto the floor of the bridge and asked the air around him, "What are you? Why are you doing this to me?"

The darkness summoned him once more. When he awoke, he saw another message:

NHYMN.

"What the Hells is a *Nhymn*?" Roelin said. Was Nhymn the name of the Other? Was this the beginning of a dialogue?

"Nhymn. Is that your name?" He waited. No seizure took him, and he was thankful but still confused. "Why did you do this to me, Nhymn?" he asked. Again, the flood of pain and shadow. When he regained consciousness, there was another message:

WE DID THIS TOGETHER.

Anger and pain boiled inside of Roelin's chest. He shouted, "No, we did not! I would never do that to my friends!"

He stood and noticed he was woozy from the blood loss.

"Nhymn, we can't talk like this," he said between breaths, holding a palm to his head. He had an idea. The storage panels on the side wall contained an old-fashioned pad of paper and markers. "If we're going to be stuck here together, we might as well get to know each other," Roelin said, returning to his pilot seat with the writing utensils. "Use this."

Darkness filled his vision once more, but this time it was painless. When he reemerged from the depths of unconsciousness, he looked down at the sheet of paper.

TAKE US TO SYMPHA.

The writing looked as though he had done it with his left hand blindfolded, but it was legible enough. Roelin smiled, still angry about the incessant demands he could not fulfill but feeling a small victory at this new ability to talk to his captor.

"Why did you choose me?" Roelin asked, ignoring her demands. His eyes closed, and without slipping into a fully unconscious state, he could feel his hand scribbling onto the paper.

YOU WILL PROTECT ME.

Roelin didn't know how to respond. He didn't want to protect Nhymn. She had forced him to do unimaginable things, *and for what*?

"Why did you make me hurt those people?" he asked flatly. He needed to know why his friends were dead. Why his wife might be dead. His anger and frustration accidentally caused him to momentarily fight the blackout that came as a response. But it won out shortly.

THEY HURT US.

"How did they hurt us?" Roelin asked.

This time there was no written response, only darkness.

When he awoke, he was no longer inside the *Astraeus*. He was lying on his back with an intense light shining into his eyes. He couldn't move at all; even his eyes remained locked in place. He felt like a dead thing.

Two people entered his line of sight wearing surgical masks. As they hovered between Roelin and the light, he recognized them.

"John!" Roelin wanted to stand and hug him. He tried to tell him he'd had a nightmare where he'd done awful things, but he could only lie there and observe through his locked perspective.

George Tanaka stood next to John. They nodded to each other. George said, "Alright, we are beginning the autopsy of the life-form we have named the Siren." George handed John a scalpel.

"I am making a lateral incision in the front neck, support tentacle," John said, moving the scalpel toward Roelin's throat.

Roelin felt the scalpel sink into his jugular. He felt blood trickle down his neck. The scientists observed him, then decided to cut deeper. John grabbed a bone saw and pushed the whirring circular blade through his sternum. Roelin wanted to scream, but he couldn't. The scientists continued the autopsy, slicing, cutting, and removing pieces from Roelin's body. He felt every part of it.

When it was over, Roelin was numb and empty. His eyes stared at the ceiling. He didn't care what George and John were discussing about the procedure. They casually walked over to a sink, removed their gloves, washed their hands, and left the room to be further cleansed of any contamination. The light clicked off.

Roelin was back in the *Astraeus*.

He was on the floor, sweaty, writhing, and bruised from flailing in pain. He sat upright and heaved ragged breaths through his mouth. He had heard enough from Nhymn that day, and left the dark bridge to return to his bunk for the night to begin his regular nightmares once again.

PRESENT DAY

Denton awakened in his bed, his thoughts of the last night possibly being a dream squashed by the soreness he felt and the bandaged stitches on his shoulder. While in the shower, he noticed the scar on his shoulder was already rapidly healing, and the dissolvable stitches retreated. His normal routine life was ending thanks to Eliana. Denton put on his work clothes and entered the dining room where his family was sitting around the breakfast table.

"A bona fide hero!" Michael said. He flicked data from his soothreader onto a display wall next to the table. It was a news video detailing the events of the night before. Denton listened to a reporter explain what had happened to the Beta Team.

They had been on a mission to a place called "the Rib Cage," a strange rock formation to the west. They had accidentally disturbed a hive of mactabilis wasps and led them back to the *Henson*. Just outside of the colony, the wasps had dug their way through the hull and stung the pilot, causing him to go into paralysis and crash the ship in the meadow.

The reporter mentioned Denton by name as "a man brave enough to run into the ship and save the survivors." The woman he had helped was interviewed as well. Lynn Fejihn, the Beta Team geologist, thanked her hero personally. Denton blushed when he saw it.

"See, she says Denton Castus of the Castus Machine Shop!" Michael pointed at the reporter. Denton sat down in his chair and tried to avoid the attention. Brynn thought he looked tired and turned to Michael.

"I think Denny has earned a day off, don't you?" she said, giving Michael a stern look. Michael's smile faded, then he gathered himself.

"Yeah, sure. Take the day off. You earned it! Maybe Ty and Jay over here can learn something from your heroic actions!" he said, and laughed heartily.

The brothers looked at each other. Denton and Tyler knew Jason didn't want to stay in the shop much longer, but their parents didn't. Jason sighed and left the room with his plate.

Brynn brought over a plate of eggs and a strange alien fruit with a blue center. She slid the plate in front of Denton and followed it up with a cup of red juice.

"Eliana Veston came by earlier. She told me to tell you to meet up with her later by the archives. She left her number," Brynn said with a smile as her eyebrows jumped up and down on her forehead. She flicked the data from her soothreader to Denton's. He plunged a forkful of eggs into his mouth through his smile.

———— ◆ ————

After breakfast, Denton wandered the colony for the first time during the daytime. It was a sunny morning, with Delta Octantis still casting shadows across the brightly lit grass and buildings. Only a smattering of clouds dotted the bright-blue sky, and a light breeze cooled him.

He walked past a school, with children scrambling to line up for their morning classes. The sound of their laughter was refreshing, especially after the shrieking wasps from the night before. A teacher counted the students and led them into the school for the day. Denton could only imagine what their itinerary would be—possibly Kamarian survival skills, science, and maybe ancient Earth history?

Denton had never been the brightest in his class. He'd grown up working in the shop with his grandfather and father, and the history of the Castus Family Legacy looming over him always. When it came to school, he couldn't concentrate. Denton wished he'd tried harder; maybe he could have broken away from the shop to do something meaningful for humanity, what little there was left of it. Perhaps Denton could have become a colony leader if he'd only applied himself. He could have made the Arrow a utopia instead of the backwater colony it was.

Like it mattered now.

Denton reached the John Veston Kamarian Archive. The building was cylindrical, stretching upward behind a small garden. There was a statue of a man standing tall before the building holding a small orb that looked like Kamaria in one hand, and tucked away in his lowered hand was an orb of the planet Earth. Denton assumed this must be John Veston, Eliana's father.

Eliana sat on the base of the statue, reading data on her soothreader. She looked up when she heard Denton approaching and flicked her hair away from her glasses, flashing a lovely, warm smile at him.

"Hey, Denny!" she said, and gave him a big hug. "How are you feeling?" She held him at arm's length and inspected him.

"A little sore, but I'll live," Denton said.

"Thank you for your help last night. I feel like if we hadn't made it there when we did, those scouts would have died."

"What exactly happened?" Denton asked. "How did those bugs get through the hull?"

Eliana tucked her arm through his, and they walked through the garden toward the archive entrance. "The scout team I am part of hasn't run into the mactabilis wasps before. So, at first, I didn't know what we were getting into," Eliana said. She pushed her glasses up onto the bridge of her nose and continued, "According to Lynn Fejihn, they discovered a hive of the wasps and did their initial scan. The mistake they made was trying to bring a deceased wasp back here. Apparently, these wasps are very protective of their dead."

"Where do scouts take specimens? To the archive?" Denton asked.

"No, no. We take specimens to the quarantine lab. It's separate from the colony. That way, if something like this happens, it doesn't hurt the rest of Odysseus. If it hadn't been so dark outside, you probably would have seen the lab from our position in the field. The *Henson* was attempting to approach the lab when the wasps worked their way into the hull and began attacking the crew."

"Scouting sounds like dangerous work," Denton said.

"Sometimes, it can be," Eliana said, "But the more we learn, the better we adapt to Kamaria. That makes it worth the risk." She pushed open the door to the archive. Denton stepped inside and looked around in awe. The archive was three stories tall, with an opening in the middle of the cylindrical space. Staircases and lift pads allowed people to access each level. In the center of the archive was a changing display of various holographic images of Kamarian life.

There was an image of Eliana and her father using the cartographer's orbs. Maps faded in and out of view, then an array of Kamarian wildlife came up, footage of creatures Denton had never seen before. They were hunting, eating, playing. It was like watching a movie. How could it all be real?

"Pretty cool, right?" Eliana said with a smirk. "Here, come check these out." She grabbed his hand and led him over to one of the first-floor wings. It was a room with displays of different ecosystems, with statues of the wildlife that lived in each.

"Are these taxidermies?" Denton asked.

"No, we didn't want to scare the natives if they visit; they are all hand-crafted sculptures."

"The natives?"

Eliana grinned and led him forward. She gestured toward a display with a sign that said, "Auk'nai," and a large bird-humanoid with outstretched wings emerging from its shoulders.

The auk'nai was adorned with beautifully colored sashes and gemstones. In its hand was a long staff with a hook on the end and decorated with various trinkets. Behind the auk'nai was a 3D window display of a city of floating, spherical platforms in a wash of tall trees.

"Meet the natives," Eliana said as she stood next to the statue with her arms behind her back and her chin held high. She used her soothreader to queue up a holographic display that would explain more about the auk'nai.

The hologram was of an older Japanese man. Denton could see he wore a name tag that said, "G. Tanaka."

"The auk'nai," the hologram explained, "is the most intelligent life-form we have discovered on Kamaria. We encountered one named Mag'Ro in the forest. He had been observing us for a full year before he judged us safe enough to approach." The display shifted to recorded footage of their first encounter. Denton saw Eliana standing in a field of glowing flowers and, just beyond her, the tall bird-man holding a hooked staff and a deceased monkey creature.

"Every auk'nai will create their own hook staff at a young age," the holograph continued. "The daunoren is a living God to the auk'nai, and they weave this spirituality into their staffs, called 'daunoren hooks.' The young citizens of Apusticus take their deceased to the northern mountains on a pilgrimage, where they place the bodies at the peak of the Spirit Song Mountain for their God to devour. This is seen as an honorable way to be treated after death." The display showed a daunoren, which Denton recognized from his family's approach to the colony.

"I've seen one before! Biggest damn bird I'd ever seen!" Denton said, pointing at the display. Eliana laughed.

"During this 'burial by devouring,' the young auk'nai take the time to cut down one of the strong, unique trees on the mountain, which is used to create the pole of a hook staff. They mine stone and metal from the caves to create the hook end." This portion of the holograph showed a slowly rotating daunoren hook staff, zooming in on the various features as they were described.

"These hook staffs are used as a tool in many facets of auk'nai life. They can be for fishing, for hunting, for fighting, and for play," the holograph of George said before transitioning into a duo of auk'nai. They were hooking their staffs together to play a game of tug-of-war, each attempting to fling the other from a small floating platform.

"We hope," the holograph of George reappeared and continued, "that one day we can merge our civilizations together. But for now, we need to keep both separate until we know more. Until then, stay curious." George's hologram gave a bow before it winked out.

"What did you think?" George Tanaka's voice came from behind them, not from the hologram. Denton spun around and saw the real-life version, a few years older than he looked in the hologram.

"That was incredible. The auk'nai are amazing," Denton said. George approached and gave him a firm handshake.

"I've heard of you, Denton. What you did last night was very brave." George looked Denton directly in the eyes. "A little reckless, but brave."

"Thank you, sir," Denton said.

"Ugh, *sir*? Have I gotten so old?" George chuckled. "Please, call me George." He smiled, wrinkling his face. "Enjoy the archives, you two. I have some things to attend to, but don't be afraid to call if you need me. Nice meeting you, Denton," George said. Then he walked out of the room.

Denton could see as George turned away that he was carrying his own mini version of a daunoren hook staff. From the end of the hand-size staff dangled a small metal replica of the *Odysseus*.

"Can we see more?" Denton asked.

"Of course! I'll give you a tour," Eliana said, and hooked her arm through his again.

Throughout their tour, Denton learned a great deal about his new home planet. In the botany hall, a hologram of Marie Viray introduced him to the exciting colors, shapes, and smells of the Kamarian botanical collection, as well as their chemical properties. There were multiple large displays full of living plants with explanations about their native habitats.

Near a display of rainforest plants, a containment field allowed the smells to come through, but not any floating bacteria or moisture that the plants gave off. There was a sparser display featuring plants from colder mountain environments. Snow fluttered from the ceiling of the display, and small-leafed plants sucked in the moisture. Denton was happy to see that there were also empty display spaces, indicating that Kamaria was still far from fully explored.

Next, they entered the geology hall. A holographic display of Faye Raike introduced them to various geodes. The history of the planet could be found in the rocks themselves. Places where there were once vast oceans and riverbeds and were now mountainous areas and canyons implied cataclysmic events in the past.

The geologists theorized that Kamaria had originally had a single moon, but something had collided with it and splintered off a smaller satellite. These two moons were named Tasker and Promiser, Tasker being the larger of the two.

Eliana pulled Denton into the scout hall with footage of all their first encounters with wildlife. Denton finally discovered what a lemurbat looked like. They were the size of an old Earth monkey, each with four beady orange eyes, long ears, a thin tail, and leathery purple skin with green and black dots much like a cheetah's pattern. One video showed a lemurbat throwing rocks at the cartographer orb Denton had fixed sometime after the video was taken.

"I think he should have paid for that service." Denton pointed at the creature in the video and turned to smile at Eliana, only to notice she wasn't near him.

Denton walked out into the main hall and saw her enter a different wing of archive called *The City of the Dead*.

"What's this?" Denton asked as he entered the wing. He noticed a holographic video of a city littered with slain auk'nai citizens. Eliana didn't answer. The video proceeded to show the area where a crypt stood, through a valley of statues. Denton saw the tall stone sentry protecting the crypt. Inside the cave, the video showed the scout team collecting samples and then finally stumbling on the alien corpse.

"The Siren," Eliana said as it was revealed. Denton saw the smashed-in skull of a creature that looked very different from everything else in the archive. The corpse lifted upward from the ground and rotated slowly in place for him to see. It had a long horn protruding from the top of its bird-like skull over a body of bone and tendrils. Razor-sharp talons lined the ends of each claw. Eliana stopped the video.

"This was the last scout mission I went on with my father," she said. Denton wasn't sure what to say. Before he could do anything, she turned and walked out of the room, so Denton followed.

Eliana led him to the remembrance hall. Names were etched into a wall of stone, with *Those We Lost* engraved above it. Denton saw nearly forty names on the list. The displays included wreckage from damaged spacecraft and statues of brave-looking pilots staring toward the sky. Denton recognized the face of Captain Roelin Raike from previous holographic messages in other rooms, but this time, the man was labeled "the murderer."

"It has been four years, and it still makes no sense," Eliana said in a faraway voice. "Roelin was like an uncle to me. My mother passed away when I was very young. The Telemachus Project staff became my surrogate family and helped my dad raise me." Eliana gently touched the name of her father on the wall of stone. "I was almost killed in the attack too."

Denton's heart dropped. "What happened that day?" he asked, looking around the remembrance hall.

"We aren't entirely sure. We think Roelin experienced some sort of psychotic break. Mandatory scans we all had to take after scout missions revealed nothing unusual. Faye was the first to start noticing something was wrong with him. She tried to help him, but in doing so, she kept his illness a secret for some time. Eventually, she asked my father for help."

Eliana paused for a moment to collect herself. "I was with her to comfort her that night. Faye couldn't find Roelin. My father found him in the quarantine lab and tried to help him." Eliana walked over to the section of the hall about Roelin. "The power was out in the quarantine lab, so we have no footage from inside. I only know what

I saw after Faye and I entered the lab."

Denton wanted to comfort Eliana, but he let her finish her story.

"Roelin ..." She hesitated. "Roelin murdered my father. Faye screamed, and before we could do much else, Roelin had pointed a gun at me. I ducked before he could shoot me, but the shot punctured the hull of the lab. Faye and I went lung-locked." Eliana rubbed her neck. "Roelin left the quarantine lab and made his way to the shipyard. He killed many colonists there and stole his warship, the *Astraeus*. We couldn't follow him fast enough, and he vanished into the Kamarian wilderness. Faye and I were rescued, and then there were months of rehabilitation and rebuilding." Eliana winced at the sting of the memories. She sighed and continued, "I was on my own. Faye shut herself away after it happened. I haven't been able to talk to her since."

Denton was done just standing by, and embraced her.

"I'm sorry," he said.

Eliana hugged him back.

"My father would have never wanted me to just give up everything. I try to honor him by pursuing knowledge and staying positive." Eliana straightened herself.

"He has plenty to be proud of." Denton nodded to her. She nodded toward the floor, then held his hand as they left the miserable room.

They continued their tour of the archives for a while before Eliana was summoned for scout business on her soothreader.

"This has been refreshing," Eliana said as she closed the notification with a wave of her hand. "Sadly, duty calls."

"Hey, how about tonight I show you something I found?" Denton offered. "Whatever time works best for you."

"Oh? Denton Castus discovering new things on Kamaria? I'm impressed." Eliana grinned and raised her eyebrows.

"Just a little corner of the colony that may have gone unnoticed. Meet me at the shop after dark."

"I'll be there," Eliana said. Denton was pleased to see her smiling again. "I look forward to it."

They shared a hug and parted ways. Denton felt like all the cells in his body were jumping and cheering, and he almost walked into the door on his way out of the archive, distracted by all the anxious energy he had built up from spending the day with Eliana.

———— ✦ ————

Eliana approached George Tanaka in the *Odysseus* construction display hall. Holograms of the spacecraft being designed and built on Mars long ago in the Sol System danced in the air.

"So, what do you think?" Eliana asked, holding her arms out to her sides as she walked toward him.

"He is definitely a curious soul," George said. "And as last night proved, he's resourceful."

"And brave. Pavel told us he held off mactabilis wasps with a particle saw."

"Speaking of," George said. He placed his hands on a table with a display of the *Odysseus* leaving the *Telemachus* and leaned forward. "With the attack last night"—George looked up from the table toward Eliana—"scouting is being placed on hold for a little while so our protocols can be reevaluated."

"What?" Eliana said, her voice raised almost to a shout. "So what do we do, twiddle our thumbs here at the colony while our new world waits outside our walls?" Eliana threw her arm to the side in a sweeping gesture.

"What happened with the wasps can't be ignored." George sighed. "I know this disappoints you. Lord knows your father wouldn't approve."

"Dad was never a fan of the council." Eliana leaned against a display. "I wish I had voting power on the council."

George gave a lighthearted laugh that sounded more like a sigh. "We'd get more done that way." He nudged her with his elbow. "I think they could be persuaded if someone found a way to guarantee events like last night couldn't happen again."

"I'll see what I can conjure up," Eliana said, and winked.

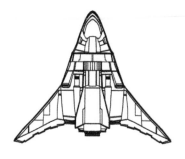

EIGHTEEN

THAT NIGHT, ELIANA MADE her way to the Castus Machine Shop to meet with Denton. She wore a casual outfit, a hooded vest over a long sweater, cargo pants, and sandals.

Ideas about how to remove the council-enforced hold on scout missions filled Eliana's head, but she couldn't seem to find an answer. It hardly even crossed her mind if this encounter with Denton Castus would be a date or not; she hadn't made time for such things since her academy days on Remus Orbital.

It wasn't that she didn't want a companion—Eliana wasn't some virgin saint—it was just the timing of it all. At Remus Orbital, she'd had her pick among many intelligent, handsome, rich boys with sticks up their asses and chips on their shoulders, but she never had been into that type of companion.

Timing had proven to be the real death of romance in Eliana's life. She was transferred from Mars to the academy, then again to the *Telemachus*, then yet again to Kamaria, a distance that took three hundred years of stasis sleep to travel. When Eliana first landed, she thought she could start her life over, settle down, and plant some roots. But lung-lock crept over the colony, and suddenly the fate of humanity rested on the shoulders of the scouts and their ability to find a cure. She'd found the cure, even though she was still unsure of what she had given up when she'd handed Mag'Ro her collider pistol that night long ago. Then fate had found a way to intervene one last time—the killing strokes of Captain Roelin Raike.

Since the day her father was murdered, Eliana felt like she was drowning in a pool of her swirling emotions. It felt like every time she was about to breach the surface, the levee would break, and her emotions would flood over her once more.

Eliana sighed and peered up into the night sky as she walked, wishing she could be more excited about this potential date she was lumbering toward. She'd just try and move through the motions and hope the moment would inspire her to forget her worries.

Denton was waiting for her outside the shop in a clean button-up shirt with a messenger bag slung over his shoulder and some loose-fitting jeans. His work boots still betrayed the pristine look he was going for, but Eliana liked that about him. He was trying to impress, yet honest in his attempt.

"Well, look at you, Mr. Castus," Eliana said with a smile. "You clean up nice."

"You ready for this?" Denton asked, returning her smile with a warm one of his own.

"I'm not sure. Depends on what *this* is."

"Follow me, I think you're going to like it," he said, and led her through the alleyway around the side of the shop. They walked over and around the loose boxes and crates until they came to the fence.

Denton pulled the messenger bag from his shoulder and removed a small tool from the main pouch. It was a handheld thermal melter.

"Breaking and entering?" Eliana asked.

"Two things," Denton said, igniting the tip of the melter and proceeding to cut a hole in the fence big enough for them to squeeze through. "First, it's not *breaking in* if it's your own family's shop." He finished cutting and held the fence open for Eliana to squeeze through. "And second, I'll fix it on the way back in." He shook his messenger bag, and the tools inside jingled. She stepped through the hole. Denton pointed to the slope. "Just over that hill."

Eliana squinted and could see a faint light coming from behind the slope. As they grew closer, they looked downhill and found Denton's secret place: a glade of glowing flowers shrouded by Kamarian trees.

"*Woah!* Do you know what those are?" Eliana asked.

"Yeah, I looked them up in the archive. Kamarian vividpetals." He smiled proudly. Eliana blushed. He was using the knowledge he'd gained from the archives to impress her, and it was adorable.

"Bravo," Eliana said, and dashed forward, laughing as she ran down the slope. Denton was caught off guard, stumbling as he chased her playfully.

Eliana made it to the vividpetal glade first. Denton's feet got away from him, and he rolled into the meadow, landing facedown in the flowers. He noticed they danced away from his impact zone, then slowly drifted back inward.

"I didn't know they could move like that," Denton said.

"Kamaria never fails to surprise," Eliana said, and lowered her hand to help him up. Denton grabbed her hand and pulled her down into the flowers. The vividpetals made room for her, then slowly encompassed them both in their warm green glow. The two laughed and stared up into the branches of the trees.

Denton noticed some sort of glowing shape moving in the branches, illuminating its path and gently dropping shimmering pollen. He squinted upward at the form but couldn't see it clearly enough.

"It's called an eventide gliderfly," Eliana said, and pointed upward at the mysterious shape. An alien butterfly as large as a house cat revealed itself. It had feathery whiskers protruding from a long snout that it used to drink up nectar from bulbs in the canopy of the trees. Denton blinked some of the glowing pollen away from his eyes as it gently drifted toward them.

"So, what do you call this place?" Eliana rolled over to look at him. He stared up into the trees, amazed by the gliderfly.

"Oh, I didn't give it a name."

"Well, I guess it's up to me. If George were here, he'd have a name. He just seems to pull them out of a hat at will." She chuckled and sat up on her butt, holding her knees with her hands. "How about Denny's Den?"

"I think I see why they don't let you name anything." He laughed.

"Hey! I haven't heard you come up with anything better!" She gave him a shove.

"Or worse either," Denton said, and they laughed together for a moment, then both paused in thought.

"How about the Glimmer Glade?"

"You know what," he said, holding a finger up and pausing for dramatic effect, "Glimmer Glade works for me."

"Glad I could help," Eliana said, smiling. The two admired the scenery a moment longer. Eliana didn't notice that she had breached the surface of her pool of emotions. She was breathing easily— smiling, even. It had happened so naturally, yet so subtly, like a continued heartbeat.

Eliana turned toward Denton's messenger bag and asked, "So what else you got in there?"

Denton reached into his bag and brought out two cold bottles of Ganymede ale, then snapped off the caps with an expert movement across his chest. "It's Castus-made Ganymede ale. Last two of their kind."

"Is that so?" She accepted the bottle and inspected it. "Well, I'm honored to drink it with you."

"Cheers," Denton said, and they clinked their bottles together and each took a hearty sip.

Eliana smacked her lips and nodded. "That's some good stuff. Shame there's not more." She took another sip.

"We'll make more, whenever we figure it out," Denton said, and continued watching the gliderfly.

"You and your brothers are pretty crafty, aren't you?"

"Yeah, we've been tinkering with stuff in the shop since we could hold a socket wrench," Denton said. "Lots of trial and error. Lots of almost blowing our hands off. But also lots of fun." He winked at her.

"It's very different from the way I grew up, it seems." Eliana's voice faltered as she spoke. A wave passed over her head inside her mental pool.

"Where are you from originally?" Denton asked.

"Martian-born, academy-raised, *Telemachus* professional." Eliana winked back.

"I'm just glad you didn't say Tvashtar. I don't know how I'd face my dad if I told him I went on a date with an Io mooner."

Eliana smiled and said, "So, this *is* a date!"

"All that schoolin', and you just figured it out? What gave it away?" Denton smiled. Then his eyes went wide and he braced himself, his palms against the grass. "Is that alright with you?"

Eliana's heart beat a little faster, and her body felt warmer. She took another sip of her beer and contained her smile as best she could. "We'll have to see, won't we?"

Denton grinned and took another sip of his beer.

Eliana noticed something else in Denton's messenger bag and asked, "What else did you bring?"

"Oh, this?" Denton pulled out his sketchpad device. "It's nothing. I just draw in my free time."

"Can I take a look? I liked your art in the garage."

"Yeah, feel free," Denton said. He handed her the sketchpad and watched her flip through it. Eliana was able to peer into Denton's life. She saw many images of Ganymede landscapes, the jagged rock formations, and the deep darks of the cold moon contrasted with the bright oranges of Jupiter on the horizon. She saw pictures of Denton's family, his brothers goofing off on the hovering rushcycle, and tender moments of his mother and father dancing to music. Eliana pointed at the dance sketch and turned it toward Denton. "I like this one the most so far," she said with a smile.

There were more technical drawings of tools, devices, and spaceships, and the schematics of the racing rushcycle he and his brothers were working on. Denton was a very detail-focused person, and the purpose of his line art was evident. After the more technical drawings, Eliana found a slew of pages with half-finished sketches. Then, finally, one glorious page in full color of the Glimmer Glade they currently sat in.

"That's when I found this place," Denton said. Eliana handed Denton back his sketchpad.

"Excellent work in there. Ever think of making it a career?"

"Career? Nah, I don't think it would work," he said. "I like to draw for myself mainly. I don't think I'd like to do it for other people."

"Well, I think they are great." She smiled. Denton blushed in response, and his flushed cheeks were exposed by the glowing vividpetals surrounding him. Eliana wondered if he didn't often receive compliments for his art. She wondered how many people even knew he could draw.

"Yeah, thanks." He paused. "Sometimes I wish I had more time for it, though."

"Oh yeah?" Eliana asked.

"Yeah. Every day, I wake up and work in the shop. Sometimes I do construction on the side, and then I go home. It's an endless circle," Denton said, waving his finger around. "No time to be me. Back on Ganymede, it helped me keep my mind off the approach of the Undriel, but here it's different. Hells, I only got the day off today by risking my life last night." He chuckled at the revelation.

Eliana asked, "Denny, do you like what you do in the shop?"

Denton hummed as he considered the question, then said, "It's okay." He winced, then admitted, "I mean, it's weird now, for me."

"What do you mean?"

"Well, on Ganymede, in the Arrow, I didn't really have a choice. The Arrow was a mining and machine-making colony. I had made my peace with it, though. Got into a rhythm. But now ..."

"Now you don't have to. Now you have options," Eliana said, finishing his thought.

"Yeah, I guess," Denton said. "But do I really? Hells, I've been pigeonholed into working in the shop again anyway. The only reason I'm not still frozen in a bed up on the *Telemachus* right now is because I can fix things."

Eliana let Denton's troubled thoughts become her own for a moment. Maybe there was a way Denton could help the colony and himself at the same time. He was a curious soul, as George had put it. He was resourceful, as the night with the wasps had shown. And Denton had a unique perspective that came from a life working on Ganymede in a machine shop.

Eliana allowed herself to be selfish for a moment. She liked him, and he made her feel human again. By helping Denton Castus find his true purpose in the colony, she could also help herself live again.

"Denny," Eliana said, choosing her words carefully. "What if I offered you a chance for something different?"

"What?"

"What if I could get you into the Scout Program?" she asked, looking Denton in the eyes.

"Are you kidding?" Denton asked, but he seemed to know the answer. "That would be—" He stopped himself.

"What do you think?" She was begging him to continue his thought. She was wondering if she'd made the right choice, putting him on the spot like this. Eliana also worried what would happen if he declined the offer, leaving her stranded not in a pool but an ocean of her own dark emotions.

"Well, my brothers and my dad ..." Denton started.

"There's plenty of good people here that could help them," Eliana stated. She almost blurted it out reflexively.

"Yeah, but it was always just us. It seems wrong to consider anything else," Denton said. Eliana's heart dropped, and she felt like her face was being pulled just a little harder by gravity. Then Denton said, "But maybe you're right."

A spark of hope. Eliana nodded and said, "Think it over. I can talk to George, and we can get you in on the scout assessment coming up."

"Thanks, I'll think about it," Denton said.

"No problem," Eliana said. The two regarded each other for a moment. "It's the least I can do, after what you did last night on the *Henson*."

"Hells, anyone would have done that," Denton said.

"But it was you. And honestly, I don't know if just anyone could run into a burning spaceship wreck and face off against giant angry alien wasps with a particle saw. So, yeah, you did a brave thing." She chuckled, then paused; she had forgotten her original problem from earlier this evening. "But scouting is on hold until we figure out a way to stop that from happening again."

"It's on hold?"

"Yeah, the council wants to keep the scouts safe, and they can't allow another expedition until we tackle this problem," Eliana said. Denton thought for a moment, still lying on his back.

"Shit, just use a taser hull," he said casually, and took another sip of his beer.

"A taser what?" Eliana jerked her head toward him.

"Yeah, a taser hull. A little trick me and my brothers cooked up." Denton sat up and used his beer as a prop as he giddily explained. "In the Arrow, rushcycle theft was common. Folks would steal the bikes and strip them for parts. To stop it, lots of people used these tethered leashes to restrain their vehicles, but those didn't work most of the time. So, my brothers and I came up with a better idea." Denton held his beer in one hand and tapped it with his other. "It's this device you can strap to any metal hull that sends a shock wave of electricity through the shell. It doesn't affect the systems of the rushcycle either. In this case, we could just modify it to work on a larger scale."

"So, creatures like the wasps would be repelled from the hull, unable to break their way in. That sounds like it might actually work." Eliana's teeth were showing through her broadening smile.

"Yeah, I thought of it after I saw you and the marines come in and save my ass. They had some sort of electrical ammo in their rifles. Killed those bugs instantly," Denton said, snapping his fingers.

"That might be the solution!" Eliana kept analyzing his idea, and it kept sounding better and better. "I have to tell George!"

"You're welcome," Denton said, smiling and taking the last gulp of his Ganymede ale. Eliana tackled him onto his back and pinned him to the ground, then kissed him on the lips. She felt lightning rush through her body. Her arms tingled, and her hair felt like it was standing up on end. The tips of her fingers felt hot and cold at the same time as she gripped the back of his neck to kiss him harder.

She finished her kiss and pulled back. "Sorry!" she yelped, and lifted herself away from him.

"Sorry, *my ass*," Denton said, and brought her in for another kiss. She felt his strong arms pull her toward him and the movement of his chest against hers. They kissed for a few heartbeats longer this time, then released, breathing heavily, as if they had been underwater.

For the next hour, they laughed and shared stories, Denton telling her of old clients with unusual requests, and Eliana weaving tales of some of the first scout missions that had taken place on Kamaria. Finally, they stood up and walked out of the Glimmer Glade, laughing and joking along the way. They passed the fence, and Denton sealed the hole he had created, making it untraceable that they had ever gone beyond it.

Once back in front of the machine shop, Eliana turned to Denton and said, "I'm going to tell George about this taser hull idea. If all goes according to plan, you have a week until the next scout assessment comes around," she said, then leaned in close to his ear. "Please consider becoming a scout. You're a perfect fit for the job." She gave him another kiss.

Denton looked down and blushed.

Eliana moved away from him, slowly releasing his hand as she gained distance. "See you around."

Eliana walked home with a spring in her step, but she was pretty sure she could fly if she wanted. Her heart was hammering in her chest, and her skin pulsed with heat. She felt like she might be emitting steam in the chilly night.

Eliana hoped above anything else that Denton would consider taking the assessment.

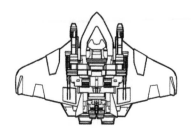

NINETEEN

FOUR YEARS AGO

DAY 200 OF ROELIN'S EXODUS

THE SIGNS OF LONG-term wilderness survival were apparent on Roelin Raike's body. His hygiene had clearly been a low priority, his hair was unkempt, and his beard had grown long and bushy. He'd removed a dead tooth at one point with tools he'd found in the medical bay, and the medicines stores were beginning to run thin.

The summer had passed. A rainy season had occurred, but he was lucky enough to not be washed away with the flooding river waterfalls. When the fish stopped coming, Roelin was forced to go out on hunting excursions.

Roelin kept his atmospheric suits maintained, but they showed signs of extensive use. Without any other way to prevent himself from going lung-locked in the open Kamarian air, the suits were his lifeline. He was extra careful to make sure he didn't go past his maximum range, or else he'd risk breathing in the unpurified air through already-strained purifiers.

Nhymn questioned Roelin incessantly, but at the same time, he managed to learn a few details about his captor. Sympha was an essential figure to her, although their exact relationship was still a mystery to Roelin. Based on the initial encounter with the gigantic monster in the jungle his first night of exodus, he assumed Nhymn and Sympha were not on good speaking terms. Roelin dreaded the thought that he would do all the work to repair the *Astraeus* only to be downed again, or perhaps die fighting. It felt like a fruitless endeavor.

Nhymn asked Roelin to elaborate on old memories; she was searching for something. She asked a lot about his wife, Faye, and summoned the familiar feelings that occurred with each memory, much like the autopsy she'd made Roelin endure, but pleasant in contrast.

He felt butterflies in his stomach when revisiting the memory of how he'd met Faye on Mars, the nervous sweat of his wedding day in a church at the base of Olympus Mons, the tenseness of a hundred battles with the Undriel, both in and out of the *Astraeus*.

The one thing Nhymn didn't seem to understand was the motivation behind these events. What had caused the battles? What was the love he felt for Faye, and why did these things happen to a human? After two hundred days, Roelin wasn't sure Nhymn would ever fully understand humanity's subtleties, or why she wanted to know so much about them.

—— ◆ ——

PRESENT DAY

Denton Castus ate breakfast at the dining room table with his family and thought about the future. Eliana's offer gestated in his mind; he thought of the exciting possibilities exploring Kamaria would bring. He thought of the sights they would see, the animals they would discover, and, most importantly, the opportunities he would have to figure out who he really was. Denton stirred his food with his fork, realizing that if he pursued this dream, he would be leaving the shop.

He would be leaving his family.

Tyler smiled and chatted about some of the exciting work they were doing, including adding taser hulls to the scouts' vessels. Eliana had passed the idea on to George, who had commissioned the Castus Machine Shop to equip their ships with modified taser devices. It put the scouting program back on track.

Jason had the same faraway look in his eyes as Denton. The shop was a hole that he couldn't dig himself out of. Jason had no direction beyond the shop; he just knew that this was not where he wanted to be.

Denton knew where he wanted to be, but he wasn't sure what he would lose to get there. He wanted to become a scout, but if he left the shop, would he be dooming Jason to more work? At least Tyler enjoyed the work. It was eating away at Denton's heart.

"What's wrong, Denny?" Brynn said. Denton looked up from his food; his face had revealed his moral struggle. He looked his mother in the eyes and winced.

"I got asked to take the scout assessment," Denton said.

"Ain't that a hoot!" Tyler said. "Those scouts must really like you. Work has been crazy here since you got them to hire us."

Jason looked up at Denton. His eyes stared through him. His mouth was open, but he said nothing. Jason seemed to be waiting for what Denton would say next.

"I was thinking of going for it," Denton said. Jason's mouth shut, and he looked away.

Michael looked across the table at Denton. He fumbled his fork in his hand and said, "What are ya saying, son?" His voice was steady but quiet.

"I …" Denton turned to face him. "I think I want to be a scout."

"You can't just leave," Tyler said. He fidgeted in his seat as his eyes darted around the surface of the table. "We need you."

"I know," Denton said. He looked down again and put his fork on his plate, then said, "It's something I think I need to do, though."

"You can't do both, can you?" Michael asked.

"I don't think so," Denton said. "But I'd try to help out when I could."

"You won't have time," Tyler said, tapping his knuckles against the table in a steady rhythm. "It's just going to be Jay and me."

Jason kept his eyes on Denton, his brow furrowed. He said nothing.

Denton looked down again. He didn't know how to proceed.

"You should go for it," Jason said flatly. Denton looked back up at him. Jason still had a stern look on his face, and he maintained steady eye contact with Denton, letting his statement sink in.

"Yeah," Brynn said. "We'll manage here. I think you should take the assessment."

"But the workload is getting heavier here," Denton said, looking at his family one at a time.

"Yeah, workload's heavier, thanks to you," Brynn said. "I think we owe it to you to let you try to be who you want to be."

"Do it, Denny," Jason said again. "You got a shot at something. You can't turn it down. If you don't do it now, you'll regret it forever."

Denton felt a weight on his heart. In a way, Jason was talking to himself. The laser-focused look on his face told Denton without words, *If you don't do it, you'll end up like me.*

"You know," Michael said with a sigh, "when I was a little kid, I found a toy gyrocopter in the garbage. Someone had thrown it out because it had crashed into something and broke. I brought it into the shop, and your grandpa sat me down and taught me how to fix it." Michael looked upward, away from everyone, with a smile on his face. He nodded and continued, "I had so much fun that day playing with that gyrocopter. I felt like I could fix anything. The world was mine, and I could build it."

Denton felt like something was tugging at the back of his throat. Michael looked at Denton. "I always wanted you boys to feel like that. I wanted you to feel like you had the power to build the world you wanted to live in."

Jason looked away toward the door.

"Denny, if this opportunity makes you feel that way, take it.

Don't worry about us, we'll be fine," Michael said.

"Thanks," Denton said. He had a hard time pushing the words past the lump in his throat.

Tyler looked at his parents and said, "Well, I want a raise if I'm doing extra work."

"You guys can split Denton's pay when he gets the job," Brynn said.

"Woah, I didn't say that," Michael said. Brynn and Tyler laughed.

"I got something I gotta do," Jason said, and stood up. "Good luck, Denny. Knock 'em dead."

"Thanks, Jay," Denton said quietly. Jason grabbed his rushcycle helmet and walked downstairs to the shop. Denton nodded as he put another forkful of food into his mouth.

He was going to take the assessment.

———◆———

A week passed, and suddenly it was the eve of the assessment. Denton had been in the archives all week. He wanted to learn everything he could about scouts and their processes before the evaluation. Eliana approached him in the chemistry hall. Holographic videos of Marie Viray working toward the Madani Cure played next to glass containers of various elements used to make the cure. Eliana gazed at the display of the gems Mag'Ro had given her as if reaching for an old memory.

"Hey, Elly," Denton said, not taking his eyes off the data.

"How do you feel about the test?" she asked.

"Feeling good about the physical test." He grinned.

"And how about the written tests?"

"Feeling … not as good." Denton deflated.

"Why is that? I've seen you in here all week."

"I don't know everything," he said. He winced and shook his head. "I don't think I'm going to pass. I'm terrible at taking tests like this."

"Do you think *I* know everything?" Eliana said. "It's not our job to know everything, Denny. It's our job to try and learn what we can."

"Well, I got a lot to learn."

"Here, I'll quiz you," she said. "First three pillars of scouting?" Eliana held up three fingers on her right hand.

"Explore, learn, and teach," he recited as Eliana dropped each finger for each correct answer.

"Great, these are the pillars upon which all scouting stands. What does it mean though?"

"We *explore* our new world to *learn* everything we can and *teach* it to others."

"Exactly. Our job is to figure things out and tell everyone. Now, how about first-contact protocol?"

"Don't panic. Assess if there is a threat. Scan the subject. Attempt basic communication, if possible. Learn everything you can. Only use force if yourself or your team is in danger and all other options have been exhausted," Denton said as he spun his finger. There was something he was forgetting.

"One more," she said.

"Don't panic?" he repeated, and Eliana chuckled.

"It's to keep an open mind. I feel like that one is the most important. Now, how about the scouting process?"

"Assess a research zone. Observe threats in the area, and, if clear, begin research. Try to disturb as little as possible. Take samples, videos, and photos. Map the area with a cartographer's orb." He paused. "Stay safe and have fun?" he said, unsure of the ending. Eliana laughed.

"Pretty good. How about if the team moves away from the ship, say a long-term scout mission that goes overnight?" she asked.

"Follow orders from Tvashtar marine escorts." Denton thought of the long-time feud the Castus family had with Tvashtar engineers and chuckled, then continued, "Secure a camping position in a safe area. Set up barrier fences and make sure each scientific workstation is locked down overnight. No unsupervised trips away from camp. Use the buddy system," Denton said.

"See? You got this! You'll be a scout in no time!" She clapped his shoulder.

"Thanks," he said, and looked down.

"It's a big step for you, I understand." Eliana put her hand on his forearm. "But I think it's the right step. You show all the qualities in a scout we are looking for." She rubbed his arm with her thumb. "Plus, you're nice to look at. I wouldn't mind having you around more." She winked.

"Thanks for the vote of confidence," Denton said with a smile.

"I'll let you get back to studying. *Keep an open mind!*" Eliana said, then kissed his cheek and walked away.

Denton nodded and sighed. The Madani Cure holographic display cycled once more, reminding him of the great things the scouts had accomplished for humanity. *Am I really up to snuff against achievements like that?* Denton wondered.

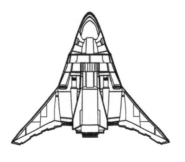

TWENTY

THE SCOUT ASSESSMENT LAB was a medium-size room with a row of desks, much like classrooms Denton had been in on Ganymede when he was a kid. Much like he was during his old Ganymede schooling, he was uncomfortable in his seat, and his eyes had a hard time parsing the questions written before him. Ten students sat in the desks around him, and only two would be chosen to become scouts. A large display screen at the front of the room signified that the end of the test was approaching.

Denton sighed through his nose, noting he had less than five seconds to spare. He clicked random answers for the final questions he hadn't read, favoring *C*'s because it felt lucky to choose the letter that also began his last name.

"Time is up, please place your stylus down," the soothing voice of Homer announced.

"Shit," Denton whispered, and put his stylus on the desk and winced. Had he correctly answered enough in the early parts of the test to make up for his guessing toward the end?

Another candidate slammed his stylus onto his desk and muttered a few swears to himself. Denton didn't know any of their names yet, but he had seen many of these colonists in the archives.

Everyone had the same ammo for this fight; Denton just hoped his gun was as good as the others.

"Alright, everyone," George Tanaka said as the display screen at the front of the room turned transparent, revealing a crew of evaluators, Eliana Veston among them. "Your score will be displayed on your soothreader. If the color of your score is green, you have passed the written portion of the scout assessment and may continue to the physical portion tomorrow. If your score is red, you have not passed, but you may retake the assessment next time there is an opening. Either way, you may leave the study room now if you wish. Expect your scores within the hour. Thank you." The microphone clicked, and the students began collecting their things.

A hard-edged woman with pale skin and a short brown soldier's mohawk stood and walked past Denton's desk. Before she made it to the door, her soothreader pinged and glowed green. She looked at it and nodded mechanically, then exited the room. She had made it to the next portion of the exam. Denton wondered how many candidates could proceed.

Another candidate bumped into Denton as he stood up from his desk. He was a clean-cut blond man dressed in a button-up shirt and slacks.

"Clumsy, moonie," he said with a sneer. Denton had heard this slur before, always from station-born citizens. This man reeked of Remus Orbital Academy sass. Denton wanted to reply with a derogatory term they used for space-station brats, "hully," but chose the high road.

"You're from that Ganymede machine shop, aren't you? My uncle is on the council. He said there wasn't any other use for Arrow colonists, you're just simply redundant," the hully said, stressing the word "redundant" to make sure every syllable hit Denton like a stone. "I'm surprised they let you in here. Not enough scraps from the Tvashtar engineers to keep you busy?" The hully laughed to himself. Denton tried to ignore him and walk past him, but the hully grabbed his arm.

"Listen here, *moonie*," the hully whispered to him with ferocity in his voice. "I'm not going to let you ruin my chances at becoming a scout. Just drop out. You know you're just muddying the water for a more qualified member of society to step in." The hully's sharp blue eyes pierced Denton.

Denton shook his arm away. The hully tipped his nose upward. A bell chimed from the hully's soothreader, and green light glowed from its screen.

"Ninety-eight percent." The hully snickered and walked out of the room.

Denton hated the hully even more for that.

"Don't let Mitch bug you," someone said from behind Denton. "All the Harlans are jerks."

"I take it you're not friends," Denton said. The candidate stuck his hand out, and Denton shook it.

"Hells no. The name's Carl Gregory," he said. He was a plump man with medium-length black hair and tanned skin. Carl pushed his glasses up the brim of his nose and added, "I grew up on Remus Orbital and have been stuck in classes with Mitch ever since we were kids. Always hated the bastard, but I just can't get away from him, so I play nice when he's around."

"I'm Denton Castus. I work at the machine shop near the shipyard."

"Hey, wait, you're the guy from the *Henson* wreck, right?" Carl said. A broad smile revealed his pearly teeth.

"Yep. That's me," Denton said. His face felt hot suddenly.

"Man, I owe you a drink. Lynn is a friend of mine. She said you saved her life."

"I just did what anyone would do."

"Humble, too!" he said, giving Denton a pat on the shoulder. Carl's soothreader lit up green, and a score of ninety-one flashed. He smiled and nodded, satisfied but not surprised. "It looks like I'm on to the next phase! Good luck!" Carl nodded and took his leave.

Denton shouldered his messenger bag and heard the ping of his soothreader. He looked down and saw a green glow, and the number seventy-two hovered in the air over his wrist.

Denton smiled. Unlike Carl, he was surprised. It wasn't a high score, but it was a passing score. He would have to compensate for it during the physical portion of the test.

Denton thought about what Mitch had said. Was he muddying the waters for more qualified candidates? The academy candidates' scores stung in comparison to his own. Was he heading into a battle he could not win? If Carl and Mitch did just as well on the physical portion as they had on the written, Denton was out.

He still had to try. It was all he could do.

———◆———

The next morning, Denton sat on a ground sail with the remaining candidates. They glided over the swaying grass of the meadow in the midmorning sun.

"This is the farthest I've been from the colony since we landed," Carl Gregory said to Denton.

"I made it over there once." Denton pointed to a dusty spot in the grass that was ripped up from the *Henson* crash. "But other than that, same here. Never been outside, really. I suppose they probably haven't either." He thrust his thumb toward the other two candidates that had passed the written exam, Mitch Harlan and a Tvashtar marine named Jess Combs. The other six had not achieved the score needed to continue, which had made Denton feel smart when he first thought about it, but then it made him nervous when he realized he'd gotten the lowest score of the passing group.

They came to a stop at the scout pavilion. It was a white, cylindrical building with a smaller structure at its side, the quarantine lab, and a fence enclosing a yard around the back. The door to the pavilion had the Telemachus Project logo above it along with its motto, "Explorarent, Disce, Docere"—or "Explore, Learn, Teach," as Denton had come to know it in Sol Common.

"Don't get comfortable, *moonie*." Mitch Harlan shoved past

Denton to make his way to the front of the group.

George Tanaka faced the candidates and said, "Welcome, everyone. This is where all scout missions begin and finish. We plan our missions here using recon satellites, targeting areas of interest or places that have a wealth of resources we can use for the colony." George paced slowly in front of the four candidates. Eliana stood behind him, checking data on her soothreader.

"This next portion of the test is to evaluate your physical abilities," he continued. "This is not a boot camp; we aren't training you to be soldiers." He looked at Jess Combs and smirked. "Not that you'd have a problem with that, right?" Jess showed no emotion. It was as if the comment had been absorbed by a robot, processed and retained. George's smirk died. He coughed and continued, "No. What we're looking for here is your ability to complete certain tasks that scouts are expected to perform. We follow the three pillars of the Kamarian Explorer's Code: explore, learn, and teach."

George gave Eliana the floor. She looked at the group and said, "Morning, candidates. First, we will have stations set up for you to learn the basics of Kamarian survival. It is up to you to learn everything you can. Then you will show us what you learned. There will be a team-based obstacle course, then the final test will be a mini-expedition with a veteran scout."

Denton was excited about the mini-expedition, thinking Eliana would be his guide. Camping in the alien wilderness underneath the new world's sky with her sounded like an excellent adventure.

"Why the obstacle course?" Carl Gregory asked.

Eliana looked over to him and said, "Our first scout mission, we were chased out of a cave by a Hells basilisk." Eliana gestured over her soothreader, and a holographic image of a horrible behemoth with a snakelike head and long arms with curled claws came to life in front of them. "So, it's not bad to know where candidates stand as far as being able to quickly get out of a situation like that."

Carl's eyebrows lifted almost into his hairline as he watched the Hells basilisk creep toward the camera's view. He nodded; that was enough information for him.

George waved the hologram away and said, "You have the full day to explore the pavilion. Feel free to talk with anyone who isn't busy. I wish we could invite you all onto the team, but the sensitive nature of scouting forces us to evaluate you this way." George smiled at the group. "Any other questions?" No one spoke, so George clapped his hands together and said, "Alright, the pavilion is yours." He gave a bow and walked into the pavilion with Eliana. The candidates followed behind.

Inside, the center of the pavilion housed a large meeting table surrounded by many chairs. Scouts looked over map data floating in holographic displays of potential new areas to explore. Denton saw Major Pavel Volkov standing with his Beta Team, a harness on his injured leg.

The walls had objectives outlined on large screens with names assigned to each. There was a station for off-loading equipment directly from the Pilgrim-class explorer vessels into a storage area. On the outer rim of the room, Denton saw various workstations for each facet of exploring: geology, biology, botany, and chemistry.

A doorway on one side of the pavilion led outside to a yard with a gym, an obstacle course, camping equipment, a viewing tower, and a gun range. The yard was encased by a tall wall to protect from outside threats, much like the rest of the colony. Denton remembered old videos of the scouting dome before the Madani Cure. This new building made the old facilities look like a flea market.

Carl turned to Denton and said, "I think I'll meet up with Lynn and say hi. I'll let her know you're around; I'm sure she'll want to see you again."

"Sounds good. I'm going to check out the yard area. I'll see you around," Denton said, and bumped fists with Carl.

Denton made his way outside into the yard. The camping equipment in the back area near the fence caught his eye, and he wandered over to check it out. A middle-aged man with dark-brown hair and a mustache was spreading out the equipment. He looked rugged, like a man who was born on a farm and had done physical work every morning right as the sun came up.

"Hey there," Denton said as he approached the man.

"Oh, hi thare. You must be one of the new candidates, yeh?" the man said with an accent Denton had heard before from clients originating from Callisto's colony, Arcas Hub. It resembled an old Earth Scottish accent. "They call me Fergus Reid when they aren't pissed." He stuck his hand out, and Denton shook it.

"I'm Denton. What's all this here?" Denton pointed at the equipment.

"Oh, this? It's actually for yoo lads. You'll be sleeping out here tonight," Fergus explained as he continued separating the metal rods and nylon tent fabric.

"You're allowed to just tell me this stuff? It's not a secret?" Denton asked.

"Wot? Course I kin! The whole point of this exploration phase is to ask questions. Would ye prefer I speak in riddles?" Fergus laughed. "No one here is trying to trick you. We can even set up a tent together, so you know what you're doing when the assessment comes."

"That sounds great. We didn't really have any outdoor equipment on Ganymede."

"*All-reet!* Well, git on it," Fergus said, pointing to a set of equipment. "Also, just between us"—he leaned in—"yeh came to the right place. Yeh'd be surprised how many folk shirk learning the basic camping stuff. I've seen a few scouts wash out after freezin' their arses off sleeping in the rain." He laughed, then gave Denton's shoulder a playful slap. "Okay, laddie. Let's learn yee. Grab the poles there."

Denton spent an hour learning the proper way to set up a tent. The whole process was very old-tech and hands-on, something Denton enjoyed a lot. With the tent up, it was time for the more advanced stuff.

"Home sweet home! Eh?" Fergus laughed. "But sorry, nylon

won't keep out a hungry *Kamarian nightsnare!*"

"Nightsnare? What's that?" Denton asked.

"Trust me, lad, you dinnae want to know," Fergus said, then chuckled. "Wait, of course yoo do! I'll let one of the biologists tell you about nightsnares. For now, you're gon'nae want to set up a fence and a fire. Kin ye grab those tool bags?" Fergus wiggled his fingers toward two small bags near where the tent bag had been before they'd set it up.

Denton held both bags in his hands and looked to Fergus for answers. "Okay, take the blue bag thare. That's the stakes for the encasement barrier. Works a lot like spaceship encasement barriers, but in reverse, ya see. You're gon'nae want to place these around the campsite. Normally there's enough for the entire scout team's site, but for this example, you'll just do it around yer personal tent."

Denton pulled out six handheld cylinders. Fergus grabbed one from him and explained, "Take it like this, and ..." He flicked his hand down quickly, and the cylinder extended into a pole two meters long with a sharp spike at one end and a blue orb on the other. "You do that with each pole. Stick them about two meters from each other in the ground and then tap the blue end at the top to turn 'em on. The orbs will find their mates and create the field between 'em, which will repel any beastie trying to come eat yeh in the night." Fergus paused. "In theory." He smiled, but it didn't reassure Denton that he wouldn't be eaten.

Denton began placing the poles and tapping their blue tips. Fergus watched him work and asked, "So, Ganymede, eh? Yer a moonie like m'self."

"Yeah, that's right," Denton said as he placed another pole.

"I would have figured yoo for a Ganny-man just by yer funny accent. I'm from Arcas Hub, Callisto," Fergus said, validating Denton's guess.

"Callisto? No wonder you have knowledge about all this camping stuff. Did you do it often?" Denton asked. Callisto was known as a garden moon back in the Sol System. It was one of the first terraformed moons refitted for human life and was an agricultural hub before the Undriel began to spread across the system.

"Camping? Laddie, I was born outside. We Arcas folk were referred to as gypsies from time to time. Roofs were optional." Fergus smiled. Denton placed the last pole.

"Sounds pretty great. In the Arrow, the only thing close to fresh air we ever got was underground in our resource farms. No bright sky to admire like here." Denton spread his arms out to indicate the nature around him, then tapped the final blue orb. The encasement barrier surrounded the tent, separating Denton and Fergus from each other.

"Perfect. Yer hired!" Fergus clapped. "Just kidding. But keep it up, and someone might say that to you in the next few days."

"So, what's in the red bag?" Denton asked, holding out the second tool bag.

"Right, last part. The red bag has tools to build a fire. During your final assessment, you'll have to find the ingredients to make a fire in the wild, but here in the pavilion, we provide you with them. See over thare?" Fergus threw his thumb behind his shoulder, indicating the pile of logs and materials. "Man's oldest invention. Let's get started."

The process was an old one, but timelessly effective. Fergus continued to offer instruction on fire making, explaining tinder, kindling, and wood-stacking formations, about which there were a few schools of thought.

Once Denton had a fire lit, Fergus congratulated him. "There you go, and that's all there is to it! You'll be sure to impress the lady scouts later when you do this on your own. Now, time to take it all down!" Fergus said.

Denton's smile faded; it had felt great to build it all up, but now it was time to remove all traces that it had ever happened.

Fergus taught Denton how to expertly take down and package away each element of the campsite, as well as how to put out the fire they had created in the most efficient way. When the fire was out, Fergus added with a grin, "You could always wee on the fire as well, if you have ta go."

"Thanks for the lesson," Denton said, shaking Fergus's hand once again.

"No problem. Make me proud, boy!" Fergus said, clapping his other hand onto Denton's shoulder. Denton walked off to explore the rest of the facility to see what he could learn.

On his way back to the interior of the pavilion, Denton walked past the obstacle course. He knew it was going to be an essential part of the assessment and thought it might be a good idea to look it over and see what was in store for him.

Every element of the course required teamwork. There was the high wall, a thin wooden board that would require one person to hold it in place while the other crossed, and a metal bar with sandbags on it that would need to be moved by two people. The last obstacle was a rope swing that slid across a tether over a pit. Whoever made it across first would have to push the swing back to their teammate.

"Daydreaming—what a great use of your time," Mitch Harlan said, interrupting Denton's train of thought. He turned to see Mitch inspecting a collider pistol at the gun range near him. "At least you're making it easy for me to beat you," he said, then shot three times into a target downrange.

Denton was no stranger to guns, and saw this as a challenge from the prissy academy boy. He approached the gun range. Mitch summoned the target back to his position, observing he had made three accurate shots close to the center.

"Not bad," Denton said. "I thought they didn't let hullies near guns. You could puncture a wall and suck everyone out into space or something."

"Watch it, moonie," Mitch said, and pushed a new target downrange. Denton approached a stand and picked up a pistol, and a holographic display prompted him to read the rules of the range. Denton put on protective eyewear and a set of earplugs. Even though he was already certified, he needed to best Mitch. A bored-looking Tvashtar marine stood nearby and observed. Denton flashed his certification through gestures on his soothreader, and the marine nodded his approval and allowed Denton to proceed.

"I'm not here to make friends, especially not with you," Mitch said with a sneer, not buying into Denton's playful teasing.

"Sounds good to me," Denton said. "Great attitude, by the way. They teach you that in that fancy academy on Remus Orbital?" He activated the collider cylinder on his pistol, causing it to rotate violently. Mitch popped off three more rounds.

"Yes, *they* did," Mitch said, looking smug as usual as he called back his target.

Denton aimed down the sights of the pistol and put himself into a stance he'd learned from his father as a young boy. He fired three shots.

Mitch exhaled deeply from his nostrils when his target reached him. "Stupid target isn't calibrated right," he said, deactivating his collider pistol and placing it down on the shelf in front of him. Before Denton's target returned, Mitch was already storming away. Denton's target had three holes right in the center. He looked over to see Mitch's grouping and found the hully had fired one near the center, then two far off the mark on the outer edges of the paper.

"Looks about right to me," Denton said to himself. The marine observer nearby heard him and chuckled. Denton felt like he had wasted a small bit of time to mess with Mitch. He had been gun certified since he was able to hold one, so shooting a target was one of the most natural things he could be doing right now.

He promised himself he wouldn't waste any more time during this phase of the assessment on Mitch's ego. It was time he went inside and learned what he could from the other stations.

The scouts inside the pavilion seemed very busy. Denton could see a group designing a new Pilgrim-class explorer vessel to replace the wrecked *Henson*. His family would most likely end up building the new ship for the scouts, and if Denton failed the assessment, he'd be included on that job.

Denton approached the chemistry station and saw complicated equations hovering in a holographic display on the wall. His gut sank, and he sighed.

"Don't worry about all that," an older woman said to him. Denton turned to see the lead chemist, Marie Viray. She looked up from her microscope and gave him a warm smile. "I think I'm the only one here who fully understands my own chicken scratch."

"How does everyone learn all this?" Denton asked, looking at the complex data.

"They don't," Marie said. "As far as what you need to memorize to pass, the protocol is key." She walked over to Denton and shook his hand. "I've heard of you, Denton Castus. We're grateful for what you did on the *Henson*." She winked. "If you've made it past the written portion of the assessment, all you have to do is pass the physical portion. From the look of you"—she scanned him top to bottom—"I'm not really worried."

"Thanks. I just look around and see so much information. It's intimidating, you know?"

"You mean, *it's fascinating.*" Her eyes flashed. "The Sol System didn't surprise me the way the Deltas Octantis system does. Kamaria is like having a new mystery novel to read every time you turn your head."

"It's exciting. Hells knows I have seen enough of the same old, same old."

"Well, Kamaria is anything but routine. Keep exploring, Denton. I wish you luck on the assessment," Marie said, then gave a smile and returned to her microscope.

Denton was happy to find so many friendly people in the pavilion. He spent the rest of the afternoon exploring all the stations and observing the activity, hoping to be involved one day.

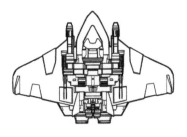

TWENTY-ONE

GEORGE TANAKA INTERRUPTED THE candidates as the sun began to set in the yard. "It is time for your first physical assessment. Tonight, you'll be sleeping outside." He gestured to the scattered camping equipment. "We would like to see you construct a shelter for the night, complete with an encasement barrier and campfire. Everything you need is here. Begin as you please." George smiled and walked away, leaving the candidates to their own devices.

Denton Castus, Carl Gregory, Jess Combs, and Mitch Harlan approached their designated camping areas and dug into the equipment bags.

"It's like we're living on ancient Earth," Carl said to Denton. "I have to admit, though, I skipped this part of the explore phase." He frowned.

"Just watch me and do as I do," Denton said.

"I might do as she does instead," Carl said, pointing to Jess, the Tvashtar marine who'd kept to herself throughout the day. She went to work without hesitation, building her tent with practiced efficiency.

"Yeah, that's probably a better idea." Denton smiled.

Mitch Harlan was muttering swears and bending poles instead of finding the correct path to success. He tossed pieces to the floor, then picked up another pole and cracked it while trying to fit it into the wrong place.

Denton watched the spectacle for a moment, then shook his head and looked down at his equipment on the grass. He looked up at Carl and said, "Alright, let's get to it."

Denton held a small pole in one hand and a large pole in the other, watching Carl to make sure he'd selected the same pieces from his kit. He showed Carl how they went together, then placed them in their correct position. Piece by piece, they went through the steps to construct their tents, and within an hour, they'd both finished setting up their campsites. Carl saluted Denton quietly and crawled into his tent.

Denton remained awake to admire the stars. He wondered which one was Sol. His mental wandering was interrupted by the frustrated grunts of Mitch Harlan, who was still desperately trying to erect his tent. He hadn't even lit his fire yet. Jess Combs was already inside her shelter for the night, leaving Denton as Mitch's sole observer. After watching Mitch struggle for a few moments, Denton's conscience got the best of him.

"Hey, Mitch. Need help?" Denton sighed.

"Damn thing is busted! They rigged my tent wrong," Mitch said, blaming everyone but himself, as usual. Denton stood up and turned off his encasement fence.

"Let me take a look," Denton offered, not wanting to aggravate Mitch any further, but he couldn't sleep if he thought Mitch was going to freeze outside. "Can I try something?"

"Be my guest. You won't get it to work, though," Mitch snarled, throwing his poles down on the ground. Denton noticed that Mitch had bent some of his poles in his ignorant fumbling. He tried to bend the poles back into position with moderate success. One pole snapped in half during his repair attempt.

"Great, good help you are," Mitch said. Denton took one of the cloth equipment bags and wrapped it around the broken pole, binding it together imperfectly. He continued to work on the tent, slowly building up the rickety equipment.

It was only after Denton finished that he noticed that Mitch's snarky comments had ceased. The tent was erected but had a heavy lean to it thanks to the damaged poles. He looked around, but Mitch was nowhere to be found. The encasement fence around Denton's tent was activated, and his fire doused.

Mitch had hijacked Denton's tent.

"The Hells!" Denton coughed and stomped over to his stolen campsite. He attempted to turn off the encasement fence by tapping the top of the pole, but his hand was flung away with such force that it spun him around and nearly dropped him to the ground. Denton wasn't getting back in there tonight. Instead of making a scene, he decided to finish the campsite Mitch had abandoned.

The wind made the ramshackle tent sway. The free nylon flapped loudly as Denton fought to fall asleep. It became apparent that Mitch had torn holes in the cloth, allowing the cold air to flow into the tent. Denton halfway considered lying outside, but eventually his body gave in, and he drifted off to sleep.

———◆———

"Good morning, candidates!" Marie Viray said as she walked into the campground with George. "We have a lot to do today, so I hope you slept …" She stopped herself when she saw Denton's tent had become more of a blanket than a shelter, having completely collapsed during the night. George frowned when he saw the abysmal work.

Jess Combs was already awake and sitting by a crackling fire. Mitch unzipped his tent and stepped out, looking well rested. "Good morning." He nodded to them both with a grin. George nodded back to him.

Carl unzipped his tent to discover Mitch in Denton's place. He looked over to see the tent Denton had inhabited for the night in complete ruins.

"Mitch!" Carl said with fire in his voice, but Mitch shot him a glare that silenced him outright. Carl holstered his comments, remembering past school days being bullied by Mitch and his little gang of brats.

Denton rose from the ground like a vampire with a few misplaced stakes in his joints. He stretched his back, aching from an awful night of sleep.

"Morning, everyone," Denton said, then lanced Mitch with a glare. Mitch looked away and whistled to himself.

"Really pioneering how we build shelters, aye, Denton?" George asked. Denton looked down and squeezed his fist tightly. George entered some data on his soothreader, causing Denton to flinch with regret.

"Right. Well, today we will assess your physical capabilities," George said. "Lifting the most weights and running the longest distance isn't the key to a good assessment score. Instead, being able to achieve certain parameters based on your own personal evaluation is the ticket. Afterward, we will split you into teams of two to run the obstacle course. Break down your equipment and follow us to the gym," George said, and gestured for them to follow. He glanced at Denton's mess again. "I suppose you're already halfway done breaking down your site."

Denton knew this hurt his chances of becoming a scout. He was raised to aid people in need, but this time, he may have harmed his chances for becoming a scout by misplacing his help. To think a guy like Mitch was going to be exploring new frontiers for the whole of humanity made Denton sick. All because Denton was too kind. He sighed and began to gather up his broken tent, along with his broken dreams.

Mitch turned to Denton with wide eyes and his brow furrowed. He didn't know how to break down the tent effectively, and it was going to hurt him now. Denton guffawed and shook his head, kneeling to roll up the tattered remains of the nylon.

Soon after, the candidates walked across the yard toward the gym area. Physical trainers met them and assessed their fitness levels. They each had a vial of blood drawn and analyzed. Then they were each handed a bag containing a workout uniform.

They got changed in the locker room and met back outside. Jess was already on a treadmill running when the three others returned. She had wireless pads strapped to various parts of her body that would give the trainers information they needed about her heart rate, lung capacity, and blood pressure

Carl rubbed his arm with his hand and asked, "Is there a time limit?"

A trainer looked away from Jess's data readouts and said, "If we get the data we need before you reach the target distance, we'll stop you."

Mitch smiled and strutted over to the treadmill next to Jess. Carl and Denton took the adjacent two treadmills and strapped on their wireless pads.

Denton got into the groove as he began his run. Although he had never formally trained, he was in good enough shape that the exercise didn't wear him out too much. Jess stepped off her treadmill first. She was about to remove her readers when a trainer stopped her.

"Please leave those on. You'll keep them on for the rest of the day."

Jess nodded, grabbed a towel, and dried herself off. Another trainer motioned her over to the weight-lifting station. They piled the weights on, and Jess pumped them upward with ease. Denton was beginning to think she was an Undriel, but it was just her Tvashtar military training. Jess Combs was built to fight impossible machines, and the results were incredible.

"Alright, Mr. Castus," the trainer said after he'd run a few kilometers, "you may move on to the weight-lifting station."

The next few hours were filled with an intense workout regimen. Jess would always finish her task first, usually followed by either Denton or Mitch, with Carl trailing behind. They lifted weights, performed leg exercises, completed rounds of sit-ups, pull-ups, and push-ups. After four hours, the scouts were given time to rest, and they made their way back to the locker room.

Carl approached Denton, his face red, and said between breaths, "I don't know if I'm going to make it."

"It wasn't a race. Just an evaluation," Denton said.

"Right, I know that. But my heart is beating a thousand times per second. I hope it doesn't disqualify me."

"Just get some rest now before the obstacle course, and I'm sure you'll be fine," Denton said. The candidates were handed another bag containing a new outfit to wear for the obstacle course.

They got changed and walked back out into the yard. Denton sat in the grass near the obstacle course, studying the layout. He was outfitted in loose-fitting pants, a long-sleeve black shirt, sturdy hiking boots with steel tips, a fake collider pistol slung into a holster on his hip, and a scout jacket with straps and compartments for tools and holsters for equipment. The coat displayed the *Telemachus* color scheme—orange, black, and white—as well as the *Telemachus* mission patch on the left portion of the chest. He had seen Eliana wearing a very similar jacket, although with an *Odysseus* mission patch instead. Denton felt important wearing the jacket, even though he knew he hadn't earned it yet.

The candidates would have the ability to use whatever they needed in the scout gear set. Denton was hoping to be teamed up with Carl; he felt like they worked together with the best.

Anyone but Mitch, he thought.

Carl approached Denton, fiddling with pieces of the uniform. He said, "It's a little tight, right?" as he adjusted the belly of his shirt.

"I assume we'll be fitted with better uniforms if we pass," Denton said. Mitch walked past them and began stretching.

"What's up, Mitch?" Carl asked.

"Oh nothing, just sizing up my opponents. I already ran this course," Mitch said. Denton shook his head and thought to himself how impossible it would be for one man to run a course built around teamwork.

Another lie from the Master Liar.

It was time to separate into teams and begin the obstacle course. Scouts from the pavilion stopped their work and came across the yard to watch. Denton spotted Eliana, and she winked at him. He winked back and smiled. Denton had to excel here. It was his only shot, and it largely depended on who he was paired up with.

"Alright, candidates!" George said, addressing them loudly enough so that the entire crowd could hear. "We have split you into teams of two by random. Team One will be Mitch Harlan …" Mitch stepped forward with a broad, toothy grin on his face. "And Carl Gregory!" Carl stepped forward, dejected.

"Team Two will be Denton Castus and Jess Combs!" The crowd of scouts clapped for the candidates. People exchanged bets and pointed at their favorites. This was not only an assessment, but also entertainment.

Denton was unsure if Jess was pleased to have him on her team. He grew up being part of a shop that was in direct competition with the moon Io, where the Tvashtar Colony operated a more successful machine business. Until now, Tvashtar had always been "the bad guys" in his mind. Jess's robotic nature didn't help dismantle this preconception either. Denton thought of her as an alien, and suddenly Eliana's voice echoed in his mind: *"Keep an open mind!"*

"Alright, teams. Head to the start area, and we'll begin the course!" George shouted, and the crowd cheered. Denton and Jess walked together with Mitch and Carl following. The congregation organized themselves into a seating area that overviewed the whole course.

"Hey, Jess, how do you feel about this?" Denton asked her, trying to pry anything out of her stony expression.

"Just do as I say," Jess replied curtly, her voice raspy and low.

"Roger that," Denton said, and worried about how to perform a team-based obstacle course with someone who barely spoke.

Mitch said to Carl, "Don't screw this up."

"Let's just get it over with." Carl sighed.

Each candidate leaned in, preparing for the sprint to the high wall. George took his position on a small platform that hovered above the course, giving him the ability to judge the contest from a better vantage point. Denton felt like an ancient gladiator facing off with an opponent made of obstacles and traps. He tried to ignore the crowd and focus on what lay ahead.

"Everyone ready?" George asked. A megaphone projected his voice for all to hear. "On your mark ..."

Denton placed his forefinger on the ground before him in a track runner's stance. He turned and saw Jess was prepped for launch like a tiger waiting to pounce on a kill. Mitch was bobbing back and forth in anticipation, and Carl only leaned his upper body forward, looking out of place among the other candidates.

"Get set ..."

Beads of sweat formed on Denton's brow, and the world seemed to slow down. He exhaled, and it felt like he was making the only sound in the universe. All other priorities went out the window for this brief moment in time. The only thing that mattered was springing forward to get up that high wall.

"Go!"

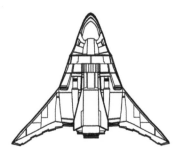

TWENTY-TWO

DENTON, MITCH, AND JESS sprang forward as Carl sloppily threw himself into a sprint. Their legs and arms pumped like engine pistons. A few breaths later, they'd covered the distance to the high wall. Jess slid toward the edge of the wall and held her hands together in a cup.

"Jump!" she shouted.

Denton obeyed, lunging one foot forward for Jess to catch. She lifted Denton as if he weighed nothing, propelling him onto the wall, just high enough for him to grab the ledge with both hands. Before Denton could scramble any higher, Jess began climbing up his body with aggressive speed. He almost lost strength and fell, but held on long enough for Jess to climb over him. When Jess reached the top of the wall, she bent over and yanked Denton upward by the back of his jacket, like a puppy being carried by its mother.

Mitch got to the wall at the same time as Jess and Denton, but Carl slowed him down. Mitch cupped his hands like Jess had done before and shouted to Carl, "Come on, *fat ass*! Get up there!"

Carl gingerly placed his foot into Mitch's cupped hands, then Mitch weakly pushed Carl up with great effort.

"Maybe I should push you up?" Carl asked. But before Carl

could lift himself onto the ledge, Mitch copied Jess's technique and climbed up Carl's body sloppily. Once he reached the top, he ran forward, leaving Carl behind.

"Thanks," Carl shouted, then muttered to himself as he hoisted onto the ledge with great effort, *"jackass."*

The next obstacle was a long wooden board over a pit of mud. Jess made it to the board first and slid it across a gap.

"Hold this!" Jess ordered; Denton obeyed. He slammed both hands down on his end of the board, and Jess climbed onto it, skimming across like a tightrope walker on ice skates. Once across, she stopped, turned, and held her end of the board.

"Come on!"

Denton jumped onto the board. His balance wasn't as refined as Jess's, and his progress was slow.

"Don't fall!" Jess shouted. Denton thought it almost sounded like concern but couldn't be sure.

"Doing my best!" was the only response he could muster as he concentrated.

Carl eventually made it to the board, where Mitch was waiting. Mitch slammed the board down and shouted, "Hold this! You can do that, right?"

Carl nodded and placed both hands on the board. Mitch jumped on and moved across as fast as he could, pulling up on Denton halfway across.

"Hey, *moonie!*" Mitch shouted, and kicked out with his right foot, knocking Denton's board sideways. Denton fell and barely caught himself, narrowly avoiding tumbling into the pit of mud below. Jess struggled to make it flat again.

"No interfering with the other team!" George shouted over the megaphone. "Another move like that, and you will be disqualified!"

Mitch sneered and finished his strafe across the board, holding it for Carl.

Jess finally pushed the board flat again, allowing Denton to scramble back on. As he did, Carl approached.

"Sorry," he said, passing him on the boardwalk.

"Not your fault," Denton grunted as he regained his footing and made his way across, finishing not long after Carl.

There was another sprint, this time with hurdles of progressively taller heights. Jess and Denton raced to catch up to Carl and Mitch, who were progressing over the hurdles well enough. They eventually passed Carl, who struggled with some of the more significant obstacles, but Mitch still held the lead. At the end of the sprint, there was a large door with big red targets floating near it.

"Shoot the targets to open the door," George said as they approached the obstacle.

Mitch slid to a stop and pulled out his fake sidearm. He shot twice, and a harmless red laser struck a target dead center and missed the other completely. The hit target ceased being red and faded to gray, but Mitch's face turned beet red. He made his third shot and struck home. The target turned gray, and his door swung open. Mitch darted through, leaving Carl lagging behind once more.

Jess and Denton dashed toward their door. They each pulled their sidearms and unleashed a shot, not pausing as they sprinted forward. Both shots hit their targets and unlocked the door. The crowd cheered with excitement as the obstacle course was coming close to an end.

The next obstacle was the two-person sandbag pull. A big metal rod with heavy bags rested on the ground in front of them. Denton and Jess slipped the rod behind their neck on their shoulders and marched forward in unison.

Mitch was attempting to do it alone, dragging part of the rod behind him but not making much progress. Carl caught up, panting.

Mitch snarled at him, "Grab the damn thing! Do I have to do *everything* myself?" Carl didn't have time to protest; he bent down and grabbed the rod, sloppily placing it onto the back of his neck. He felt the rod hit his neck hard, and it knocked him halfway to his knees.

"Come on, get up! Do not ruin this for me!" Mitch shouted. Carl summoned his remaining strength and carried the weight.

Jess and Denton placed their rod onto the harness at the end of the track and continued on to the last portion of the course, the tethered rope swing over a deep mud pit. As they sprinted forward, Denton shouted to Jess, "You first!"

Jess nodded, and launched herself onto the rope, allowing it to slide across the tether and swing her to the other side.

"Think fast," George said into the megaphone.

Drones emerged from the pit, buzzing like the alien wasps Denton had encountered on the *Henson*. Each had a red target on its side, like the locks for the door earlier in the course. Denton watched as one of the drones turned its gaze toward Jess and fired a rubber ball at a high velocity. It clipped Jess's leg, spinning her on the rope and causing her to slip. She caught herself as she continued to slide.

Denton grabbed his fake pistol and shot the drone in the side. It faded to gray like the targets before, then lazily floated back to its base station. Two more drones emerged, and Denton worked to keep them from harassing Jess.

Mitch and Carl had caught up. Carl almost tumbled into the pit as Mitch beat him to the tether. The drones buzzed in the air and began aiming at Mitch.

"You know," Carl said to Denton as he reluctantly aimed his fake pistol at the drone, "I should just let these things take him out."

"I won't tell him if you don't," Denton said, shooting another drone away from Jess. They shared a laugh as they kept the targets off their teammates. Jess made it across the gap and shoved the tether back to Denton. She grabbed her false gun to take her turn protecting him during his slide.

Denton caught the tether in his outstretched hand, turned to Carl, and said, "See you on the other side," then leaped forward as Carl saluted.

Mitch cleared the gap and shoved the tether back across. He didn't wait to shoot drones. Instead, he bolted toward the finish line. Denton spun on his rope to face Carl. The tether stopped a few meters away from the ledge Carl was standing on.

"Ah damn," Denton whispered. There was no way Carl could make the jump.

To Denton's surprise, Carl took a few steps back and braced himself to jump. He sprang forward with one hand outstretched to catch the rope. He managed to catch the very bottom of the line, holding on tightly as he began to slide along the tether like a flailing fish at the end of a hook.

Denton finished his slide and joined Jess in a race to the finish line.

Carl was getting close to the other end of the gap, but he was too low to make it over the top. With another wild swing, he flew from the rope and smashed hard into the ledge with his leg outstretched. He screamed out for an instant as he heard his leg snap with the force of the impact.

Carl lost all control and fell into the mud pit upside down, his leg bent improperly to the side. He lay on his back, gasping for air.

The on-site medical staff rushed to Carl's side. Most people in the audience were not aware of his broken leg, and continued cheering after a moment of collective, "Ohhh, that looks like it hurt!"

Denton, Jess, and Mitch crossed the finish line.

"Team two wins the race!" George Tanaka announced from the megaphone platform.

Carl was being removed from the mud pit via a stretcher.

"Useless," Mitch spat into the grass near the finish line. Denton ignored him and rushed over to Carl's side.

"What happened?" Denton asked. Carl was covered in mud, and his leg was braced.

"I screwed up. It looks like I'm the one going back to the colony for now. Sorry, man," Carl said through whiplashes of pain. The medical staff hovered him away. Denton was quickly surrounded by people who had bet on his win. Jess was lifted on the shoulders of another group nearby and carried away while Mitch sneered. Denton glared at him.

Mitch shrugged and walked away.

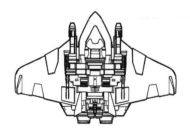

TWENTY-THREE

AFTER THE EXCITEMENT OF the day had passed, the remaining candidates returned to their campsites. The tents were already erected and the fires lit to reward the candidates after a hard day of physical stress, with one less campsite present. Carl Gregory had been sent back to the colony to heal his broken leg.

The orange glow of the campfire joined with the deep blue of the night in a soothing entanglement of light. The smell of burning firewood filled the air, and the sound of the campfires crackling brought peace to those with restless minds.

Denton rested by his fire, drawing in his sketchpad and looking inward. He couldn't help but wonder if he would have been sent home if Carl hadn't gotten injured. Mitch's little bait-and-switch trick with the tents the night before certainly didn't make Denton look good, and his test scores were lower than the others.

"Knock, knock." Eliana Veston approached Denton's encasement fence with a bottle of wine in one hand and two thin glasses in the other.

"What's the password?" Denton asked.

"I brought alcohol," Eliana said with a smile.

"That'll do." Denton deactivated his fence, and Eliana gave him a kiss on the lips.

"You shared your Ganymede ale with me, so I figured I would share some Arcas wine with you." She tilted her head toward the bottle, allowing her hair to dangle loosely from her forehead.

"Fair enough," he said with a smile. "You're not going to get in trouble for being here, are you?"

"I pulled rank," she said, pouring the sweet red wine into the glasses. She planted herself next to Denton.

Eliana handed a glass to him and held up her own. "To making it past the obstacle course and the physical assessment. Cheers." She clinked her glass against his. Eliana took a gentle sip of her wine, but Denton slurped down the whole drink in two chugs. He raised his eyebrows and let out a weak cough.

"Not what I was expecting," he said, holding his glass forward for more.

"You're not much of a wine drinker, are you?" She smirked and poured him more. "Arcas Hub on Callisto made the best wine in the Sol System. They shipped us some on the *Telemachus*, and we still have a few barrels left. I know some of the elderly Arcas Hub veterans are determined to find a way to make more of it here on Kamaria. There's even a small tester winery in the colony. So far, lots of tests, not a lot of results." She took another small sip.

"Every test makes this place a little more like home," Denton said, taking a gentle sip like he had seen her do. He let out an overexaggerated sigh and smacked his lips.

"True," Eliana said, and gulped down the rest of her wine. Denton raised his eyebrows and guffawed. "Just catching up to you," she said with a grin and a flick of her hair as she poured herself another glass.

"You know, something about this ..." Denton said, winking at Eliana. "Almost seems like yer setting me up to get a little tipsy."

"Oh, more than tipsy." Eliana bit her lower lip and tilted Denton's glass to his lips. "Drink up, Castus."

Denton finished the glass, and as Eliana turned to grab the bottle to pour him more, he leaned over and kissed her neck.

"That's the spirit," Eliana said with a wide grin. She used her forefinger to pull Denton's chin up to her face. Denton obliged and kissed her thoroughly.

The petting became more intense. Eliana put one hand on the back of Denton's head and moved her fingers through his hair. She searched his chest with her other hand.

For a moment, she pulled her lips away and pressed her forehead against his. They locked eyes, and without saying anything else, Denton reached over to his tent and unzipped it. They hid away as the campfire continued to crackle under the light of a hundred billion distant stars.

———— ◆ ————

The next morning, Delta Octantis cast its light across the yard, sending long shadows out across the grass. Denton was awake with his scout uniform on. He pushed the remainder of the wood from the smoldering fire around with an iron poker. Eliana sat near him with a blanket over her shoulders and a glow on her face.

"Here they come," she said, pointing across the yard at a group of silhouettes.

"I guess you're not my teacher, then," Denton said, watching the figures approach.

"Oh please! After last night, we'd get nothing done, and you'd learn nothing from the experience." Eliana pushed him playfully.

"I wouldn't say I'd learn *nothing*, exactly." Denton winked. Eliana blushed.

"Go on, Denny." Eliana stood and shed her blanket, revealing her outfit from the previous day. She gave him a long kiss on the lips.

They released each other, then Denton dumped a pitcher of water onto the dying fire. It hissed as he grabbed his bag and walked across the yard.

Jess Combs was marching not far from him. He nodded to her, and she nodded back with a smile. He felt like he understood Jess now that they had bonded during the assessment.

Mitch trudged up, carrying three bags with him across the field, two more than either Denton or Jess had. He struggled with the awkwardness of the bags. Usually, Denton would have offered to help, but with Mitch, that had backfired once already.

The three remaining candidates approached the four shadowed figures. Denton recognized them all. George Tanaka, Fergus Reid, Sergeant Clint Foster, and Major Pavel Volkov.

George stepped forward. "Good morning, candidates. Today will be your final assessment. These three veteran scouts will be your guides and judges." George waved a hand to indicate his companions. "You will begin with a hike away from the colony to separate locations. There, you will have to demonstrate what you have learned thus far and apply your knowledge fully. You will spend the night outdoors in the Kamarian wilderness. Each guide has a comm link to the colony central should there be an emergency, but otherwise, you will be isolated. Stay safe and good luck. See you tomorrow afternoon." George bowed and walked back toward the pavilion.

"Combs, you're with me," Clint Foster said in his synthesized voice. Jess nodded and approached him. Clint handed her a camping bag with a freshly rolled-up tent strapped to the top. The two Tvashtar marines marched away together without exchanging another word.

That left Fergus and Pavel. Denton hoped Fergus would be his guide so he'd have the chance to explain what had happened with the tent situation the first night.

"Harlan. Yer with me, boyo," Fergus said, dashing Denton's hopes. "Drop those candy bags you got there. You won't be need'n 'em."

Mitch looked around. "Is there a locker, or—"

"Drop 'em!" Fergus shouted with more authority. Mitch hesitated, then sighed and dropped his extra baggage, which hit the ground with a resounding clang. Fergus handed him a camping bag, and they walked off. Denton could hear Mitch explaining why he needed all his bags as Fergus offered silence in return.

"Just us two, comrade," Pavel said, holding out another camping bag.

"Want me to drop my stuff?" Denton said, having only the one small bag with his sketchpad and supplies.

"Not necessary. We just like mess'n with that hully," Pavel said.

Denton grinned and adjusted his bag to rest on his left side, tucked under the camping bag he'd strapped to his back. He pointed at Pavel's leg harness. "You going to be alright with that?"

"Oh, this?" Pavel said, eyeing his leg. "I'll be fine. Not problem."

They joined the other two pairs near the colony gateway. A guard standing on top of the parapet waved to the scouts and opened the gate, revealing the Kamarian wilderness beyond. The purple grass waved in the light breeze, inviting the candidates to explore.

The three veterans nodded to each other and began marching outward. Jess and Clint marched to the west, Mitch and Fergus to the north, and Denton and Pavel to the east.

The thin dirt path they followed was easily traversable; it had been created by colonist hunters over four years of hiking to hunting grounds while Denton had been asleep on ice on the *Telemachus*. A sleep the others were still dreaming through.

Denton enjoyed the sunlight and the feeling of the wild breeze rushing over the tall purple grass that surrounded him. For four kilometers, they said nothing and simply enjoyed the fresh morning air and scenery.

The path led into a forest in the distance. The leaves of the forest trees were a deep crimson.

"You know," Pavel said, breaking the silence, "I never got chance to thank you."

"Oh, it was nothing. I'm sure you would have done the same for me," Denton said, embarrassed by the unexpected kindness.

"Perhaps. But your bravery that night on the *Henson* saved my life. I owe you," Pavel said, looking over his shoulder briefly as they hiked the trail.

Denton nodded. "You're welcome."

They entered the alien forest. It was the first time Denton had been surrounded by so much life, a grand departure from the cold, dead rocks of Ganymede.

The forest was an explosion of color. The tree trunks were violet with pulsing lights flowing gently into the crimson leaves above. The grass changed from purple to deep blue with softly glowing stones scattered throughout. The dirt path was white, highlighting a clear passage through the forest. Twinkling alien gnats buzzed about, creating a shifting glimmer layer on the ground.

"This place is called the Timber Chase," Pavel said.

They walked for another kilometer, and the path sloped downward to meet a mellow river. Beautiful colors shimmered in the water as if a kaleidoscope were constantly shifting just beneath the surface.

"River dancers," Pavel said. "Is school of pencil-thin fish. They change color by shifting which fins they swim with."

"Looks like a rainbow," Denton said, "or at least pictures of rainbows—I've never seen one in person."

They found a welcoming riverbank next to a cliff wall. A circular pond caught part of the river in its placid swirl, emptying on the other side of the bank.

A honking sound was coming from ahead through a swath of bushes. Pavel halted and put a finger to his lips. He pushed part of the bush to the side and pointed across the river to a herd of four-legged, deerlike creatures.

The creatures had feathers all over their bodies and small trunks at the end of their snouts. They flapped their long ears, batting away gnats as they grazed and drank from the river. The creatures sounded like a flock of honking geese.

"Nurn. I see them here from time to time. We don't hunt them here, or else we'll never see them again," Pavel said, leaning against a rock. They watched the nurn continue about their business. He jerked his head toward the herd and said, "Go ahead. Scan them."

Denton smiled wide with excitement as he lifted his bioscope and aimed it at the nurn he suspected was the herd leader. The alpha nurn was adorned with flashy red, blue, and green feathers. It had a single long antler thrusting outward from the back of its skull. Denton activated the bioscope and scanned it. The scope buzzed back to him with a small analysis on his soothreader.

"Good work." Pavel smiled.

The alpha nurn cawed out with a rhythmic honk, and the herd perked up. The creatures slowly paraded away from the riverbank. When the last one left, Pavel got back to his feet.

"Alright, let us set up camp," he said, shuffling into the clearing. "Show me what you got, comrade."

"What, no help?" Denton asked.

"Can't. Handicapped, remember?" Pavel smiled back as he patted his harnessed leg.

Denton unpacked and rolled out the gear for the tent. Since he had functional equipment and plenty of experience this time, he had the tent up within fifteen minutes. Pavel was pleased with the result.

"Great job. Now, build fire. Plenty of wood here," Pavel said as he plopped himself down near the tent. He reached into his backpack and pulled out a paperback novel. Denton grabbed a few dry twigs and glanced at the book in Pavel's hands. The text looked unfamiliar, but if he had to guess, it was possibly pre-Sol Common Russian lettering.

"Wow, old fashioned. How'd you get your hands on that?" Denton asked.

"A gift from my father and his father before him. I keep it always."

"It looks brand new."

"*Da*. Radiation conditioner back in my home. Keeps things from decaying. I brought with me for journey," Pavel said, not glancing up from his book. "I read this book thousand times." He smiled and turned a page.

"It's nice to see someone who appreciates the classics," Denton said.

"*Da*. When I read it, I think of ancestors who also read it. Is like we are all here together, flipping through pages," Pavel said. Denton enjoyed the romantic view of reading the old book and thought of the Castus Machine Shop on Ganymede. In a way, the book and the shop both preserved memories.

"What's it about?"

"Man surviving ancient Russian winter. It's called, *Kogda vse poteryano, Solntse Voskhodit*—or in Sol Common, *When All Is Lost, the Sun Shall Rise*—by Victor Sokolov," Pavel said, flipping another page. "It makes me wonder what Earth was like. Mars was cold, but never like here in book."

"I've never been to Mars. Then again, never been anywhere really."

"*Da*, moonie," Pavel said, smiling and looking up at Denton.

"Hey, watch it, *Marshman*," Denton said with a laugh.

"So, moonies do have word for Martians." Pavel chuckled, having never heard the derogatory word for his people. "*Da*, pretty good, pretty good. How's fire coming along, moonie? Marshman would be warm by now."

"Got everything I need, one minute." Denton pulled out his magnesium fire-starting tool and a knife. With a few scrapes, the fire was healthy and crackling.

"Good job. Place the fence poles, don't activate yet. We have fishing to do," Pavel said. Denton pulled out the blue bag and began placing the poles but not touching the blue orbed tips.

Pavel got back to his feet and pulled a box from his backpack. As Denton finished his assignment, Pavel opened the box and brought out two cylindrical rods. He shook them quickly up and down, allowing them to spring open into a fishing pole. From there, he grabbed a reel and clicked it into place on the handle.

"Go on, take reel and get fishing," Pavel said, threading his line through the pole and tying a hook to the end. Denton followed his example.

"Have you fished before?" Pavel asked as he sat on a boulder near the river outlet.

"No, I'm just sort of winging it right now," Denton admitted, finishing the preparations on his pole and joining the old major near the water. Denton took a deep breath, appreciating the smell of the riverbed: fresh mud and water mixing into a pleasant scent.

"Well, trick is patience. Once you feel pulling on end of rod ..." Pavel was explaining, but noticed something was already beginning to tug on Denton's pole.

"Woah, I feel it!" Denton shouted. "Now what?"

"Don't panic. Wait for bigger tug, then pull back and upward, as hard as you can." They waited for a breath longer. Denton felt the rod yank toward the water and ripped backward on the pole. His line began rapidly extending.

"*Da!* Grab reel!" Pavel shouted. Denton slammed his hand onto the spinning reel. The line halted its wild extension, and he felt the pull of the whole rod threatening to take him into the river. Pavel cheered, "*Da!* Reel in!"

Denton grunted as he pulled backward on the pole; the fish was putting up a tough fight. The rod jerked side to side, but Denton held fast and kept reeling it in. Soon, a giant fish was batting around, knocking against the surface of the water.

"Good! Good!" Pavel said, pumping his fists with excitement.

The alien fish launched itself out of the water. It was much larger than Denton had expected, with a meter-long body covered in colorful fins. On its flank were small holes filled with needlelike objects.

"Duck!" Pavel shouted.

"What?" Denton didn't react fast enough and was struck in the face, neck, and chest with tiny barbs that the fish had flicked outward. He shouted in pain and bobbled the fishing rod, but caught himself before dropping the rod entirely. Denton began reeling in the line harder.

"You little *jerk!*"

The fish splashed wildly but finally tired itself out. Denton pulled it ashore and laid it on the riverbank. He watched as the holes on the side of the fish filled with more needles. His eyes widened, and he covered his face with his arm instinctively.

Pavel thrust a knife into the fish's head. It flailed weakly a moment longer, then became still. Denton removed the barbs from his face, leaving small, bloody holes.

"Battleship pike. Well done!" Pavel laughed with excitement. "That's good meal."

"Good, I'm glad," Denton said, not masking his contempt for the fish, and removing another barb from his skin.

"Let's continue, we'll cook him soon. I'll teach you," Pavel said, returning to his own fishing rod. Denton put the pike in a bucket near his feet and cast out another line. He remembered reading about people fishing on old Earth, but he could have sworn the process was supposed to be relaxing. He watched his line bob in the water, curious what else they would catch tonight.

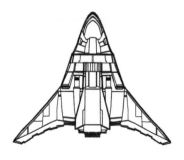

TWENTY-FOUR

DELTA OCTANTIS DIPPED BELOW the horizon, and Kamaria's dueling moons, Tasker and Promiser, shined with a crescent-shaped light high in the sky. Beneath the stars and the faint wisps of pre-summer clouds, Denton Castus and Pavel Volkov sat next to a fire, cooking their catch of the day and sharing stories. The encasement fence softly hummed around their campsite as the night air cooled the explorers from the heat of the day.

"Well, comrade. I think you'd be great addition to team," Pavel said, "and I thought you only moon baby first time I saw you." He snickered.

Denton smiled and poked the fire. "You really think I'd make a good scout?"

"Well, if it was up to me, you are in. Depends on how others do," Pavel said. "George favors Remus Orbital candidates. Mitch has a shot. Test scores were good. Others favor military obedience. Candidate Jess Combs is Tvashtar marine."

Military obedience was a way of life in Tvashtar Colony. The colony was on Io, Jupiter's most volcanically active moon. Tvashtar colonists joined the military when they came of age, serving a mandatory four years. Most of them fell into it as a career, having not many other options on Io besides working in the refineries and machine shops, something Denton could relate to.

"And I'm just a moon baby." Denton sighed.

Ganymede had been Denton's weakness all along. His education wasn't anywhere near as robust as that of a Remus Orbital student, and working in a machine shop for his father didn't exactly make him militantly obedient, as a variety of public mischief reports would corroborate.

"Really, is anyone's dinner. You show promise in your own weird moonie way," Pavel said, waving his fork in circles as he eyed Denton.

"I hope you're right. It's almost a little unfair that we can get a taste of Kamaria outside of the colony and then be forced to go back to our old lives. It should be open to everyone," Denton said, poking the fire with a stick and thinking of the poor souls still sleeping on the *Telemachus* in orbit. It made Denton appreciate the sights he was privileged to see.

"You sound like John Veston." Pavel smiled, biting a chunk of the battleship pike from his fork. "He would have liked you." He finished chewing, then looked up at Denton. "His daughter sure does, aye, comrade?" Pavel burst into laughter, forcing Denton to blush.

After his overlong outburst, Pavel calmed himself down.

"I agree," he said. "But is dangerous out here. If everyone could just run around, there would be problems for humanity. We need to build numbers back home first and solidify position with auk'nai before we make freedoms."

"Where are the auk'nai?" Denton asked.

"Auk'nai? About three hours' flight from colony. Only scouts allowed to talk to auk'nai. Is why we assess so much before we let in. Don't want to piss them off."

"Are they dangerous?" Denton asked with his eyebrows raised.

"*Da*, as dangerous as you and me if they want to be. They also have tricks we don't. Can read minds." Pavel tapped a finger against his skull. "Never lie to auk'nai. Call you out every time. Lying isn't a thing they do." He took another bite of his dinner.

"They sound amazing," Denton said.

"I hope you meet them one day." Pavel smiled. "Alright, comrade, turning in. Douse fire when you're done for night. Check fence too. *Spokoynoy nochi*," Pavel said, slipping into an ancient Russian language.

He zipped himself into the tent, leaving Denton alone in the night.

After some time, Denton heard a chirping noise. He examined the area, hoping to find some sort of animal he could scan with his bioscope. He looked straight up into the overhanging trees and felt his skin crawl.

Two glowing eyes shined back at him through the darkness of the branches. Denton lifted his bioscope out of his hip holster and scanned. As the scope aimed toward the eyes, they flickered colors back, each eye its own rapidly changing hue. The scan completed, and the readout appeared on his soothreader. Denton's heart sank.

The chirping continued, and the rapidly flashing eyes returned to a red state. On Denton's wrist was an analysis for a quadrupedal predator called a panthasaur. It silently lowered itself into the light of the campfire. Eyes protruded out the sides of a long snout on eyestalks, with long, jagged teeth jutting wildly from its mouth. Its orange and red skin was smooth like a salamander's, but its body was bulky like a jaguar's.

"*Psst!* Don't move," Pavel whispered from inside the tent, unzipping only enough to see.

"It can't get past the fence, right?" Denton asked, but he was answered when the panthasaur dropped into the camp zone with a thud. It was the size of an old Earth mountain lion.

"Only if it comes from above the fence. Is not dome," Pavel said, then stuck one finger from the hole in the zipper he had made, pointing. "It wants our fish, but will rip your face off if it thinks it needs to."

The panthasaur flicked out frills from the side of its head, warning Denton to back away from the remains of the battleship pike.

"All yours, buddy," Denton said, putting both hands up and stepping backward slowly.

"Shut fence off. Once it has what it wants, it will go to den. We don't want it running into fence on the way out and getting really pissed off," Pavel whispered.

Denton backed up and reached toward the blue orb on top of the encasement fence post. He misjudged his reach and poked the fence with his bare hand. The force of the shock launched his hand forward toward the panthasaur. The beast's eyes flashed colors, and the frills flicked in and out wildly. The chirping ceased and was replaced with a howl that rolled in pitch and tone. The panthasaur unhinged its jaw and displayed its long, vicious teeth to Denton.

"There, there now. Sorry about that." Denton tried to calm the predator, wincing as he attempted to ignore his stinging hand. He reached back again, and this time accurately deactivated the encasement fence. The fence blinked off, but the panthasaur didn't seem to notice, moving its head from side to side in an intimidating display.

Eventually, it learned it had the upper hand and moved forward a few paces, snatching up the remains of the battleship pike as well as the other leftover fish they were saving for breakfast. Its neck bulged with the weight of its meal, and it growled its high-pitched, rolling shriek once more as if to say, *Don't even think about following me.* It then slid off into the darkness like a tooth-and-taloned shadow.

Pavel unzipped the tent and made sure the panthasaur had exited the area. Denton slapped the top of the fence again, reactivating it as the creature left. He put his hands on his knees and exhaled sharply. Pavel patted Denton on the shoulder.

"Honestly, thought it was going to rip your face off." Pavel made a gesture with his hands like a monster attacking its prey with a protruding jaw. "But instead, it helped clean campsite. Not bad."

Pavel laughed and slapped him on the back.

Denton let out a laugh that was more like a relieved sigh, shaking his hand to get the feeling back in his fingertips. Pavel poured a bucket of water on the fire, letting the hiss fill the quiet night air.

"Alright, time to rest. He won't be coming back. Panthasaur live downriver. Probably heard your moon baby cries when pike barbed you earlier."

Denton shook off the adrenaline from the encounter, awed by the experience. He entered the tent and sealed it.

———◆———

"Denton, wake up, come see," Pavel whispered, leaning into the unzipped entrance of the tent and waving Denton forward.

It was dawn, and the fresh morning air made its way into the tent through the open zipper. The encasement fence was deactivated, and Pavel had moved to a nearby hill. Denton pulled on his jacket and slipped on his boots to join the scout.

On the other side of the hill, past the winding river, the forest cleared, and the morning mist hung over the grass. Denton saw animals grazing in the fog, some familiar, like the nurn from the day prior, but others he had never seen before. There was a group of three massive beasts, each hefty like an elephant but with long necks like a giraffe's and heads crowned with horns. They pulled fruit from the top of nearby trees and blew out trumpet sounds.

"Arcophants," Pavel said with a glint in his eye like a child seeing a firefly for the first time. He gestured to Denton to scan the animals. With each scan, Denton's knowledge of the world around him expanded, making him feel like part of the world rather than just an observer.

Next to the arcophants, hulk weevils scooped up mud and filtered it through their massive bodies. These insects were enormous like buffalo, grazing the field and searching with massive antennas. They grunted and bumped into each other, shaking off dried mud.

Pavel leaned over to Denton. "Those are my favorite." He giggled with innocent glee.

Scurrying about in packs of six were something the bioscope called "hueginn." Denton recognized the name of these creatures from a dish his mother prepared from time to time. Their meat tasted much like pork, but their appearance was far from a pig's. The hueginn had shells like a snail, but instead of a slug, a fat, hairy creature protruded from the opening in the front of the shell. They had elongated necks like a llama and scavenged the ground for food with two long arms, moving along the grass on four little legs. They added to the orchestra of the morning feast with their flute-like calls.

A young nurn pranced around a young hueginn, honking and fluting in their play. It was a peace that Denton had never seen in the cold, dead rocks of Ganymede. He could imagine himself waking up to views like this every day and never growing tired of it.

"Every time I come here, I make sure to wake up early to see this. They do it all spring and summer. Is beautiful, yeah?" Pavel asked.

"For sure. Thanks for showing me."

"I told you, I owed you," Pavel said. "Is not much …"

"It's plenty," Denton said with a smile.

"Well, as much as it pains me to say it, we must head back soon. You did well, comrade," Pavel said, giving Denton a hard clap on the back, almost knocking him forward. The old major made his way back down the hill to the campsite, but Denton stayed a moment longer, hoping this wasn't going to be the last time he would see something like this.

———— ◆ ————

As they hiked through the afternoon, Denton took one last look backward at the Timber Chase. With every step, Denton worried he would have to return to his repetitive life.

The other teams came into view as they reconvened back by the gate. Jess Combs and Sergeant Clint Foster were ahead of them, marching together silently. Mitch Harlan and Fergus Reid trudged through the tall grass farther back. Fergus was swinging his arms and shouting angrily, a muffled sound that could be heard even at this distance.

Denton and Pavel approached the gate, where Pavel and Clint walked over to the side to discuss what they'd learned and their evaluations. Mitch and Fergus arrived fifteen minutes later.

"Can we get on with it? I'm ready to be done with this tumor," Fergus said, wasting no time waving his arms to the gatekeeper. The gates began to open.

Denton glanced over at Mitch; he looked like Hells. He was dirty, with a large bruise on his arm. His clothes were covered in dry mud and he had scrapes on his face. His eyes were sunken, with paths through the dirt on his cheeks that outlined recently fallen tears.

"What the Hells happened to you?" Denton asked.

"We took the hard trail. I had to help Fergus—" Mitch began to say, but Fergus cut him off.

"Enough with the lies, *boyo!*" Fergus shouted. "All night, this little pink-eyed flutter cup sat and lied. You should have seen how Mr. Wonderful here attempted to build the tent! We had to sleep outside, which is something I don't mind. But something I *do* mind is hearing this wee baby cryin' about it all night!" Fergus said. "It made me question how he managed to get the tent up the first night of the assessment. Let's just say you can'nae *fake it until you make it* in the scouts! Bean face here is not getting a pass from me!"

Mitch began to say something in his defense but then lowered his head, defeated as tears welled up in his eyes. Denton felt a little sad for Mitch, but at the same time, it felt like justice for what had happened to Carl Gregory.

The gates finished opening, revealing George Tanaka, Marie Viray, Eliana Veston, General Martin Raughts, and Helen Davies, the colony leader.

Denton was surprised to see Ms. Davies there. She was short and stern, and kept her hands behind her back, only bringing one out to greet the candidates. General Raughts stood stoically behind her. He had been colony leader before the *Telemachus* arrived, but after the incident with Captain Roelin Raike, Helen Davies had moved into his position.

"Welcome back, candidates," Helen said. "You must all be tired from the hike. Please feel free to have lunch and wash up while we evaluate your progress. We'll have our decision in a few hours." She shook each of their hands as they passed her.

The candidates walked through a tunnel of their trainers, each congratulating them on their hard work. Eliana grabbed Denton and kissed him on the lips, almost knocking him backward from the force of it. He caught himself and hugged her.

"Well done," Eliana said, and looped her arm around his as they made their way back with the others. "You'll need to tell me all about your trip with Pavel."

Denton smiled fondly as he remembered the beautiful hike, the nurn drinking by the riverside, fishing with Pavel, the harrowing encounter with the panthasaur, and the sight of the animals grazing in the misty open meadow.

He had just been on his first real adventure, and he hoped it wouldn't be his last.

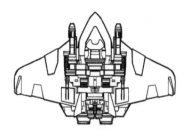

TWENTY-FIVE

DENTON APPROACHED THE CASTUS Machine Shop wearing his new scout jacket. With Mitch Harlan exposed as a liar, Denton and Jess Combs had been selected to join the program, effective immediately. As part of the deal, Denton was given his own one-bedroom apartment on the other side of the colony.

The garage door was open, and Denton's family was outside enjoying the cool night air. Tyler saw him coming and stood up from his seat and put an arm forward, palm out. "Hey, listen, buddy. We're closed for the night," he said with a grin.

"I guess I'll just take my business down the road to those Tvashtar guys, then," Denton said, spreading his arms out.

"This friggin' guy." Tyler gave him a friendly hug and clapped his hands against his arms. "Looks like you made it!"

Michael and Brynn joined them, each holding glasses of whiskey. "That's my boy!" Michael said.

"Come here," Brynn said, then brought Denton in for a big hug. "We're so proud of you."

Tyler poured another glass of whiskey and handed it to Denton. "We should be celebratin'! Cheers to Dent!" They clinked glasses and each took a deep gulp.

Denton asked, "Where's Jay?"

"Your brother has been a ghost lately," Michael said. "Been hard to keep track of him. We only know he comes back here to sleep and sometimes work."

"He's up to somethin'. We just ain't sure what," Tyler added. Denton knew of Jason's desire to do more than work in the shop, but Jason was prone to finding comfort in drinks. Gallivanting around the bar scene of the colony would not be out of character for Jason Castus.

"I'm sure he'll come around when he feels it's right." Denton sighed.

"Yeah," Michael said. "Come on, have a seat. We want to hear about the assessment!"

Denton pulled up a chair and told them about the whole process. They drank and chatted into the night.

In the morning, Denton packed his things to move to his new apartment. He didn't have much, having only lived in the new version of their shop for a few months, but it still felt strange to be leaving his family. In a way, this move across the colony seemed farther than the move from Ganymede to Kamaria.

Michael drove Denton down the road to the new apartment. It was in a grouping of buildings, each around ten stories tall. Michael parked the hover truck and got out, looking upward and shielding his eyes from the afternoon sun.

Eliana Veston was waiting for them as Denton and Michael stepped out of the truck. Denton slung a backpack over his shoulder and hefted a box in his arms. He turned to his father, who nodded and looked at the ground.

"Well, congrats, son," Michael said. "I have to get back to the shop. We're interviewing some replacements for you today. Don't know what the Hells I'm s'posed to ask them, but we'll figure it out."

"Thanks, Dad," Denton said.

Michael turned to Eliana and added, "He's your problem now."

"Oh darn." Eliana smiled.

Michael said his goodbyes, got in his truck, and drove back

toward the machine shop.

Denton felt like a part of him was still in that truck with his father. He'd left the shop many times on a day-to-day basis, but this felt different. He was a dog let off the leash for the first time, which was both exhilarating and terrifying.

"You ready?" Eliana asked. Denton nodded and grabbed his box of belongings.

They took the elevator up four floors and then walked down a hallway. The number "402" was listed on his door. Eliana nodded to Denton and said, "Your soothreader has already been given access."

Denton waved his hand at the door, and it slid open. He walked inside.

It was a modest one-bedroom unit. In the living room, a window faced the center of the colony, with a couch and a vid screen for colony news. One side of the living room had a small kitchen with a sink, some cabinets, a refrigerator, and an all-in-one food prepper.

An open door revealed a small bathroom and shower, and a closed door led to the bedroom. Denton walked into his room and saw a queen-size bed under a window next to a dresser and a closet for his things. He put the box on the bed and looked around.

"Where does my roommate sleep?" Denton asked.

"You have a roommate?" Eliana asked.

"Don't I?"

"Denny, as far as I'm aware, this is all yours."

"Really?" he asked.

"Yeah. Each of these one-bedroom units houses one or two people, depending on if they have a significant other or not."

Denton sat down on the end of the bed and slowly ran his hand through his hair. He smiled and let his eyes drop to the floor.

"What's up?" Eliana asked with a smile. "You got something going on in that head of yours. I can see it."

"It's just …" He looked around. "I never had this much room to myself before. Back in the Arrow, I shared a room with both my brothers. Here in the new shop, I was sharing a room with Tyler. It's just always been crowded in my family."

"Kamaria has its perks," Eliana said, and sat down on the bed next to him.

"This whole experience, I never thought I'd have an opportunity like this," Denton said. "Working in the shop, I never felt right. It was like …" He twisted his hands in the air. "It was like being at a party full of people and feeling alone. I had my family there, people who loved me, but I still just felt like I needed to leave and find my own people."

"Did you find them?" she asked.

"I think I might have," Denton said, and kissed her.

———— ✦ ————

Denton's new life was busy.

For the first few months of his scout career, he spent his mornings organizing collected data and samples, fixing scout tools, catching up on current Kamarian knowledge, and taking time to get to know the rest of the scouts.

After they had earned their stripes in the pavilion, Denton and Jess were given roles on the Beta Scout Team, where they worked directly under Major Pavel Volkov. Beta Team's primary goal was to assist in the advancement of the colony, while Alpha Team worked to further understand Kamaria.

While a replacement for the *Henson* was being constructed, the Beta Scout Team requisitioned Fergus Reid's personal ship, the *Viridios*. It originally had been used to transport cargo between the Jupiter colonies. The ship wasn't sleek like the *Henson* had been, but it worked perfectly as a pack mule, carrying lumber, metals, and other assets the Beta Team gathered during their missions to bring back to the colony.

After work, Denton would spend time with Eliana. He was beginning to imagine a future with her in a way he'd never done with previous girlfriends. It had taken the end of the Sol System to bring them together under the light of an alien star. Eliana had shown him his real purpose, a gift unlike any other.

As summer on Kamaria was ending, the eve of Silence Day approached. It was the day of mourning for those lost during the massacre helmed by Roelin Raike.

It was the anniversary of the day Eliana's father was murdered.

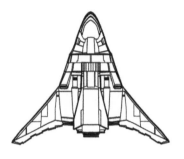

TWENTY-SIX

ELIANA VESTON WAS BEGINNING to think she had moved on. The lie didn't feel like a lie anymore. She had truly believed her father's murder was behind her. Denton Castus had come along, and at first, he'd been a fun distraction from the reality of the world, but now he was becoming something much more important to her. Helping Denton find himself on their strange new planet had also led to her own self-discoveries.

But today was Silence Day. A day of remembrance that Eliana wished she could forget permanently. If she could ignore it, it would be like it had never happened.

It would be like her father was still here.

Eliana started her day early; she had been through this four times now. The first time, she had gone to the graveyard to visit her father's tombstone, but by doing so, she had put herself on display. Crowds had gathered at the cemetery to pay their respects—most were fellow sufferers, having lost their own loved ones in that massacre. But Eliana was special; she was the only living daughter of John Veston, the leader of the Telemachus Project. They would watch her respectfully from a distance, but she could still feel their eyes on her. It was hard to feel anything but the pressure in her chest with the weight of observation upon her. So she'd made a deal with herself to visit her father's grave another day, when people went back to their routines and left the graveyard to the dead.

Eliana made her way to the scout pavilion to get some work done and take her mind off of things. Her objective was to just make it through the day, to do anything but think about what this anniversary meant. Her soothreader buzzed with notifications, but she didn't care; she didn't want to read well-wishes from her teammates.

The ground sail raced over the meadow toward the pavilion. Out here in the wilderness, she felt at peace. If she didn't have to bring an escort with her to go for a hike, she'd be alone in the wild without a care in the world. Eliana craved a hermit's life.

A notification from Denton pinged Eliana's soothreader, but she didn't open it. She didn't want to hear him coddle her. She didn't want to make her problems into his problem, unsure if he would even accept them. Maybe he'd leave her too.

She entered the pavilion and the lights came on, assuring Eliana that she was, indeed, alone.

"Homer," Eliana asked her mechanical half-brother, "bring up the newest satellite data, please."

"Of course, Dr. Veston," Homer responded. The vid screen blipped on, and a top-down view of various environments appeared. Other team members had highlighted some areas as points of interest for future scout excursions.

Eliana didn't notice herself drift away from their highlighted areas. Her mind was full of rambling about what the day signified, why the massacre had happened … *Why can't everyone just leave it be? Why can't we all just move on? Why can't we find—*

Denton pinged Eliana's soothreader again, breaking her concentration long enough for her to notice what she was doing. She had shifted the satellite data back in time to the day of the massacre.

Eliana was looking for signs of Captain Roelin Raike.

They had searched these images before, so thoroughly that she could picture each of them in her head. Eliana wasn't sure if Roelin had planned the perfect escape, or if he was just lucky that the satellites weren't in the right positions in orbit to catch it. There were no clues; Roelin had been entirely swallowed by the planet that night. Eliana was left only with her questions and her sorrow.

"Elly?" Denton's voice startled Eliana. She turned to see him and sighed. Denton continued, "I'm sorry. I tried to ping you. When I couldn't get ahold of you, I figured I'd prepare some stuff for tomorrow."

Eliana's shook her head. She knew what he was going to say. It would be that same old "sorry for your loss" crap she'd been hearing from everyone for the last four years.

"How are you holding up?" Denton asked.

"I'm *fine*," Eliana lied. "You don't need to check on me, or coddle me, or comfort me. I'm *fine*." She sifted through more satellite images rapidly as she spoke, the gloss of tears blurring her vision. "I don't want to hear it. That old 'I can't imagine what you're going through.' They can't know, of course they can't. So why do they have to say it?"

Denton got closer to Eliana, and she turned and sneered at him. "*You* weren't even there. *You* were sleeping cozily in your little bed, flying in a machine my father built. *You* slept while he bled to death. *You* don't know what I'm dealing with, so don't—"

Denton embraced her.

Eliana's breath fluttered in her chest. She raised her fists, then unclenched them and wrapped her arms around his back. She sobbed freely as she held Denton, burying her head in the crook of his neck and shoulder.

"I wasn't here then. But I am here now," Denton said.

Eliana allowed the last ragged breaths to pass from her as a wave of calm washed over her. The surging sea of her mind had become a quiet pond.

At the end of the day, Denton walked Eliana back home. They passed the candlelight vigil near the John Veston Kamarian Archive, noticing how the soft blue holographic ghosts of those who were lost that day contrasted with the warm orange glow of the candles.

When they arrived at her apartment, Eliana turned to Denton and smiled weakly. "Thank you for being with me today," she said.

"I can stay, if you'd like," he offered.

Eliana shook her head. "I'm exhausted. I'm just going to go to bed and be done with this awful day." She kissed him, holding her lips against his for an extended moment.

"Good night," Denton said with a nod.

"Good night," Eliana replied, then gently shut the door.

———◆———

It was still early in the evening, and Denton wasn't tired, so he decided to go for a walk.

The soft Kamarian breeze gently blew a few stray leaves through the street. The twin moons cast their light, which splintered off into a scattering of stars.

Something caught Denton's eye on a parapet on the colony wall. He squinted when he noticed a woman standing there, looking outward into the Kamarian frontier. She wore a loose blanket over her shoulders that waved quietly in the wind.

The mysterious woman turned to leave, hesitating when she noticed Denton looking at her. He quickly averted his gaze to not spook her, but knew he was too late. He had made eye contact, and it was enough for him to recognize her.

It was Faye Raike, Roelin's wife. Denton remembered her from the geology display in the archive. As hard as Silence Day was for Eliana, Denton thought it might be even harder for Faye. Her husband had betrayed all of humanity that day.

Yet Roelin was gone, and she remained.

Faye paid no attention to Denton; she walked away to some unknown destination, fading into the night.

"Long time, no see," a voice came from behind Denton. He turned and saw his brother Jason. It had been months since they had last seen each other.

"Where the Hells have you been?" Denton asked, and they shared a brotherly embrace.

"I could tell ya, but I bet where you have been is more interesting." Jason chuckled and walked with Denton.

"Mom and Dad don't know what you've been up to," Denton said.

"Ty does," he said.

"Ty does?" Denton jerked his head. "Hells, why does Ty know and I don't?"

"I would have told you, but you were too busy saving those people on the *Henson* and becoming a scout."

"Out with it!" Denton said with a smile.

Jason grinned and flicked a few gestures over his soothreader. When he finished, a text prompt displayed: *Contract Approved.* Jason nodded toward it and explained, "I had been tryin' for months now to do something. Get myself out of the shop and make my own way, like you did. I actually tried to do this on Ganymede too, but that damn Councilman Blaise shot it down. Here, though, he was outnumbered."

"What is it?" Denton was dying from the anticipation.

"I got approved to build the colony a rushcycle racetrack," Jason said with a smile.

Denton's face lit up. "That's *awesome!*" he said, and clapped his hand against Jason's shoulder. "You can finally put that beast of a bike to good use!"

"That's the plan. But I figure this will also help Mom and Dad's shop. If I race there and do well, it's like free advertising." Jason smiled and nodded.

"I'm happy for you. This is *your* future, not Grandpa's or Dad's—it's yours."

"It's thanks to you. Once you told everyone you were thinking of becoming a scout, it took the edge off the knife. It inspired me to go out and get something done."

Denton smiled. "How's Ty feel about it?"

"Ty?" Jason chuckled. "Ty wants to run the shop! Can you believe that? It's like he's not even our brother or something. But that's his choice; he wants to take over and keep the Castus Machine Shop alive."

"Ain't that something," Denton said quietly.

The brothers stopped in front of a bar, the Laughing Lemurbat. There was a holographic video loop of a lemurbat chugging away at a juice bulb, something those creatures were known to do. Jason walked toward the door and said, "Come on, let's get a drink. I'm buyin'."

Denton nodded and walked into the bar.

Tomorrow would be a better day.

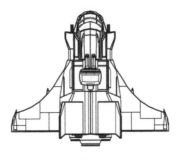

TWENTY-SEVEN

THREE YEARS AGO

DAY 510 OF ROELIN'S EXODUS

ROELIN WAS UNRECOGNIZABLE FROM his former self. A Landing Day had passed during his exile, and the fish had migrated through his part of the stream directly into his net. He tried to make the alien fish last for as long as he could, preserving some of their meat in his smoking hut and keeping the rest alive in a small pond he had created off to the side of the stream.

Roelin also unearthed laser stones as he terraformed the yard around the *Astraeus*. The unstable fonts of electrical energy had their uses. Roelin created an adapter to funnel some of the electricity into the ship. It didn't give the ship enough power to lift off, but it provided him with light and helped maintain the air purifiers.

Nhymn started asking more and more questions about human deaths. She wanted to know why humans died, what happened after they perished, if they faded away or if they remained, like she had.

Roelin couldn't answer.

Each time he failed to respond in a satisfying way, Nhymn would hurt him, slicing through his mind and raking her phantom talons across his memories. Roelin felt like he remembered less about who he was as time went on. Nhymn was devouring his history.

To Roelin, the man he'd been on Mars was a stranger, the man in Odysseus Colony was a second stranger, and the man trapped in the Kamarian wilderness was a third man he didn't know.

Roelin walked onto the bridge and checked off another repair. He inspected his list. Every time he saw something on it he could not repair, he would underline it in red. The red underlines were piling up, each one an anchor to this jungle prison.

Roelin's vision was ripped into the abyss as Nhymn stepped into his mind once again without warning. He awoke on his knees on the floor, the pad of paper in front of him. At the rate she was questioning him, he would soon be out of backup notepads. He picked it up and read the message.

WHY DID THE HUMANS COME HERE? Nhymn asked in ink.

"There was a war, we were being chased out," Roelin said aloud. Roelin had not been around to witness the end of the Undriel war, but he knew the machines would inevitably win. Toward the end of the Telemachus project, it became clear that mission parameters had shifted from *space exploration* to *escape and survive.*

A blink, and more text appeared.

WHAT CHASED THE HUMANS? Nhymn had written.

Roelin didn't like this question; he had this itching in the back of his mind that Nhymn was planning something. He felt like the less she knew about the Undriel, the better.

"I don't have time for this," Roelin said, standing up. "I'll tell you later." He left the pad of paper on the floor and exited the bridge to do maintenance on an air purifier on the outer hull.

PRESENT DAY

It was a beautiful morning in Odysseus Colony, contrasting the bleakness of Silence Day two weeks before. Autumn had come, and the leaves near the colony were beginning to turn brown and shed from their branches. Denton, Jess, and Pavel were loading the *Viridios* with equipment, preparing for another salvage mission. Pavel pushed a hover mule up the access ramp, then turned to the new recruits.

"You two have been doing well," Pavel said to them as he clapped dust off his hands. "I have told you this, no?"

Jess nodded and smiled. Over the months, the Tvashtar marine had remained strong and silent, but her humanity was starting to show in small gestures.

Denton pushed a crate into position in the *Viridios* cargo hold and said, "Thanks, Pavel." He pivoted to go back down the ramp and grab more supplies, and noticed George Tanaka approaching.

"Just in time," Pavel said, smiling. Denton looked over his shoulder at the old major. Something was going on. Jess nodded toward George, and he returned the nod.

"Good morning, Major Volkov," George said.

"*Dobroe*, George," Pavel greeted him, mixing in his old language. "Think they are ready, *da*?"

"Hey, what's up?" Denton asked anyone who would answer.

"The auk'nai have requested we visit them. I think it's about time you two met the natives. They don't ask us to do this often," George said. Denton's eyebrows launched to the top of his head in surprise. Jess lifted her chin and grinned. George turned to Pavel and asked, "Will that be alright, Major?"

"Beta will miss them. But as my fad-ther used to always say, *I'll do the work myself*." Pavel clapped Denton on the back. "Go ahead, you two."

Jess saluted Pavel, and he saluted her in return. She left the ramp, and Denton almost thought she was skipping very subtly.

"Thanks, George," Denton said, a little unsure of what to do with himself.

George nodded. "Go talk to Eliana about preparations. We leave in one hour," he said, then bowed to Pavel and took his leave.

————— ◆ —————

One hour later, the *Rogers* was loaded and ready to fly.

"Apusticus, here we come," Lieutenant Commander Rocco Gainax said over the comm channel.

In the main passenger cabin, Denton looked out his port-side window as the colony shrunk in view. George leaned over to him and asked, "How much do you know about the auk'nai?"

"Only the broad strokes, really. I know how their spirituality is attached to the daunoren. Also, the hook staffs," Denton said, lifting a finger toward George's handheld daunoren whistle. "Actually, I've meant to ask about that little one you have there."

"This? It's like a whistle, actually." George twirled the whistle in his hand and held it out for Denton to inspect. "They gave us these to summon them when we arrive at the designated meeting place. You'll see when we get there. The auk'nai used to keep a lookout near the Timber Chase too; in case we needed their help, we could whistle for them. But they haven't done that since the night of the incident."

Denton glanced toward Eliana. She gazed out the window with a faraway look in her eyes.

George continued, "The lookout witnessed the incident from the trees and reported back to Apusticus about it. They have been scarce ever since. In fact, this will be the first time we've seen them in over a year."

"Do they like us?" Denton asked.

"To be honest, we aren't entirely sure," George said, and slipped the whistle back into a pouch in his scout jacket. "Sometimes I feel like we make great strides toward unity, and other times, I feel like they keep us at arm's length."

"It's better than it was when we first landed," Eliana said. "Their original leader, Ve'trenn, didn't trust humanity. But Mag'Ro has become the new leader of Apusticus, and he's more accepting of us."

"That's true," Marie Viray said, leaning over the armrest of her seat to face them. "You know, Denton, Eliana here convinced Mag'Ro to give us the elements we needed to cure lung-lock. She's a hero."

Denton smiled and gripped Eliana's hand, and she smiled back. Marie winked and returned to her usual sitting position.

"I trust you, Denton, but I want to reiterate something," George said. "We don't know what the auk'nai have planned for us when we reach their city. I want you to be careful, and remember, the auk'nai can read your intentions. You can't lie to an auk'nai, not even a little lie."

"I understand. I'm just going to follow your lead," Denton said.

"I know you will. I wouldn't have asked you to join us if I didn't think so." George smiled.

Rocco interrupted them over the comm channel: "We will be making our descent into Apusticus airspace now. Please have a seat, everyone."

"Here we go," George said.

The *Rogers* drifted down to the ground just outside of an alien forest. The mighty trees were solid ivory, with veins of shimmering blue running up their vast expanse. A crown of large, bright-blue leaves shaded the forest floor from the autumn sunlight, casting a waving pattern of light across the blue-green grass below and creating an underwater-esque atmosphere. There were no trails here, only a section to the side of the landing zone that looked like it had been used previously by scout teams as a campground. There were no auk'nai structures to see from here; they would need to travel into the forest to find them.

The ramp lowered, and the scouts began exiting the *Rogers*, carrying workstations and equipment down into the camping area. The Tvashtar marines on the expedition were Sergeant Clint Foster, Lance Corporal Andrew Louis, and new recruit Lance Corporal Jess Combs. They wore combat suits with jump-jets and a full marine kit. They scanned the area to make sure it was safe for everyone.

There was no urgency; this was not Clint and Andrew's first visit.

The scientists exited shortly afterward, lead biologist and linguistics expert George Tanaka; lead chemist and botanist Marie Viray; lead geologist Lynn Fejihn; lead medical officer Dr. Eliana Veston; and humble mechanic Denton Castus, who felt a little out of place among the others.

Denton walked with Eliana and asked, "What is this forest called?"

"The Azure Vault. Pretty, isn't it?" Eliana pointed at the blue veins that ran up the humongous tree trunks. "You see those? The trees draw minerals from the ground with their roots. Lynn says those roots are all over the mines below the city."

Denton was hypnotized by the shimmering light. He was interrupted as a ground sail exited the *Rogers*. Denton noticed a strange device attached to the flanks of the sail. It didn't look like anything he had come across in his years as a mechanical engineer. George walked down the ramp, fiddling with his daunoren whistle as he moved away from the leading group.

"George is going to ring the doorbell," Eliana said to Denton, flicking her chin toward the tree line.

George waved the whistle over his head, and it let out a loud birdcall as air moved through it. George whistled out three times in succession, then held the whistle down behind his back in both hands.

A large, shadowy shape dropped from the trees. It descended from the canopy rapidly, then flung its wingspan open to slow its drop. It was an auk'nai, the first Denton had ever seen in person. Its broad wings flapped, slowing its fall and gracefully allowing the three-meter-tall bird-man to land unharmed.

This auk'nai had bright-blue feathers that matched the leaves of the Azure Vault behind him. It wore bone-white sashes interwoven with brilliantly colored gems. Its beak was sleek and sharp. Long ears protruded from the sides of its head.

It held a daunoren hook that stood as tall as the auk'nai itself.

The staff portion of the hook was a combination of different elements: jagged bones, smooth metals, and some rocky materials. Denton knew the whole staff was built over time as the auk'nai who owned it aged, becoming a sort of an autobiography for the wielder. Gems were also fixed into the staff, some protruding sharply and others hanging loosely. Although it was beautifully colored, the long hook reminded Denton of the Grim Reaper's sickle.

"We have come as you requested," George said, and bowed. The team approached George and the auk'nai. As each scout approached, the bird-man's ears twitched and his beak tilted toward them. Denton felt a pang of fear strike him when the sharp beak faced him; he was being recognized by the face of Kamaria, and he felt small beneath its gaze.

"You bring with you those whose songs are unknown to Apusticus," the auk'nai said with a deep grumble in his voice.

"Ah yes, our new recruits." George gestured for the newest scouts to step forward. "Nock'lu, meet Denton Castus and Jess Combs."

Nock'lu cawed and tilted his head, inspecting Denton. When he was satisfied, he flicked his gaze to Jess. Nock'lu's ears twittered and he cooed.

"A warrior. Nock'lu sees reflection on her surface."

Jess nodded and smiled.

"Denton is a mechanical engineer," George said. "He might have some insight that could be useful to your people."

Nock'lu let out a caw that sounded like the auk'nai equivalent of a chuckle. Denton felt a little offended, and Nock'lu must have picked up on it, because he halted the laughter and nodded to George.

"Follow Nock'lu," the auk'nai said. "Mag'Ro is waiting."

Nock'lu cawed and pushed downward with his massive wings, launching himself into the air and blowing grass and dust everywhere. George coughed and waved his hand to clear the dust. "The auk'nai don't have any phrases for 'goodbye,' so when it's time to go, they just"—he thrust a thumb into the sky—"*vamoose.*"

The scouts walked over to the ground sail and boarded it. There was a loud whistle from the sky; Nock'lu was ready to lead them into the forest. The ground sail pulled forward into the woods. There was no premade trail, as this forest belonged to the natives, and they had no use for them.

Nock'lu displayed his flight skills by diving downward and acrobatically rolling between the trees. The ground sail followed slowly through the thick of the forest.

"Show-off," George muttered with a smile.

In a few places, Denton wasn't sure if the ground sail would fit between the trunks. To his surprise, the vehicle lifted higher off the ground to fit through less tight spaces along the lengths of the tree trunks.

"How is it doing that? I thought our hover tech only had a maximum height of about a meter?" Denton asked.

"It's auk'nai technology," Eliana said. "We upgraded our ground sails to give them some new tricks." She tapped the side of the vehicle. "A little gift from them to us. We use these special ground sails to reach their city in the treetops. You'll see."

Denton inspected the unfamiliar device he'd noticed earlier and started to realize his role on the team. The auk'nai were not some race of tribal birds; they were an advanced species with their own machines. No one else on the team had a background in engineering. Suddenly, Denton felt both proud of himself and worried. Sure, he was the lead engineer of the Alpha Scout Team today, but if he didn't understand how auk'nai technology worked, he would be about as useless as a pistol with no collider cylinder.

The forest separated around a dried-up creek bed where the sails could increase speed, using the creek as a natural path. Denton saw strange creatures observing them as they passed. They looked like old Earth apes, with long arms and legs and a curled tail. They were covered in short yellow fur, and their heads resembled a chameleon's, with a hood on the crown and coned eye sockets that allowed the eyes to examine their surroundings independently of each other. Two of these strange ape-lizards swung close to the ground sail, grabbing low-hanging branches of the trees to swing forward. Nock'lu cawed at one of the creatures, and it barked back and scuttled off into the forest away from the sail.

"The auk'nai call those yommies," Eliana said, pointing at the swinging creatures. "They eat these big grubs that grow on the forest floor here that are kind of a nuisance to the auk'nai."

The forest began to fill with lovely birdsong, like a choir of angels. Denton squinted his eyes and saw that a crowd of auk'nai natives were standing near the tree line up ahead, watching the scouts approach and singing together.

Structures floating high above became more visible. Circular platforms hung motionless in the air, hiding just under the canopy. The birdsong grew louder and louder, like a welcoming cheer. The ground sail stopped below one of the large, hanging platforms.

Lynn Fejihn stepped off the ground sail and waved. "This is where I get off. See you all later tonight!"

Sergeant Clint Foster adjusted the rifle strapped to his shoulder and joined the geologist. He nodded to Jess and said with his synthetic voice box, "I'll escort this group. You stick with Louis here and do what he says."

Lance Corporal Andrew Louis said, "I'll show her the ropes."

Jess nodded. Clint led Lynn away from the sail as a pink-feathered auk'nai with a duckbill-shaped beak joined them.

"Where are they going?" Denton asked Eliana with a whisper.

"The auk'nai mines are a short walk that way. Lynn will be working with them today," she whispered back.

"We ready?" Lance Corporal Andrew Louis asked the remaining crew.

"Take us up," George said.

Andrew pulled a crank on the unique device strapped to the side of the sail, and they began to rise into the air. Denton grabbed the railing and gripped it until his knuckles turned white. Eliana reassured him with a considerate shoulder rub.

"Hope you're not afraid of heights," George said, raising his eyebrows. Denton laughed nervously and watched the ground fall farther and farther away from him. His nerves were replaced with astonishment as they surmounted the lip of the circular floating platform, revealing the city of Apusticus.

There was a vast network of broad platforms, some at different elevations, each adorned with a series of auk'nai structures. Many buildings had floating elements, such as roofs hovering just above walls and perches drifting in midair. The structures were brightly colored and incorporated large gemstones into the design, making the entire city look like a beautiful, glimmering painting.

Denton had never seen antigravity technology this refined. Human-based hover technology usually caused the object to wobble in place, or drift ever so slightly, but these structures were motionless. It was as if the auk'nai had built the city using the air as scaffolding.

The auk'nai cheered, creating a sound that was like a flock of musical instruments, beautiful and loud. A group flew down to meet them on the platform.

"Watch your step," Marie said, grabbing one of the auk'nai's long, outstretched arms and allowing it to pull her safely onto the platform. One by one, the scouts exited the ground sails and entered the city.

Denton's eye was caught by an extravagant fountain, unlike anything he had ever seen in human engineering. The water flowed from a central vessel upward to a sizeable gemstone that reflected light onto other floating gems. The flow cascaded downward in arcs, bouncing off intricately designed pieces of architecture that rotated as they caught the water and deposited it into a pool below.

A large, red-feathered auk'nai wearing a decorative hood adorned with glowing stones approached them with an escort. The leader's daunoren staff was more intricate than the others'. Denton noticed some human technology built into the staff, including a few collider cylinders. He wondered what they were for, and how they'd gotten there.

"Eliana," the tremendous leader auk'nai said in a deep voice with a low tuba sound behind it.

"Mag'Ro, I've missed you," Eliana said. To Denton's surprise, the auk'nai held his hand outward, and she shook it. He recognized the name from the archives. Mag'Ro was the auk'nai observer who'd made first contact with Eliana five years ago. Since then, he had succeeded the previous leader of Apusticus and made dealing with humans a priority.

"Nock'lu spoke of your new ones." He tilted his beak toward Denton and Jess.

"Yes, these are our new recruits, Denton Castus and Jess Combs. They are good friends and would like to learn about your culture," Eliana said.

Mag'Ro cooed, then said, "New ones are welcome today."

"Mag'Ro, we are unsure why you summoned us," George said. "Do you need our help?"

"Mag'Ro wishes to show the humans something, but it is not ready now," he said, referring to himself in the third person, which Denton was realizing all auk'nai did. It could just be a glitch in translation from auk'nai to Sol Common, or perhaps it had something to do with their mental capabilities. If every auk'nai in the city of Apusticus referred to themselves in the first person, it would be hard to know who was talking to who, or which thoughts were your own.

"Should we come back at a better time?" Eliana asked.

"No." Mag'Ro grunted, then he gestured to one of his escorts. The smaller of Mag'Ro's companions, an auk'nai with black and green feathers, circled Denton with curiosity. It had glinting purple eyes, and blue sashes with only a few minor gemstones. The small auk'nai seemed to be a juvenile, less experienced than the formidable Mag'Ro.

"Talulo will escort you around Apusticus while Mag'Ro finishes preparations." The smaller auk'nai twitched its ears toward Mag'Ro, then cooed.

"Marie," Mag'Ro's other companion spoke up. The plump auk'nai with orange feathers and purple sashes waddled over to Marie Viray. It had a duckbill as well, differentiating it in appearance from Mag'Ro, Nock'lu, and Talulo.

"Marie, please follow Galifern," it said. "Want fresh human eyes on an experiment."

"Okay, Galifern," Marie said. "I'll see you all later," she said, and followed the waddling auk'nai into a nearby structure.

"That's the city chemist," Eliana leaned over to tell Denton. "They work together to learn new things about Kamaria. The auk'nai have a unique insight into science."

"I noticed his beak is different," Denton said, trapping his hand near his nose.

"Auk'nai with a duckbill like that are female."

"How does she manage to get around in a place like this?" Denton asked.

"She is rather plump." Eliana sighed. "But the auk'nai compensate for their citizens who may be physically incapable of flying between city segments. Like older citizens or those who lost their power of flight." She pointed to the other end of the platform they stood on. "Bridges link each platform together."

Denton squinted and saw a bridge that looked like floating stepping-stones, no railing protecting the traveler from a fall. He winced as he watched a few young auk'nai children scurry across them with ease.

"We also gifted her a surveyor craft a few years ago," Eliana continued. "It allows her to visit areas outside of the town and collect her own samples. Before, Galifern relied on others to get what she needed, with varying degrees of success. Just one of the ways we have been sharing technology with our new neighbors."

Mag'Ro leaned over to Talulo and spoke in their native language, a fast-paced dialect with birdsong mixed in. Talulo turned toward the group as Mag'Ro launched himself into the sky, his floating gemstones trailing in his wake.

"Talulo will lead you now," the small auk'nai said, "Follow this way."

Auk'nai citizens eyed them from windows and perches as the humans walked through the city. Each looked unique, having different configurations of colorful sashes and gems to complement their beautiful feathers. They went about their daily tasks, carrying alien objects to various destinations, trading food for materials, organizing groups for hunting.

"Go ahead and ask Talulo any questions you have," George said to the new recruits. "It's a good opportunity to learn."

Jess took the initiative and asked, "Talulo, what do the auk'nai use for currency?"

Talulo tilted his head as he translated the question, then said, "Auk'nai trade in three ways. One is through contribution to the city. It is known in the song of Apusticus how much an auk'nai is worth through work. If an auk'nai is a better worker, an auk'nai may receive more."

They walked past what Denton could only assume was the auk'nai version of a machine shop. Inside, he saw alien mining equipment, much different in appearance than human engineering, but similar enough to recognize their purpose. The exteriors were made with a type of metal Denton didn't recognize. The machines glimmered as they walked past.

"The second auk'nai trade is through information," Talulo cooed. "If auk'nai brings new learnings to Apusticus, the song grows more beautiful. Mag'Ro brought great learnings to Apusticus, so great we made him auk'nai leader."

The group came to a large building that looked like an upside-down pyramid. An opening in the front would be the scouts' entrance, but Talulo flapped upward and hopped through a hole a floor above them.

"What's the third currency?" Denton asked.

"Gems," Eliana said. "Each gem has its own song, and therefore its own worth."

"That's a lot of songs." Denton said.

"Tell me about it." Eliana smirked.

The scouts walked through the first-floor entrance into a room of floating pools. Steam flowed away from the water, and Denton could see large eggs slowly rotating inside each.

"Auk'nai nursery," Talulo said.

"They have never let us in here before," Eliana said, and gripped Denton's jacket sleeve and squeezed.

"Come and learn," Talulo said, flying up to a waterbed above them.

"Step onto this platform," Eliana said, grabbing Denton's shoulder and pulling him close to her. The others joined them on the platform and waited.

The floor under their feet lifted away from its origin and floated toward Talulo. Denton and Jess looked down in wonder and watched as they moved past rows of hovering water pools.

"That never gets old," Lance Corporal Andrew Louis said, and nudged Jess with his elbow. "I always feel it in my guts." He chuckled. Now that the platform had reached the waterbed Talulo was on, Denton could see what he wanted to show them.

Water drained from an egg pool and traveled through the open air to a vessel on the opposite wall, like a tentacle of liquid retreating into a cave. The eggs descended with the water until they lay gently on a soft bed of gel. The steam boiled away, and as the egg cooled, a small piece of it chipped off.

"Amazing!" George said, and flipped a small camera up on the shoulder of his jacket. It made a beep as he began recording the event. The small hole in the egg cracked more, with a tap on the other side of the shell proceeding each crack. A beak tip slammed through one of the shells. Soon after, the other two eggs began their own hatching process.

The cracks became a large hole. A female auk'nai landed on the edge of the empty pool, her feathers white and yellow. The auk'nai nurse hesitated to attend to the newborns when she saw the humans.

She looked at Talulo, and he said something to her in auk'nai.

The auk'nai nurse hesitated a moment longer, examining them, then began helping the eggs hatch by pulling away loose portions of shell. Soon, they could see a black shape inside flailing its head and beak toward an unseen shell in its blind, newborn state.

Talulo continued speaking to the nurse in auk'nai as they hatched the other two eggs, another black one and a white one. The chicks flailed their soft, chubby, featherless arms. Each was about the size of a newborn calf, and they reminded Denton of newborn human babies more than hatchling birds from old Earth.

"Two boys and a girl. How wonderful," Eliana said.

"Come this way," Talulo said, lifting one of the babies and plopping it, wet and wiggling, into Denton's arms. Everyone was surprised by the suddenness of the action, Denton most of all.

"Hold him tightly!" George said nervously. Denton got a good grip on the baby boy he was holding. The newborn slammed its beak against his chest a few times; Denton could feel the small sting even through his scout jacket.

"Take this one," Talulo said, handing the baby girl to Jess. The floppy, uncoordinated baby squirmed in her grasp, but she held her with no visible problems. The auk'nai nurse gently handled the last newborn boy with a grace earned from years of experience. She flapped her wings and floated downward. Talulo twitched his head, and the platform began to lower.

Denton wrangled his newborn auk'nai as he whispered to Eliana, "Is he controlling the platform with his mind?"

Eliana raised her eyebrows and flicked her nose toward the opposite wall. "You see over there?" she said, referring to a perch with a few young auk'nai standing by a series of levers. "Talulo tells them to move the platform telepathically. They can't move objects with their minds or anything, but they can speak to each other this way."

Denton peeked over the edge of the moving platform and saw they were approaching their destination.

A large pen hung in midair under a large, warm gemstone. The nurse placed the baby boy into the enclosure. Denton saw other newborns in various stages of infancy wiggling around inside. Some looked awkward, with small feathers sticking out of their skin like tiny needles, and Denton could see they had various eye colors. It seemed like auk'nai coloration was random by birth.

"Put the new one here," Talulo said, gesturing to Denton to put the chick into the pen. Denton nodded and struggled to put the wiggling newborn into the enclosure. The chick plopped down and flailed for a moment before tiring itself out and resting. The infant auk'nai looked up at Denton, opening his eyes for the first time and grunting. He blinked his large green eyes against the harsh light. He looked angry, almost annoyed by the experience of being born.

Jess moved forward to place the baby girl in the enclosure, but Talulo stopped her. "No, no," Talulo said. He closed his eyes for a moment, and the platform lowered once again to a separate pen.

Female auk'nai hatchlings bounced around inside. Jess nodded and placed the female newborn into the pen with no problems. The little infant was much calmer than her brother. Another newborn wiggled its way over and leaned its head against the newcomer. The two calmly fell asleep—much less chaos compared to the boys' pen above.

Jess asked, "How do the parents know which baby is their own?"

Talulo said, "They sing the song of their *loopahs*."

"Loopahs?" Denton asked Eliana.

"Auk'nai word for 'parents,'" she said.

Talulo whistled with excitement. He flapped his wings but didn't leave the ground. "Insightful for humans?" he asked George.

"Yes! We learned a lot. Thanks for the tour, Talulo." George said. He thumbed the recorder on his shoulder. The light blinked from red to green as it began uploading data to the *Rogers*.

"Talulo will show humans more," Talulo said, lifting off and flying out the door. The scouts had to wait for their platform to lower all the way back down to the main floor to exit.

"Good job, you two. You handled those newborns well," George said, eyeing Jess and Denton.

"I'm just glad I didn't let the little guy get away from me," Denton said. His heart skipped a beat and pulsed a sting through his body as he imagined what would have happened if he'd dropped the newborn.

"It was fun," Jess said. The experience seemed to open her up in a way Denton had not observed in the past months.

"See, there's nothing to it," Eliana said with a smile.

The platform landed, and the team stepped off.

Outside, Talulo flew through the city, looping his flight path in his excitement and singing. Auk'nai filled the buildings and skies above them. The light shining through the canopy made all the scattered gems in the city glow and reflect color everywhere. Denton and Eliana were at the back of their group, enjoying the stroll.

A few auk'nai on their path turned to look at them, still curious about their new neighbors. Denton thought that humans probably seemed bland to the auk'nai. Scout uniforms were black, white, and orange, while auk'nai were walking kaleidoscopes.

An auk'nai with a strange insect leeching onto its head walked past with a vacant look in its eyes. Its feathers were mottled, and there was a visible scar on its chest. The auk'nai wore no sashes or gems.

"Talulo, what's his story?" Denton asked.

Talulo looked at the sullen auk'nai and let out a low caw. "Arrilstar the Murderer." Then he looked back at the humans and tilted his head. "Auk'nai justice. Different from human justice."

"How so?" Jess asked.

"See j'etthoda." Talulo gestured to the leech on the murderer's head. "Auk'nai know the songs of thieves and murderers. J'etthoda makes Arrilstar servant to the city. When the song of Apusticus decides the time is served for crime, j'etthoda is eaten and the criminal gets to sing the song again."

"You don't lock them up?" Denton asked.

Talulo cawed, almost disgusted. "And let murderer sit locked in a cell, nothing done for the song of Apusticus?" Talulo twitched his beak. "J'etthoda keeps singing while criminal learns how bad crime was."

"Who did Arrilstar murder?" Eliana asked. She had not been aware of this facet of auk'nai life before.

"Ve'trenn," Talulo said curtly.

Eliana stopped walking and went cold. "Your previous colony leader?"

Talulo cooed, "Yes, Apusticus loved the song of Ve'trenn. He is sorely missed. Arrilstar was Ve'trenn's advisor alongside Mag'Ro. When Mag'Ro was picked to be Ve'Trenn's successor, Arrilstar killed him. It is in the song."

Eliana remembered Mag'Ro mentioning Ve'trenn the night she'd exchanged the collider pistol for the gems. Maybe Mag'Ro was trying to save his leader and mentor. Perhaps it was this exchange that caused Mag'Ro to be the chosen successor over Arrilstar, and thus forced Arrilstar's hand to violence. She had many questions, but asking in broad daylight on a populated city street didn't seem appropriate.

Arrilstar the Murderer moved past them like a zombie. Denton noticed Eliana had trailed behind to keep watching the murderer. He took her hand and smiled. Eliana snapped out of her trance and rejoined the group.

The scouts passed in front of an outdoor school where young auk'nai perched on floating rods in front of an elderly schoolmaster. He had a disassembled daunoren staff before him and was holding pieces up for the class to see. The teacher said nothing aloud. The students simply followed his movements with their eyes.

"How does that work?" Denton asked, pointing at the class.

Talulo answered, "Speaking is a right earned through pilgrimage. Until young ones go on their journey and build their own daunoren hook, they are spoken to only through the unsung song."

Talulo led the scouts to the auk'nai laboratory, which was run by Galifern. Inside, Marie Viray studied the plump orange auk'nai's data. The lab contained floating work shelves holding various alien vessels of fluids and powders.

Denton noticed some familiar chemistry equipment—microscopes, centrifuges, hot plates, burners, and distillation glassware—which implied the human influence on the lab. His eyes caught the surveyor craft in the corner.

The craft was the most familiar thing to him in the room. Talulo hopped over to Denton and considered him, twitching his birdlike head this way and that.

Denton noticed he was being observed and said, "Sorry, it's just that my brothers and I fix these." He still felt the need to explain himself to a creature that he knew could read his thoughts.

"Denton fixes tools?" Talulo asked.

"They call us mechanical engineers. We build and fix machinery," Denton explained. Talulo's eyes widened, and he whistled in excitement. Denton considered this a good thing and asked, "How about you, Talulo? What do you do here in Apusticus? It's not just showing humans around, is it?"

Talulo grabbed his daunoren staff and ran his long, taloned fingers across its length. "Talulo is unbound. Talulo tried fishing, but the fish did not bite Talulo's bait. Now does what Mag'Ro tells Talulo to do." The auk'nai cooed weakly. Denton knew the feeling. He, too, had not known where his place was. "Come on. Talulo will show humans more."

Talulo flapped himself over to the other side of the room. The lab was connected to a greenhouse complete with a garden. Talulo walked them through the garden where they witnessed water floating between growing plants hanging by invisible tethers in intricate, colorful pots. Denton could tell the auk'nai appreciated art.

Talulo led the team out of the greenhouse and farther into the city. Mag'Ro rejoined them, landing near George and chatting with him. Talulo hopped backward toward Denton and Eliana.

"I think Talulo likes you," Eliana said to Denton.

"I think so too." Denton laughed and watched Talulo bounce around and whistle.

Mag'Ro waved the scouts over to a ledge on the platform and beckoned with his deep voice, "It is ready. Come and see." Mag'Ro used his enormous hooked staff to point over the ridge of the city. They could see the forest floor of the Azure Vault, still dancing with light as if it were underwater.

Denton peered over the balcony, containing his anxiety at the vertigo of the drop just beyond the lip of the platform. Bushes swayed and leaves were rocked loose from nearby trees as disarray filled the tranquil forest. Auk'nai urgently whistled and shrieked at each other, a contrast to the cheerful birdsong that had welcomed them into Apusticus.

From the foliage, a massive reptilian monster emerged.

It was a ten-meter-tall quadruped with a long snout filled with a row of sharp, jagged teeth. It had six eyes fixed at the front of the muzzle. At the back of the beast's head were two elongated spikes that projected past its outstretched neck. The spine was covered in more spikes and hard scales that acted like battle armor.

The monster let out a booming roar, shaking the platform they stood on. Nearby auk'nai squawked in fear and stopped whatever they were doing to watch the monster pound the forest floor.

"A titanovore!" Lance Corporal Andrew Louis shouted.

Two auk'nai warriors appeared near the tree line, slashing their daunoren hooks at the titanovore's exposed areas. One hook had a sizeable blunt hammer at the top, and the other dangled a chain with a spiked ball on the end.

These warriors were very different in appearance from regular auk'nai civilians. Their feathers were painted white to blend in with the forest. They wore chain-mail sashes around their bodies, made with the unique metal Denton had seen earlier in the mining equipment. Machinery covered their faces and beaks, each with a long barrel sticking outward like a rifle strapped to their head.

"That's Pyla and Hazunda, but what do they have on their faces?" Eliana asked.

Pyla launched her arm forward, and the flail chain swung

around the titanovore's neck, embedding the spiked ball in its leathery skin after a final twist. Wasting no time, she hurled the other end of her daunoren staff like a spear, striking deep into a nearby tree. The titanovore was pinned in place but continued to lash out with its claws and tail. It snapped ferociously at the air, hoping to catch one of the warriors in its maw.

Hazunda flew above the titanovore's head, then crashed downward at breakneck speed, smashing his hammer into the monster's head just above its eyes. Its armored scales fell loosely to the forest floor, exposing a significant weakness.

Mag'Ro leaned forward and said to Eliana, "See now." The titanovore swung its front claw in a devastating arc, almost striking Hazunda. He dropped altitude to avoid the claw, planting his feet on the ground, then recoiled, bursting upward into the sky and leaving behind a trail of blue leaves.

Denton watched as Hazunda's beak barrel began to glow white hot. It looked like the inside of a collider pistol but without a casing. Somehow, the auk'nai had learned how to charge particles without the need for a collider cylinder.

Denton looked over at Mag'Ro's daunoren staff, remembering the array of collider cylinders built into it. That staff was possibly a prototype for the weapons being displayed in the fight below.

The titanovore rallied, shrieking as it broke loose from the tree that held it captive. Hazunda fired his face cannon, striking the monster in the side of the neck but missing the target on top of the head.

Now the titanovore was loose, and it spun wildly, swinging outward with its long tail. It collided with Hazunda, sending him spiraling wildly into the air. The scouts collectively gasped. Hazunda pivoted and flapped his wings hard, catching himself in midair just before he would have slammed into a tree.

Pyla pulled the spear end of her staff away from the tree and propelled herself into the titanovore's neck once more. She slammed the sharp end into the wound created by Hazunda's particle blast.

The titanovore squealed in pain as blood ejected from the gash around the spear.

Hazunda charged his face cannon once more, taking careful consideration to not accidentally shoot Pyla. The particle was fully charged, and with one more steadying flap of his wings, he fired.

There was an audible clap as the particle blast struck the head wound directly, spraying blood outward against the pristine white trees and onto Pyla. The roaring stopped abruptly, and the monster wobbled. Pyla detached herself from the monster's neck and joined Hazunda in the air. They watched as the beast toppled to the ground, lifeless. Cheering erupted from the city above them—even most of the scouts were clapping and hooting.

Denton turned to see that George and Eliana weren't thrilled by the excitement of the hunt. He wondered how anyone could watch that display and not be impressed. The auk'nai warriors landed on the ground near their kill. Pyla stabbed it once more in the eye to confirm it was dead. A team of auk'nai launched themselves from the city platform to join the warriors on the forest floor. They would break down the body and transport the meat up to the city for all citizens of Apusticus to enjoy.

"Now I see why they brought us here," George whispered to himself, loud enough for Denton to hear.

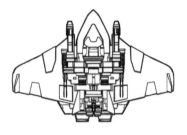

TWENTY-EIGHT

AFTER A LONG DAY in the city of Apusticus, the team returned to the *Rogers* spacecraft. They built a campfire and relaxed under the stars, surrounded by an encasement barrier for safety. Denton drew in his sketchpad, inspired by the fantastic sights of the city. He drew Talulo, with his sharp beak and huge eyes and ears, cloaked in a blue sash. Denton felt a kinship with the young auk'nai that he had not expected. Apparently, finding your place in the universe wasn't unique to Ganymede folk.

Eliana peeked over his shoulder at the drawing and said, "That's really good. You know, if you make enough of these, we can publish them in the archive."

"You think so? I never considered that," Denton said, focusing on the sketch. He switched his stylus to a paintbrush setting and began coloring the sashes, feeling it would be an injustice to leave the color out of a drawing of an auk'nai.

One by one, the scouts around the fire turned away to rest for the night. Eliana was the last holdout with Denton.

"I'm going to get some shut-eye. Will you be alright putting out the fire when you're ready?" Eliana asked.

"No problem." Denton smiled. Eliana kissed his lips and drifted toward their tent. Denton wondered if he could somehow procure a gemstone for her, but from what he could tell, the auk'nai prized them dearly. Denton stood up, stretched, and smothered the fire with a bucket of water. He put his sketchpad into his backpack, then heard a whistle come from beyond the encasement barrier.

Denton shouldered his bag and went to investigate. It was hard to see now that the fire had been put out, so he clicked a button on his scout jacket, and a small flashlight on his right breast pocket illuminated his path. The whistle came once more. Denton shook his head in disbelief as he recognized Talulo just beyond the barrier.

"Talulo? What are you doing here?" he asked.

"Denton fixes machines," Talulo whispered. "Can Denton fix a thing for Talulo?"

"Fix a thing? What are you talking about?" Denton asked, trying to keep his voice down so he wouldn't wake the others.

"Denton fix a thing for Talulo, just one small thing." Talulo purred as he begged.

"Where is the thing you need me to fix?" Denton asked, looking over his shoulder to make sure no one was around.

"By the mountain," Talulo grunted, and jerked his head in the direction of the mountain in the distance.

"*What?* I can't go there!"

"Sure we can," George Tanaka said from behind Denton. He emerged from his tent already dressed and ready for a hike. Denton looked wide-eyed at George. "It's alright, Denton. Let's go together. Talulo, can you lead us?"

Talulo whistled and bobbed his head.

"Well, let's go." George smiled and waved Denton over. "We'll take the surveyor. Grab your tools, please."

———— ◆ ————

Denton piloted the surveyor as George leaned back in his seat and admired the night sky. It was a small two-person skimmer that hovered just above the ground like the one the colonists had loaned to Galifern. Denton's workbench trailed behind the surveyor. Talulo flew ahead of them, guiding them across the meadow to the base of the mountain. He rolled and flipped as he flew, exploding with excitement.

Denton was concerned he wouldn't be able to fix whatever alien device Talulo wanted him to repair.

"Couldn't sleep?" George asked Denton as they drove.

"Actually, I was just thinking of heading in before Talulo caught me. I almost missed all of this," Denton said. "Whatever *this* is."

"Good thing we didn't. I always like to follow an adventure when I see one."

"Are we breaking the code?" Denton asked nervously. "We don't have a Tvashtar marine escort with us."

"Nonsense, I have the Hero of the *Henson* with me. I'll be perfectly safe." George smiled. "Relax. We've scouted in this area quite a few times."

"That's good." Denton sighed with relief.

"So, what do you think of them?" George waved a hand at Talulo as he danced in the sky.

"They are amazing. I can't believe what I'm seeing. Thanks for taking me with your team today."

"Not just today. This is a permanent thing now. I already cleared it with Major Volkov." George patted Denton on the shoulder. "You're an Alpha Team member now—Jess too. Congratulations."

"It's an honor," Denton said with a broad grin. *Denton Castus: Alpha Team scout.* He had officially made it a reality.

The mountain loomed closer. A hazy green mist hung above the rocks, fog from the day illuminated by sun geodes and laser stones, like a low-hanging aurora.

"Earlier today, when we watched those auk'nai take down that monster—"

"A titanovore," George interrupted.

"Right. You seemed upset."

"You didn't catch what Mag'Ro was doing?" George sighed. "The auk'nai don't trust us. They seldom allow us into their city, and when they do, we usually have to give them something. It's been a one-sided relationship." George turned to Denton and said, "Mag'Ro was demonstrating his power today. He was showing us how he reverse engineered our technology for their own use, and that he could do great violence with it if provoked."

"I recognized the technology on their heads ... faces? Beak cannons?" Denton wasn't sure what to call their face-mounted weapons, gesturing with one hand at his own face to illustrate what he was trying to say.

"Your guess is as good as mine as to what they call those things. It was the first time I saw them too." He considered for a moment and smiled. "We'll call them 'peck rifles' for now."

"That works."

"Did Eliana ever tell you how she got the gemstones from Mag'Ro during the early days of lung-lock?" George asked, one eyebrow crooked upward.

"She convinced him, so I imagine she had something really clever to say." Denton shrugged.

"She gave Mag'Ro a collider pistol," George said. "And we just now see how he used that weapon. It's a little secret between us scouts. If the council knew what Eliana did, they would be furious." George sighed. "A perk of being human, we can lie to each other."

"So now the auk'nai know how our technology works," Denton said, putting it together, "and we can't lie to them, and they can read our intentions. That's a lot of advantages in their corner. How much do we know about their own technology?"

"Only what we gleaned from the gems Eliana received, and just how the planet works. Which is to say, not much." George shrugged, then pointed a finger at Denton. "That's where you can come in handy, Hero of the *Henson*. Whatever this thing is that Talulo needs us to fix, I want you to learn as much as you can from it. Anything we can learn about their technology helps even the playing field."

"Are the auk'nai enemies?" Denton asked.

"I don't think so, but it's better to be prepared than surprised," George said.

Talulo landed in the grass in front of them, and Denton slowed the surveyor to a stop.

"Very close. Up this way." Talulo waved a hand toward the base of the mountain. They hopped off the surveyor, and Denton unhooked his workbench, then followed George and Talulo up the slope.

Talulo made the hike seem easy, but Denton and George were fighting to catch their breath toward the end. They arrived at their destination in the foothills of the mountain. There was a hole carved into the stone, no higher than Denton's knee. Talulo hopped in front of the tunnel and bobbed his head, grunting with excitement.

George huffed and pointed. "Okay, what are we doing here?"

"Talulo will call friend," Talulo said, and he poked his head into the hole and whistled. When Talulo pulled his head away, there was a dim blue light coming from deep within the tunnel.

Denton leaned over to George and asked, "Do you know what's going on?"

"Not a clue. The auk'nai haven't asked us to do anything like this before," George said, then pulled his shoulder-mounted camera into position and clicked the record button. Denton noticed this and un-holstered his bioscope, excited that he might make his first real discovery on Kamaria.

"*Ah*, here is Talulo's friend," Talulo said. He stepped back a few paces and waited. The light from the hole was interrupted by whatever was coming forward. Part of Denton considered that maybe he should bring out his pistol instead, but his calmer half prevailed. *Keep an open mind.* A moment later, a small creature squeezed itself from the hole and stood upright on its hind legs.

"Well, look at that." George chuckled. "What is this little guy called?"

The funny creature had big, bulging black eyes protruding from the top of its head, like a frog's, and a snout shaped like a tube. Its long, scaly neck terminated on furry shoulders, and it had padded feet. A flat, leathery tail much like a beaver's protruded from its rear end. The little creature held a device in its hands.

"Blek is a wizz'ik," Talulo introduced the small creature. The wizz'ik looked nervous, shifting its weight back and forth and gripping its little device.

"Well, good evening, Blek." George bent down to the wizz'ik's level. "My name is George." Blek inspected George, blinking each eye separately. Denton scanned the wizz'ik with his bioscope. Oddly, according to Homer's initial readout, this little creature was edible. But lucky for Blek, no one was interested.

"Go, Blek." Talulo nudged Blek forward. The wizz'ik held its hand forward.

"Oh, what's this? A handshake?" George chuckled and shook the tiny, weird hand. Blek then hurriedly put both his hands back on the device.

"Is that the thing you want me to fix?" Denton asked.

"Show Denton," Talulo encouraged the wizz'ik. Blek moved forward and held his hand out again for a handshake from Denton.

"No, Blek! *The device!*" Talulo urged. Blek honked with insecurity, then held out the device.

Denton took it. The tiny thing fit right in the palm of his hand. He turned it over to inspect it thoroughly and laughed when he recognized it. It was a handheld particle shocker. These devices were used to change liquid state—one shock could turn water into ice or gas instantly. Denton had used them daily on Ganymede, converting purified moon ice into cold drinking water or into vapor to humidify a dry room in the shop.

"Hey, wait a minute! Where did you get this?" Denton asked. "It's a particle shocker, this is one of our tools."

"Talulo took from human workbench during last visit," Talulo said, pointing at Denton's workbench as an example. There was that famous auk'nai honesty.

"Talulo, you know better than to steal from us," George said, shaking his head. "If you wanted something, you could ask."

"Talulo knows this," Talulo said. "But Blek—he needed it."

Blek twiddled his fingers together nervously and let out a tiny honk as he hid behind Talulo.

"It's alright. But from now on, ask us, please," George said, and Talulo bobbed his head in acknowledgment. Blek watched Talulo nod, and mimicked him.

"Okay, so what did Blek need this for?" Denton asked as he inspected the shocker, looking for the problem.

"Talulo will demonstrate," Talulo said, and reached into a sash on his side. He dug out a vicious-looking centipede-like creature with large pincers. It had a larvae middle section that gyrated and convulsed.

"Hells!" Denton spat in surprise as he bobbled the shocker in his hands.

"This is a m'unjo," Talulo explained, carefully holding the horrible insect. "When m'unjo is shocked, stones come out."

Denton held the broken particle shocker in one hand and scanned the hideous centipede with his bioscope. The m'unjo was not edible. In fact, it was acidic.

"Want me to stun it?" George asked. "It might have the same effect." Talulo nodded and dropped the m'unjo. The insect coiled up like a cobra and hissed at its attackers. George unholstered his collider pistol and set it to stun.

George let loose an electrical bolt right into the m'unjo, and it thrashed about in pain, then regurgitated a small gemstone. Talulo reached down and grabbed the gem quickly. The rest of the m'unjo began dissolving itself in some sort of acidic chemical reaction.

"Woah!" Denton said, and stepped back a pace to avoid getting any of the bubbling worm juice on his boots. That explained the bioscope readout. Blek, now happy the m'unjo was dead, scurried over to scoop up the bubbling acid with his tubular snout. Denton and George winced at the grotesqueness of this activity.

"Okay, I think I get it," George said, holding back from gagging. "So, Blek here shocks these m'unjo inside his tunnel there and collects the gems to give to you, and he"—George watched as Blek finished slurping the worm juice—"he eats the juice?"

"That isn't the whole song," Talulo said. "M'unjo blood helps Blek make his home bigger. Burns through rocks."

"Blek uses the acidic blood as a mining tool," Denton said curtly. He inspected the particle shocker further, flipping open a small compartment and noticing some frayed wires.

"Denton sings the whole song," Talulo said. "Blek and Talulo both gain."

"A mutually beneficial relationship," George said. "But why don't you just get the gems from the m'unjo yourself, Talulo?" he asked.

"M'unjo live in the rocks." Talulo pointed at the tunnel. "Talulo has no mining tools."

Denton understood. Talulo was not able to acquire gems like many of his auk'nai brothers and sisters, so he'd found a way to get his own without their help. The catch was that it required human technology and wizz'ik ingenuity. Talulo's little scheme was now a multi-species effort. It didn't sound easy, but it appeared to have achieved moderate success.

"Let me see what I can do," Denton said, and walked over to his hovering workbench. George stayed with Talulo and Blek to chat, learning as much as he could from this unique encounter.

Denton leaned against the workbench and summoned a soldering iron from inside one of the compartments. From there, he turned on a magnifying lens and flashlight to get a close look at the work to be done. After a few minutes of soldering and moving wires carefully, Denton held the particle shocker at arm's length and activated it, satisfied with the white pulse of light that flicked out from the toothed end.

"All set," Denton said, and he twirled the shocker in his hand, handing the butt end to Blek. The little wizz'ik clapped his hands and honked. Talulo whistled and sang with happiness.

George clapped a hand onto Denton's shoulder. "Great work!"

"Blek, get Denton a good one," Talulo said to the wizz'ik. Blek turned and launched himself headfirst into his rock tunnel.

A moment later, there was a hiss, a zap, and then a bubbling noise emitted from the tunnel, followed by a generous slurping sound. Blek emerged, wiping his snout with his forearm like an old man wiping milk away from his mustache. He held a sparkling blue-and-yellow gemstone up to Denton.

"For me?" Denton asked. Talulo nodded and observed the gemstone with envy.

"That stone sings a beautiful song, Denton." Talulo said, grunting and pointing. "Eliana will enjoy the tune."

Denton blushed. George turned to him with his eyebrows raised. "Well, there you go." He chuckled. George tapped a finger against the side of his head, reminding Denton the auk'nai could read their intentions.

"Thanks, I'm sure she'll love it," Denton said, and took the gift from the tiny hand. He regretted it immediately; the acidic residue on the exterior of the gem burned his palm as he touched it. He bobbled the gemstone in his hand, then caught it with his sleeve. Blek honked and clapped, amused by Denton's minor pain.

With the m'unjo sauce rubbed off, Denton held the gemstone up to the dueling Kamarian moons. He peered through the beautiful raw stone and watched it reflect the twilight blue.

"Blek, it was nice meeting you." George tickled the bottom of Blek's chin under his snout, which resulted in a delightful honk and a little dance from the creature.

Talulo whistled with joy.

"We should head back," George said.

Denton took another look at the raw gemstone and pocketed it in his scout jacket before heading down the slope after George. The twin moons danced in the sky above the surveyor as it cruised back to the campsite.

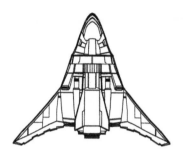

TWENTY-NINE

AT SUNRISE, THE SCOUTS began breaking down their campsites. Denton and Eliana worked together, separating the tent equipment and cleaning their area. George walked over to the nearby hover mule and plopped his gear onto its surface. As Eliana collapsed the tent poles, she turned to Denton and asked, "So, what were you two up to last night?"

"Us two? What do you mean?" Denton asked as he rolled the nylon tent into a cylinder, doing his best to play dumb.

"Don't lie to me, Denton Castus. You can't lie to an auk'nai *or* to a woman," Eliana said, and shoved him playfully.

"Denton escorted me for a midnight stroll around the valley," George said. "I was going to go alone, but he offered to walk with me. Nothing nefarious, Elly."

"Something funky is going on here, and I'm going to figure it out." She squinted her eyes and darted an accusing finger between them. "You just wait and see." Eliana backed away from them and left to go instruct her team of medical staff.

"I think she bought it," Denton said, and rubbed his hands together as he stood up from his task. George shook his head.

"So, what are you going to do with that gem?" George asked.

"I have an idea, but it's a secret." Denton winked and thumbed his jacket pocket to ensure the gem was still safely there.

"Keeping secrets from your partner in crime. That's bad business." George laughed. A sharp whistle from the sky interrupted them. They looked up to see an auk'nai circling above. George stepped into an open area away from Denton and waved his daunoren whistle. Dust and grass kicked up as Talulo landed in front of George. Denton and Eliana walked over to join in on the conversation.

"Morning, Talulo. What brings you here?" George asked.

"Talulo would like to help you learn the song of the jungle," the young auk'nai said. "Easy to get lost in the jungle. Talulo knows the tune, and in return, you teach Talulo human ways."

Denton remembered that information was a form of currency among auk'nai.

"Did Mag'Ro send you to do this?" Eliana asked.

"Mag'Ro does not know. Talulo does this for friends." Talulo cooed.

"We can return tomorrow with supplies if that works well for you?" George asked respectfully. Talulo cooed again and nodded his beak, then launched himself into the sky.

"New scout tomorrow, then?" Denton asked.

"Sounds that way. We'll have to take a smaller team, though. Kamarian jungles are dangerous. With fewer people, we can remain undetected more easily." George kept his eyes on the auk'nai as he vanished into the tall blue canopy of the Azure Vault.

———◆———

Hours later, the team returned from Apusticus and wrapped up their assignments. Night blanketed Odysseus Colony. Clouds hung in the air, blotting out the moonlight. The autumn breeze swept clusters of leaves around as if a maid were tidying up a house.

Denton walked to the Castus Machine Shop. He reached into his pocket and pulled out the raw gemstone he'd received from

Talulo and Blek the night before, wondering if anyone would be awake at this late hour.

The shop was quiet and dark as Denton entered. He turned the lights on with a command from his soothreader and watched them flicker to life. Denton ran a hand across a workbench as he moved through the garage, inspecting the gemstone he held in his other hand. This garage had been his life, but that seemed so long ago.

There was a loud shuffle coming from the kitchen. Denton suddenly felt like an intruder.

"Damn rat monster again!" It was the familiar voice of his father and the equally familiar sound of a blunder-blaster being pumped. Michael Castus flung himself from the kitchen wearing only a tank top and boxer shorts. He aimed an old buckshot particle weapon at Denton.

"Oh, it's just you." Michael sighed with relief. He pumped the gun once more to deactivate it, then placed it down on the workbench to his right. "Thought you were one of them little bastards that's been terrorizing my shop."

"What little bastards?" Denton asked.

"It's like a flying rat-octopus thing." Michael waved his hand toward the ceiling. "They got into the shop about a week ago and have been eatin' some of our tools. I've been sleepin' in the kitchen, hoping to catch one in the act."

"Sounds like a bully bloke," Denton said. "Those things can eat through anything."

"Anyway, what's up, Dent?" Michael asked. "It's a little late for a visit, isn't it?"

Denton held the raw gemstone up for his father to see and said, "I need some help. If you're up for it."

"Oh yeah? What do you have in mind?"

"I want to refine this and forge it into a ring." Denton paused for a breath before he added, "For Eliana."

Michael grinned, showing all his teeth through his tangled mess of beard. He nodded and said, "You know, I always liked her more than I liked you."

"Sounds about right." Denton laughed.

"You hear that, Brynn?" Michael shouted, not turning his head.

Brynn Castus emerged from the kitchen in her pajamas. She shuffled over to Denton and gave him a big hug. "Yes, I did. This is amazing!"

When Brynn released Denton from the embrace, Michael said, "Alright, let's get started."

A few hours later, Denton had designed the ring on his sketchpad, Michael had forged the ring with a Ganymede Palladium ingot, and Brynn had cut the raw gemstone to fit the centerpiece. The ring was ready.

"Ain't that the prettiest damn thing. If Eliana doesn't say yes, I will," Michael said.

Denton held it in his hand. His design was influenced by the mystical fountain in Apusticus, with interweaving pieces leading up to a stone. He couldn't make the gem float, but he could simulate the feelings it gave him with his design.

"Thank you, both of you. I think Elly's gonna love it," Denton said.

"No problem, Denny," Michael said, and looked at Brynn. "Let's just hope it fits."

"Yeah, no kidding," Denton said, plopping the ring in his jacket pocket. He was about to put the tools away and say good night when he heard a strange clucking noise coming from the corner of the garage.

A pile of tools fell over, and a weird little animal jumped out from the rubble. It had no arms, only two wings that led into a ratlike tail. The creature's face had one big eyeball and tentacles dangling from its oily chin. It grasped a socket wrench in its undulating maw.

"Hells! Get my blunder-blaster!" Michael shouted, pushing Denton aside to rush the bully bloke. The bully growled a muddy, bubbling snarl. It gobbled up a socket wrench before flying off toward the roof and squeezing between some rafters, evading Michael once again.

"I'll get you next time, you bastard! You hear me?" he shouted, shaking his fist at his archnemesis.

After some time spent putting the tools away, Denton said good night and went back to his apartment.

THIRTY

THREE YEARS AGO

DAY 520 OF ROELIN'S EXODUS

CAPTAIN ROELIN RAIKE SAT up in his bed and held a hand to his forehead. He felt dizzy, on the verge of vomiting. He shifted his body and hung his feet over the side of the bed, noticing the bloody bandage on his arm.

"Damn it!" Roelin shouted. Nhymn had not gored him like this since one of their first conversations. He reached over to a bottle filled with purified water and chugged the entirety of it. As he waited for the dizziness to fade, he searched the bunk room for a message Nhymn had made with his blood and found nothing.

Eventually, Roelin stood and left the bunk room. The hallway between the bunk and the bridge was free of bloody scrawlings as well, so he continued on with his routine, sure he would stumble upon another question from his mental captor.

The door to the command bridge slid open, and Roelin stepped in. He felt his neck tense up. His fingers tingled, and his breaths became short and shallow. Across the walls, written in his own blood, were questions.

WHAT IS THE UNDRIEL?

WHERE ARE THE UNDRIEL?

HOW DID THE UNDRIEL RID THEMSELVES OF THE HUMANS?

And the most unsettling of all:

WHEN WILL THE UNDRIEL ARRIVE?

Roelin was paralyzed. Nhymn had finally turned the mental lock and opened the door in his mind that revealed the Undriel. Roelin knew now he could hide no secrets from her. Nhymn would dig out whatever answers she needed in time.

Roelin fell backward out of the room through the open doorway. He was still weak from blood loss, and the shock had caused him to lose his balance. Seeing how much blood she had used to write with made him feel even more disoriented. Roelin lay on his back in the hallway and stared at the flickering light above.

He heard the footsteps of a large creature slowly walking toward him.

Has something gotten past the perimeter trap and entered the ship?

How did it get through the air lock?

Roelin watched as a creature with an ivory-beaked skull and a sharp bone horn slowly moved over him, then stared down at her prisoner. Her open eye sockets dripped black tar.

Nhymn was real now.

The Siren pressed a heavy, taloned foot down on Roelin's chest, and he heaved under the weight. She was physically touching him, completing the sensory overload. She bent down, oozing her hot ebony bile onto his face.

In Roelin's mind, he could hear Nhymn whisper, *"No more secrets. Fix this ship. Take us to Sympha."*

Roelin's torture was about to become more real than it had ever been during the past two years. Nhymn removed her foot from Roelin's chest and stepped over him, her taloned claws scratching the floor as she ambled down the hall. She moved back into the darkness and faded away.

Nhymn was *real*.

———— ♦ ————

PRESENT DAY

The Kamarian jungle breathed.

Flat alien leaves sprouting from obscure trees rolled in the humid air as if treading water in an ocean of heat. Smaller creatures observed the human scout team through perches in the vines, vanishing from sight the moment they were discovered. Shadows concealed the jungle floor, with spears of light pushing through the dense upper canopy. The shady trees had jet-black trunks that bled a crimson sap. Long, wine-red leaves draped from their branches.

Sergeant Clint Foster and his fellow marine escorts, Andrew Louis and Jess Combs, walked ahead of the team. Their machetes sliced through the thick vegetation, carving the first human trail in the alien wilderness.

The team was smaller than a typical scouting expedition, just eight scouts and one auk'nai tracker. George Tanaka and Marie Viray led the scientific portion of the team, scanning everything they saw with their bioscopes and sharing notes.

Eliana was the field doctor. She carried a special medical kit with a high-range receiver that, if needed, could contact Lieutenant Commander Rocco Gainax on the *Rogers* in an emergency.

Denton and Fergus were on hand to assist with anything the rest of the team needed, filling in a generalist role. Denton trailed a hover mule behind him through the foliage of the jungle filled with camping equipment and rations for the journey. Fergus had a small guitar slung to his backpack, something he liked to bring with him to play around the campfire.

Talulo was their tour guide. He was proud to help his new

human friends study the ancient jungles under the Sharp Top, the mountain peak known for its hooklike appearance.

Eliana brushed her hand against one of the dark jungle tree trunks, admiring the macabre timber. She reached up and felt a flat crimson leaf in her hand. It felt waxy yet dripped moisture in beads.

Denton brought the hover mule over to her and admired the tree with her. He said, "These bleeding trees almost give the jungle a haunted-house vibe."

"I think it's beautiful in its own grim way," Eliana said as if she were in a dream. She walked away from the tree, letting her hand trail behind her as she investigated the upper canopy. She turned toward George and Marie and asked, "Do we have a name for these trees?"

Marie lowered her bioscope and said, "Poe heartlings."

"Fitting." Eliana smiled. She looked toward the marines as they hacked away at the thick foliage. Beyond the soldiers, mist shrouded the jungle.

"Poe heartlings," Denton echoed, looking up into the ghoulish trees.

Fergus chuckled and said, "I'm gon'nae go ahead and keep callin' 'em creepy, if ye don't mind."

Clint Foster swung his machete once more and stopped abruptly. He held his hand outward, alerting the team to stay quiet until he could further assess the situation. Talulo hopped forward and poked his head over the sergeant's shoulder, ignorant to the meaning of human gestures.

"*Hey!* Sarge said to keep still!" Lance Corporal Andrew Louis hissed at the auk'nai.

Talulo let out a loud caw. Ahead, lemurbats scurried away from the carcass of a large dead animal. Talulo turned to Andrew and grunted, "Only lemurbats picking at dead things."

"It's not the lemurbats that worry me," Clint said, his synthetic voice box emphasizing his warning.

It was the gigantic carcass of an arcophant. The skin had been

261

ripped to shreds, exposing dried blood and viscera. Angry lemurbats barked at the scouts from the trees, challenging those who would try to steal their loot.

"Lemurbats do this?" Andrew asked. "Didn't think the little bastards ate meat."

George approached the arcophant carcass, "No, they didn't kill this animal. They do scavenge, though. Criminals of opportunity." He bioscanned the body. "You have to be a pretty capable predator to take down an arcophant," George said as he waved his finger at some ripped-up foliage and debris from the struggle, "especially if it had its herd with it."

"Dray'va," Talulo grunted, inspecting a footprint. Three long-clawed toes in the front, one in the back. Claw marks on the body and the ground, and wounds in the Poe heartlings told the story of a vicious predator.

George turned toward Talulo and said, "We haven't seen a dray'va. What can you tell us, Talulo?"

"Very dangerous, dray'va hunt in duos," Talulo said, turning and sniffing the arcophant remains. "We leave before dray'va come back."

"Aw, man, I wanted a good fight." Andrew spat on the carcass.

As they continued through the jungle, the team discovered many new plants. Marie scanned everything she could and read the analysis Homer returned. She sighed happily and said, "I could probably come here every day for the rest of my life and not have enough time to scan all the beautiful plant life here."

George said, "I could say the same about the wildlife as well. This place is an endless feast. How about we retire to a nice tree house?"

"Sure! You build it, and I'll live in it," Marie said, playfully shoving George as they laughed.

The Poe heartlings came to an end, revealing a forest of trumpet-shaped trees. They were as tall as buildings, with splintered fractal shapes like blood vessels made of vegetation. Their bases were an aqua green that faded to crimson at their bell-shaped extremities.

Here, the jungle sloped downward into an arched rock formation that led to a lower jungle level below. To each side were more rock archways acting like alien staircases covered in trumpet trees. Scouts had seen formations like this before on Kamaria; they called them "rib cages." It was as if some giant beast had died and decayed into the jungle itself.

On their way down the rock archway, they disturbed a flock of eventide gliderflies. The beautiful alien butterflies lit up the jungle for them as they lowered farther into its depths. Eliana grabbed Denton's arm as they walked.

"It's like the Glimmer Glade," Eliana said, reminiscing about their secret hideaway back at Odysseus Colony. Denton rubbed her hand and smiled at her.

"Look," Talulo said, pointing forward.

"Incredible," Marie said, her mouth hanging open.

The jungle ahead was a parade of marching flora, the trees uprooting and replanting themselves. The golden child of botany and biology: a walking tree.

"Follow Talulo. Come and see," the auk'nai said, and flew toward the jungle parade. Marie looked at George with her eyes widened in excitement, then took off in a hurry toward the tree creatures. George smiled and ran after them. Clint gestured toward Andrew and Jess to stay on the hill and keep an eye out for danger.

"Yeah, sure, we'll babysit," Andrew said, and leaned against a rock. Jess shouldered her particle rifle and admired the view with a warm smile.

Fergus nudged Denton and winked. "Let's be very careful where we get our wood for the campfires tonight, yah ken?"

Denton laughed through his nose and nodded.

Eliana and Denton walked closer to the parade.

The herd of walking trees marched in a row through the jungle, sunlight streaming through their dense canopy. Each tree was unique, and had clearly grown in whichever way it needed to best absorb sunlight and walk away from the shade. They all had multiple enormous legs, like giant cellar spiders. The scouts had to crane their necks to see where the legs joined together.

The trees took their time, and their slow pace made it safe to walk among them. Marie and George pointed at various parts of the trees' bodies as they made their observations. Eyestalks with glowing eyeballs floating in bulbous pods popped out of many areas between sliding pieces of tree bark, giving the trees complete 360-degree vision.

"So, George." Marie put her elbow on his shoulder, leaning against him as they both admired the parade. "What do we call our baby?"

"Our baby?" George said, confused.

"Well, it's a plant, but it's also an animal. This one is both our departments. What do we call it?" she said.

"The honor is yours," George said, inviting her to name them.

Marie considered the creatures for a moment, then offered, "Colossal timbermen."

George nodded his approval, then spread his arms out and walked closer to the newly named subjects, "Good afternoon, timbermen!"

The timbermen paid no attention to the tiny invader, marching forward to find light and water. The parade extended as far as they could see. They seemed very careful to not knock down their immobile brothers, only stepping into the spaces between the trumpet-shaped trees. Their blunt-ended feet smashed into the dirt, obliterating small vegetation but leaving the jungle floor fertile in circular patches in the wake of their march.

Lemurbats scurried into the dirt patches and ate up any exposed grubs. Satisfied, they would scramble back up the timbermen legs and hurry into small cubbyholes in the bark.

"I bet the timbermen appreciate the lemurbats acting as a cleaning crew, eating all the bugs," Denton said.

Eliana nodded and said, "A mutually beneficial relationship."

"Excellent observation," George said with a proud smile.

Marie pointed upward and grabbed George's shoulder. "Look up there!" She pointed toward a lemurbat hollow.

A mother lemurbat had returned to deliver grubs to her young. Hanging from the ceiling of the hollow was a timberman eyestalk. As the mother entered the hollow, the eyestalk spurted out a mist of pollen, coating the grubs and the mother on her way in.

"I bet that's how timbermen reproduce," Marie said. "The lemurbats eat the pollen on their grubs, and when they jump down to collect more, they fertilize the fresh dirt below."

"Fascinating," George agreed.

"A parade of life," Eliana stated.

Denton craned his neck to stare straight up, noticing the birds flying in and out of holes higher up the timberman trunks. The parade was a walking ecosystem. "How far do they travel?" he asked Talulo.

Talulo flew up to a knee joint on one of the timbermen and fished out a grub to eat. "Trees come here in winter, leave in summer," he said between bites.

"They migrate?" Denton asked.

Fergus recognized the behavior. "Ah, like Callisto geese," he said, referring to the domesticated birds introduced to the garden moon he'd come from. Many old Earth animals had found a second life on Callisto, but most had been left behind in the scramble of the *Telemachus* exodus. No one knew if the Undriel had a specific fate designed for the animals of the Sol System.

The team stayed with the parade for the rest of the afternoon. Marie and George took photos and samples from the timbermen. Talulo continued to show them more things about the timbermen, having spent many days in his youth among their branches.

———◆———

The sun receded over the Kamarian jungle, and the last light remaining was a campfire surrounded by humans. Fergus played his guitar and sang old songs his grandfather had taught him as a boy. Talulo joined him by whistling and hooting. Denton, Eliana, George, and Marie sipped on juicy jungle bulbs and discussed their findings of the day. Andrew, Clint, and Jess kept watch on the perimeter, sharing war stories and comparing scars.

The campsite rested in an open clearing near a rocky ledge just outside of the jungle. The area may have been burned by a wildfire in the past. Twisted dead trees regained some life as vines coiled around their carcasses. The stars twinkled above them like an eternal tide washing in.

Fergus and Talulo's song ended, and everyone clapped. George asked, "Talulo, what do the auk'nai call this place?"

Talulo whistled out a birdcall, then translated, "In Sol Common, the Tangle Maze. Did you humans like it?"

"Yes, we find it fascinating," Marie said. "In one day, we have almost doubled the entries in our database of Kamaria's flora. I'm in heaven."

"We have our excellent navigator to thank for this adventure." Denton raised his juice bulb to Talulo. The young auk'nai whistled and bobbed his head in appreciation.

"To Talulo." Fergus stood. "May your feathers stay fluffy and your beak stay sharp. Or something." The group shared a laugh, and each took a gulp of their bulbs.

Eventually, the night came to an end.

Denton and Eliana were the last two awake. Eliana cleaned their camping zone, picking up loose garbage and incinerating it in the mobile combustor.

Denton grabbed a bucket of water, preparing to douse the last stubborn flames of the campfire. Just as he was about to tip the bucket and smother the fire, he saw something near the tree line of the jungle.

Just beyond the encasement fence was his mother, Brynn Castus, as clear as the fire before him.

"Mom?" he shouted in confusion.

Eliana turned quickly to see Denton walking toward the encasement barrier, reaching to turn it off.

"No, wait!" she shouted, and grabbed Denton's hand just before he could deactivate the fence. Andrew was on watch and heard the commotion. He walked across the campsite, one hand on the pistol that rested on his hip.

"My mom's out there! How the Hells is that possible?" Denton shouted. He looked out into the dark jungle again and confirmed it. Brynn was standing just behind the tree line.

"Denton, calm down! That's *not* your mother!" Eliana shouted at him, trying to get to him through his panic.

"Then, who is that?" Denton asked, watching his mother take a step forward out of the foliage. She had not said a word as she'd stepped closer to the fence. Denton could see the unnatural look in her eyes. It was as if something was wearing his mother as a costume, and it didn't fit right. When people recognized each other, even in pictures, there was always a particular sort of life behind their eyes. That life was not here.

"Elly, what is that?" Denton moved his hand away from the containment fence button, now scared of the approaching farce. Brynn took another step closer, with a vacant stare like a deer haunted by the headlights of an oncoming semitruck.

"It's called a Kamarian nightsnare," Andrew said as he removed his pistol from the holster. "I say go ahead and open the fence, let me kill the thing."

Eliana put her hand on Andrew's pistol. "*No!* It's doing nothing wrong. We can handle this."

"Suit yourself." Andrew looked at the creature one last time. "Fuckin' creepy. Looks just like my ex-girlfriend," he said, and walked back to his post.

"That's my mom, *jerk!*" Denton shouted, although he regretted it immediately, realizing that this creature was only a poor imitation of her. Andrew didn't care; he returned to his mindless entertainment on his soothreader on the other side of the camp.

Eliana put a hand on Denton's arm. "No, the nightsnare has the same mental capability that the auk'nai have. The only difference is it doesn't absorb mental information. It reflects it. The snare has no idea what it's projecting back at you. It only knows you see something that can lure you into a vulnerable position."

"We're being hunted?" Denton didn't take his eyes off the horrible monster beyond the fence.

Eliana glared at the nightsnare, but it wasn't Brynn Castus she saw. The glowing eyes of a demonic Roelin Raike stared back at her. He wore his combat suit without the helmet. The suit looked as it did on the night he'd murdered her father, covered in his blood. Roelin stepped forward, but Eliana stood her ground.

"We're safe, just keep the fence up, and he can't get in," Eliana said flatly. They watched the phantom move further into the light, and it became more obvious that it was a horrifying homunculus instead of a real human.

A twig snapped in the forest behind the nightsnare, and it jerked its head to the side to see the source of the noise. Something in the forest squealed in fright. The snare launched itself back into the jungle, transforming into a brown monstrosity with long, clawed arms and a mouth that zippered up from its pelvis to the top of its head. The foliage shook with a struggle, followed by a hushed silence. The hunter had caught its prey.

"He's gone," Eliana said.

"*He?*" Denton asked. He wondered what form the snare had taken to lure Eliana.

She turned back to the fire, grabbing the water bucket from the ground. "We should get some sleep, we hike out tomorrow," Eliana said, then dumped the water on the fire, snuffing the life out of it.

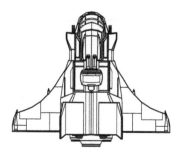

THIRTY-ONE

TWO YEARS AGO

DAY 820 OF ROELIN'S EXODUS

ROELIN WAS CURSED, A husk of his former self. Every time he attempted to resist the Siren's persuasion, he failed.

There were several attempts at suicide.

Roelin once tried to hang himself, only to awaken sitting in the chair he was going to step off with a shredded rope in his hands. The gun he was going to use to paint over Nhymn's incessant questioning with his own bloody stain was thrown across the room. An attempt to starve himself to death resulted in awakening to the remnants of some dead animal ripped to pieces before him. He had no clue where it had come from, but he appeared to have eaten it raw.

He had found a way to digest things humans had no right eating. The cells in his body were evolving to fit the needs of the Siren, creating some sort of cockroach out of Roelin Raike.

Roelin was no longer a man, and therefore, he could not die as one.

Nhymn knew everything about him now, and Roelin knew nothing more about her. She had all the cards in the deck, and Roelin was handing her his chips. Life was a blur—

repairs were made, equipment maintained, nightmares every night, and questions every day—no greater torture could be done to man.

One morning on the bridge, Roelin realized he may be able to get the *Astraeus* operational enough to return to the colony. Nhymn had shown Roelin where Sympha would be, but it was double the distance he needed to return to Odysseus Colony.

Roelin knew he'd left Odysseus a mass murderer, and that upon return, he was capable of even more violence. But the crazed part of his mind knew it was the only way to break the cycle he was locked into. Roelin had to risk it. He hoped the colony could defend itself against whatever monster he had become.

The only impossible part would be convincing Nhymn to allow him to do it.

———— ◆ ————

PRESENT DAY

Denton awoke to the smell of freshly brewed coffee and the wispy breeze of the cliffside air. He opened his tent to see Fergus pouring himself a cup of the brew and taking in the view.

"Morning, lad!" Fergus said, and offered Denton a cup.

"Thanks," Denton said as he took the coffee and tested its heat on his lip. Satisfied with the temperature, he took in a gulp and sighed. "Good stuff."

"Aye. Only the best." Fergus winked and took a sip of his own cup. They peered out over the cliff ledge to the jungle below. An expanse of alien trees and rock formations spread to the horizon. A fog hung in the canopy, and wispy tendrils of mist reached from the treetops like long fingers grabbing for the sun.

The jungle covered the side of the mountain nearly all the way to its hooklike peak. Denton had never seen a summit quite like it before; it was a shape unique to Kamaria. Large waterfalls cascaded down the side of the knife-edged crest, resulting in a large lake at the mountain's base. Perhaps it would make a good target for an expedition.

Kamarian birds fluttered from the misty canopy as the distant call of whatever exotic beast roared them into action. From this distance, the bellows of monsters did not stir panic in Denton and Fergus.

The sound of liquid splattering against a rock in a steady stream interrupted the peace of the morning. Lance Corporal Andrew Louis was relieving himself just beyond the tents. The marine snorted in mucus from his nose and hawked out a large wad of spit at the target he was thoroughly lubricating. It made a violent, wet splat.

Denton sighed. "Well, time to get packed up anyway."

Fergus nodded and moved to his tent as the others began coming out into the sunlight. Eliana emerged and grabbed a cup of coffee. "Morning," she said quietly. Denton gave her a quick kiss on the cheek. They heard a whistle coming from below the cliff edge. Talulo ascended into the sky before them, twirling majestically. He opened his wingspan and allowed himself to drift gracefully down onto the ledge.

"Talulo found breakfast. A favorite among Apusticus," Talulo announced with a grunt. He bobbled pear-shaped fruits in his arms in front of them.

Marie Viray clapped her hands and exclaimed, "Excellent work." She took the fruit over to the hover mule and removed a knife from her hip holster. "I'll cut these up for a nice breakfast while you take down the campsite," she said to George as he exited their tent.

"Oh, is that right?" George said. Marie held the knife upward and raised her eyebrows. George put his hands up and said, "Oh, that *is* right." He smiled.

The scouts spent their time packing up equipment and getting ready for the hike back to the *Rogers*. Denton shouldered his backpack and checked the hover mule. The mule had proven it could take on any terrain, having navigated the jungle floor with no issues on the hike in. After a breakfast provided by their auk'nai escort, they were ready to hike back to the *Rogers* spacecraft.

"Everyone all set?" Sergeant Clint Foster asked, pulling his rifle up and resting it on his shoulder, barrel toward the sky. Andrew and Jess nodded at him.

"Looks that way," George said, double-checking the area to make sure they'd left nothing behind.

"Alright, everyone," Clint said. "Let's head back. I'm sure Rocco missed us."

Freshly caffeinated from the coffee, Fergus played his guitar while Talulo sang a song in auk'nai. Only George could understand a handful of the words, but the others appreciated the beauty and upbeat nature of the song.

Once they entered the dense jungle, the music stopped. The natural jungle noises filled the air, echoing off the thick canopy. A creature hooted, birds twittered, and bugs clicked. Each footfall added to the jungle orchestra. As they hiked, the high-noon sun burned off the low-hanging fog, revealing more of the undergrowth.

They reached the area where the colossal timbermen had been marching the day before, now only a path of mashed-up mud. If they had not witnessed the parade, they would have never guessed it had happened. The trumpet trees remained unmolested by the ceremony, standing tall and proud under the rays of sun that poked through the upper canopy.

Eliana stared forward with a vacant look in her eyes. Denton had noticed that she had been quiet since the encounter with the nightsnare the night before. Had the snare used the form of her father to try and lure her? Denton felt it was better not to ask.

They came to the natural stone archways that led to the upper jungle. The *Rogers* was only a short hike beyond this point. Clint led the team forward with Jess and Andrew bringing up the rear. Denton peered over the ledge and watched as the lower jungle layer fell away from them as they ascended the rib cage of rock.

Denton noticed podlike shapes drooping from some of the trumpet trees. He nudged George and asked, "Were those there when we first came through here?"

George squinted and looked at the hanging pods. He unholstered his bioscope and began to lift it when a vibration began rolling through the jungle. Small rocks chipped away from the stone archway they stood upon, and the trees in the distance started to shake.

"Aye, what's all this?" Fergus asked.

The loud roar of a hundred beasts charging through the jungle below filled the air. Denton peered over to see a stampede of enormous red monsters, each with three large horns protruding from their snouts and tufts of long yellow hair tracing their spines. They crashed into each other as they ran in a panic. One of the beasts bashed into the side of the stone archway, knocking the scout team off-balance.

"Hold on to something!" Clint shouted.

A familiar roar filled the jungle. Talulo's ears perked up, and he shrunk into himself in fear. Eliana looked wide-eyed at Denton and shouted, "Titanovore!"

A crash in the trees announced its arrival. The massive quadruped snapped its jaws at the stampede, looking for purchase. It chased the red beasts under the stone archway, crashing about wildly. Denton heard a screeching sound and looked up.

The pods hanging from the trumpet trees were not pods at all. They were giant, bat-like creatures awoken by the commotion in the jungle. They had huge black eyes and thin snouts filled with sharp teeth. One screeched and propelled itself from a tree, almost colliding with Denton as it attempted to flee the chaos.

"Everyone, look out!" Denton shouted.

More of the bats left their perches and filled the air around them. Another bat knocked into Denton, almost shoving him off the stone archway. He caught himself on his side near the ledge and looked over to see the red beasts continuing their stampede below. A titanovore smashed into a trumpet tree and uprooted it. The tree fell, crashing into more trees and sending up more bats.

Marie shouted, "We have to get out of here! *We have to—*"

Marie was swept sideways by a giant bat creature and sent over the edge of the stone archway. Denton watched her disappear into a tangle of trees below.

"Marie!" George shouted, and fell to his knees. Jess caught him before he could jump off after her in a fruitless attempt to save her.

"Fire on the fliers!" Clint ordered. The marines began shooting at the bats, hoping to force them to move around the scouts instead of through them.

Denton thought quickly. He grabbed the hover mule and banged his fist against a side compartment, revealing a long rope. He snatched the rope and tied it to a boulder.

"Denton, wait!" Eliana shouted, but he was moving too quickly. Denton gripped the rope tightly and hopped from the ledge, aiming for the area where he had seen Marie fall. Halfway down, Denton stopped his descent to remain still as a titanovore rushed past him after its prey. The stampede had moved on farther into the jungle. He only hoped that Marie had not already been crushed by the beasts.

Denton slid through the canopy of the lower jungle, knocking through branches. He landed on the ground hard, kicking up dust and dead leaves with the impact. Denton unholstered his pistol to ward off any predators that may have been attracted to the noise of the stampede. His eyes darted around, searching for Marie.

Marie was curled on the ground in the fetal position. Her arm and leg were bent in unnatural directions, clearly broken from the impact. Denton went to her side and checked her pulse, reassured when he heard her groan from the injury. Talulo whistled from above and landed near them with a loud thud. He knelt next to Marie and let out a sad bird chortle.

"Marie, we're here!" Denton said to her. He shouted to the scouts above, "She's alive. But she's hurt bad." Then he looked at

Talulo and said, "Go get Eliana."

The auk'nai nodded and launched himself upward into the canopy.

Denton didn't hear Eliana come down the rope and approach them. She joined Denton near Marie and opened her medical kit. First, she fixed Marie's neck in place with a neck brace.

"Help me move her," Eliana said. Together, they shifted Marie, laying her on her back. Eliana gave Marie a shot in the arm for the pain, then went to work getting her bones realigned as best she could. When Marie was stabilized, Eliana removed two rods from her kit and shook them, causing the rods to extend.

"Put this on her side," Eliana said. Denton placed the rod lengthwise next to Marie. Eliana clicked a button on her end of the rod, and Denton followed her example. An encasement field shimmered into existence and propped Marie up from the jungle floor, grabbing a few fallen leaves with it. Eliana twisted a dial on the side of her rod, and Marie lifted upward into the air horizontally. Denton recognized a device on the end of the rod that looked similar to the device on the ground sail.

"We have her on a stretcher." Eliana yelled upward to the rest of the team. "Talulo will need to raise her up."

"We're ready." Fergus shouted from above. Talulo rejoined Eliana and Denton, nodding his beak toward Marie's hurt body like a puppy worried for its master.

"Keep Marie steady," Eliana said to Talulo. He cooed and twisted the dial on the auk'nai device on the stretcher. They rose steadily from the ground, Talulo hovering as close as possible to Marie as they ascended.

"Good thinking with the rope," Eliana said.

"I hope it's enough," Denton said.

Talulo got Marie safely to the top.

"You first," Denton said, holding the rope for Eliana. She nodded and began climbing as the team above pulled her up to hasten the process. Denton waited for it to return.

Denton noticed he didn't hear anything after Eliana had left. There was a slight breeze, and even though he could see the jungle foliage swaying, he heard nothing. He turned around to inspect the area further, confused.

Near the trumpet trees, Denton saw a shape in the shadows. He thought it might be one of the horned beasts that had ravaged the jungle, so he pulled out his pistol, keeping it in his right hand near his hip.

A low-tone hum quietly reached Denton. The shape emerged from the darkness, a giant walking skeleton held together by tentacles. It had a bull-shaped skull with horns and one eyeless socket like a bottomless black pit. The creature took the shape of a mythical centaur, with four skeletal hooves marching the monster forward into the light and a long upper body with two muscular arms that terminated in sharp talons.

Denton recognized it from archive footage during his studies for the scout assessment. It was the stone sentry from the crypt outside the City of the Dead. But this was no immobile statue; it eased toward him with eerily slow, precise movements.

Denton felt like he couldn't move, and sweat began to bead on his forehead. The sentry stood over him now, drenching him in shadow. It bent forward and leveled its head with Denton's. He couldn't look away from the abyssal eye socket that was dripping with blackness.

Denton's eyes widened, his head jerked backward, and his pupils vibrated like gelatin orbs. Denton wanted to shriek in agony, feeling like his spine was going to snap just under the base of his skull. He became engulfed in darkness.

Then, he was no longer in the jungle. Denton was standing in a field of grass.

He turned, looking for the jungle and his friends. Denton found nothing but an empty field. The breeze kicked up, and the gusts of wind whipped past him, forcing him to whirl back around. He allowed his eyes to focus.

Before him was the crypt near the City of the Dead. The opening of the cave looked like a vicious maw ready to devour him. The howling winds attempted to suck him into the cave. His feet slid forward in the wet grass.

Denton felt something slam into the back of his head.

The rope had been tossed down from the upper ledge and collided with his head. Denton was back in the Tangle Maze on his knees among the leaves of the jungle floor. He felt like he had just seen something but couldn't recall what it was, like the fading memory of a terrible nightmare. He shook his head, searching the area, but he was alone.

"You alright down there, kid?" Andrew called from above.

"Yeah, coming up!" Denton shouted, noticing he had his pistol in his right hand. He slid it back into its holster and grabbed the rope. He climbed up, minding the pain in his head the whole way.

Just beyond the trumpet trees, the sentry watched Denton ascend. In the shadows of the tree, it crumbled to dust and was swept away into oblivion by the gentle breeze.

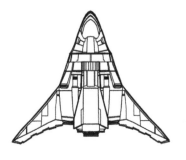

THIRTY-TWO

"STAY WITH ME, MARIE!" Eliana gasped, panting as she maintained her pace with the rest of the team while checking Marie's pulse on the hover stretcher. They broke through the tree line and rushed toward the *Rogers* spacecraft.

Rocco Gainax was standing on the ramp. "The med bay is ready. What's her status?" he asked as they scrambled past him.

"Won't know the full extent of her injuries until we get her inside. Better start packing up just in case," Eliana said.

"On it," Sergeant Clint Foster said. Denton, George, Andrew, and Jess began to gather the scouting equipment scattered around the *Rogers*. Fergus was about to join them when Eliana stopped him.

"I need your help," she said.

"Of course," Fergus said, and pushed Marie's stretcher from behind into the bay. Fergus was the only other scout on the team with medical training.

Denton had just grabbed a crate of supplies and was pushing it toward the ship when he noticed Talulo talking to a small wizz'ik near the tree line. Denton shouted, "Talulo! We are leaving!"

"Talulo will fly back to Apusticus, do what you must," Talulo said, then pointed at the wizz'ik. "This is Talulo's new friend, Puppo!

She likes your ship!" Talulo cooed, then added, "Puppo says she liked the bigger ship more, though."

George grabbed another piece of equipment and stopped. *"Bigger ship?"* he whispered to himself.

The only ships they had used on their scouting trips were Pilgrim-class explorers. The *Odysseus's* approach vector would not have flown over this region, and the *Telemachus*, although still in stationary orbit, was not observable from Kamaria's surface.

"*Bigger* ship?" George repeated to himself. There was only one other ship it could have been. George's eyes widened.

"The *Astraeus*?" George shouted as he turned toward Talulo and Puppo.

"Possibly," Talulo said with a chortle. "Puppo says she saw it sail through the sky many orbits ago."

"Where?" George forgot Marie's emergency and left the equipment on the ground. He walked briskly up to them. "Where did she see the *Astraeus*?"

Denton saw George drop the equipment and shouted, "George! We have to go!" Talulo shrunk into himself, his brow raised like a puppy who had been caught chewing on the furniture. He turned to the wizz'ik and asked George's question, then turned back to George with the answer.

"Toward the mountain," Talulo grunted. He pointed to the south. "Sharp Top."

"Oh my God," George said. *"Roelin."*

"We need to get back to the colony," Denton said.

"Roelin is over that mountain!" George shouted. The *Rogers's* engines roared to life, filling the area with turbulent wind and dust.

"George!" Denton tried to reason.

"No, we need to go to Roelin."

"George, Marie is hurt. She could die!"

George's eyes darted around as he lowered his gaze to the ground. "Damn it all." he clenched his fists. Denton walked with George up the ramp, raising it behind them.

Talulo waited outside, wondering what he had done wrong.

———— ✦ ————

An hour later, Eliana and Fergus stepped out of the medical bay, drying their hands off with a towel. Eliana said, "Marie's stable, for now." She looked around the cargo bay of the *Rogers* at all the tense faces. "What's going on? Why haven't we taken off?"

There was a pregnant pause. No one said anything, but Eliana could sense that they all had something to say. She looked over to Denton. He sighed, but before he could speak, George said, "We got our first lead on Roelin's location."

Eliana dropped the towel she was drying her hands with. Hearing his name knocked her soul from her body. She felt like she had drifted away from herself and had closed her eyes, yet she stood with her eyes and mouth open, looking at George. She couldn't find words.

"What does that mean?" Fergus asked.

"It means—" George began.

"It means we might find some answers," Eliana said in a hushed tone. "We need to find him. Where is he?"

"Somewhere near the Sharp Top," George said.

"We can't. Marie needs our help," Denton reminded everyone. Eliana's eyes snapped toward him. She felt anger wash over her. She looked up and inhaled deeply, bringing herself back into rational thought.

"Marie will be fine," Fergus said. "I'll keep an eye on her."

"Do we have enough supplies?" Eliana asked the group.

Clint shared a glance with Andrew and Jess, and they nodded. He turned to Eliana and nodded to her.

"I'll talk with Talulo and see if he can navigate for us," George said.

"You *really* think that psycho is still alive?" Andrew asked. Eliana and George lanced him with a glare. Andrew didn't care, and continued, "What do you think, Sarge?"

Clint sighed and rubbed his hand against the scar near his throat, the injury that Roelin had given him the night of the massacre. He said with his synthetic voice box, "I don't know. The odds are not good for him."

"Roelin wasn't around for the lung-lock cure, correct?" Jess Combs asked.

"Right," George said. "We might find a ship log that can explain what he did that night. Even bones can provide answers."

Denton grunted and rubbed the side of his head. Eliana approached him and put a hand on his shoulder, attempting to soothe him. He was sweating.

"We should rest before we do anything. Take some time to prepare," Eliana said resolutely.

"We'll head out in the morning," Clint said.

"I'll go have that talk with Talulo. Maybe he can get us more information from that wizz'ik," George said, and walked toward the access door.

"Right." Fergus nodded and looked toward the floor. "I'll keep an eye on Marie. I want nothing to do with this Roelin business."

Eliana remembered Fergus on that night four years ago. He'd seen Dr. Wynter's murder, and he was the one who'd brought Eliana and Faye back from lung-lock, saving their lives. Fergus had earned his right to avoid seeing the monster Roelin Raike again.

"I just need to lie down," Denton said, inhaling sharply through his nose. He walked past Eliana toward the bunk room. The marines huddled together and began discussing the protocol going forward.

Eliana was alone in the cargo bay of the *Rogers*. Whenever she was alone, she felt like someone was standing behind her, ready to grab her. It was the uneasy sensation of being a survivor, like the world around her was prepared to correct itself and erase her. Eliana shuddered. She went outside to join George and Talulo.

Denton entered the bunk room, his head throbbing. He pushed the base of his wrist against his head, but no matter what he did, the pain was ceaseless. A low tone began growing in volume. He lay on his back and crushed his eyelids together.

He was pulled into unconsciousness.

THIRTY-THREE

DENTON FELT IT ON his eyelids first.

Crisp bursts of air followed by waves of heat. Snow and rain hit his face, only to evaporate before he could exhale. There was the sensation of a finger pressed hard against the middle of his brow. He winced with the building pain, blinking out a tear as he opened his eyes.

The cave near the City of the Dead loomed before Denton. He had never been here before—no one had since the first expedition more than four years prior. The clouds appeared and dissipated, the grass grew and died, the seasons came and went in a relentless display of time. A thousand years passed in a matter of heartbeats. There were no stone statues in the field before the cave like he had remembered from archive footage. Instead, it was just nature, living and dying in perpetuity.

The only constant was the cave, remaining steadfast as time charged forward.

Denton stood from the grass and walked toward the cave's entrance. Although the rapidly changing seasons blasted him with bursts of warmth and cold, the cave offered only a dull, damp air that clung to him.

Denton stepped in.

Hiding beneath a shroud of swirling mist, an ebony ooze covered the floor like a murky blanket. Denton was careful not to slip as he made his way down the slope.

Denton struggled to remember the data from the archives, trying to predict what he would find in the depths of the cave and prepare himself. If his memory was accurate, there would be a pile of bones and the mummified corpse of the Siren. The strange corpse's horned bird-skull-shaped head would be crushed in. As he made his way through the mist, he found the bone pile but no corpse beneath it. He inspected the pile of bones more closely.

Each bone was unique. There were probably thousands of configurations that could be assembled from the selection available. The mist lapped up the side of the pile as if attempting to reach the summit of the alabaster mountain.

Denton heard gurgling coming from the slime and saw something forming. The ooze seemed to be piling up in a small area—building something. The thing was so tiny Denton had to strain his eyes to see it.

An ivory skull began to push itself way from the slime. It was like watching a plant grow in a time-lapse video, although it was hard to gauge exactly how long this was taking. First, there was a horn, then the ridge of a beak appeared. Denton recognized it as the Siren's skull, unfractured by whatever violence had ended the creature long ago.

There was more gurgling from the muck. Denton stepped back to watch another skull develop in the mist, this time into a shape unlike anything he had ever seen before. It was different than the Siren's head but similar in some ways as well, like a half-sister.

The skull was rounded at the top, with two large eye sockets forming below the humps, finishing in a point at the bottom. It reminded Denton of a child's drawing of a human heart.

Once the two skulls had completed forming, small tentacles grew from their bases. Denton watched as the skulls wiggled and flailed around. In the back of his mind, he heard the echoes of children laughing. He continued to watch as the little creatures grew.

Eventually, the skulls became more competent on their tentacle legs and began moving around with more purpose. Denton could hear them both speaking to each other in his mind, each with their own voice.

Although their language was alien, he managed to understand it somehow. The words sounded wrong, but their meaning was still coming through. He wondered if this was how the auk'nai understood humans. The skulls had names for each other; the bird-shaped one with the horn was called Nhymn, and her sister with the heart-shaped skull was Sympha.

Nhymn and Sympha played in the muck, giggling and rolling around with their tentacles flailing. Denton shielded his eyes as he noticed sunlight coming through the cave's entrance. It was a steady, bright light.

Time had returned to its normal pace outside the cave.

Nhymn and Sympha faced the sunlight. Sympha wiggled her way toward the slope. Nhymn grabbed Sympha with a tentacle and tugged her back into the comfort of the dark cave. Sympha struggled, then batted Nhymn on the top of the skull with a tentacle until she released her. Sympha wormed her way up the slope and out into the sunlight, leaving Nhymn behind.

Nhymn hesitantly began to move toward the slope but stopped herself before scaling it. She turned toward Denton and shrunk into herself. Denton was unsure if she was looking directly at him or not. He thought he'd been a phantom observer this whole time, but perhaps he was wrong. His presence could possibly be felt here.

Nhymn scrambled up the slope and out into the sunlight after her sister. Denton began to follow her, but as he got closer to the entrance, the sunlight blinded him.

He lifted his arms to shield his eyes from the impossibly bright light.

Denton sat up in the bunk room of the *Rogers*. It was dark, with only the dim glow of the door panel light breaking through the blackness. He tasted copper on his tongue and pushed his hand against his nose, feeling wetness there. He stumbled his way toward the door and could hear the soft breathing of others sleeping in the bunk room. As he made his way through the darkness, he was careful not to wake them.

Once Denton made it to the light of the cargo bay, he looked down at his wet hand. Blood covered his fingers. He approached a mirror near one of the lockers and saw a stream of blood trickling from his nose. He reached for a nearby rag and wiped it away.

Denton's head felt better.

"Oh, you're up too," Rocco Gainax said as he entered the room.

"Who else is awake?" Denton asked.

"Just Dr. Veston. George went down just a few minutes ago," Rocco said. "She's on the roof if you wanted to see her. It's safe, I have the perimeter up."

"Thanks," Denton said. He made his way outside to join her.

Eliana sat under the stars on the roof of the *Rogers*. She couldn't sleep knowing Roelin was so close. The man who'd stabbed her father to death lurked in the jungle. He was a nightmare but also her only chance for peace. Eliana needed to know what had happened that night. The questions had burned in her soul for four years.

"Don't scratch the paint," Denton said. Eliana looked toward him, and for a moment, she smiled. He sat next to her.

"Are you feeling better?" Eliana asked.

"Yes, I don't know what that was all about. I had the strangest dream …" he said, his voice trailing off as he tried to recollect the dream and failed.

They shared a silence, listening to the distant sounds of jungle creatures. The twin moons, Tasker and Promiser, drifted quietly toward the horizon.

"Talulo," Eliana said, breaking the silence, "said he could track the wizz'iks' movements in the past through some sort of auk'nai science."

"Auk'nai can see *the past?*" Denton asked with amazement and concern.

"He'll help us find where Roelin is," she said, her eyes drifting back toward the stars. "Maybe he can even see what happened that night."

Denton nodded and looked into her eyes. "Are you doing alright?"

Eliana tilted her head and furrowed her brow. "I ..." She let her jaw hang open as she winced. Denton gripped her tightly and rubbed her shoulder. "We've been looking for so long," Eliana said. "I can't believe we finally found a lead."

"What do you think you'll find?" Denton asked.

"Who knows," she said. "Maybe nothing, maybe just a wreckage and no answers. But the thing we'll find for certain is some closure."

"Sounds peaceful."

"Yes," Eliana said, and leaned her head against his shoulder. "Peace at last."

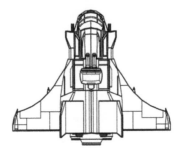

THIRTY-FOUR

ONE MONTH AGO

DAY 1,460 OF ROELIN'S EXODUS

THE *ASTRAEUS* WAITED PATIENTLY in the jungle. The Undertaker-class warfighter had forgotten itself as a space vessel and had long since become part of Kamaria. Tubes funneled out from the hulking vessel like roots seeking the laser stone fonts, keeping the ship and its human occupant alive. Jungle foliage spread over the hull, with leaves shading the wreckage from the sun. In the grassy yard around the *Astraeus*, crates were scattered as time unorganized their contents. The smoker lay dormant, and a water purifier churned, filtering away the deadly bacteria and providing a container of potable drinking fluid.

Inside, the air was pure but musty with age. Sunlight faintly wormed its way in from outside through grime-covered windows. Debris littered the floor from years of a man losing his mind. Clothes, equipment, rotting food, and dust lined the walls of the hallways.

Inside the bunk room, Captain Roelin Raike awakened once more. He sat up in his bed and wiped dried blood away from his nose. He was nude and didn't notice the scars and bruises on his emaciated body anymore.

Roelin pulled a loose T-shirt onto his thin frame to keep himself warm. The *Odysseus* mission patch was a reminder of a different man who had once used this vessel as a war machine.

These days, it was nothing more than a hermit's prison.

Roelin entered the bridge and checked his list of repairs. He had done his best over the past year to hide his real plan from Nhymn, but he couldn't know if he was successful or not.

The Siren's presence was beginning to affect him more deeply now. Roelin could feel changes in his body that he couldn't explain. Sometimes he could feel Sympha's presence on the planet, like a blanket for a fevered mind. She was in a cold, dark place that Roelin had never seen with his own eyes, with green lights pulsing in shadows.

A bang on the roof of the hull distracted Roelin. He listened for a moment longer, but it didn't repeat. He made a mental note to inspect it, but Roelin knew what he really had to do.

Today, Roelin would finally go home.

Roelin exited the bridge and donned a civilian atmospheric suit. Outside, he hauled his toolbox over to a panel on the front of the *Astraeus*. As he rounded the nose of the ship, two lemurbats scurried away. Roelin's eyes widened as he saw what they had done.

"Shit," Roelin grunted, and ran to the open panel.

The panel was marred by lemurbat mischief. Their sharp little teeth had frayed the wires, and some screws and metal pieces lay in the jungle grass below. Worst yet, fluid leaked from a pipe.

"No, God no," Roelin said through gritted teeth and slammed his tool bag to the ground with enough force to kick up dust. He fell to his knees and froze, unsure what to do next.

Nhymn stepped out from the shadow of a nearby tree.

"What were you planning, Roelin?" Nhymn whispered into his mind, hissing like a serpent. The question was an attack. Roelin knew she was already aware of his plan, she just wanted to force him to admit it.

"I was fixing the ship," Roelin said, futilely attempting to lie but defeated, "like you wanted."

"Not like I wanted," Nhymn hissed. She thrust her ghostly, worm-skinned arm toward his forehead. Roelin arched back violently. He felt as if his spine would snap if he put up any resistance.

Nhymn circled the hopeless prisoner, tracing a taloned claw around his helmet as she moved around him. *"Humans and their lies. You still betray me even though this planet will not tolerate it."* She leaned toward him, her beak close to Roelin's nose. *"I can taste your thoughts. I can eat your dreams. There is nothing you can think that I can't devour."* Nhymn pushed further into his mind.

Roelin coughed blood, then, with immense effort, began to push back against her. He could feel the struggle in his mind, like arm wrestling a machine.

Nhymn was caught off guard. She pushed once again but lost her grip on his mind as Roelin lifted himself off his knees. He stood taller than her. Nhymn slunk back into her shadow to watch the disobedient prisoner like a cornered viper.

"You feel it too," Roelin huffed. "You've changed me. And now I'm more powerful than you anticipated." He flexed his hand. "I'm going to fix this damn ship. Then we are going back to Odysseus Colony, whether you tolerate it or not." He stared down at the beak and horned skull, his eyes glowing with malice through the visor of his helmet.

When Roelin's point had been made, he walked away from Nhymn, something he had never been able to do before. He felt like he had left her in the shadow, liberated his body from her control.

Roelin smiled, flashing his remaining teeth to the world. The muscles on his face ached. It had been so long since he'd had a reason to smile. For the first time in years, Roelin felt like he'd won. A gurgle from his stomach reminded him of the fact that he was still starving in an alien jungle.

Food supplies were running low. Roelin had been working

overtime on the *Astraeus* and hadn't made it out to hunt. He felt ambitious and wanted to celebrate his newfound power to hold back Nhymn. Even if his plan to go home was put off for a while, this victory needed something special.

He wanted nurn steak for dinner.

———— • ————

Roelin hacked his way into the jungle until late in the afternoon. He made his way to a place he didn't often hunt, a valley of tall grass higher up on the mountain. He had seen nurn grazing there before and hoped they would be back.

Roelin's kit included a particle rifle, a machete, a collider pistol, and a backpack of repair gear in case he slipped and needed to fix his suit. His combat suit required maintenance, so Roelin wore a civilian atmospheric suit in its place. The suit made him more vulnerable, but he didn't care, he felt invincible. He only wished it had jump-jets, which would make getting around the jungle much more comfortable. Regardless of the risks, he had a spring in his step from his victory over Nhymn. He practically floated through the jungle.

The sun went down, and the dueling Kamarian moons, Tasker and Promiser, hung in sickle-shaped crescents above the cliffside. Roelin hacked further into the jungle with his machete, stopping when he heard the honking of nurn in the distance. He smiled.

Time to get dinner.

Roelin pulled his rifle from his shoulder and crept through the trees as quietly as he could. There was a spot in the brush with a view of the meadow. He gently pushed aside a leafy branch to get a better look.

In the twilight, meadow sailors glowed a soft orange as they glided above the tall grass, sucking in alien gnats. Near the sailors, a group of nurn chomped away at the succulent leaves, honking with pleasure. It was a peaceful scene, made more peaceful by the lack of Nhymn's presence.

Roelin monitored the herd dynamic. Two juvenile nurn played

together, leaping and bumping each other while honking like geese, their beautiful blue feathers glinting moonlight like sparkling star reflections on the ocean. A few pulled grass up with their flat teeth, using their trunk-like snouts to twist and yank. One sat away from the others, lying on its side with its long neck upright, head scanning the horizon. A long antler protruded from the back of its head, signifying its role in the herd. This was the alpha nurn, the protector. If predators arrived, she would alert the others, and it would be time to leave, but Roelin remained undetected.

Even before his exile, Roelin had noticed that hunting animals on Kamaria was more relaxed than hunting on terraformed Mars. The wildlife of Kamaria had never encountered humans before, so they didn't know what to fear. It gave Roelin an edge.

One of the grazing nurn strayed from the rest of the herd. Roelin flicked a switch on the rifle with his thumb, and the collider cylinder faintly hummed as it spun, charging a particle to lance his prey with.

Roelin aimed, steadied himself, and squeezed the trigger.

In the flash from the particle burst, Roelin saw Dr. Cassandra Wynter in the meadow. The bolt of light smashed through her helmet visor, sending fragments of shattered glass and blood into the air in a wild arc.

It was only for a haunting instant.

The weak cry of the dying nurn snapped Roelin back to reality. The herd scattered and the meadow sailors floated away, the peaceful meadow emptied. Roelin had brought violence here too.

He'd struck the target right through its center mass; it died a moment after it hit the ground. Roelin shouldered his rifle and stepped out into the bright moonlight. There was a roar from some distant monster, clearly alarmed by the sound of the rifle blast. Roelin didn't care; he was only trying to return to his cheerful mood before the vision of Dr. Wynter had reminded him of his past transgressions.

Roelin knelt next to his kill, pulling out his skinning knife to get to work removing the internal organs and windpipe. He fought back the visions of John Veston lying on the ground and being repeatedly stabbed by arms that were not under his own control. In the distance, another roar, and the loud shrieking of a nurn. Roelin was still too busy fighting his personal demons to notice.

The machete sank into the deceased nurn.

A shadow cast a long pillar of darkness over Roelin, waving slowly. Roelin traced the shadow to a tall rock formation where he found his witness, a silhouette against the twilight.

It was a three-meter-tall reptilian creature with hauntingly white and blue scales that gleamed in the moonlight. Blood-red eyes glowed as they observed Roelin. The beast had the frame of a silverback gorilla, but with a large, menacing tail that swayed back and forth like a metronome. Two long, thin horns protruded out of the back of its skull near the muscular neck. It hunched forward on two powerful arms that terminated in sharpened claws, and flicked its long tongue in and out of its serrated-toothed jaw, tasting the night air.

The auk'nai call these predators *dray'va*.

Roelin slowly pulled his machete from the body of the nurn and considered his options. Turning his back to the dray'va could cause the beast to chase him, like a bear or a lion. Trying to make himself appear big and imposing was risky. As he spun through ideas, he was interrupted by a guttural growl in the tall grass two meters from him.

Roelin snapped his eyes down into the grass and saw the two glowing violet eyes of a second dray'va. Its deep-emerald scales perfectly camouflaged it in the tall grass. It rolled back its upper lip to reveal jagged teeth in a vicious smile and began to prowl forward on long arms braced to pounce.

Roelin gasped. He turned to run but was tackled to the ground. He lay on his stomach as the emerald dray'va pinned him with a massive claw.

Through Roelin's visor, he could only see the long snout of the predator sniffing him. The emerald dray'va turned toward his hunting partner and barked. The ivory dray'va barked back with excitement and leaped down from the moonlit rock.

"Shit," Roelin whispered to himself. He didn't have much time. Once Ivory arrived, Emerald would begin to tear into him. Roelin still had his machete, and although he was pinned on his back by one long, powerful arm, the beast's other arm supported all of its weight.

Roelin slapped the machete into Emerald's support arm, and the beast crashed to the ground with a shriek. Quickly, Roelin scrambled to his feet and brought the machete down in a vicious arc, slicing into Emerald's neck, which threw blood into the air. Emerald shrieked loudly and scrambled into the tall grass, vanishing from Roelin's view.

Roelin turned his attention to Ivory, shouldering his machete in favor of his rifle.

Ivory had closed the distance between the moonlit rock and Roelin quickly and pounced like a roaring rocket. Roelin had his rifle in hand but didn't have time to accurately aim. He squeezed off two shots as he fell backward, narrowly dodging Ivory's attack.

Ivory hit the ground behind him. Roelin's shots had failed to meet their target. The beast ducked behind a boulder and out of view. Roelin knew he didn't stand a chance out in the open and scanned his surroundings. His best bet would be to hide within the trumpet-shaped trees half a kilometer from his position.

Before Roelin could run, he caught movement out of the corner of his eye. Ivory had scaled the tall boulder to his right and launched from it with its sturdy hind legs. Roelin was unprepared again, and he scrambled to avoid being crushed.

Claws struck the shoulder pad of his suit, ripping away the outer layer and exposing the undersuit beneath. It wasn't deep enough to allow the deadly air to seep in and force Roelin to go lung-lock. Ivory landed in the dirt again and rolled with the impact. Roelin stepped backward and desperately attempted to bring his rifle up to aim.

Ivory gurgled and spat something at a high velocity. A glob of thick spit struck Roelin's rifle, and the goo ate away at his gun, burning through the collider cylinder and causing it to fizz violently with electricity. It threatened to burst.

Roelin hurled the rifle at Ivory, but it ducked under the gun as it sailed past. The rifle smashed into the ground behind the dray'va and violently combusted. The creature was distracted by the explosion, which gave Roelin time to flee.

Hearing the scramble of the heavily suited man, Ivory turned and continued to pursue Roelin. He listened to the pounding of claws against the dirt as Ivory rapidly gained on him. Roelin knew he'd be beaten in this foot race.

Roelin grabbed his collider pistol with his left hand, his right hand grabbing his machete. He spun to face his pursuer, gun forward and machete ready to swing. Claws and teeth rushed toward him with incredible speed. Roelin punched out two shots with the pistol, striking Ivory in the shoulder. The monster didn't slow down; it was filled with blind rage.

The beast swung one of its giant claws at Roelin. He ducked, falling onto his ass. Roelin brought the pistol up once more to shoot, but Ivory swiped at it with its other claw, knocking the gun away.

Roelin scooted backward on the ground.

Ivory raised its massive arms above its horned head. Roelin's eyes widened as he watched Ivory swing its fists downward. He reflexively bunched himself up as the fists smashed into the ground where his helmeted head had just been. Dirt and debris kicked up from the impact of the fists. Ivory raised its fists high once more, readying for another strike.

Roelin slapped the button on the side of his helmet, activating the headlamp. The bright torchlight worked like a flash grenade. Ivory's pupils shrank instantly as the intense light blinded the beast. It scratched at its eyes, trying to liberate itself from the false fireflies that invaded its vision. Roelin scrambled to his feet and hustled for the forest.

Once he made it into the trumpet-shaped trees, Roelin thought that he may have gotten away from his reptilian pursuers. He ran until he couldn't run any farther, then he ran some more.

Eventually, he slid behind a boulder and heaved violently. Part of him prayed the Siren would come to save him, somehow. After all, she had an interest in their mutual survival. So, where was Nhymn now?

"Nhymn, are you there?" Roelin asked the wilderness, but there was no response.

Had he finally rid himself of the Siren only to die in the Kamarian jungle? He felt stupid. Roelin was a war hero. He had fought impossible enemies before—he was smart about the way he tackled problems. And yet—he was stuck behind a tree in a civilian atmospheric suit with no weapons except for a machete, all because he wanted a steak.

The silence was interrupted by the shaking of the bushes to his right, and an emerald claw sprung from the brush and smashed into Roelin's chest. Roelin rolled away and got to his feet. The outer layer of his suit's chest plate sustained three deep scratches, but again he dodged the lung-lock bullet. He stood in a small clearing in the trumpet trees, waiting for the beast.

Emerald emerged from the bushes, blood dripping from the neck wound Roelin had given it earlier. Saliva drooled from its snarling mouth, and its violet eyes glowed in the dark night. It was clear it wanted to even the score.

Roelin backed away, gripping his machete, his final form of defense. His heart sank when he heard something large crash into the grass behind him. He whirled around to see Ivory baring its fangs. The duo of dray'vas circled him like sharks in blood-filled water. Their tongues lapped the air, searching to taste their dinner before it was ready to be devoured.

Roelin thought of Faye. He was so close to making his way back to her. Back at the ship, he'd wanted it to all be over, but now he yearned for just a little more time. He was outnumbered and surrounded.

The dray'vas pounced.

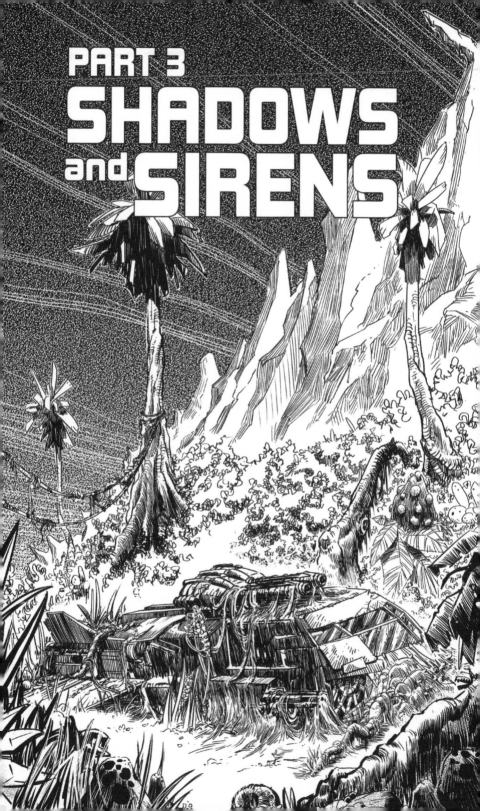

PART 3
SHADOWS and SIRENS

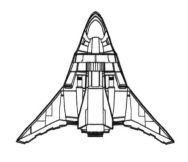

THIRTY-FIVE

PRESENT DAY

IT WAS THE DAY Eliana had both anticipated and dreaded for four years. She was awake before the others, already packing her equipment in the medical bay for the mission ahead. On a nearby recovery bed, Marie slept silently, lulled to slumber by machines casting out their soft, steady beeps.

In Eliana's mind, she knew Roelin must be dead, so bringing a gun seemed redundant. There was the part of her that wanted him to still be alive, if only to answer her questions. She wanted a good answer, a straight answer, a satisfying explanation that would calm her restless spirit. For this reason, Eliana stuffed syringes of the Madani Cure into her field medical kit.

Fergus stepped into the medical bay with two cups of coffee. He nodded silently and handed her one of the cups. She accepted the offering and silently mouthed the words, *"Thank you."*

Fergus nodded and flicked his head toward the bay door, and Eliana left the room with him. She entered the cargo bay of the *Rogers* and found the team was nearly ready to go. There was only the sound of equipment rustling and zippers fastening as they prepared in silence.

Denton tightened a strap on his backpack and approached Eliana. He said nothing, but the look in his eyes told her that he would be with her every step of the way. Eliana smiled and entered his embrace. The atmosphere reminded her of her father's funeral, very somber, very choreographed. Back then, Eliana didn't have Denton. He was sailing through the stars in a deep sleep when all the calamity had happened in the colony. She wished he'd been there with her that day four years ago, if only to give her a warm hug like this.

Sergeant Clint Foster shouldered his particle rifle and nodded to Andrew and Jess. The Tvashtar marines were ready for anything.

"I dare that bastard to try and fool us again," Andrew said, clicking his collider pistol into his hip holster. "He'll be sorry."

"That's enough," George said. He gave the marine a glare that could freeze stars. Andrew shook his head and elbowed Jess, looking for support. She only turned away and left Andrew to his own tauntings.

Rocco Gainax stepped into the room from the command bridge and said, "Talulo's back. He's waiting for you outside."

"We'll be right out," George said. He turned toward Fergus and nodded with an unsteady candor.

"I'll keep a good eye on Marie. You lot just worry about findin' Roelin," Fergus said, answering George's unspoken question. George sniffed, nodded more firmly this time, and walked out the door to the access ramp, the marines following close behind.

Eliana and Denton were the last to leave. As Eliana stepped through the doorway, she heard Fergus quietly tell Denton, "Keep an eye on those trigger-happy marines, lad. They lost a fight years ago and 'ave a score ta settle."

"I'll try," Denton said. "See you later."

"Stay safe out thare," Fergus said, sipping his coffee as the ramp closed behind them.

Eliana and Denton joined the others outside near Talulo. Denton brought a hover mule filled with tools to fix the *Astraeus* if they were to find it. They hoped if the old warship wasn't able to fly, maybe they could salvage a flight recorder and find some answers.

The team stood around Talulo at the base of the *Rogers*'s access ramp. The auk'nai was digging around inside a satchel he'd brought back from Apusticus, and the scouts could hear glass vials clinking together.

"Where do we begin?" George asked.

"Tra'oi'due," Talulo said as he fished out some vials of mysterious liquids. "Talulo needs to see where Puppo has been. That way, we find the *Astraeus* and Roelin."

"You said the wizz'ik had seen the *Astraeus* near the Sharp Top," George said. "Shouldn't we just head there?"

"Yes," Talulo said, slinging his daunoren hook staff over his shoulder between his wings and kneeling down and placing the vials on the dirt. "Sharp Top is a big mountain. Tra'oi'due will lead us right to Roelin. No need to guess the tune." The auk'nai grunted and set a wooden bowl on the ground near the glass vials.

Talulo began mixing two of the potions, creating a violet ooze that flickered with swirls of orange. Eliana watched bubbles start to form, thinking Marie would have loved to have watched this chemical reaction.

The auk'nai lifted a vial of white liquid above his head and slowly dripped the contents into each of his eyes. He winced as smoke began to emit from his pupils as if he had started a fire inside them.

Talulo's eyes changed color rapidly from red to blue to yellow. He coughed, then removed a dead m'unjo centipede from his satchel and devoured it like a rabid dog.

"Woah, wait." Denton attempted to stop Talulo from eating the acidic centipede creature, but it happened so quickly, he was powerless to prevent it. Eliana saw the look of horror on Denton's face and wondered where he had seen one of those before.

The auk'nai quickly collected the wooden bowl of violet and orange ooze and gurgled it down. More smoke as thick as vomit came from his mouth. It combined with the smoke from his pupils. It smelled like concentrated sulfur. Eliana's eyes began to water, and she cupped a hand over her mouth and nose.

Talulo reached forward and placed both hands on the ground in front of him, stretching his wings out over himself and creating shade over his upper body. Smoke filled his makeshift umbrella, and his wing feathers rustled as he inhaled the gas.

"This is stupid!" Andrew shouted. "He's get'n high." He thrust a hand toward Talulo.

"Shut up," Clint Foster said with a coldness in his synthetic voice that seemed to command more authority than usual.

"Yes, sir," Andrew said, and stepped to the back of the group of observers.

"Permission to speak freely, sir?" Jess asked.

"Go ahead," Clint said.

"Are we really going to go with this tactic?" Jess asked. Sergeant Clint Foster frowned; he, too, wasn't sure how viable this strategy was. This mission relied heavily on their faith in Talulo's abilities.

"Here's my plan," Clint said. "I'm going to follow whatever this auk'nai tells me to do, and you two are going to follow me. Is that clear?" It wasn't a question. The marines replied in unison.

"*Sir, yes, sir!*"

Talulo threw open his wings, releasing the plume of smoke into the air. His eyes were solid white like large marbles. A gentle spill of smoke oozed from behind his eyelids, but it didn't seem to cause Talulo any visible pain. He was calm, as if the torture had never happened.

"You okay, buddy?" Denton asked. Talulo opened his beak and twitched his ears as if listening to something very far away.

"I see Puppo's song. Follow this way." Talulo cooed and walked in the direction of the Sharp Top. Andrew and Jess shared a look of disbelief. Clint followed the auk'nai without checking to make sure his fellow marines were right behind him.

"Oh, *come on.*" Andrew huffed.

"Semper yoga," Jess said, reminding Andrew to remain "always flexible."

Andrew fell in line. The scouts followed their guide through the jungle, unsure if this trick was just a young auk'nai chasing a high or chasing the past.

"Always keep an open mind," Denton said quietly to Eliana. She nodded and reached for his hand. He grasped it firmly, and they walked together, following Talulo into the wilderness.

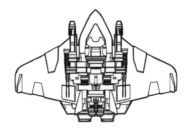

THIRTY-SIX

THE HIKE CONTINUED THROUGHOUT the afternoon, leading the team upward through dense jungle and cliffside ledges. Talulo silently followed his visions of the past as his eyes continued to faintly emit smoke.

Denton pulled the hover mule full of tools behind him as they traversed the jungle. He was beginning to feel the strain of the hike, and looked around to see if anyone else was as winded as he was. George didn't let his age show; he walked uphill with a steady, silent grace. Eliana remained deep in thought, and she felt distant to Denton even though they were hiking side by side. The storm in her mind grew as they got closer to the *Astraeus*. The Tvashtar marines had no trouble with the intensity of the hike, chatting casually as they hauled their heavy combat gear.

"So, what's the game plan if we find this psycho alive?" Andrew asked, lifting his rifle to sit behind his head on his shoulder blades as he looked out from the ledge of a cliff.

Jess said, "I think the lung-lock would have taken him by now."

"Yeah, but let's pretend it didn't," Andrew said. "That means we get to kill him ourselves and become heroes back in the colony."

"This isn't about fame," Jess said.

"Maybe not to you," Andrew huffed, "but I wouldn't mind bragging rights."

Clint said, "Cowardly acts meet cowardly ends. Roelin didn't have the supplies to stay alive this long out here. If I thought he were alive, we would have brought more marines." Clint rubbed the old scar on his neck.

Denton saw Eliana wince at the talk of killing Roelin. He whispered to her, "Don't let them bother you. We'll see what we see, and we won't know anything more until then. That's all hot air coming out of those marines."

"Yeah," Eliana said, keeping her eyes on Talulo. "It's just the way they are talking about him. I remember Roelin so differently. That horrible night was the exception, not the rule. Roelin was a war hero before he …" Eliana bobbed her head and sighed. "I just need answers. I need to know why he killed my father and all those people."

Denton rubbed her shoulder with his free hand, pulling the hover mule full of tools behind him with his other. They walked together in silence for a moment, letting the jungle breeze brush past them as they climbed higher up the mountain.

The sunset signaled to the team that it was time to make camp, and they chose a spot on an outcropping near the cliffside. The jungle tree line bordered their campsite on one side, with a bare cliff ledge facing outward toward the stars on the other. The Milky Way spread across the expanse before them, similar to how it had appeared in the Sol System.

Denton slammed down his last encasement fence post and waved to Jess, who activated the fence. The marines would keep watch for the night in shifts. George sat with Clint near their campfire to discuss plans for the next morning. Eliana had already set up their tent and gone to sleep. Denton was sore from the long hike and the anticipation of repeating it the next day. He decided to join her for some rest.

With the tent sealed behind him, Denton turned toward his cot and was pulled into slumber before his head even hit the pillow.

————— ◆ —————

"This again." Denton sighed to himself as he sat up in the grassy field in front of the cave near the City of the Dead.

These dreams felt like he was a tourist in some unknown land instead of a sleeping man dreaming of a faraway place. He could feel the cold, the breeze, and he could even feel time sliding by him in some strange way; it tickled slightly. Right now, the hairs on the back of his neck stood rigid. He spun on his heels.

Nhymn, the Siren he had come to know from the previous dream, stood within arm's reach. She was grown now, as she had been when the scouts had found her carcass on the expedition years ago.

The Siren's long horn above her sharp beak pointed directly at Denton's head, right between his eyes. Gnarled teeth grew out of her carapace, covering all the hard places of her body like thorny armor. Her worm-skin arms were pulled inward, and she was massaging her claws together. The tentacles that climbed out from her shoulder blades reached toward Denton with the barbed spikes that protruded from their ends. She took a step closer, planting her taloned foot down just in front of him.

Can she see me? Denton wondered with horror.

Nhymn was so close, Denton could feel her presence in his mind. He assumed he had gone unnoticed as a phantom in this dream world, but perhaps he had judged that incorrectly. He swallowed hard as sweat dripped from his brow. Nhymn's tentacle traced its way up his body, starting near his foot and running up his leg, past his belly and chest, over his neck, and up to his chin. The Siren could spike his throat right now if she wanted to.

Denton was at her mercy.

He noticed another presence tickling his mind. It was the signature of Nhymn's sister, Sympha. He could understand their vocabulary in his subconscious. Sympha had something to show Nhymn and wanted her to come into the cave and see it.

Nhymn perked her head up, looking over Denton. She stepped around him and entered the maw of the cave.

Denton followed Nhymn.

Down in the misty shadow space, Nhymn found Sympha standing in front of something she had created. Denton recognized it as the stone sentry from the jungle, but he wasn't sure how he knew.

Sparks of memories flickered in his mind. He knew the sentry was in the jungle and had done something to him, but what it was exactly, he wasn't sure. It was hazy, as if something were standing in front of the window into that memory.

Sympha had grown as well. She was as tall as Nhymn, and her head was now more curved and heart shaped, although her large eye sockets weren't dripping tar like her sister's did. Sympha floated a meter above the ground, expelling a mist of some sort that propelled her smoothly through the air, as if she were swimming. It was beautiful in a way, like witnessing a graceful sea creature. Her bottom half was a swarm of tentacles, and hoops of bone grew from her torso below four green worm-skin arms.

Sympha was excited to show Nhymn this new creation; she had named the stone sentry Karx.

Karx had a bull-shaped skull with one cyclopean eye socket. His frame was centaur-like in shape. His worm skin had a blue hue, and blocks of bone armored his body. Karx watched Nhymn as she circled him.

Nhymn asked what this creature was exactly. Sympha explained that she had learned to create life. This confused Nhymn, so Sympha offered to show her an example. She floated to a cave wall and ripped a few rocks away, then placed the rocks onto the oozing floor.

Sympha leaned in carefully and expelled a gentle green mist from her open skull cavities. Within moments of being enveloped in the mist, the rocks began to chatter. Electrical energy began to emit from the ooze and slither over the pile of rocks. The rocks rolled around inside the ball of electricity, constraining themselves together into a small creature with three rock legs and a long neck with a stone face. With the frame built, Sympha gently placed her hand on the stone head and pressed inward. She gathered herself for a moment. A pulse of green light erupted from her spine, flooding her whole body. It surged into the small thing she had built.

The tiny construct began to move around awkwardly, like a newborn calf. Sympha squealed in excitement, and Nhymn wrung her claws together with happiness.

More friends!

Sympha explained that she called these stone constructs nezzarforms, and that the nezzarforms would help them build whatever they wanted. Sympha encouraged Nhymn to try and make one too. Nhymn rushed toward the cave wall, kicking up black matter as she stomped forward in haste. She slashed away at the wall, slicing clean chunks of rock onto the floor as if she had cut through butter with a hot knife. Nhymn sloppily pushed the rocks together and held her head close to her misshapen construct.

Tar dripped from her large open eye sockets onto the tiny figure, but nothing stirred. Sympha looked confused, and Nhymn grew frustrated. She tried again, but there was no green mist, no stirring, no life—only tar.

Nhymn kept pushing herself but grew increasingly impatient with the process. In a fit of anger, she slashed the tiny pile of rocks into oblivion and roared with rage.

Sympha told her to keep trying. Nhymn slashed more rocks from the wall and built up another pile. Sympha summoned Karx to her side, and together they left the cave to allow Nhymn to concentrate.

The light outside the cave began to come and go rapidly with the passing of days; time was sliding past again, and Denton could feel it vibrating in his bone marrow. As time passed by, he watched Nhymn move about the cave. Tiny mounds of rocks would rise and fall. Some would be thrown across the room or sliced in half, but none came to life. Time moved so quickly that Denton figured decades had gone by. Nhymn never left the cave, just kept trying to create a construct to impress her sister. She failed for what seemed like a century.

Suddenly, time skidded back to its normal progression. Mounds of rocks littered the floor of the cave. Denton searched for Nhymn but could not find her. In his mind, he could feel her immense sadness. After searching further, he found Nhymn behind the pile of skulls that she'd been born under.

She was curled up on the ground, half covered in mist. She emitted a great sense of despair, which was palpable. She had failed to create life for far too long and knew it was never going to happen. Nhymn was jealous of her sister and would give anything to be like her for a moment.

She felt beyond useless.

A harsh cry came from outside the cave. Nhymn bolted upright. Sympha was in trouble and calling for help. Nhymn raced up the slope of the cave and back into the light. Denton attempted to follow, but as he got closer to the entrance, the light grew so bright that it engulfed him fully.

———— ✦ ————

Denton awakened inside the tent. He looked for Eliana but instead found only an empty sleeping bag. He felt something wet on his upper lip. He reached up and wiped away the blood that had dripped from his nostrils.

These nosebleeds were becoming more frequent. Denton decided that, after the mission was over, he'd go in for a checkup. He didn't want to worry Eliana before then. He bent forward and unzipped the tent.

It was still dark outside, and Denton could see the galaxy twinkling in the Kamarian night. Insects sang each other lullabies in the jungle trees. In the distance, waterfalls relentlessly crashed away at the jungle below. Denton looked toward the campfire and saw the marines on watch. Andrew lay against a rock, sleeping and snoring.

Jess stirred the fire with a stick, and looked up when she heard Denton. She flicked her head toward the rocky outcropping just beyond the tents.

Eliana was sitting cross-legged on a boulder, watching Talulo. The auk'nai was perched on a small dead tree, observing the stars. His daunoren staff hung on a nearby branch, silhouetted in the night. Denton quietly walked over to sit next to Eliana, and she opened her blanket to him. He accepted the offer and sat shoulder to shoulder with her.

"He's still looking into the past, isn't he?" Denton asked, flicking his chin toward Talulo.

"Yeah. The way it changes him, I hope he isn't hurt by the experience," Eliana said. "We owe him a great deal for this."

Denton nodded, and the two sat for a moment, absorbing each other's body heat. Denton wondered out loud, "Do you think he can see the past of the stars?"

"We all can do that, technically. A lot of these stars no longer exist by the time their light reaches us. It's a sky full of memories."

"I guess you're right," Denton said, admiring how poetic that sounded. "You know, I never bothered to find out which one was Sol."

"It's this one, here." She traced her finger across a few stars in the sky. "The Lantern constellation. My dad and I named it." She sighed. Denton rubbed her shoulder under the blanket as they both looked at their old star.

"From here, it looks just like all the others," Denton said.

"I used to think the same thing," Eliana said. "But now I feel like that constellation is a guardian angel watching down over us." She squeezed Denton's hand tightly. "I'm worried about finding Roelin."

Denton rubbed her shoulder. Her worry was understandable; if they found Roelin's corpse but no answers, she'd still be stranded in an ocean of questions. If they found Roelin alive, it would be an entirely different problem to worry about.

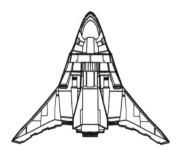

THIRTY-SEVEN

IN THE MORNING, THE team ate a quick breakfast, packed up the campsite, and continued on their journey. Talulo led the way, plodding his daunoren staff into the dirt with each hastened step as he followed the phantom projection of the wizz'ik Puppo through the foliage. The auk'nai's eyes remained hazed over with the effects of his tracking drug still coursing through him.

The team came to an outcropping of tall trumpet trees. Talulo knelt to observe something. He watched the area as if figures moved in front of his white glossed-over eyes. He hopped backward, his wings expanded in alert.

"What is it?" Sergeant Clint Foster asked, signaling the marines to aim their guns at the tree line.

"Talulo sees a human," Talulo said, his eyes darting around.

Denton scanned the surroundings and knew Talulo meant he was seeing a person who had been there in the past. There was chaos in the clearing, scratch marks still healing on bark, tufts of mossy grass scraped away from a battle, and dried blood, lots of dried blood. Denton turned to Eliana and saw her wide-eyed expression. She whispered, "Oh no."

"Is it Roelin?" George asked. He thumbed his soothreader and displayed an image of him. "Do you see this man?"

Talulo flapped backward and took a quick glance at George's soothreader projection. He cawed and grunted, "It is the man Roelin. His song is strong here."

The auk'nai flapped sideways reflexively, dodging whatever had happened here in the past.

"What's happening?" Clint asked.

Talulo knelt and kept his head low, darting his beak around as he watched the replay of whatever carnage had occurred here. He grunted, "Roelin was attacked by two dray'va."

"Shit, they got to him first," Andrew muttered.

Talulo's beak darted around. "Roelin is a strong warrior." Talulo stood up and shuffled over to a tree.

Eliana raced over and picked something up off the ground. She held up small fragments of amber glass from a civilian atmospheric suit.

"That's part of a helmet visor, isn't it?" George asked. He looked down and whispered, "Lung-lock."

Talulo's eyes darted over to a large boulder. "No, George. Roelin fixed his helmet."

"What, how?" George asked with renewed hope.

"Dray'va cracked Roelin's mask against tree, but did not shatter it." Talulo grunted, then picked up a vial of used repair sealant from behind the boulder. "Roelin sealed his mask before air could enter and end his song."

George smiled and looked at Eliana.

Talulo flapped his wings and brought himself over to a bush. They watched as he pushed the foliage aside to reveal the ripped-to-pieces carcass of an emerald-scaled dray'va.

"This song is confusing to Talulo," the auk'nai said. "Dray'va don't cannibalize each other. But this one killed its partner as the man Roelin watched."

Talulo hopped backward, his smoking white eyes widened, and he cawed in fear. He fell back, pulling his daunoren staff upward to shield himself from an invisible attacker.

"Talulo!" Eliana shouted, and ran to his side.

"Is he going lung-lock?" Denton asked as he rushed over to them. "Can auk'nai even go lung-lock?"

"No, it's impossible," Eliana said.

"*Ahn'ah'rahn'eem!*" Talulo gasped. "*Neh! Hrett'ti'lo!*"

George stepped forward and tried to find Talulo's attacker in the empty air. "*Hrett'ti'lo* means 'monster' in auk'nai."

"Guns up, marines," Clint said. Jess and Andrew helped form a triangular perimeter around the civilians in the team.

"*Ahn'ah'rahn'eem!*" Talulo shouted. "*Ahn'ah'rahn'eem!*"

"Something about a nightmare?" George asked. "That's the word Mag'Ro used for the City of the Dead."

Talulo began to seize up, his body twitched, and his feathers flexed rapidly.

"Shit!" Eliana shouted, and grabbed Talulo's satchel, turning it over and emptying the contents. On the ground were a few odds and ends from his potion creation: the stirring bowl, a few grubs, some stray jewels, and a glass orb with green powder inside.

Talulo slammed his fist down hard on the glass orb, releasing a plume of green and purple smoke. He curled his head toward the smoke and inhaled sharply. After a moment, he lay still, shuddering with the aftershock.

"Are you alright?" George asked, holding his hand out toward the auk'nai.

"There is … evil here …" Talulo rasped out through coughs. Once the smoke cleared, Talulo stood up, his eyes back to their standard bright violet.

"You can no longer see the past, can you?" Eliana asked.

"No, the *Tra'oi'due* has ended," Talulo said, and lowered his ears, ashamed that he was no longer useful. He clutched his daunoren staff to keep himself upright.

"You did great, Talulo," George said.

Clint said, "It should be easy enough to track him the old-fashioned way now. Look." He pointed toward broken branches and footprints. There was blood splattered inside some of the prints and against the brush.

"Whose blood is that?" Eliana asked.

George scanned it with a bioscope and said, "It's not human. It's matching the readout of the dray'va carcass over there."

"There are some boot prints near the blood trail here leading up into that meadow," Jess said, pointing up the sloping trumpet forest.

"That's our heading, let's move out," Clint Foster said, and began marching away from the ripped-up clearing.

Eliana and Denton looked at each other. Eliana's eyes looked like polished glass, a spark of hope mixed with dread over what might happen. She pressed her lips together firmly and held Denton's gaze. This was it, it was real. Roelin was close, the signs were all here, and now there were bread crumbs to lead the team directly to him.

———— ◆ ————

The trumpet forest opened to a cliffside meadow. The midday light burned moisture from the tall grass, creating plumes of mist that wisped into the air. As they moved through the tall grass, Andrew bent down and pulled an abandoned standard-issue collider pistol from the mud.

Another bread crumb.

"Here's one for the trophy case," Andrew whispered to himself. Eliana was the only one in earshot. She considered the weapon with her eyes and ignored the man holding it.

A desperate alien carrion bird picked away at the long-dead carcass of a nurn. Clint scared the bird off and got a closer look at the remains. There was a significant purple burn mark on the bones and remaining flesh, the signature of a particle blast.

"Roelin did this, see here." Clint pushed the bones into view so George and Eliana could see. "That's a particle impact wound right through the rib cage."

"Good shot," Andrew said, looking over their shoulders. He

traced the angle of the shot toward an outcropping of Poe heartlings in the distance.

"I think he went that way, Sarge." Andrew nodded toward the trees. Clint stood and began walking.

George observed the carcass of the downed nurn before stepping away to join the marines. He asked, "Why shoot the nurn and not take it with him?"

Jess shrugged. "Maybe he enjoys it?"

Denton noticed more signs of distress in the area around the nurn and said, "I think he found himself in some trouble." He flicked his chin toward a burst particle rifle's remains in the dirt nearby. It had the telltale signs of a ruptured collider cylinder. The grass around it was scorched from the violence of the explosion.

They crossed through forests of Poe heartlings and scrambled up rocky ledges, following the trail of boot prints and dried blood. Where the soil was softer, Roelin's footprints could be seen alongside those of a clawed creature.

"Dray'va," Talulo said.

"Was he being hunted?" Denton asked.

"Talulo doesn't know." Talulo lowered his ears and squeezed his staff in both hands.

"We assume these tracks were made at the same time," Eliana said. "But what if they weren't? Maybe this dray'va was following Roelin."

"True," George said. "Or maybe he was following it? If the dray'va had a fresh kill, maybe Roelin saw it as an opportunity to steal some."

"Heads on a swivel, everyone," Clint said. "We either have a murderer or a monster out there."

Talulo's ears perked up, and he squinted. He whistled and flapped his large wings to boost himself ahead of the team.

"Talulo, wait!" George shouted, following him with a short sprint. As they overcame the slope, George saw it too.

The *Astraeus*.

The derelict Undertaker-class warship rested in a small clearing. Roelin's home for all these years. The ship was overtaken by Kamarian plant life but remained mostly intact. It waited in the shade under a cliff ledge, hidden from satellite view.

A waterfall from a higher ledge flowed into a medium-size pond, which continued on as a stream farther into the jungle. Poe heartlings hung lazily over the pond, forming a peacefully quiet scene of a hermit's home.

A variety of tools and crates were spread across the yard. Laser stones pulsing with electricity were harnessed by makeshift machinery, siphoning power into the ship. Small Kamarian birds tweeted in the afternoon light.

Eliana joined George and stood at his side with her mouth open. The peaceful scene clashed with her last encounter with the man who lived here. It reminded her of the graveyard near Odysseus Colony on a warm afternoon. It was quiet, but it had a dark history.

To Eliana, the *Astraeus* held the answers she had been seeking for four years. It held the reasons her father was stabbed to death by one of his good friends. It held the end of her restless nights and the beginning of her journey forward in life.

"All these years, he was right here," Eliana whispered.

George was in awe. He had just as many questions that needed resolutions as Eliana. He slowly moved forward toward the edge of the clearing.

Talulo's sharp eyes caught a glint of light from a small thread just above the forest floor. He bent down near the tree, discovering a thin wire. He wasn't sure what it could possibly be, but it felt out of place. He put his finger on the wire and traced the line toward a nearby tree.

The auk'nai was ignored by the rest of the team as they all approached the clearing. It was a mythical place, a legend come to life. A *real* place that held a *real* bogeyman.

Talulo traced the wire to its source and found a grenade tied to the base of a Poe heartling. The wire clipped tightly to the pin mechanism, and tripping the wire would set the trap off violently. Talulo wasn't sure what the object was. He turned to George and noticed he was about to step through the wire. His eyes widened as he heard the click.

The pinging of the metal pin wrenching from its position in the housing of the grenade was the last sound the team heard before the explosion rocked the jungle.

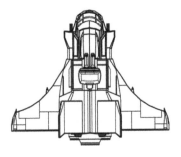

THIRTY-EIGHT

"SHIT! SHIT! *SHIT!*" SOMEONE shouted through the haze of chaos that enveloped the team.

Denton's ears rang with a high-pitched squeal. He slowly pushed himself up from the ground and inspected his surroundings. His face felt hot. Sharp pinpoints of searing pain lit up his body, and the world seemed to follow his eye movements one second too late. Denton reached over to the hover mule to stabilize himself from the dizzy world around him, but found that it had gone missing.

Eliana knelt over George, tying a tight tourniquet around his arm to stop the flow of blood that poured from the old man.

Talulo lay facedown, unmoving. Clint and Jess frantically battled the fire that continued to smolder from the feathers on the auk'nai's badly damaged wings. Andrew stood with his rifle raised, waiting for an ambush.

"Shit! Shit! Shit!" Andrew shouted, his eyes wide with fear.

Denton's vision realigned, and he shook the concussion off as best he could. He ran to Eliana's side and asked, "What do you need me to do?"

Eliana was entirely focused on keeping George alive. He had been knocked sideways by the blast of the grenade and had taken a large chunk of a fractured Poe heartling branch to his arm. Denton saw the bloody fragments of wood that Eliana had already removed, noticing there were even more in George's side.

"Grab him," Eliana said sternly. "The *Astraeus* may have more tools inside. We need to operate on these two quick, or they are going to die."

"Got him," Denton said as he grabbed the shoulder straps of George's scout jacket and began pulling him across the grass yard toward the old warship.

Andrew shouted in protest, "That maniac could be in there!"

"Then *do your job!*" Eliana shouted back, grabbing Talulo's arm and beginning to pull. "We don't have time!"

"Step aside," Clint Foster's synthetic voice interrupted her. He pushed Eliana away and grabbed Talulo under his arms. He felt the burn from feathers that continued to smolder. Clint turned toward Jess and said, "Go with Dr. Veston and secure the *Astraeus* while Denton and I get the wounded to the medical bay. Lance Corporal, establish a perimeter around the ship."

The two Tvashtar marines nodded and proceeded to follow orders. Jess and Eliana took off in a sprint toward the *Astraeus*, with Jess expertly scanning the yard with her rifle as they ran full speed toward the warship.

Eliana made it to the outer hatch first and attempted to open it up with a series of input codes. Jess kept her rifle aimed at the door. When the command failed, Eliana slammed her fist against the door panel, and it shuddered, then activated. The door thrust open with violent speed, and Jess went in first to clear the interior. Eliana waited behind for Denton and Clint to catch up with their wounded in tow.

Jess Combs was dusted off with a weakened quarantine blast in the air lock, then allowed access to the main ship. Once inside, there was an eerie silence, interrupted only by the metal of her boots clicking against the floor and the steady hum of the collider cylinder on her rifle. She walked through halls littered with debris, remaining on high alert. Jess could see grisly remains of something chewed to pieces beyond recognition. It reminded her of scenes she had witnessed during the war with the Undriel.

Jess remembered what Talulo had said about the dray'va and realized a beast may have been using the ship as a nest, perhaps having eaten Roelin long ago. She moved past the chewed remains and continued down the hall.

She opened one door at a time, thrusting her rifle into the room and checking each corner before deeming it safe for the others. The medical bay was in shambles, and Jess was unsure if there was anything left in there that would be useful, but it was devoid of threat, and that would have to do for now. She'd let Eliana decide how to use the bay.

The final room was the command bridge. With the lack of hostiles in all previous areas, the likelihood of someone being on the bridge was much higher. Jess readied herself and reached with her left hand to open the door. It flung open, and she stepped in. Jess moved through the room quickly, whipping her rifle around corners and checking every shadow with her torchlight.

Empty.

"*Astraeus* is clear," Jess said into her soothreader. It was so quiet, she could hear the outer door opening and the others stampeding into the medical bay. Now that she knew the ship was empty, Jess took in her surroundings with a more narrow focus. There were words scrawled in blood on the walls.

WHAT IS THE UNDRIEL?

WHERE ARE THE UNDRIEL?

HOW DID THE UNDRIEL RID THEMSELVES OF THE HUMANS?

WHEN WILL THE UNDRIEL ARRIVE?

Jess's spine tingled with the thought of the Undriel coming to Kamaria. It was not the first time the horrible idea had crossed her mind; nightmares of the war had conjured that possibility for Jess before. It had been three hundred years in real time for the universe, but to those who'd fought the machines, it didn't feel nearly that long ago.

The floor was littered with various papers, some crumpled and others lying flat. Each sheet had words written on them, many referencing the Undriel. She picked up a notepad that had odd questions written on it.

THEY HURT US.

WHY DID THE HUMANS COME HERE?

HOW WERE THE HUMANS CHASED OUT?

One phrase was repeated on many of the papers:

TAKE US TO SYMPHA.

Jess put the papers down and walked out of the room to rejoin the team inside the medical bay. Eliana, Sergeant Clint Foster, Denton, and the two wounded were inside, moving around in haste. Talulo was facedown on one table, and George lay on his back on the other. Eliana was expertly moving between them. She had removed all the wood fragments from George's body and had used suture foam to stabilize him. The old man's right arm was heavily bandaged.

Talulo's wings had been completely ripped apart by the grenade blast, and the smell of smoldering bird feathers and flesh filled the air. Eliana knew she couldn't save his wings and that leaving them heightened the risk infection. She hunted the medical bay for a bone saw but could not locate one.

"We need something to cut his wings off," Eliana said to the room. Clint quickly pulled a large combat knife from a sheath on his belt and handed it over. Eliana shook her head. "If we can't find anything else, we'll use that. But look for something like a saw."

"In the hover mule," Denton said, "I have a few metal cutting saws. Those should work."

"Go get one," Eliana said, then added: "Denny, be careful."

Denton nodded and hurriedly left the room. Talulo began to spasm and howl loudly. His cries echoed off the walls of the *Astraeus*.

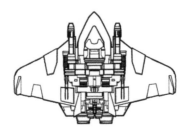

THIRTY-NINE

DENTON PUSHED THROUGH THE outer hatch of the *Astraeus* and almost knocked Andrew down on his way over to the hover mule.

"Watch it, kid!" Andrew said as Denton moved past him. "Hey! Where the Hells are you going?"

Denton slid himself over a crate in the yard and yelled over his shoulder, "We need the hover mule!"

"I'm not abandoning my post! You're on your own!" Andrew's shouts grew distant as Denton got closer to the tree line. Remnants of Talulo's daunoren staff littered the ground, some pieces embedded in the nearby Poe heartlings. Denton wished he had time to collect the treasured fragments for their auk'nai companion, but Talulo's life was on the line.

Denton found the mule on its side in a bush a few meters away. It was stuck between two trees, so he braced one leg against a tree to get the leverage he needed and heaved until he got the mule upright. Denton kicked on the glider, and the mule boosted itself into a hovering position, spurting bursts of mud and sticks out as it cleared its boosters. He pushed the mule toward the *Astraeus* as fast as he could—there was no time to waste.

———◆———

"I thought you took off," Andrew said smugly. Denton quickly moved the hover mule across the clearing, but he had to navigate around the various crates and devices scattered in the yard.

Denton glared up at Andrew in time to see a particle blast knock the marine sideways. Andrew screamed as a smoking hole ripped through his shoulder armor, causing him to lose his grip on his rifle.

"Shit!" Denton shouted ,and ducked behind a crate just in time to see a few particle shots collide with the ground where he had been standing, sending blasts of dirt upward with each impact. Andrew used his good arm to crawl toward his rifle. Denton lifted his soothreader to his face and flicked on the comm channel. He shouted, "Andrew's been shot!"

Denton slammed his fist against the panel on the mule, and a drawer slid open, revealing a collider pistol. He grabbed it and pulled back the hammer, causing the collider cylinder to whir violently.

Another shot ricocheted off the crate near him, gouging a large chunk out of the corner. Denton wasn't safe here. These crates would shield him from view, but they may not entirely block a particle shot. It was better than being out in the open, but not by much.

"I'm pinned down!" Denton shouted to Andrew, who had moved out of his line of sight.

"Stay down, *kid*!" Andrew shouted as he gripped the handle of his rifle and activated the collider cylinder. He used every swear he could think of as he rolled behind part of the *Astraeus* to block himself from more particle blasts. "Where are you, you bastard," Andrew muttered to himself, flicking his wrist to activate a mirror setting on his wrist-mounted soothreader. He angled his hand so get a view around the side of the *Astraeus* and found a shadow moving in the tree line. "Found you."

A figure with a rifle was among the trees, aiming his sights on Denton. Andrew braced himself against the ship to steady his aim. He peered down the scope on his gun and whispered, "Buddy, you're going to make me famous."

The thumping of metal coming from the top of the *Astraeus* diverted Andrew's attention.

Running across the top of the *Astraeus* was a large, ivory-scaled, reptilian beast. It pounded forward with its enormous front arms and lean back legs, swinging a long tail in its wake. The dray'va leaped from the top of the ship and smashed down on Andrew's back, crumpling his spine. He could barely scream out in pain as the beast's vicious maw collapsed down on his head, crushing his skull like a watermelon and spraying the contents onto the grass. The dray'va pulled upward, removing what little flesh still clung to the rest of Andrew's shoulders.

"Holy *Hells!*" Denton's heart sank into his gut at the sight of Andrew's abrupt death. He knew if he didn't act now, he'd be next. Denton flung his arm out from the side of the crate and let loose three shots that missed the dray'va but forced it to move.

If the beast hadn't known Denton's position before, it sure did now. The dray'va rushed toward him, tearing up the yard with its enormous claws.

More shots rang out, but this time, they weren't being aimed at Denton. Clint Foster and Jess Combs emerged from the outer hatch of the *Astraeus* firing. Jess used her jump-jet to duck a blast from the jungle tree line and returned fire. Clint shot the dray'va once in the back. The beast roared in pain and rushed into the jungle and out of sight.

Sergeant Clint Foster looked at Andrew's body and gasped. He focused on the tree line the dray'va had vanished beyond and shouted, "Denton! You still here?"

"Still here! Watch out, he's out there!" Denton shouted back.

"I noticed!" Jess said, and launched a round of particle shots into the jungle trees. Chunks of wood and foliage were ripped from their bases and cluttered the air. Jess jump-jetted her way behind a tall stack of crates and waited to see if there was a response.

With a loud clank, the large turret of the *Astraeus* jolted to life and spun toward the yard.

"Heads up!" Jess shouted. The turret turned toward Jess and fired a particle blast designed to take out Undriel battlecraft in space.

The recoil rocked the whole ship, liberating dust and dirt from the plants that had claimed the warship as their own. Jess rolled away in time to watch the blast explode on her previous position, creating an impact crater and sending more dirt and debris into the sky.

———— ◆ ————

Inside the *Astraeus*, Eliana felt the shake of the turret being fired. Any medical supplies that remained on the shelves fell to the floor with a clang, and dust shook itself away from every surface. She knew right away something was wrong and pulled her soothreader toward her face. "What's going on?" she asked into the comm channel, fearing the worst.

"Lock yourself in the medical bay! Do not let anyone in," Sergeant Clint Foster ordered her sternly, the sound of particle blasts echoing behind his voice. Another rocking of the large turret gun being fired shook Eliana.

Eliana ran to the door and input the commands on the terminal to lock herself and the wounded in. Talulo groaned in pain, letting out a rolling birdcall that announced his agony. She turned and saw his heavily damaged wings and knew she had no time to wait for the hover mule with the metal cutting saws. Eliana grabbed the combat knife Clint had left behind and held Talulo's wings as steadily as she could.

"I'm so sorry, Talulo," she said quietly.

———— ◆ ————

The turret gun spun toward Clint's position and blasted out another shot. The blast just missed him, colliding instead with the pond and causing a colossal fountain of water to spray into the air, but it passed close enough to push him sideways. Clint flew five meters and rolled on the ground.

The dray'va rushed him instantly. Clint rolled onto his belly to push himself up, and the beast pounced. Jess Combs used her jump-jet to propel a dropkick into the dray'va's side, knocking it sideways.

She landed near the sergeant and let out a volley of particle blasts at the beast. It scrambled away, taking a few shots to its flank. It vanished beyond the tree line, leaving behind only a roar.

"Get up, Sergeant!" Jess shouted, and reached one hand out to Clint, keeping the other on her rifle, aimed at the tree line in case the beast returned. The marines were back on their feet in time to jump-jet in separate directions as the *Astraeus* blasted out another shot from its large particle turret.

"Everyone still up?" Clint spoke into the comm on his soothreader.

"Yes, sir," Jess said, and made a quick wave from her new position behind a crate.

"Still breathing," Denton said, anxiously checking the trees in case the dray'va returned. Then he shouted, "Look!"

Captain Roelin Raike emerged from the tree line, spraying particle blasts toward all three of their positions. He was equipped in a combat suit that was worn down and damaged from the time spent in exodus. As quickly as he came into view, he vanished around the back of the *Astraeus*. A loud roar came from the tree line, announcing the team was surrounded.

The particle turret spun toward Clint once more, and he shouted, "Everyone, move!"

The turret blasted directly into the center of the combat arena, causing Clint, Jess, and Denton to scatter. Clint jump-jetted toward the *Astraeus*, banging into its hull with his shoulder. Jess jump-jetted toward the tree line, rolling her landing. Denton was pushed backward by the strength of the blast. The hover mule lazily glided into position next to him, and he pulled it behind another set of crates.

Clint pulled a grenade from his belt and jump-jetted onto the top of the *Astraeus*, planting himself next to the large turret. He was met with the butt end of a rifle to the nose before he could pull the pin on the grenade. Clint stumbled backward, nearly falling from the *Astraeus* but catching himself with a well-timed jump-jet boost.

The dray'va tackled Jess near the tree line, pinning one of her arms to the ground. Jess flicked her free hand, producing a sharp, rotating saw blade on her knuckle that she slammed into the beast's jaw.

Denton saw both marines struggling and acted quickly. He had only one clear choice: Clint was blocking his line of sight to Roelin, so he aimed at the dray'va pinning Jess. Denton let loose a round of shots, striking the dray'va in the back and sending arcs of blood flying into the air. The beast rolled in pain and scrambled back into the trees, vanishing once more. *The damn beast just won't die!* Denton thought as he tried to track where it went.

"Sarge!" Jess shouted.

Cint Foster jump-jetted into Roelin Raike's body, tackling him against the ship's hull out of sight of Denton and Jess. Clint didn't have time to reach his sidearm, so he flicked his hand and brought out the knuckle saw blade. He punched downward toward Roelin's helmet, hoping to smash his visor and cause Roelin to go lung-lock, but Roelin was too fast. With supernatural speed, Roelin dodged the blade, and Clint's fist got lodged into the ship's hull.

Before Clint could yank his hand free, Roelin gestured over his soothreader. The large particle turret spun, smashing into Clint and breaking his arm as it flung him across the bow. Clint caught himself before falling off the ship but had no time to react as Roelin jump-jetted onto him. Still recoiling from his now-broken arm, Clint could only watch as Roelin removed the pins from the grenades still left on the sergeant's belt and kicked him into the yard in one movement.

Clint hit the ground in front of Jess and Denton, then exploded.

"Fuck!" Jess Combs shouted, and ducked behind a crate as gore splattered the yard. Denton found cover on the other side of the combat arena. Roelin jumped off the top of the *Astraeus* and landed in a position by the nose of the ship.

Denton had a line of sight on Roelin, and lifted his collider pistol to line up a shot, then hesitated. Looming over Roelin was the phantom image of Nhymn. The Siren from his dreams, here in reality.

How is this possible?

The large particle turret whirred, aiming its barrel straight at Denton. He knew he only had time for one move. Denton could shoot Roelin and be killed by the turret. Or he could go with plan B, which wasn't much better.

Denton opted for plan B.

Denton launched himself on top of the hover mule and began gliding across the yard straight toward Roelin and the Siren. The turret blasted off another shot, missing Denton and the mule but striking close enough to send them flying the remaining distance. Denton landed on the base of his shoulders first, then rolled into the bush near Roelin's position, and the mule clattered against the ground, then smashed into a nearby Poe heartling, expelling most of its contents in the process.

Denton looked up and saw Roelin reaching toward him. Denton squeezed off one sloppy shot from his pistol, which Roelin easily dodged. Roelin snatched the gun away from Denton's hand as quickly as a cobra striking a mouse, then smashed the pistol across Denton's face.

Everything went fuzzy, then there was a heavy pressure inside Denton's mind as if Roelin had pressed his boot against his skull. Denton thought he was going to black out, but suddenly the pressure ceased. Roelin recoiled and asked with a voice humming with unnatural resonance, "What are you?"

"What?" Denton gasped between breaths.

There was no time to answer as particle shots rang out. Roelin pulled Denton upward and held him in front of his body as a human shield. Jess Combs stopped shooting and watched from her concealed position in the yard.

Roelin threw Denton so hard, he felt like he was in a car crash. He tumbled into the dirt and landed on his stomach. Denton spat out some blood, then brought himself to a knee. Before he could stand and turn toward Roelin, he heard the massive turret gun spinning toward him. Denton was on his knees in the open, with no way to move fast enough to escape the enormous turret blast. The smoldering crater where Clint Foster had exploded still drafted smoke into Denton's nostrils, showing him exactly how screwed he was.

"Hells," Denton grunted through gritted teeth as he froze, unsure of what to do. He lifted his arms in surrender as sweat dripped from his brow. *This is it.* He winced, bracing himself for destruction.

"Wait!" Jess Combs called out. "Hold your fire!" She threw her rifle and pistol out into the yard and stepped out from her position with her hands raised above her head.

Roelin Raike came out into the open and pressed the barrel of his rifle against Denton's head. Denton winced and sucked in air, bracing for death.

"Remove your soothreaders," Roelin said in a voice that hummed with alien vibration. Jess reached for her wrist, unclasped her soothreader, and tossed it into the grass. She nodded for Denton to do the same, and he lowered his arms, removed his soothreader, and threw it where Jess had done the same. Roelin let out a guttural hum that sounded adjacent to pleasure.

Denton looked at the field, the mess they had made. Clint's remains were nothing more than a few scraps of burnt armor, and Andrew's corpse lay headless near the outer hatch. Jess had managed to spare Denton's life, but for how long?

The ivory dray'va reemerged from the jungle and joined Roelin. Somehow, Roelin had trained the beast to do his bidding. He used his free hand to pat the creature's head. *"Good, Dol'Gohm."*

The beast had a name.

"Move," Roelin hissed, then marched Jess and Denton into the *Astraeus,* leaving the carnage outside.

FORTY

THE SHAKING STOPPED.

Inside the medical bay, Eliana was cut off from the carnage outside. She frantically tried to contact the others. "Denny? Clint? Jess? Is anyone there?" she asked over the comm channel on her soothreader, but there was no reply.

Eliana considered going outside to find them, but she was afraid of what she would discover. She had seen her father's murder, and it had destroyed her. If Denton …

No. She had to remain calm. Eliana hummed the tune to the Martian lullaby, "Far Away, Yet Also Near" like her mother had when she was a child, but it wasn't helping much. George lay with a bandaged arm in stable condition, and Talulo rested, now wingless. She had left his broken, burnt wings in the corner of the room, but their presence only reminded her of the pain that Talulo would find when he awoke.

The door to the medical bay pinged green, then opened. Eliana locked it, but the captain of the ship could easily override her locks.

Roelin Raike stepped into the room wearing a combat suit covered in dried blood. Eliana froze as pinpricks of shock tickled their way up her spine to the base of her neck.

Roelin stepped forward, and Eliana snatched the combat knife she'd used to amputate Talulo's wings. She pointed it at him, and although she had tears in her eyes, her face was all fire and fury.

"Don't touch them!" Eliana ordered the nightmare man. For a moment, it looked as though he'd obey. Then he removed his helmet and slammed it down on the end of the table.

"Ro-Roelin—" Eliana stuttered when she saw his face. This wasn't the Roelin she remembered from the early days of the Odysseus Colony. This man before her was gaunt, with a disheveled beard and messy long hair.

This man's eyes vibrated unnaturally.

After recovering from the initial shock, Eliana held the knife with more authority. She mouthed the words, *"Stay back,"* but could not put a voice to them.

Roelin raised his rifle in one hand.

Eliana inhaled sharply, allowing one tear to slip from her eye as she braced herself for the particle blast. Roelin had shot at her before, but this time, at this range, there was no way he could miss.

Yet, he did nothing. Roelin only twitched.

———•———

In the month since Roelin had been attacked by the duo of dray'vas, he had endured Hells. At the moment the beasts were going to tear him to pieces, the Siren had stepped in. Nhymn had charmed one of the beasts and now used Dol'Gohm as an enforcer to outpower Roelin. To show Roelin what true obedience looked like, Nhymn had forced the Dol'Gohm to kill its emerald-scaled companion.

Since then, Roelin had to feed Dol'Gohm. If Roelin did anything Nhymn didn't approve of, she would not only harm him in his mind, but would make sure Dol'Gohm hurt him in the physical realm as well.

Dol'Gohm also acted as a mental enhancer, feeding power into Nhymn's control. When the beast was near, Nhymn was unstoppable, but when Dol'Gohm moved away from Roelin's body, Roelin could feel some of his mental power return.

Roelin had been on a hunt with Dol'Gohm when the perimeter trap went off. The sound summoned him back to the *Astraeus*, and there he saw the first humans he had seen in four years. Real people, right in front of him.

Nhymn felt outnumbered. She needed to even the odds, so she took control of Roelin's body once more. Roelin was forced to watch Dol'Gohm crush that marine's spine and eat his head, and as he killed the sergeant with the grenade explosion, and to do nothing as he pushed that young man in front of the large particle turret to coerce the last marine to surrender.

Nhymn had read enough of the man named Denton's mind to know he could repair the *Astraeus*. The man was a mechanical engineer who had worked on spaceships for most of his life. Roelin also sensed fear and confusion in Nhymn in that moment. Something about Denton Castus scared Nhymn, and when the Siren was scared, she was sloppy.

Nhymn had left Dol'Gohm outside, which left her wide open to Roelin's mental attack. Using all the power he could muster inside his own mind, Roelin prevented Nhymn from shooting Eliana. He couldn't make the Siren put the gun down, but he could stop her from pulling the trigger.

Nhymn held her ground, pushing back against the waves of energy Roelin was sending forth. *"This is a fight you cannot win, Roelin,"* Nhymn's sinister alien voice echoed in the invisible chambers of the mental battlefield.

"Then we will stay paralyzed! I call that a win!" Roelin shouted back into the chasm of their shared mind.

"An impasse." Nhymn sighed. *"You still manage to surprise me, Roelin."* Nhymn forced a wave of mental energy at Roelin that stuttered his control.

Roelin's hand gripped the rifle tighter, almost squeezing the trigger. Eliana gasped, noticing the movement. A tear rolled from her eye and fell down her cheek.

"Roe ... *Please* ..." Eliana whimpered.

Roelin knew that if he gave one inch, Nhymn would squeeze the trigger and kill Eliana. Their wills struggled against each other, both seeking to gain momentum and failing.

"*If you kill her,*" Roelin said in his mind, "*I will fight you every instant going forward. You won't be able to scratch your nose without pushing through me. Every breath you breathe through my lungs will be a battle, every blink a war.*"

After some time, Nhymn said, "*I won't kill the girl if you take us to Sympha.*"

"*Not just her, you won't kill* anyone *else! This has gone on far enough!*" Roelin struggled through the waves of energy, but he held firm. Roelin gave one last plea: "*If you spare them, I will cooperate. I will take you to Sympha.*"

There was a silence. The mental waves of energy went calm.

"*I concede,*" Nhymn said.

"*Prove it,*" Roelin said.

Roelin's rifle barrel lowered to the floor, away from Eliana. He felt the Siren fade into the chasms of his mind. She was still in control of his body, but he could feel her violent intentions deteriorate. The deal was legitimate, but Roelin remained alert. "*You better honor this deal!*" Roelin shouted into the darkness of his mind.

The darkness did not answer back.

———— ◆ ————

"Roelin ..." Eliana whispered. Another tear rolled down her cheek and onto the floor. Roelin shook his head. "What *are* you?" Eliana asked as more tears formed. She shrunk back in horror and confusion. Eliana had come for answers but had only found more questions.

Roelin said nothing and approached Eliana, keeping his vibrating eyes on her as he grabbed the soothreader on her wrist and removed it with a forceful yank. He loomed over her.

"Hmmm …" Roelin mumbled, and turned his attention to Eliana's medical kit. He reached over and opened it, pulling out the syringe of the Madani Cure.

"Do you know what that is?" Eliana asked, hesitantly. "It's the cure to lung-lock. I brought it in case—" She watched as Roelin slammed the cure into his neck and smashed down on the plunger.

Roelin stumbled backward two steps, then regained his footing. His eyes ceased vibrating for the briefest moment, then ramped back into chaos. Roelin shook his head violently from side to side, reacting to the side effects of the cure to lung-lock.

Roelin moved away from Eliana to conceal himself in shadow. He exited the medical bay and locked access to the area, using his command overrides to prevent her from leaving the room.

Eliana slunk down to the floor, allowing herself to sob. She reached for her medical kit. All the telltales for life signatures for the other scouts not present in the room with her showed flatlines. The removal of their soothreaders destroyed her ability to monitor their health remotely. There was only the steady beep of her own pulse and the pulses of George and Talulo.

Eliana summoned her courage and acted. The medical kit allowed her to ping their location to the *Rogers* in cases of emergencies, so she opened a manual toggle lock and switched the GPS on to ping Lieutenant Commander Rocco Gainax. Eliana input a message in the small keyboard on the side panel:

Astraeus found at this location. Dangerous. Call for backup from Odysseus Colony. Do not approach alone.

Eliana shut the medical kit and sat on the floor. Her back to the wall, she allowed only a few more tears to liberate themselves from her eyes. She wiped them away. It was quiet now. She continued to listen to the metronome of beeps from George and Talulo.

Eliana had saved them for now, and that was all she could do.

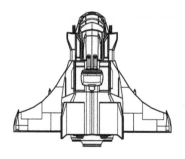

FORTY-ONE

THE AIR WAS CRISP. Roelin felt it in his lungs.

He stood outside the *Astraeus* with his helmet off for the first time since arriving on Kamaria. The man with the vibrating eyes laughed maniacally into the night, shaking the stars with his hilarity. It was a new sensation to Roelin Raike, but a familiar one to Nhymn. The scent of the jungle filled his nostrils, then the smell of decay invaded his senses.

Dol'Gohm was devouring what remained of Lance Corporal Andrew Louis. The huge beast ripped limbs from the deceased man and greedily gobbled them up. Nhymn released control of Roelin—she wanted him to watch.

"What have you *done* ..." Roelin whispered as he slunk to his knees, weak from fighting the possession. His eyes dripped tears as he silently watched Dol'Gohm consume the first human he had seen in four years.

Roelin lowered his head to the grass in defeat.

Nhymn stepped out from behind him, putting herself in front of his view but not blocking the carnage of Dol'Gohm's meal.

"The young one," Nhymn whispered, and flashed an image of Denton Castus into Roelin's mind, *"fixes starships."*

"Good, you got what you wanted," Roelin weakly muttered.

"Now let me die."

"No, Roelin. You have a larger role to play here. There is a reason I chose you." Nhymn peered into Roelin with her large bird-skull head and deep eye chasms. *"You're a warrior, Roelin. The best. Better than … "* Nhymn's phantom hand drifted toward Andrew's remains. *"I'll need you with me when we get to Sympha."*

"Leave these people out of it," Roelin said, meeting her gaze with his own stern glare.

"As I conceded before, if you cooperate with me," Nhymn said, *"I will not harm these humans."*

Roelin said nothing and looked back down at the grass. He considered the situation they were in for a moment. He knew he couldn't defy Nhymn for long, especially with Dol'Gohm strengthening her hold over him like a generator feeding power into a machine. Nhymn's offer allowed the others to remain safe, as far as he could trust the Siren. Roelin knew she was a deceiver, but he had no other options.

"We stick to the deal," Roelin said.

"Good," Nhymn said. The Siren rushed herself into his mind once more. Roelin's eyes faded again to darkness. He stood mechanically and marched back into the *Astraeus*.

———— ✦ ————

"Damn it!" Jess Combs banged her hand against the metal wall of the brig she was trapped in with Denton. It was a dark and musty room, with bones of various animals littering the cell next to theirs, and the stink was foul. An encasement barrier hummed, keeping the prisoners from the door.

"Shit," Denton whispered to himself. The situation was becoming more and more perilous. He'd thought they would make it to the *Astraeus* and find a skeleton sitting in the pilot's chair, rotting away after a tremendous crash. Denton said, "You probably should have shot Roelin instead of saving me."

"I wasn't going to just let him kill you," Jess said as she paced back and forth next to the encasement barrier. She huffed and whispered, "Shit."

"I'm grateful for that. I just don't know if I was worth it." Denton sighed.

Jess knelt next to Denton and gave him a stern look. When Denton had first met Jess, he'd thought she was more like a robot. She'd seemed so cold and distant. But at this moment, Jess wasn't a robot; her eyes were glossy with the threat of tears. And she wasn't distant—instead, she put a hand on his shoulder.

"Everyone is worth it," Jess said. She stood up. "There was someone I fought in the war with who I cared deeply for. We fell in love even with the Undriel tearing everything down around us. Emily was always so optimistic about how we'd win the war, and everything would go back to *the way it was*." Jess wrung her hands together. "I didn't want it to go back to *the way it was*. The *way it was* sucked. People fought each other for money and land instead of fighting machines to survive. But now I see what she saw. It was never about the way it was, it was always about the way it could be." Jess nodded. "After coming to Kamaria and seeing how life can be without greed toxifying our species, I now see she was right all along. I just wish Emily was still here to say, *I told you so*."

"I'm sorry for your loss," Denton said.

"Emily died protecting a civilian transport from the Undriel." Jess looked down into her hands. "She gave her life in a war that felt impossible, for people she had never met before. All because the way it could be was worth the cost. I had to try and save you, Denton. And I'm glad I did."

Denton nodded. "Thank you, Jess."

"Just doing my job." Jess nodded back.

The clanging of boots echoed down the hall. The door to the brig slid open.

Captain Roelin Raike stood in the doorway, a harsh shadow against the light from the hall. Denton could see Nhymn's ghostly form hovering just above Roelin's shoulders and wondered if Jess could see her too.

Roelin approached the cell and scanned a data pad with his soothreader. The encasement barrier blipped off.

Jess Combs made her move.

She launched herself from a crouched position. Roelin, two steps ahead, dodged the lunge and grabbed her bicep. He slammed his elbow hard into Jess's chin with a resounding crack. Roelin gripped Jess's bicep and yanked outward—the popping noise it made signified her arm was dislocated. Jess shouted in anguish as Roelin prepared to strike her once more.

"Stop!" Roelin shouted, confusing both Jess and Denton. Roelin shoved Jess back into the cell, allowing her to slump over and hold her uninjured arm against her broken jaw.

Roelin and the Siren both turned their heads to face Denton.

"Easy now," Denton tried to reason with his hands up. He tried to squirm away but wasn't fast enough to dodge the lightning-quick grab of Roelin's arm. Denton was shoved into the hallway. The brig door slammed behind him, leaving Jess alone with the hum of the barrier and the bones of long-dead animals in the dark, musty cell.

In the hallway of the *Astraeus*, the hazy light revealed the Siren more clearly to Denton. Roelin turned toward him, and Denton noticed that his eyes looked like vibrating gelatin orbs, the pupils swirling and undulating unnaturally. Denton barely held back from screaming at the sight of it. Roelin was indeed a nightmare, exactly as Fergus had described.

"What do you want from me?" Denton asked.

"You fix starships," Roelin said with a voice infused with alien vibration.

"Yeah." Denton scanned the dilapidated metal hallway. "You want me to fix the *Astraeus*?"

Roelin nodded his head. Denton knew this was going to be the repair job of his life, and he suddenly wished for his old routine days to return. He was worried about Eliana, and her face flashed in his mind.

"She is alive," Roelin said. "Cooperate, and she will remain that way."

Denton kept his eye on Roelin's hand as it hovered just above the collider pistol strapped to his hip. Denton wasn't exactly sure what was happening, but he was going to have to take this sick man's word for law.

"Alright," Denton said, uneasy in the presence of the man and the ghost. "Keep her safe, and I'll fix your ship. When I finish, you let us go, and you'll never see us again."

Roelin and Nhymn peered at him. "Perfect."

Denton suddenly felt the pressure of what he had to do. Everyone's lives depended on him doing this job to perfection. Roelin waved his arm toward the outer hatch, and Denton walked out the door.

The Milky Way was spread across the Kamarian sky as Denton walked ahead of Roelin toward the bow of the *Astraeus*. All that remained in the blood-stained grass where Andrew's body once lay was a smattering of gore and tattered combat armor. Denton remembered the beast that had killed the lance corporal. Dol'Gohm was probably out there in the shadows of the jungle, watching and waiting. A cold sweat formed on Denton's brow.

The front panel of the *Astraeus* was in a bad state. Denton could see that Roelin had attempted to repair it but lacked the knowledge required to get the job done right.

Denton needed his tools from the hover mule, but once again, the mule was missing. He turned around, scanning the area. He remembered gliding across the yard on the mule and being thrown from it when the large turret shot at him.

He found the mule smashed into the side of a Poe heartling, his tools scattered on the ground around it. "I gotta get my equipment," Denton said, waving a hand at the mess of items.

"Go ahead," Roelin said in a haunting whisper.

Denton walked over to the mule and grabbed the handle. He pulled hard, straining himself, but there was no movement. The mule was stuck firmly in the tree. He tried again, getting the mule to budge slightly. Roelin pushed Denton aside, grabbed the handle, and brutally jerked the mule free from the tree with one swift rip. The mule slammed into the dirt and kicked up a cloud of dust.

"Uh, thanks," Denton said awkwardly, and powered up the mule. It lifted off the ground and hovered in place with an injured wobble. For a moment, he appreciated the sturdiness of the hover mule; even after being blown up twice, the old machine still had life in it.

Roelin sat down on a nearby crate and trained his pistol on Denton's back. Denton heard a growl as he knelt to retrieve a wrench. The ivory-scaled dray'va that had slain Andrew emerged slowly from a bush. It had wounds all over its body from the multiple particle blasts it had sustained. The beast seemed to heal quickly—some of the holes were already sealed. Its large eyes vibrated just like its master's, and its lips peeled back to reveal a maw full of bloodied, jagged teeth.

Dol'Gohm stepped around Denton and walked toward Roelin, then hunched down next to him like a large dog waiting for some scraps of food. Roelin's hand patted the back of the dray'va's head at the base of its skull where two large spikes emerged.

"Now, fix the Astraeus," Roelin commanded.

"You got it." Denton nodded, grabbed the wrench, and walked over to the work area. Denton plugged a cable from the mule into the front panel of the *Astraeus*. A diagnostic report flickered on a data screen on the injured mule, and several pieces reported they needed to be replaced with parts that could be manufactured in the mule's replicator. Roelin lacked access to a replicator and didn't realize precisely how dead in the water he really had been.

The part that worried Denton the most was that the software on the *Astraeus* would need to cycle, which was a long process for an Undertaker-class warship in this condition. Would Nhymn give him the time necessary for that? Or when he finished with the repairs and began the cycle, would she deem him useless and decide to execute everyone? Denton was going to have to make himself useful even after the repairs were completed if he hoped to keep everyone alive.

"Here we go," Denton whispered to himself, and began replicating the ship parts he would need. The replicator hummed, creating the smaller pieces first. He grabbed a few replicated fuses and brought them to his work area, removing the old dead fuses and plugging in the new functional pieces. Then he decided to try something.

"Nhymn," Denton said, looking out of the side of his eye at the phantom hovering over Roelin. The Siren loosened its grip on Roelin for the briefest moment; Denton saw the light come back into the gaunt man's eyes, and he gasped like a man recovering from drowning. Roelin quickly sank back into the abyss. Denton continued, "That's your name, right?"

Roelin stood up, and Dol'Gohm growled. Roelin adjusted the pistol in his hand but remained silent. Denton snapped his attention back to the broken panel. He jerked a piece away and tossed it over his shoulder into the grass. "Your sister is Sympha, isn't she?"

Roelin moved forward rapidly and shoved the gun against Denton's head, and Denton's eyes widened. The weapon began to twitch against his skin. Roelin shoved the barrel forward into Denton's head, knocking him to the ground.

Denton looked up at the Siren, who was glowing with anger. Gnarled, bony spikes protruding from her hardened ivory carapace glistened in the twilight, and her worm-skin arms ending in a phalanx of razor-like talons flexed with rage. Nhymn was heaving in anger.

"What are you?" It was no longer Roelin's voice at all. The voice had come into Denton's mind directly, a sound he was familiar with from his nightmares. *"Something is wrong,"* she hissed with suspicion.

Denton's head was thrown backward, arching his spine to its limit. He tried to shout in pain but was muffled by Nhymn's mental probing. She pushed further into his mind until, suddenly, her arm was thrown backward as if she'd touched an encasement barrier. Nhymn looked down at her taloned hand, then at Denton, who was heaving on the ground.

"No more talking. Fix this ship," Nhymn said, keeping Roelin's gun aimed at Denton.

In the abyss of Roelin's mind, he watched the young man work. *How the Hells did he just repel Nhymn?*

For a moment, Roelin felt hope.

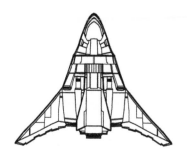

FORTY-TWO

HOURS PASSED, BUT TO Eliana, it felt like years inside the medical bay of the *Astraeus*. She wondered if the others were still alive. *Is Roelin killing them? Is he going to kill us all?*

"Ugh," George Tanaka groaned, and shifted on his table. "Where am I?"

Eliana came to his side and clutched his hand. "George, can you hear me?"

"Elly, is that—" George stopped himself as he took in his surroundings. "Where are we?"

"The medical bay of the *Astraeus*," Eliana said, checking his pupils with a flashlight.

"Are we going back to Odysseus Colony?"

"No. Something happened. We aren't safe." She squeezed his hand.

"What's going on? I remember seeing the *Astraeus*, then ..." George trailed off. "Talulo?" George turned his head and saw the wingless, unconscious auk'nai on the table beside him. "Oh God! Is he ...?"

"Talulo is stable." She sighed. "I had to amputate his wings. A perimeter trap went off, and he took most of the impact. It hit you pretty hard as well. We dragged you into the *Astraeus*, and I managed to stabilize you both. But be careful with your right arm, it took a lot of shrapnel." Eliana pulled up a holographic display of George's fractured arm.

"What about Roelin?" George asked, ignoring the scans of his arm.

"He was in here." She looked toward the floor. "Something's wrong with him. His eyes ..." She fluttered her fingers in front of her face. "He's dangerous, George. I don't know if the others made it. We're locked in here."

George rested his head down on the table, staring straight up at the ceiling. "So, Roelin survived."

"I'm not sure he did, actually. Whoever that was that came in here didn't look like the Roelin we knew."

Eliana's medical kit pinged, a green light blinking on its exterior. She opened the kit and saw a message from Lieutenant Commander Rocco Gainax.

REINFORCEMENTS ARE COMING. HOLD TIGHT. ETA SIX HOURS.

———————— ◆ ————————

Denton worked through the night on various parts of the derelict Undertaker-class warship. The final pieces came together on the bridge of the *Astraeus*. Roelin and Dol'Gohm loomed over him as he worked away on an engine panel under the platform of the pilot's seat. Denton used a screw thimble to fix the last remaining mechanism inside, then attached a cable from the panel to the hover mule to get a final assessment.

The bridge's holographic command graphs activated, illuminating the room with a hazy blue light. System readouts flickered from yellow to green. It gave an estimated maximum range the ship could fly in its current state.

Nhymn's phantom form hovered above Roelin's body, scanning the various data screens. She silently analyzed what she observed, and

Denton felt like his life was on the line again. If this wasn't satisfactory work, she might choose to end him right there. Hells, she may even decide to do so if he was successful. Denton waited for verification, but there wasn't any.

"It—" Denton began. Roelin snapped his head toward him. Denton continued, "The *Astraeus* needs to cycle its power. It will take a few hours. After that, it should fly."

"*Should?*" Nhymn hissed.

"It *will* fly," Denton said, reinforcing his statement. Roelin smiled. It was the only indication that Denton may have done well.

"So, what now?" Denton asked. "Will you let us go?"

There was no answer. Denton gulped, hoping he hadn't just aided Nhymn for nothing. "Will you go find Sympha?"

Nhymn whirled her head toward him, and Roelin's smile faded into an expression of pure rage. She approached Denton and grabbed his arm. *"Say that name again, and I will kill you and everyone else here,"* Nhymn shouted into his mind. Roelin grabbed Denton and thrust him out into the hallway.

Roelin escorted Denton to the brig and threw him back into the cell. Jess was seated against the wall, her arm and jaw hanging at unnatural angles. She coughed and winced in pain. Roelin turned away from the cell and left the brig, sealing the door behind him.

"Jess! Are you alright?" Denton rushed to her side, hovering his hands over her, wanting to help but unsure how. He could fix the ship, but fixing people was a whole different game. Eliana would know what to do, but she was locked away somewhere.

Jess coughed again and attempted to talk through a broken jaw, her speech slurred. "I'll hhh-livve," she said, and gestured to her shoulder. "Help pushhh."

Denton put his hand on Jess's shoulder with a flat palm. They nodded to each other, ready for the next step. Denton shoved forward, and an audible popping noise resounded as the bones jumped back into position. Jess huffed through her nose, hard. She used her good hand to touch her hanging jaw and winced.

Denton shook his head and said, "Elly might be able to fix it."

Jess nodded, and Denton took a seat next to her against the wall. He thumbed his jacket pocket and pulled out the ring he and his parents had created for Eliana. Denton hoped she was safe, but he had no way of knowing for sure. He only had the word of a violent alien phantom.

"The *Astraeus* is functional again. We might be let go soon," Denton said. Jess huffed. Denton continued, "We'll know in a few hours."

Denton was exhausted from the all-night repairs. He felt the urge to remain awake, but something beyond his control dragged him into a slumber. It was as if the life was pulled out of him.

FORTY-THREE

THE WIND RUSHED PAST Denton from behind. His eyes were closed, and no matter how hard he pushed to open them, they wouldn't budge. His arms drifted upward loosely, and his legs seemed to dangle. Denton realized he was falling from some great height. A scream filled the void around him, forcing Denton to cover his ears to fruitlessly try to hide from the immense sound.

Then, suddenly, silence.

Denton lay on his back for a moment to collect himself and slowly opened his eyes. He was in the dream world once more, but this time, it was different. His violent entrance into this place had been brought on by an outside force. Denton knew these were no longer just dreams, they were something else.

The cave outside of the City of the Dead loomed before Denton again. Time moved at its average pace, in no rush to slide through eons like it had been before. He looked down to see small creatures made of stone and electricity wandering around. These little nezzarforms seemed to be building the larger stone statues that Denton had become familiar with in the archive footage. The little workers were cute, in their own odd way.

A high-pitched scream forced Denton to sit up quick and cover his ears.

The sound of something slamming hard against the ground grew louder and more rapid, approaching Denton from behind. He jerked his head in time to see Nhymn rushing toward him at an incredible speed. She tore up grass and burst through any nezzarforms that strayed into her path. Denton covered his face to protect himself.

Nhymn passed through him like a baseball thrown through an open window. Denton lowered his arms and watched her sprint away toward the source of the scream. Then he scrambled to his feet to catch up, breaking into a dash to chase the Siren.

They ran deep into the Kamarian forest. Denton noticed there was no auk'nai City of the Dead hovering above them, as he had seen in the archival footage. This vision must have been from before the city was built.

There was a clearing ahead filled with broken Poe heartling branches and the carnage of a brawl. Nhymn burst through another swath of brush and into the clearing.

The stone sentry, Karx, was pinned against a tree. A yellow-scaled dray'va was ripping away at one of his horselike legs. Karx attempted to slash at the beast, but the sentry's attacks only angered it further.

Sympha was cornered against a boulder by a second dray'va with crimson scales. The beast had a taloned claw gripped around one of Sympha's floating tentacles, forcing her to the ground so she couldn't fly away. It clamped down on another tentacle with its maw, sending Sympha into a shrieking frenzy.

"*Stop!*" Nhymn shouted, and pounced onto the back of the crimson dray'va. Their voices were more precise in Denton's mind now, as if the visions had adapted to him.

Nhymn clawed away at the hard scales on Crimson's back, but the beast wouldn't release her twin sister. Crimson thrust its head back, stabbing into Nhymn with its long horns and knocking her away. Nhymn tried again, lunging forward and jabbing her horn into Crimson's back.

Crimson squealed but continued to hold Sympha down. The beast rolled sideways like a crocodile, tumbling Sympha into the dirt and knocking Nhymn away. Nhymn recoiled in time to be swiped hard with Crimson's tail and thrown into a nearby tree.

The yellow dray'va clawed at Karx's skull, leaving deep cuts. Karx howled in pain, struggling to free himself to save his creator.

Crimson clamped down once more on Sympha's tentacle, spraying her blood through its sharp teeth. Sympha let out another shriek of pain.

"Stop! I beg you ... " Nhymn whimpered. She felt despair so deep that Denton could feel it too. It was like someone was standing on his chest and threatening to cave in his sternum.

The despair shifted into infinite anger. Denton felt a rush of heat that started in his heart and surged into his extremities. His fingers tingled, and his arms went from feeling like jelly to like sharp swords. His mind whirred like a machine. Nhymn got to her feet and angled herself at the crimson dray'va.

Crimson arched his neck back, preparing to lunge at Sympha's throat tendrils. Denton thought he felt an explosion inside of his body, as if his arms, legs, and head were propelled away from his torso.

"STOP!" Nhymn shouted, her voice boomed like a jet going supersonic. Crimson froze, its maw still open as its eyes exploded into torrents of blood. The eyeless beast lowered its head and released Sympha from its grasp with a haunting calmness.

Sympha was scared and confused. She grabbed her wounded tentacle in both claws and held it close like a panicked child clutching a teddy bear for comfort.

Nhymn stood with her talons outstretched toward Crimson. She emitted the Siren equivalent of laughter, and Denton could feel the wild hysteria inside him. Crimson echoed these noises with an eerie series of grunts. Yellow stopped clawing and biting at Karx and turned toward its hunting partner.

Nhymn turned toward Yellow, and Crimson did the same, like a puppet obeying its puppeteer. Yellow's eyes darted between them both. Nhymn pulled her hand back, then thrust it forward with lightning speed.

Before Yellow could react, Crimson tackled it to the ground. Crimson's jaw smashed into Yellow's throat and ripped it wide open, sending wild streaks of blood into the air. Nhymn moved closer to the violence with her arm outstretched. She had finally discovered her power.

"All this time, it was not my place to create." Nhymn laughed. *"I was put here to control."* This revelation filled her with ecstasy; it flowed through her blood vessels with a tickling heat. Crimson ripped Yellow to pieces, blood and viscera covering a mess of bones. Nhymn laughed more and then released her control of Crimson.

"Nhymn …" Sympha whispered as she watched the carnage. Crimson shrieked and clawed at the empty sockets where its eyes had been. It rolled around wildly in the grass, splashing in the blood of its hunting partner. Nhymn howled in laughter at the spectacle. Crimson clamored off into the forest and out of sight. It would not survive long without the use of its vision, but Nhymn didn't care. She calmed herself down and looked at her claws, feeling the newly discovered power within them.

Sympha floated over to Karx and blew mist into his wounds, stopping the bleeding but leaving behind the scars from the fight. Sympha helped Karx to his feet, paying careful attention to his damaged rear leg. Sympha and Karx left Nhymn in the forest with the bloody corpse of Yellow, unsure of what would come next.

Denton followed Sympha and Karx through the dream forest. He stumbled when time shifted without warning. Sympha and Karx vanished, and others appeared in their place.

Denton watched a group of ancient auk'nai discover the area and build the platforms that the Alpha Scout Team would eventually call the City of the Dead. There was an abundance of life, a thriving auk'nai metropolis expanding and flourishing over the rapidly shifting time. Denton expected that decades must have washed by as he walked through the forest and watched as the floating city was erected above him.

Time slowed down once more to normal. Denton was still in the forest, standing under a floating city platform, but something felt wrong.

No auk'nai were moving about. It was too quiet. He could feel Nhymn, Sympha, and Karx approach from the bushes behind him. Nhymn wanted to show them something; she was excited.

Nhymn walked up beside Denton. She stood taller now, the gnarled spikes on her carapace more extended than they had been before. She beckoned the others to follow her as she jumped up the side of a tall tree and clawed her way high enough to leap onto the floating platform.

Sympha gracefully floated upward, pulling a few loose rocks and leaves from the ground with her as she defied gravity. Her features had become softer, her carapace had rounder curves than before, and she emitted a motherly aura when she passed Denton. He felt comforted for the first time during one of these visions.

Karx was deteriorating. The sentry didn't seem to be an actual Siren, but was something more than a regular nezzarform. Denton was unsure of Karx's place here. The sentry's carapace looked cracked, and loose skin hung from his arms at odd angles. Karx jabbed his claws into the tree and pulled himself up with great effort. They had all now vanished behind the lip of the upper platform.

Denton climbed up after the Sirens and their sentry and eventually made it onto the platform on his hands and knees. He felt the pressure of a thousand eyes watching him and looked up. The entire auk'nai city stood before Denton like a full auditorium waiting for a presentation to begin. Nhymn had perfected using her power of control. Each auk'nai had her signature vibrating eyes.

Denton had seen Nhymn's condition in the present-day reality—she was a parasite leaching off of Roelin for control. But here, in this vision of the past, she was the puppeteer of a kidnapped army. Nhymn was in her prime.

"What is this?" Sympha asked as she watched the crowd. *"I have seen these creatures before, and they have not acted this way."*

"Watch, sister," Nhymn said, and raised her claw, palm facing the city of puppets. She spread her talons apart, and the auk'nai lifted their hands in unison, mimicking her gesture. Nhymn pushed her arms out to her sides, and the auk'nai did as well. She raised one arm up, and lowered the other toward the floor, and the auk'nai copied. Nhymn then turned to face her sister, and the auk'nai looked at Sympha as well.

"Isn't it amazing?" Nhymn asked.

"This is unnatural. These creatures need—" Sympha began, but Nhymn interrupted her.

"Watch!" Nhymn hissed, and pushed her claws out toward the crowd, then pulled inward.

A few auk'nai emerged from the group carrying oddly shaped stones. Denton recognized the shapes: they were similar to the stone nezzarforms that waddled about in front of the cave, only larger.

"These creatures can help you create larger nezzarforms," Nhymn said with pride.

The five auk'nai stepped forward to the lip of a platform and hopped across to the adjacent platform. The last auk'nai, smaller than the rest, misjudged the distance and toppled sideways, falling from the platform. In its puppet-like trance, it failed to spread its wings and cease its fall.

"Stupid thing!" Nhymn hissed as the little auk'nai fell, nothing more than an interruption to her perfect performance. The auk'nai landed headfirst on the boulders on the forest floor, its long neck snapping. It twitched, then let out one last gasp, expiring in the dirt with blood oozing from its beak. Denton recognized the scene. Three hundred years from this moment, the Alpha Scout Team would find that body perfectly preserved during their initial exploration of the City of the Dead.

"Nhymn!" Sympha shouted, horrified. *"You must let them go, it isn't good for them!"*

"What?" Nhymn took a step back in shock. The auk'nai mirrored her pain, reaching for their chests weakly as if their hearts were collectively going to fail. Nhymn pleaded, *"Are you not impressed, Sympha? I did this for you."* The atmosphere changed. Something unnatural was happening.

"Nhymn, please! Release them! This is wrong!" Sympha begged.

Nhymn's pain shifted into immense anger. It was unfair! Sympha had this beautiful power to create, and she was telling Nhymn that her own ability to control was *wrong?* Nhymn was always wrong, wasn't she? Nhymn was still the weaker sister. She couldn't create, she couldn't float, she couldn't love anything the way Sympha did. Why did Sympha get all the beauty in this world while Nhymn was tossed the scraps?

It was unfair!

"Stop? No," Nhymn said. She would never stop.

"Sister, please! It is not our place to control the wills of others!" Sympha pleaded.

"Isn't it, though?" Nhymn hissed, and stepped toward Sympha. *"It is precisely my place! It is the only thing I was given in this world! I should be able to control whatever I please!"* Nhymn shouted. *"I should even be able to control YOU!"*

There was an eruption of screaming as the auk'nai attacked each other without remorse. The violence was indiscriminate. Auk'nai butchered their neighbors, brothers, sisters, mothers, fathers, and children. Beaks stabbed into chests, claws ripped out throats. Blood spilled and sprayed.

"No! No! What are you doing?" Sympha shouted in anguish. She turned to Nhymn one last time and watched as the puppeteer orchestrated the show. Sympha had no choice: *"Karx! Stop her!"*

Karx charged Nhymn, pounding forward with all four of his horselike legs and rearing his long, muscular arm backward for a massive swing.

Nhymn sensed this and acted accordingly. She was one step ahead of Karx, pushing herself down and around the attack, then flicked her hand toward the auk'nai mob.

Six bloodied auk'nai soared toward Karx. The first one drop-kicked him sideways while the others struck him from all angles. The six crazed auk'nai continued to beat Karx to the ground.

Although the world was busy killing itself around them, Nhymn was alone with Sympha now.

"Nhymn, wait!" Sympha pleaded, and tried to float away.

"No, Sympha." Nhymn thrust her hand toward Sympha and forced her to the ground using only her superior mental strength. *"If you can't see what a wonder my power is, I will have to make you see it!"*

Sympha felt the waves of control slip over her, like high tide in a sea of razors. Sympha pushed back as much as she could, but the waves kept crashing relentlessly. Nhymn was shouting in their minds, and Denton fell to his knees from the sound ringing through his skull.

"It is UNFAIR! You should have loved this. We could have built something together." Nhymn's hand shook with rage as she pushed further into Sympha's mind. *"No matter. I will do it myself. I will keep this planet and all things within it. It will be my garden, and it will have no shelter for you."* She thrust her claw downward, standing over her sister. Sympha's large skull began to breathe out the green life-giving mist, which drifted lazily up toward Nhymn's hand.

Nhymn watched the mist rise and dance along her forearm. Denton felt the sensation on his arm as well, like cold water running over a sunburn. It was refreshing, although it came with a sting. For the briefest moment, Nhymn eased her control, entranced by the green mist's power. The violent crowd grew silent. The forest breeze whistled uninterrupted.

The break of control was all Karx needed to evade his aggressors. Before Nhymn could turn to face him, Karx knocked her to the ground. The world stood still.

Sympha lay on the ground next to Nhymn, still recovering from the mental assault. She turned her head to watch as Karx reared back onto his hind legs.

"Wait!" Sympha shouted, but she was too late. Karx smashed down with his mighty front hoof, destroying Nhymn's skull.

Hot tar shot out from under Karx's hoof as Nhymn's body flailed in agony. Sympha screeched in horror as she watched her sister thrash against the platform.

Sympha pushed Karx away and grabbed Nhymn's dying body.

"Nhymn." She begged Nhymn not to die but could not control death itself. She breathed the green mist toward her sister's smashed skull, but there was no response. Nhymn's flailing ceased, and her body went limp. Sympha curled Nhymn into her chest, shaking with a mix of rage and sadness. She exploded into a wave of green mist, covering the entire city in a blanket of the unique bacteria, preserving the scene for all of eternity.

The few auk'nai not killed in the slaughter looked up at the mist that was slowly falling over broken and bloody bodies. They had witnessed the whole event, watched as their own families were ripped apart by bodies they did not fully control. They cried out in torment, holding any pieces of their loved ones they still recognized.

Sympha held her sister awhile longer while Karx stood ever vigilant near her. Night fell over the city, and slowly, the surviving auk'nai dispersed from the evil place. It had finally become what it was in the scout videos Denton had watched: the City of the Dead.

Sympha stood and ordered Karx to carry Nhymn. He obeyed and lifted the limp body from the platform, leaving behind only a puddle of tar and some bone fragments. They traveled back to the cave.

The valley before the cave entrance was littered with tall, lifeless nezzarform statues. The little stone workers that built the statues watched the funeral progression. Karx carried the body into the cave while Sympha waited outside. The stars continued to swirl, just as they had done for eons, and eventually, Karx emerged from the cave alone.

"You will stay here. Watch over her," Sympha said with a sadness Denton could feel in his chest. *"Protect the little ones."*

Sympha floated away into the night, leaving behind her eternal sentry to guard her sister's grave. Time sped up once more, and Denton watched as Karx stood utterly still for hundreds of years, calcifying into a stone sentry.

Then the valley was quiet, and one by one, the tiny workers faded into the statues they'd built, becoming nothing more than lifeless rocks. Denton was now alone, so he wondered why the dream didn't release him. His thoughts were disturbed by howling coming from inside the cave.

The light of the two moons illuminated the interior of the cave as Denton descended the stone ramp. The howling grew louder as he walked farther into the abyss.

Before him, Nhymn's broken body lay preserved by the same bacteria Sympha had coated the city in. But the howling continued to echo from around him. *Where's it coming from?*

Out of the corner of his eye, shapes were moving in the low-hanging mist of the cave crypt. He turned his head to find a shape moving through the swirling mist. He concentrated and allowed his eyes to adjust.

After a while, Denton saw them.

Nhymn's phantom, much like the one he had seen controlling Roelin in the *Astraeus*, was being chased by a thousand lesser ghosts. Other spirits that had strived for life and failed where Sympha and Nhymn had succeeded.

They tackled her and ripped her apart as she shrieked in agony. Time sped up, and Denton watched as sunlight filled the cave in a heartbeat, then as moonlight filled it once more. Again, Nhymn's phantom was chased and attacked by the lesser ghosts. The sun came, the night came, Nhymn was destroyed. Again and again, it happened; he watched it happen a thousand times. Sun, moon, destruction, repeat. It felt like Denton would witness it repeating for eternity. Nhymn's relentless howls fell on the deaf ears of Karx, who remained silent outside. There was nothing that could be done.

The sun rose once more, and unexpectedly, it remained. Denton assumed time had returned to normal. He heard footsteps echoing from the entrance of the cave and a familiar voice he never thought he'd hear in this dreamscape. "There's a faint amount of electricity running through the slime on the floor here," George Tanaka said.

The Alpha Scout Team entered the cave in full atmospheric gear. Captain Roelin Raike and Eliana Veston were at the front of the group. Roelin shifted his weapon directly toward Denton, and for a moment, Denton wondered if he should say something. *Can you see me?* Roelin moved away, which answered Denton's question, but Eliana hesitated a moment longer.

"Elly, you have to turn back. Leave this place," Denton said as he moved closer to Eliana, but she shivered and hurried toward Roelin. He followed them, wanting to protect them from what lay ahead, but he was helpless to do so.

"There's something over here," John Veston said. Denton was taken aback seeing John Veston alive and exploring, having never met Eliana's father in the real world. John was dead, and yet, Denton was haunting *him*. Was this how John saw the world now? Was John with them in the real world in the same way that Denton was with them in this dream?

Denton believed he was being shown this for a reason, although he wasn't sure why. Perhaps it was just his unconscious mind flickering through old memories of the archive footage. He remained in the cave and watched as the rest of the scout team joined John near Nhymn's corpse. George knelt to scan the Siren with his bioscope. Roelin continued to search the cave, nervously shifting his weapon around.

George knelt over Nhymn's body and said, "Incredible." He pointed at the eye sockets on the corpse. "These large openings have a slimy interior. It's a lot like the walls of this cave." He then proceeded to give his theory on how the Siren's biology worked.

The slime was a new way for the unique creature to sense the world. Denton almost chuckled, knowing that was only half of it. George had no idea how advanced the Sirens were, capable of creating and controlling life itself. It was as if George had only figured out how a tongue worked but failed to see the brain behind it. He couldn't fault the biologist. Denton wouldn't have known either without seeing it firsthand.

Denton saw her then, Nhymn's phantom crouching in the fog. She was hiding from her relentless ghostly pursuers when she saw Roelin. Denton wasn't quick enough to stop what happened next.

"Watch out!" Denton reached his hand out to try and stop Nhymn as she launched herself toward Roelin. For a moment, Denton felt as though he'd grasped her, slowing down her lunge but not enough to stop it entirely.

Nhymn vanished into Roelin's helmet as he reflexively tried to block his face. The gesture was useless as she had already worked her way into his mind. Denton had a sinking feeling that he could have prevented everything that happened next if he'd been faster. Was he really there? Was he supposed to intercept Nhymn at that moment? Was that the purpose of all this?

"Hey, Roe," Eliana said, "everything okay over there?"

Roelin grunted and shook his head as the lesser ghosts in the cave wailed in anger. They had watched Nhymn steal her way into life a second time, and their jealousy was palpable. Roelin grunted, "It's so loud."

"What?" Eliana asked. Roelin answered her by stumbling backward and coughing raggedly. Eliana ran over to him.

Denton fell to one knee. That was it, the moment Roelin became possessed. They'd called it a mental breakdown, but it wasn't that at all. Denton watched silently as Eliana inspected Roelin and found nothing wrong with him.

"Elly, you have to quarantine Roelin. He's going to do horrible things if you don't," Denton tried to urge Eliana, and he could see that she sensed him on some level. "If you don't stop him, *he's going to kill your father.*"

Humans use rea

Denton reached for Eliana's arm, and she jerked away from him. He hung his head, defeated.

The scene played out as it had years before. Denton solemnly followed the scouts as they exited the cave. He watched them leave, finally seeing the *Rogers* fly upward above the tall trees in the forest surrounding the City of the Dead.

Then there was silence.

Denton pondered what he had just seen. Why was he being shown this? Karx stepped forward stiffly, fighting his calcified joints and shaking off loose rocks built up from centuries of standing still. He watched the ship leave, then he began to walk away. Nhymn wasn't there anymore, the little ones had all faded to stone, the sentry had failed his task. So Karx left, and Denton followed.

"I neeed yourrr helppp ..." a deep voice said in his mind. He looked at Karx as the sentry continued his slow hike.

"Karx?" Denton asked. The stone sentry looked over its shoulder as if to acknowledge Denton's accuracy. "You need my help? Is that why you showed me this?" Denton asked.

"I did nooot show you thisss ..." Karx rumbled. *"Yooou cameee herrre on yourrr ownnn ..."*

"What?" Denton shook his head in confusion. "No, it was you, right? In the Tangle Maze. You gave me these visions. I remember that now."

"Theeen thaaat isss where I gooo nowww ..." Karx shifted direction, heading north instead of west.

"Wait, you didn't know that?" Denton stopped walking for a moment. "Did I just do this to *myself?*"

Karx nodded. *"Sheee mussst bee stopped ... You seee thaaat nowww ..."*

"This sounds like your problem. She wants to see Sympha," Denton said. Karx looked down at the ground as he dejectedly continued his slow march.

"I faaailed herrr ..." the low voice said. *"Weee arrre alll innn dangerrr ..."*

359

"What can we do?" Denton asked. He noticed they were now standing in the Tangle Maze. This place was nowhere near the cave; his dream continued to play tricks with time and space.

Beyond the bushes, the stampede of giant red beasts and titanovores pounded through the jungle. It was so loud that Denton had to cover his ears. When the stampede had nearly passed, Marie Viray's body crashed to the jungle floor in a heap. Denton wanted to run to her, but he remembered this scene.

The real-world versions of Denton and Eliana rappelled down and stabilized Marie. After Talulo raised Marie's wounded body to the upper ledge, Eliana followed, leaving Denton alone.

But he wasn't alone, he saw that now. Denton watched himself.

Karx turned his attention from Denton's phantom form to his physical one. He poked his head through the bushes. Denton once again felt the sting of the soul transfer from Karx's physical body to Denton's. Even in phantom form, Denton was brought to his knee. When the pain stopped, Denton's physical body climbed back up the rope, unaware of what had occurred. Karx turned toward Denton's phantom as he began to crumble away.

"*Helppp meee stoppp herrr ...*" Karx said.

"How?" Denton asked.

Karx sighed as he disintegrated.

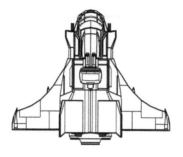

FORTY-FOUR

DENTON SLOWLY OPENED HIS eyes, overwhelmed with the sensation that he was vibrating. Jess Combs's face came into focus, her broken jaw still hanging at an unnatural angle, her eyes wide, and sweat beading on her brow. The marine was shaking Denton back to consciousness.

"Yourrr eyeshhh," Jess gurgled through her jaw injury. She removed her uninjured hand from Denton's shoulder to point two fingers at her eyes. "They were shake-king."

Denton reacquainted himself with the *Astraeus*'s brig cell. He pushed himself upright against the wall and lifted a hand to his nose to brush away the blood that had leaked during his dreaming.

There was a warm, wet sensation running down the sides of Denton's neck. He brushed his hand just under his left earlobe to find more blood. That was new. He felt like a donkey had kicked the inside of his skull.

Denton remembered everything now. The last words Karx had said to him warned him of the danger they faced and that he needed Denton's help. Denton grabbed part of his jacket and wiped as much blood away from his neck and nose as he could.

"What time is it?" Denton asked.

Jess shrugged her good shoulder in response.

"How long was I …" He paused, trying to think of the right word. He wiggled his fingers in front of his eyes and said, "*Shaking? Is that what you said?*"

"Hourshh. Are you infected?" Jess spat blood-filled saliva onto the floor.

The lights snapped on inside the brig, and the *Astraeus* shuddered to life. The room lit up with various HUD displays, a rainbow of alerts and notifications.

"Looks like the power cycle is complete," Denton said, sharing a concerned look with Jess. Footsteps echoed from the hallway, followed by the hydraulic door lifting to reveal Roelin Raike and, to Denton, the phantom form of Nhymn. He knew her thoroughly now and what she was capable of. Nhymn had to be stopped. Karx had asked for help, but what was he supposed to do?

"*The machine lives again,*" Roelin hissed, a smile visible on his face under his vibrating pupils. Jess saw Roelin's grisly face for the first time in the light, and she turned to Denton. To Jess, Roelin's vibrating eyes were no different than the way Denton's eyes shook while he was unconscious. Denton saw the look Jess was giving him.

She thinks I'm like him. Denton was chilled by the thought, and worse yet, he wondered, *Is she right?*

"Jess, I can expla—" Denton began, but Roelin cut him off.

"Come with me," Roelin said, keeping one hand on the trigger of the particle rifle tucked under his elbow. "Do as I say, and do it quickly."

Denton reached down to help Jess stand, but she shrugged him away and lifted herself up. The marine walked out of the cell with her crooked chin held high. Roelin pushed Denton to follow her and hurried them toward the air lock.

The ivory-scaled reptilian beast, Dol'Gohm, watched the prisoners from a shadow in the hallway. It growled through its snarling teeth. Its wounds had completely healed.

Roelin opened the hatches, revealing the morning sunlight

outside. No one else was there, only the familiar yard scattered with tools, debris from the skirmish, and the leftover viscera of Jess's fellow marines.

"Where are Eliana and the others?" Denton asked.

Roelin kicked Jess away from the door and out onto the grass. She grunted as she landed on her knees. Jess turned to face the hatch in time to see it slam closed, with Denton still inside with Roelin.

"What's going on? We had a deal!" Denton shouted at Nhymn.

I would be a fool to let you go, Nhymn said into Denton's mind. *If the ship breaks down again, I would be right back where I started.* Roelin grabbed Denton by the shoulder and dragged him back down the hallway. Roelin's hand slapped the control pad for the door of the medical bay, and it lifted open.

"Denny," Eliana yelped as Denton was thrown into the room. George and Talulo, finally conscious, watched him enter. They only saw a glimpse of Roelin before the door slammed shut once more, sealing the surviving scouts inside of the medical bay.

Denton scrambled toward Eliana, and the two embraced each other ferociously. Eliana broke the hug and held Denton at arm's length.

"Where are the marines?" she asked.

"Jess was kicked off the ship just now," Denton said, and he looked away from her. "The other marines are ..." He trailed off. Eliana knew what he meant to say and pulled him in tight for another embrace. The ship shuddered again.

"What just happened?" George asked.

"The engines just started," Denton answered.

———◆———

Jess Combs clamored to one knee and watched as the *Astraeus*'s engines warmed up. There was a superheated rush of air as the thrusters fired, lifting the hulking Undertaker-class warfighter up from its grave. Jess had to push back against the force of the thrust to avoid falling over. Vines and other foliage stretched and snapped, and dirt shook loose and created a cloud of dust. Small animals that had made their homes on the exterior of the ship scurried away. The *Astraeus* was alive once more, and facing Jess Combs like a growling dragon.

Jess looked down from the ship as she lifted her arm to shield herself from the intense rush of debris whipping by her face. She saw the pile of gore that had once been Lance Corporal Andrew Louis, and spotted his soothreader. Jess knelt and grabbed the reader, shaking away the loose skin that still clung to it. She held it close to her face, attempting to block out the sound of the hulking warship's return to life.

"Is anyone there? Can anyone read me?" said the voice of Rocco Gainax over the soothreader's communication channel.

"I read you!" Jess shouted, pushing her fist against her broken jaw and grunting.

"Reinforcements have arrived as requested! Just need a signal of your exact location."

Jess watched as the *Astraeus* rose higher and higher, almost clearing the canopy. The aft thrusters ignited and lurched the ship forward, avoiding a collision with the rocky ledge above that had concealed its position from satellites for so long.

"*Hole-lee* shit!" Rocco announced over the soothreader as he watched the *Astraeus* rise. The Pilgrim-class explorer the *Rogers* had no weaponry to fight the *Astraeus*, but the two Matadors that flanked it could take on the old beast with their skilled pilots. Lieutenants Eric Murphy and Luca Vincente answered Rocco's call for reinforcements. They were unsure of what they would be facing due to the limited information.

"Is that what I think it is?" Lieutenant Eric Murphy asked. "You didn't say anything about fighting a warship, Rocco."

"Ey, this just got a whole lot more complicated," Lieutenant Luca Vincente said, and checked his weapons systems.

"I'm under *Astraush*," Jess said through her broken jaw.

"I'm coming to get you, hang tight," Rocco said.

"We'll take care of the *Astraeus*," Eric said, then nodded to his wingman, Luca.

"Advancing on target," Luca said.

The Matadors cut through the air like a flock of swords.

FORTY-FIVE

ROELIN'S BODY SAT IN the captain's seat of the *Astraeus*, but Nhymn was the pilot. She sensed the presence of her pursuers' minds like annoying gnats ruining her picnic.

"No, no, no!" Nhymn shouted in Roelin's mind. She pushed Roelin's hands toward the toggles and activated the turret cannon.

"We had a deal, Nhymn!" Roelin shouted at Nhymn from the dark recesses of his mental prison. She shoved him deeper into the darkness; her drive to complete her objective and her proximity to her mental enhancer, Dol'Gohm, overpowered anything Roelin could do. He could shout in the dark, but he couldn't stop Nhymn now. Those who chased her from outside the *Astraeus* were not included in their deal, as far as Nhymn was concerned.

The turret whirred to life and pivoted toward the approaching Matador fighters. The *Astraeus* shook as the turret fired, sending a hypercharged blast of particles ripping through the air.

"Incoming," Lieutenant Eric Murphy shouted as he rolled to avoid being hit by the blast. The *Astraeus*'s aft engines roared and thrust the ship south.

"Stay on him!" Lieutenant Luca Vincente shouted, and cut hard to the right to pursue the *Astraeus*. Eric cut left and continued from the flank.

"Heads up, Jess," Rocco Gainax said as he brought the *Rogers* toward her position. "Fergus, get her a ladder."

"On it," Fergus said as he ran to the stern of the ship. He lowered the access ramp and threw down a long tow rope. Jess approached the tow line, grabbed hold with her good arm, and wrapped a length of it around her waist.

She tugged the tow rope hard to let Fergus know she was ready. He raised the towline up into the ship, lifting Jess into the *Rogers*. Once aboard, she untied herself.

"Where are the others?" Fergus asked, shutting the access ramp and eyeing Jess's haphazardly hanging jaw.

"Hosst-tiges." Jess shook her head in pain and frustration at the injury. "*Astraeush.*"

"Hostages on the *Astraeus*?" Fergus repeated to make sure he'd heard her correctly. Jess nodded, and Fergus pinged Rocco on the ship's comm channel. "You hear that, Rocco? Tell yer boys not to shoot down the *Astraeus*."

Rocco understood. "Homer, give me control," Rocco commanded, and queued the comm link to the Matadors. "Listen up, we have hostages on the *Astraeus*. Take precautions to ensure their safety."

"Got it," Lieutenant Murphy responded.

Fergus Reid inspected Jess's jaw injury. "Let's get that look't at straightaway," he said as he guided her toward a table in the medical bay. Marie Viray was sitting in a wheelchair inside, ready to help.

"Where are George and the others?" Marie asked. Jess shook her head as she lay down on the table.

Fergus gave Marie a wide-eyed look, then nodded somberly. "It's up to those pilots now."

———— • ————

The jungle rushed under the *Astraeus* like a raging river as the fighters tore through the sky. Nhymn searched Roelin's mind for aerial combat strategies; she knew she could only hold off the pursuers for so long before they inevitably shot her down, but if she could dodge them until she got close enough to Sympha's location, she'd win.

Nhymn followed her senses, sniffing out Sympha's location with her mind. The path was clear, but the journey would be impossible with the fighters in tow. The *Astraeus*'s turret cannon pivoted toward the Matadors and sent out two massive blasts in succession, knocking the *Astraeus* left and right with the momentum of the powerful blasts.

"Widen out," Lieutenant Murphy shouted. Both Matadors rolled away from each other, creating a large gap between them with the *Astraeus* in the middle. Nhymn would have to fully rotate the turret cannon to aim at one at a time.

Nhymn pulled some tricks from the corners of Roelin's mind. There were cannons on each side of the hull that could be controlled from the bridge. She set the ship to autopilot and hopped away from the pilot seat, pushing Roelin's body into a battle station on the port side of the bridge and using Roelin's soothreader to control the turret cannon. Port hull guns could shoot at one fighter while the starboard flank was covered by the turret gun.

The *Astraeus* wouldn't maneuver while on autopilot, but Nhymn bet the odds the fighters would be reluctant to shoot the *Astraeus* down with hostages on board. She knew their most significant weakness was their care for each other.

Another blast from the large turret lanced toward Vincente's Matador. He raised his fighter's nose upward, losing a small amount of speed but gaining altitude in the process. The turret needed a few moments to adjust its trajectory because of the new height.

The port-side cannons of the *Astraeus* rang out shots through the sky toward Murphy's Matador. He raced against the particle shots, just barely avoiding being clipped from behind. He pushed his Matador to its limit, then pitched right, passing the *Astraeus* so closely that Nhymn felt the buzz inside the bridge.

Nhymn couldn't lead Murphy with the cannons at that speed, sending particle shots blasting wildly into the jungle below.

"Launching toe-stubber," Lieutenant Murphy said as he passed under the nose of the *Astraeus*, leaving himself only a fraction of a second to accurately launch the device. A hatch on the top of his

Matador slid open, and a puck ejected upward, latching itself on to the underside of the *Astraeus*.

Murphy pushed past the nose of the *Astraeus* and joined Vincente on the starboard side of the ship. Nhymn looked ahead and saw the edge of the jungle in the distance. Beyond the tree line was a vast desert of crimson and ebony sand. Dunes snaked, curving inward and outward, creating a ripple-like effect as seen from overhead. Nhymn saw the horizon begin to rise and noticed her engines were cut. The toe-stubber had stalled the *Astraeus*, but the altitude and speed they were racing at propelled it into a glide.

Nhymn wasn't done yet. The engines were cut, but the guns were not. She commanded the turret gun to face the port side, then fired all the cannons at once. The *Astraeus* began to barrel roll wildly, pushing Roelin hard into the seat as the guns on the port side fired hundreds of particle shots in a circular pattern.

"Scramble!" Lieutenant Vincent shouted. The two fighters began evasive maneuvers to avoid the random pattern of particle fire. On the bridge of the *Astraeus*, Dol'Gohm grabbed part of the pilot's seat, tearing its claws through some of the leather backings as it searched for a stable hold. The beast's claws failed, and it was thrown against the starboard sidewall, pinned by the force of the wild spin.

Inside the medical bay, Eliana, Denton, George, and Talulo began to float.

"What is th—" George started to ask but was cut off when the ship spun and flung everyone in the room against the wall. Contents that were once loose propelled themselves against any surface they encountered as if possessed by magic. The combat knife Eliana had used to cut Talulo's wings free plunged itself into the wall, slicing through Denton's cheek and splashing his blood in the process. They could do nothing but obey the spin.

The pressure from the violent barrel roll caused the toe-stubber to dislodge from its position on the underside of the *Astraeus*. The autopilot reconnected the power to the engines and worked overtime to stop the roll. Roelin aided the autopilot by spinning the turret starboard and firing a few high-powered blasts. The *Astraeus* lurched and roared as it regained its balance.

Nhymn laughed—she had beaten the odds again. She pushed Roelin back into the pilot's seat to take control of the warship as it approached the desert canyons below.

She felt invincible.

In the medical bay, Eliana, Denton, George, and Talulo fell to the floor, unpinned from their positions against the wall.

"*Shit!* Damn thing near took my head off!" Denton said, and held his bloody cheek. He looked upward to see the combat knife still lodged in the wall, his blood a portrait of crimson on the otherwise stark-white backdrop.

"Keep pressure on it," Eliana shouted. She snatched her medical kit from the floor, then got to work on Denton's wound immediately.

Below the ship, dunes gave way to rocky plateaus and canyons. The *Astraeus* port-side wing scraped hard against a cliff edge, kicking up a swath of debris in its wake. Nhymn pulled back hard on the flight stick, urging the *Astraeus* to raise its nose.

"No joy. Bogey still airborne," Lieutenant Murphy said from his Matador as they continued their high-speed pursuit of the *Astraeus*.

"Moving in," Lieutenant Vincente replied.

"We got your back," Rocco said, pushing the *Rogers* to catch up to the chase. He wanted to be close in case he could provide assistance. Without weapons on the explorer vessel, there wasn't much else he could do.

"The *Astraeus* is entering the canyon," Lieutenant Vincente notified Rocco and Murphy as the chase continued down into a sizeable crimson canyon. A river flowed through the canyon under repeating archways of rock that resembled a giant's rib cage.

Here, Nhymn could focus on evading. She let the turret gun do the work on its own and sacrificed using the outer hull cannons entirely. She would be harder to hit and impossible to toe-stub again.

"We're going to have to catch it with the draglines," Lieutenant

Vincente suggested. The draglines were designed to lift downed ships away from a battlefield, not generally used to lasso warships in midflight.

"Clip its wings, catch the main cabin," Lieutenant Murphy added. The fighters dipped into the canyon behind the *Astraeus* just as its turret gun let out another blast of energy.

"Shit!" Lieutenant Vincente shouted as he rolled away from the particle lance. The blast rocked the canyon wall behind them, sending a cascade of rock and dust outward from the impact zone.

"Sympha, you're so close," Nhymn said. She could feel her sister stronger than ever. She had planned this day for four years, locked inside Roelin's body. She would not let these humans stop her now.

"What the Hells is that?" Rocco asked. On the canyon floor, a pulse of green electricity emerged from an underground tunnel. It surged over the ground like an overflowing bucket. As quickly as it came, it vanished.

Another blast from the *Astraeus* rocked through the canyon. Lieutenant Murphy pitched upward to avoid taking the impact.

"Do it now," Lieutenant Murphy shouted as he slammed his finger against the trigger on his flight stick. The machine gun rotated, launching an array of particle bullets into the *Astraeus*'s starboard wing. Shrapnel flew as the wing began to disintegrate. Lieutenant Vincente followed the order and proceeded to tear through the portside wing.

The *Astraeus* began to destabilize. Nhymn pivoted the cannon toward Lieutenant Vincente's Matador and let out another blast. The pilot rolled his ship while shooting, sending a few shots through the rear engine and upward into the turret gun itself. There was an explosion as the turret gun took damage, rocking the whole ship. Nhymn attempted to pivot the turret once more, but it wouldn't move. It could shoot, but it was locked in the rear position.

"There we go," Lieutenant Vincente shouted with excitement.

"Good maneuver! Keep on those wings," Lieutenant Murphy said.

"Something's not right," Rocco said, interrupting their celebratory moment. The canyon floor began to glow with a thousand tiny green lights, almost as if the stars from the cosmos had fallen into the river, "You guys seeing this?"

"A little busy," Lieutenant Vincente shouted, and rolled his ship back into position behind the port-side wing of the *Astraeus*. Rocco watched as some of the tiny lights began to glow brighter.

A bolt of green lightning launched up from the canyon floor.

"Holy *sh*—" Lieutenant Vincente shouted as the green lightning bolt licked through the *Astraeus*. The electrical energy hung in the air long enough that it passed through Lieutenant Vincente's Matador as well, causing both ships to destabilize.

"I'm losing control here!" Lieutenant Vincente shouted. He looked up as his ship wobbled its way into the path of the *Astraeus*'s large particle turret.

"*Perfect,*" Nhymn hissed. She shot off another blast, ripping through the starboard side of Lieutenant Vincente's fighter. Fire and smoke replaced his wing, and the ship began to roll wildly.

"Eject!" Lieutenant Murphy called out.

Lieutenant Vincente pulled the eject cable, and the windscreen of his Matador blew off. The pilot's seat launched itself from the ship. He managed to stabilize himself with the jump-jets equipped to his seat as the parachute deployed. Lieutenant Vincente watched his Matador spiral into the glowing river and explode.

Rocco watched Vincente go down and shouted, "I'm coming to get you! Hang tight."

Another lightning bolt emerged from the river, causing Lieutenant Murphy to employ evasive maneuvers. He shouted, "I'm staying on target!" and continued his pursuit.

———◆———

Lieutenant Vincente's ejection seat slammed into the riverbank. He pulled himself free from the chair and yanked a rip cord under the armrest. A plume of orange smoke filled the air, alerting the *Rogers* to his location. He watched as his wingman and the *Astraeus* cut around a bend in the canyon.

"All you now, Murph," Lieutenant Vincente said, and watched for the *Rogers*, shielding his eyes from the sun with his hand. There was a humming noise, the sound an electrical wire makes when it has been charged.

"Vincente, watch out!" Rocco warned.

Lieutenant Vincente spun around to face a monster made of stone and electricity. The enormous nezzarform had a cavernous cyclopean hole that served as an eye. It moved toward him with heavy, slow lurches.

"Hey, watch it," Vincente shouted. He pulled his sidearm from its holster, then noticed more stone monsters surrounding his position. "Stay back!" Vincente pleaded.

Nezzarforms emerged from the river itself, sparkling with electricity and sending waves of energy over the water's surface.

"I warned you!" Vincente took a shot at one of the nezzarforms, watching as rock chipped away from its chest piece. The nezzarform's cyclopean orifice began to glow brightly. A bolt of lightning blasted outward from its face hole, hitting Vincente directly in the chest.

Vincente was thrown backward into another stone monster with such force that he broke his left shoulder. He gasped in the sand, desperately trying to catch his breath. The nezzarform behind him raised a massive arm made of jagged rock. Vincente's screams were cut off as the arm crashed down on his torso, smashing him like a bug. The other nezzarforms piled in, pummeling Vincente's body with their heavy stone arms until there was nothing but a crater in the dirt.

"No! Damn it!" Rocco slammed his fists against his armrest. He watched as the nezzarforms bashed Lieutenant Luca Vincente to dust. The *Rogers* had just begun to descend on his position when the stone monsters had arrived.

Rocco didn't have time to collect Vincente's body. The nezzarforms finished with the lieutenant and turned their attention on the *Rogers*. Their bodies began to glow white hot. Rocco knew the lightning bolts would follow. He thrust the *Rogers* upward, out of the canyon and high enough into the sky to hopefully avoid being struck by the lances of electricity.

———— ◆ ————

"NHYMN, COME NO CLOSER," the voice of Sympha echoed in Roelin's mind. Nhymn pushed toward where she could feel her sister's presence the strongest. The *Astraeus* shook again with the impacts of Lieutenant Murphy's assault on the wings.

The *Astraeus* was tattered and flying on plumes of smoke. Nhymn could see a few brightly glowing lights up ahead and knew a volley of lightning was heading their way. She tilted the *Astraeus* to the starboard side, putting Lieutenant Murphy in the path of the turret cannon.

She launched a volley of particle blasts from the turret, forcing Lieutenant Murphy to make an evasive maneuver that put him at risk of the lightning bolts from the nezzarforms ahead.

"Hells," Lieutenant Murphy shouted as three bolts slashed through his Matador. His teeth felt like they would vibrate out of his mouth.

The Matador pulled to the side of the canyon, scraping against the cliff wall and blowing the entire port-side wing off in the process. He pulled the ejection cord.

Lieutenant Murphy was lucky enough to be ejected above the lip of the canyon. He landed, pulling himself from the seat and setting off his smoke signal for the *Rogers*. His Matador tumbled into the ravine below, exploding into a whirling fireball of debris.

"You can't hide from me," Nhymn said.

The canyon was coming to an end just ahead, terminating in a waterfall that poured into the river below from an upper plateau. Three electrical bolts lanced the ship from the ground, throwing the *Astraeus* into a wild, destabilized wobble. Nhymn held on to the flight stick with all of Roelin's might.

"There!" Nhymn felt it. Just ahead, there was an opening shrouded by the waterfall. All she had to do was keep the ship steady and let gravity do the rest of the work.

Inside the medical bay of the *Astraeus*, Eliana finished stitching Denton's cheek, having maintained her accuracy with the suture needle even during the turbulence. George held on to the table in the middle of the room to keep himself from falling over. Talulo seemed to have no trouble at all standing in the middle of the bay during the rocky maneuvering.

Eliana held a cloth pad against Denton's sutured cheek.

"Elly. If we—" Denton said, and Eliana quieted him with a kiss on the lips. He held her close. She could see tears beginning to form in his eyes. Eliana fought back tears of her own. The *Astraeus* shuddered, then slammed hard into something, flinging everyone wildly around the medical bay.

"The *Astraeus* is, uh…" Lieutenant Murphy didn't know what to make of it. The Undertaker-class warship had vanished behind the waterfall at the end of the canyon. No explosion had followed. He looked down into the chasm and watched as each of the green lights dimmed, then winked off.

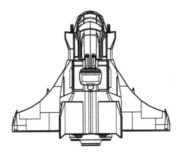

FORTY-SIX

THE *ASTRAEUS* CAREENED THROUGH the waterfall and slammed hard against a rocky slope. The Undertaker-class warfighter entered a hidden tunnel, losing the already-tattered remains of the port-side wing, with the starboard-side wing barely hanging on from the onslaught of its Matador pursuers. There was no engine power or thrust, which had both been disabled from the bolts of green lightning that passed through the ship before breaching the cave threshold.

The *Astraeus* crashed hard into a boulder, sending the ship tumbling end over end until it rocked itself to a fiery stop. Glass cracked, and electricity popped from exposed paneling. The war machine groaned as a fire began to spread.

The *Astraeus*'s final resting place was at the bottom of a colossal underground hollow, awash in sparkling emerald lights. Nearby, a broad, rocky pathway led to a massive structure that clung to the roof of the cavern.

A river boiling with electrical energy raged under the giant stone pathway, cascading through waterfalls under the grand hanging palace. Green light slowly pulsed up the sides of the structure, giving it the appearance of a beating alabaster heart.

This was the artery of Kamaria.

Inside the command bridge of the wreckage, Nhymn laughed and slowly lifted Roelin's head, bringing his body into an upright position against the back of the pilot's seat. Dol'Gohm raised his reptilian head from behind a battle station; the beast was thrown around the cabin during the crash, but its scaly body protected him from any significant damage. Dol'Gohm growled with anticipation.

It was showtime.

Nhymn unbuckled Roelin from the pilot's seat and stood, surprised to find the whole ship was tilted 45 degrees. She found her balance, then reached for her combat gear.

"NHYMN," Sympha's voice boomed in her mind. An immense green light filled the cavern and pulsed through the rocks, washing over the *Astraeus*. After a moment of darkness, tiny lights ignited around the cave.

Nhymn knew these lights were Sympha's nezzarforms preparing an attack.

Sympha called out again, *"YOU SHOULD NOT HAVE COME HERE."* But they both knew that Nhymn had no intention of leaving. She moved Roelin around the bridge and collected grenades, two collider pistols, a rifle taken from Andrew Louis's corpse, combat body armor with a jump-jet, and a machete. Dol'Gohm followed its master around like an obedient dog.

Roelin's eyes vibrated and undulated. Inside his mind, he was screaming at the top of his lungs for it all to stop, but it wasn't going to stop, not now. Not when Nhymn was so close to Sympha.

There was a fire lining the hallway of the *Astraeus*, lighting it a deep, flickering orange and clouding it with thick black smoke. Pipes had burst, debris scattered, and metal shards poked through the walls at random angles.

Nhymn navigated the wreckage, pushing past it until she was able to slide Roelin's body down the slope toward the air lock. She pried the door open and left the *Astraeus* behind. Nhymn, Roelin, and Dol'Gohm walked up the stone pathway hanging over the electrical river, ready for a war.

Smoke filled the medical bay.

Denton tried to get the door open as Eliana helped George and Talulo to their feet. Everyone was bruised and dirty from the violence of the wreck, but there was no time to assess their injuries—their air was running thin.

"Piece of crap. Come on!" Denton shouted as he kicked the door open, but it resisted his attack and held itself firmly shut. He scrambled to think of a solution and looked toward the control panel, noticing it hung open in a tangle of metal and wires.

"There we go! Just gotta …" Denton said to himself as he reached inside the broken panel, knowing which wires to reconnect. With a jolt, the door opened, but not far enough for anyone to pass through it. Denton stuffed his left shoulder into the opening, pushing upward with all his might. It resisted at first, then gave in to his pressure with a loud thunk. "Time to go!" Denton shouted over the roar of the fire.

Eliana, Talulo, and George ran ahead toward the open air lock. Denton turned the other direction, unsure if Roelin was still on board. He wasn't about to let Roelin die of smoke inhalation. Denton ran up the slope toward the bridge, through the debris in the hallway, and found the door was already open.

Inside, the windscreen was destroyed, with smoke tracing the ceiling and spilling out of the room through the broken glass. Denton saw the green lights, the electrical river, and the enormous hanging palace with its emerald pulsing rays, but he didn't see Roelin, Nhymn, or their pet, Dol'Gohm.

Denton spotted his collider pistol lying on the floor against the wall. "Glad to see you here," he said, and took the gun, slamming it back into the holster on his belt as he left the bridge.

There were more popping noises as Denton reentered the hallway. He knew the fuel line had been ruptured, and the *Astraeus's* engine was a ticking time bomb. Denton leaped forward, scrambled through the debris, then slid on his side down the sloped hallway toward the air lock. He bounced off some clutter and tumbled forward through the open hatch. Outside, he saw the others and shouted, "Move back! *It's going to—*"

The *Astraeus* exploded, sending red-hot fire shooting straight up into the emerald-lit cavern. Denton grabbed Eliana by the jacket and hopped behind a boulder, with Talulo and George following their example. Panels and large metal pieces of the *Astraeus* sprang outward from the old ship.

One more giant explosion came as the rest of the ship caught fire, the debris raining away like fiery leaves on an autumn day. Then there was only the crackle as the skeleton of the Undertaker-class warfighter, the *Astraeus*, rested on its funeral pyre.

George stepped forward, his face pale with shock. Looking at the burning remnants, he asked, "Oh God, was Roelin inside?"

"No," Denton said. "I checked. He wasn't there."

"Look, he's over there," Talulo said, pointing toward the stone ramp. There was a show of lights: white-hot beams from a particle rifle and green electrical bolts from stone nezzarforms.

Roelin was moving toward the hanging palace, lashing out at anything that crossed his path. A flash of shadow silhouetted in the light show was all there was to see of Dol'Gohm lunging between nezzarforms, ripping their stone limbs from their electrical tethers.

The team flinched as a grenade went off on the ramp, casting a trio of nezzarforms into the electrical river below. Roelin made it up the ramp, then used another explosive to enter the palace.

Denton looked at his friends. Talulo looked back at him, but Eliana and George didn't take their eyes off where Roelin had entered the palace.

"What now?" Denton asked.

George and Eliana looked at each other, then to Denton.

"We have to finish this," Eliana said. "We need to get Roelin."

"I had a feeling you'd say that," Denton said, then turned toward Talulo, "Are you coming with us? This isn't really your fight."

Talulo looked at his wingless shoulders, then down to the cave floor. Eliana approached him and looked him in the eyes. She said nothing out loud, but Denton knew she was saying everything she had to with her thoughts.

"You don't have to follow us," George said. "There is daylight coming from beyond that waterfall. You can follow this stone ramp up and get to the surface."

Talulo looked back toward the ramp, seeing the flickering, dim glow of daylight behind the waterfall.

"My flight." Talulo's voice weakened, and he mumbled in his native language before continuing. "Eliana cut my flight."

"Your wings were ripped apart by the grenade trap, there was too much risk of infection. If I didn't amputate, you would have died," Eliana said before her eyes became glossy. "I wish there was another way. I'm so sorry, Talulo."

"Eliana cut Talulo." The auk'nai squinted as if trying to understand. "But, she saves Talulo." Talulo looked into an empty space between the scouts, the place he could find his logic. His beak jerked toward Eliana, and he said, "The unsung song Talulo hears is sad, but sings with truth." He looked Eliana in the eye. "Friends still listen to the song, even when it is sad. It is necessary."

"Talulo … I…"

"Friends intend to head toward a danger?" Talulo asked.

"Yes, we do," Eliana said. "You don't have to join us. Like Denton said, this isn't your fight."

"Eliana saved Talulo's life, and although the song is sad, the song has a chance to become joyous again in the future because of Eliana's actions. Talulo will go with friends into danger." Talulo cooed. "We find the man Roelin."

Eliana hugged Talulo. The auk'nai was shocked, as this was not a gesture his race was familiar with, but he returned the hug all the same.

"Let's go get Roelin, then," Denton said, checking his collider pistol and activating the cylinder.

FORTY-SEVEN

"TURN BACK!" SYMPHA'S VOICE warned Nhymn, and again, her caution went unheard. Nhymn moved Roelin's body into the hanging alabaster palace. Roelin wasn't sure if anyone else inside the *Astraeus* had survived the crash, but the farther Nhymn moved his body away from the wreckage, the safer any survivors were. Roelin made no moves to stop Nhymn; he allowed her to play in this candy store she so desperately wanted to be in. Nhymn was free to find her sister and free to use any force necessary to do so.

The walls and floors of the alabaster palace were bone white, with jutting stalagmites thrusting upward toward another interior hanging structure. This central structure was connected by a spiraling stone ramp, and the surrounding shell wall contained rocky ledges with nezzarforms sputtering to life. The center of the floor was an open pit with a swirling whirlpool of rushing water and electricity that churned violently below.

The nezzarforms began to glow.

Lightning flashed, and Nhymn jump-jetted away in time to watch the deadly bolts explode on the ground where she had been standing, leaving behind a steaming crater in a shower of pebbles.

Nhymn returned fire with Roelin's particle rifle, striking one of the nezzarforms directly in its cyclopean eye and causing it to explode into rubble and dust.

The nezzarforms forced Nhymn and Dol'Gohm into cover behind a stalagmite, blasting away at it and sending chunks spraying into the swirling pool below. Nhymn knew she wouldn't be able to take cover long and had to shake up her strategy.

Nhymn turned to Dol'Gohm, and at once, the creature understood her plan. The dray'va bounded away from their cover behind the stalagmite, deftly dodging bolts as it flanked the nezzarforms on the upper ledge.

One of the nezzarforms was struck from the side by Dol'Gohm. The mighty beast shoved the rock construct into the large pit in the middle of the room. It collided with the rocky lip of the central gap and broke into pieces, slapping rocks into the electrified whirlpool below.

Green pulses of energy rushed upward from the floor toward the hanging structure again, and Nhymn knew Sympha would be there. She could taste her presence in the air.

A burst of lightning destroyed the top half of the stalagmite Nhymn hid behind, and she jump-jetted away from the toppling stone pillar. She rolled at the end of her leap and returned fire, striking the sniping nezzarform in its center mass and causing it to stagger backward long enough for Dol'Gohm to intercept it and tear its stone head off. Electricity licked over the beast's scales, but Dol'Gohm paid it no mind.

Nhymn commanded Dol'Gohm to climb the outer shelves as she scaled the spiral ramp in the center of the room, and the beast obeyed with a sharp-toothed grin. Dol'Gohm leaped onto a stalagmite closest to the lowest shelf, then springboarded off, tackling another nezzarform and giving Nhymn time to make her move.

———◆———

Eliana, Denton, George, and Talulo entered the interior chamber moments after Nhymn exited, witnessing the destruction she'd left behind. Denton kept his pistol ready, unsure of what to make of the stone corpses sputtering on the floor.

"Roelin. God, what have you done?" Eliana whispered to herself. Green pulses of light slowly lapped up into the central hanging structure above the chasm hole. There was only the hum of the electricity, the whirring of the vortex below, and the smell of charred stone.

"What is this place?" George asked. Denton looked past the stone corpses at the rest of the room. He watched the spiraling abyss and took in the shape.

"If I didn't know any better"—Denton paused, trying to think of the right words—"I'd say this looks like some sort of engine."

"Engine?" George asked. "Like part of a spaceship?"

"Maybe," Denton said. "That could be the intake down there." He pointed at the whirlpool below, then at various parts of the structure. "And that's shaped like a compression cylinder—" Green energy lifted from the floor to the ceiling, loading into the central partition of the structure. "Maybe that's a combustion chamber?"

Eliana said, "That's where Roelin's heading."

"If Roelin's heading there, that's where we are going," George said, and moved forward toward the spiral ramp.

"Just to be clear. You want to head *into* the combustion chamber?" Denton asked rhetorically, then shrugged. "Well, as long as they don't feel like takin' this thing out for a spin, we should be alright."

The team jogged up the ramp, eventually coming to a gap. It looked unnatural, like it had been created during the chaos of the fight. There was the telltale circular shape of a grenade blast lining the sidewall of the interior structure.

"Looks like Roelin covered his tracks," Eliana said as she looked over the edge into the whirlpool below.

Talulo hopped across the gap with ease, unafraid of the dizzying height. The others were reluctant.

"Talulo, can you help us across?" Eliana asked. "Just try and catch us as we run and jump."

"Yes," Talulo said.

"Okay, you go first, George," Eliana said.

"Wait, me? Why do I have to go first?" George cradled his injured right arm.

"Age before beauty," Eliana said, and raised her eyebrows. George looked to Denton for help, and he shrugged.

"Ah fine. You win," George huffed. He walked a few meters back as he braced himself for the task, then took one last deep breath and sprinted forward with surprising speed for his age.

George leaped across, but his jump was too short. Talulo grabbed George by the back of his jacket and lifted him up onto his side of the spiral ramp.

"See!" George huffed, shaking off the adrenaline. "Not so hard."

Denton turned to Eliana and said, "It's like the scout obstacle course."

"Yeah, sure," Eliana said, and stepped back a couple paces. She got into a sprinter's stance and took a few deep breaths. Before she could begin her run, the room shook violently.

The pulsing green lights that moved upward toward the structure rapidly sucked inward into their central point. An eerie silence followed, and Eliana and Denton looked up for answers.

"What was that?" Eliana asked.

The green energy burst outward from the central interior structure and spread across the whole palace like a tidal wave of light. The heat washed over them, vibrating the room with immense power. Once again, there was silence.

"Is everyone alright?" George asked.

"Still breathing," Denton said, patting his chest and legs.

"Yeah, I think ..." Eliana said.

The nezzarform debris started to rumble. One of the stone corpses twitched, then rose from the ground so quickly and unnaturally, everyone on the team jumped in surprise. Stone parts rolled back toward their designated positions as the nezzarforms reassembled themselves. The scouts suddenly found themselves surrounded by reconstructed nezzarforms, resurrected by whatever unknown energy was coursing through the alabaster palace. The dead had risen.

"That can't be good," Denton said, checking his pistol.

"Hurry, *jump!*" George urged them as a nezzarform standing on the outer shelf began to charge a blast.

Eliana and Denton sprinted toward the gap, leaping across just as the bolt of green energy blasted the ramp behind them. Eliana slammed into Talulo, knocking the auk'nai onto his back. Denton flew past George and rolled toward the edge of the ramp, catching himself with one arm as he dangled from the side of the spiral staircase.

"Hells!" Denton shouted, and lifted his pistol. He shot off a round of particle blasts toward the sniping nezzarform on the outer shelf of the structure, striking it in the chest and head. The nezzarform exploded once more, flinging bits of rock at Denton.

George and Eliana grabbed Denton and lifted him onto the ramp.

"We must hurry, a doorway is ahead," Talulo shouted. They dashed up the slope toward an opening at the top, their entrance to the central hanging structure. Nezzarforms shot more bursts in their direction, crumbling the remains of the ramp behind them.

"In here! *Here!*" Talulo shouted. He was the first to make it to the central structure's entrance, with the others only a breath later. Another assault of blasts rocked the door behind them, causing a landslide and blocking their escape.

"Hole-lee Hells!" Denton huffed out.

"No turning back now," Eliana said.

"Even if we find Roelin, how are we going to get out of here?" George asked.

"We'll figure it out as we go along," Denton said. Eliana stepped forward into the new room, the sound of her footsteps echoing off the grand walls.

"Woah," Eliana gasped.

They stood in a hallway built for gods.

The ceiling loomed over the team roughly three hundred meters up. It was as if they'd walked into a giant cathedral. It was shaped like the tip of a spear, the point at the very top and center, with curved edges cascading down toward the floor. The walls were made of the same crystalline alabaster as the rooms before it; the hallway went so deep that it became obscured in a haze. The immense corridor curled to the left, blocking their view of where it led.

If Denton's engine theory was correct, this hallway would lead to two chambers on each side, possibly more, and one central room. Green energy began to flow along the floor again like a gently lapping tide pool. It gave them a heading.

In the distance, they could hear the echoes of a battle. The particle shots and lightning bolts exploding sounded small in such an ample space. The team moved forward toward the action, their footsteps lost in the sounds of battle.

———— ◆ ————

"NHYMN, STOP! YOU CAN'T GO THROUGH WITH THIS!" Sympha begged. Nhymn and Dol'Gohm didn't care. They continued to shoot and tear their way through the stone protectors. The nezzarforms they destroyed stood to fight again, only to be ripped apart once more. It was a feeling Nhymn had experienced in the past, during her time as a ghost among ghosts in the cave. The nezzarforms could get back up and fight Nhymn a thousand more times, and Nhymn would always be there to tear them down to rubble.

Nhymn had been preparing for this day for centuries.

The hallway emptied into another massive room. Thick fog shrouded its interior, but Nhymn could tell Sympha was hiding there.

A taloned hand the size of the *Astraeus* emerged from the fog and planted its palm against the floor. A green mist showered from it, the fingers compressed, then the hand lifted upward, revealing a colossal stone nezzarform. This construct was taller and more formidable than any they had encountered previously. The massive hand vanished back behind the fog, leaving only the immense guardian standing in its place.

The nezzarform was centaur-like in shape—Nhymn recognized the frame as similar to Karx's, but much taller. Her sister's pet, the one who had stomped her life out of her body. Although this was not Karx, she would vent her anger onto it as if it had been.

The centaur's arms were long, sharp blades of alabaster stone. Its massive, clawed hoof stepped forward as the single hollow in its face cavity began to charge with energy.

Lightning burst forward.

Nhymn leaped to the side, away from the impact zone. Dol'Gohm dodged to the other side of the hallway, recoiling like a snake ready to lash out with its fangs. To both of their surprise, the impact area erupted with a secondary blast, showering them with rubble.

"Climb," Nhymn whispered into Dol'Gohm's mind. The dray'va leaped onto the wall and scrambled along its edge. The centaur focused on Nhymn and pumped all four hooves to propel its massive body forward, scraping its bladed arm against the alabaster floor.

The centaur swung its blade. Nhymn activated her jump-jet, propelling herself away from the slash. She slammed hard against the ground on Roelin's shoulder.

The centaur turned and prepared to lunge again. Nhymn stood to face it like a matador and whispered, "Now!"

Dol'Gohm leaped from the sidewall onto the centaur's head. The beast clawed away at the cyclopean eye, allowing the electricity to pass over its scales. The centaur shook its head around violently to try to release the dray'va. The glow was nearing its climax, readying the bolt that would follow.

Nhymn saw an opportunity. She unclipped Roelin's last

grenade, thumbing the pin away with one movement. The centaur shook its head one last time as Nhymn launched the grenade into the glowing cyclopean hollow.

The grenade exploded close to Dol'Gohm's head, obliterating the dray'va's upper half and igniting the charged energy in the centaur's face. The resulting firework display of explosions and debris bathed the room in harsh white and blue light.

The centaur crumpled into itself, pulling the remaining pieces of Dol'Gohm with it before exploding violently. Nhymn covered Roelin's head as rubble and blood washed over their shared body.

Nhymn spared no love for her fallen pet. Dol'Gohm had served its purpose.

"NHYMN!" Sympha cried out. Nhymn turned toward the fog-filled room. She entered the massive, hollow chamber and watched as green lights emerged from the fog. There was a life-form lurking within the haze that was so enormous it made the centaur look like a child's toy.

"Sympha," Nhymn said with a wispy wonder. "We have a world to save together."

Nhymn had finally reunited with her sister after hundreds of years of torture in the cave. She felt Sympha's presence like a warm pool of water.

Roelin's body locked in place, refusing to take one more step.

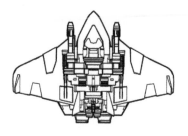

FORTY-EIGHT

"*I KNOW WHAT YOU'RE planning, Nhymn!*" Roelin shouted from inside their shared mind. "*I saw it!*"

Roelin's foot twitched, then jolted forward a step.

"*You think you can stop me now? Here?*" Nhymn challenged.

"*Dol'Gohm is gone! You wasted your last advantage!*"

"*You think, after everything we've been through, I will let a puny thing like you stop me?*" Nhymn hissed, and another foot jerked forward. Roelin's body disobeyed his own mind, slowly giving Nhymn more control.

Roelin was slipping.

"*Your part in this is over,*" Nhymn said, taking one more step forward.

"*NHYMN! DON'T—*" Sympha cried out.

"*I'll do the rest myself!*" Nhymn shouted as Roelin's body fell to his knees.

Roelin's body curved backward so fast it snapped some of his lower vertebrae with a resounding crack. Sympha's head emerged from the thick, dark fog, green lights sprouting from small hollows scattered around her colossal eye sockets.

Nhymn's essence launched from her human prison and smashed into Sympha's tremendous skull, knocking her head back into the fog. Roelin remained on his knees in his broken position on the floor, alone in his mind and gasping in anguish.

Sympha's screams shook the entire palace. Stalactites fell from the ceiling, dust burst from ages of buildup on the rocks, boulders loosened and crashed violently into the floor. Sympha's body flailed wildly as Nhymn eviscerated her mind.

A pulse of energy shot out from the fog and resurrected the stone nezzarforms. They rose, but their electricity flickered, and their bodies twitched as they took painful steps toward Sympha. Their electrical tethers oscillated from green to violet. A nezzarform was struck by a falling boulder seven meters from Roelin's body as the palace was becoming unstable in the chaos.

Denton, Eliana, George, and Talulo ran as fast as they could down the rest of the hallway. The nezzarforms that were recently resurrected fell apart and reassembled rapidly. A boulder liberated itself from the ceiling and crashed down onto the floor next to Eliana, but she continued her sprint as if it hadn't happened.

Ahead of them, an immense centaur-shaped nezzarform pounded back and forth, smashing into the sides of the hallway and stomping craters into the floor in its wild, confused state. It, too, had been recently resurrected, but the glitch in their world had driven the nezzarforms into a broken frenzy. The scouts dashed through the legs of the massive stone construct as it smashed the hall around it. Denton looked back over his shoulder and saw the centaur crumble to pieces, destroying the floor they had traversed over just a moment ago.

"Roelin!" Eliana shouted when they entered the fog-filled chamber. She dashed to him, putting everything she could into her sprint.

Roelin gurgled on his own blood, sitting in his broken position on his knees. Eliana leaned his upper body forward, allowing a torrent of blood to spill onto the floor from his mouth. Roelin gasped.

"My legs," Roelin grunted, and spat more blood onto the

chamber floor. "I can't feel my legs."

Denton entered the room with George and Talulo. They slowed their sprint to a jog, then to a standstill as they watched the green and violet lights swirl in the darkness.

"We're too late ..." Denton whispered.

A massive, clawed hand swung wildly forward from the fog, then sank back into it, like an abyssal monster surfacing and retreating. A cathedral-size tentacle swung overhead, spilling tendrils of fog out over the room. The shrieking was ceaseless as the mental battle continued. George went to Eliana and Roelin as Talulo kept an eye on the frenzied nezzarforms.

"*Sheee hasss donnne ittt ...* " the voice of Karx said in Denton's mind.

"What happens now?" Denton said to himself—the room was too loud for anyone else to hear him.

"*Obliterationnn ...* "

The room became silent. The sound of blood dripping from Roelin's face and splattering on the floor mimicked a ticking clock. The nezzarforms stood and watched the dark fog, motionless. Their electrical tethers had changed to a royal-violet hue.

They awaited their new master.

An enormous claw emerged from the dark fog and planted itself to the right of the team with a thunderous pounding. A second claw emerged and planted itself on the left. Then, two more claws placed themselves next to their counterparts. Massive tentacles rolled outward from the fog, knocking the haze away from the center of the room like smoke on a lake. These tentacles terminated in a mess of hooked talons.

Sympha's head came forward out of the center of the fog, though it was not her heart-shaped bone skull. Instead, it was Nhymn's head, reborn in her sister's vessel. She had shattered her sister's skull and reassembled it to match her own visage. Purple mist seethed through cracks in her sharp beak and horn.

"*At last ...* " Nhymn whispered in their minds. The immensity of the monster before them was incongruent with such an innocent whisper. Denton felt his skin prickle.

"Sympha?" Denton asked, although he knew the answer. Eliana, George, and Talulo looked at him with confusion.

Nhymn turned her abyssal eye sockets toward Denton. *"You,"* she whispered. *"I remember you now."*

Denton's skin turned bone white. Nhymn pushed her head farther out of the fog, revealing a series of thorned tentacles that acted as a phalanx of necks.

"You were there. Back in the early times. I remember your"—she hesitated on the word—*"shade."*

"Denny, what is it talking about?" Eliana asked in a hushed whisper as she trembled.

Denton didn't know how to respond. Had his visions of the Sirens been more than dreams? Had he time traveled somehow? Karx told Denton he'd brought himself there ... but how?

"Karx." Nhymn let out a gurgling, alien chuckle. It was a fragmented sound, like bones clicking against wet meat. *"I see you in there, Karx."*

"Nhymnnn ..." Karx spoke through Denton's mouth. Eliana gasped, George's eyes widened, and Talulo's ears whipped back against his head and he shrunk down, scared and confused.

"Whattt haveee youuu donnne?" Karx asked.

"Only what you have done before me, Karx," Nhymn whispered. She lifted all four of her immense claws and pulled twisted black nezzarforms from the floor. *"And now, I have become life itself."* The twisted nezzarforms ignited in violet energy and stumbled forward. *"I have become the Decider."* Nhymn's hands pounded the ground, and she pulled up more nezzarforms. *"The Creator and Annihilator."*

"The *Nightmare*," Roelin gasped and looked up at Nhymn, but he couldn't stand to face her. She ignored her previous vessel. Roelin was nothing to her now, just discarded trash.

"Sympha made you," Nhymn whispered to Karx. She waved a finger forward toward Denton. *"I now unmake you."* One of the new,

twisted nezzarforms charged a purple blast in its hollowed-out face and launched the bolt of energy at Denton. It struck him in the chest, casting him back into the alabaster wall with brutal force.

"Denton!" Eliana shouted, and rushed toward him.

Nhymn laughed wildly. She'd just gotten her first real taste of the destructive power she now harnessed. She reached upward with all four of her claws and raked them against the cave ceiling, sending boulders and dust smashing down.

"Talulo! Help me!" George shouted. They grabbed Roelin's arms and dragged him over to Eliana and Denton, away from the center of the room where the chaos was most destructive.

The room fell apart as Nhymn dug further into the ceiling. Eliana didn't care—she compressed Denton's chest, then breathed into his mouth.

Light broke into the cave, revealing all of Nhymn's new body. She stood upright, floating on an array of tentacles, filling the colossal room from floor to ceiling. Her bony carapace was spiked with sharp horns. With every twitch and pulse, she grew larger.

"Damn it, breathe!" Eliana had tears in her eyes. She pumped Denton's chest and breathed into his mouth until Denton coughed raggedly and gasped for air.

"Elly, what …" Denton pulled away, still trying to catch his breath. Something caught his eye near Eliana's head. He watched as the engagement ring he'd created for her slowly drifted upward, away from his pocket. It gracefully rotated in midair.

"What the …?" Denton whispered weakly. He snatched the ring out of the air before Eliana could see it.

"It isn't safe here," Eliana said, her hair floating in wispy tendrils above her head. All around them, items were beginning to float upward. Denton turned to Nhymn and saw that she, too, was floating through the hole she'd carved out of the palace ceiling.

The rules had changed.

"Hold on to something!" George shouted, but it was no use; everything, including their bodies, began to move upward through the palace. They joined the army of twisted nezzarforms rising from the floor and floating through open air toward the surface.

———◦———

"Hey, guys." Fergus Reid watched a dust storm flickering with purple energy form in the dunes outside his passenger window on the *Rogers*. "Come take a look at this."

Rocco, Jess, Marie, and Lieutenant Eric Murphy looked up from their hologram of plans to see what Fergus was talking about.

"What in the Hells is that?" Jess said, gritting the words out through her newly installed jaw brace. They watched as rocks began to float over the desert. A colossal monster pulled itself to the surface, surrounded by creatures that looked like twisted black rocks held together with purple energy. They spilled out of the hole in the ground like ants out of a hill.

"Scanners indicate the team's life signatures!" Rocco said, pointing at the heads-up display of the team. The enhanced scanners of the *Rogers* pinpointed George, Eliana, Denton, Talulo, and Roelin.

"Go on, then! Let's get them!" Fergus shouted. There was no time to waste.

"On it," Rocco said, igniting the engines. The *Rogers* lifted off the plateau of the canyon edge and launched toward the new crater.

———◦———

Nhymn stretched out her enormous arms in the light of Delta Octantis. She could finally feel it again. Sympha's frame, although larger than Nhymn had ever been in her first life, was still more familiar than the soft, small structure of Captain Roelin Raike. The sun was hot on her tendrils and claws. The air was dry on her inner skull socket. Her way of observing the world around her was clearer than using that idiot's eyeballs, ears, and nose. She was whole again.

More than whole, she was powerful.

———— ◆ ————

Denton, Eliana, George, Talulo, and Roelin were thrown onto the rim of the crater Nhymn had made. All around them, nezzarforms rose out of the ground and rushed forward to march along with their new master. A sandstorm rose around Nhymn as she moved through the red dunes, carving out a new path.

Talulo laid Roelin against a rock on a small outcropping of boulders near the dunes. Denton crumpled down beside him. They watched as Nhymn moved away. Where was she heading now? What would she do next?

"Obliteration," Karx's warning echoed in Denton's mind. Although he'd almost been killed by the lightning blast, Denton still felt Karx's presence inside of him, hidden away. But the phantom sentry was silent now, and that made Denton nervous.

"Down here!" George shouted to the sky. He stood on a tall rock ledge and waved to the *Rogers* as it lowered its landing gear and ramp. Jess Combs and Fergus Reid walked down the ramp to help them.

"Is he—" Jess shouted her half question and pointed at Roelin's unconscious body.

"Roelin needs medical attention," Eliana interrupted her. "If I don't take care of him now, we get no answers,"

Jess hesitated, then nodded. "If he survives, put him in quarantine, Rocco's orders."

Eliana nodded. With George and Fergus's help, she brought Roelin on board toward the medical bay. Talulo walked up the ramp ahead of Denton.

As Denton scaled the ramp, Jess put a gun to his chest.

"What the—?" Denton asked in shock.

"You're going to quarantine," Jess shouted over the engine noise. "I don't know what I saw you do in the brig on the *Astraeus*, but as far as I'm concerned, you're contaminated like Roelin."

"I can explain," Denton shouted.

"You bet your ass you're going to explain! Quarantine, *now!*"

Jess wouldn't budge.

Denton lifted his arms and complied. Jess marched him to the quarantine hatch and punched in the code. The door flung open, and Denton walked inside. He sat down on a bench and watched Jess seal the hatch and leave.

The ramp raised, and the *Rogers* lifted into the desert sky.

As the Pilgrim-class explorer sailed through the sky, it passed the towering monster and its growing army of twisted nezzarforms. Denton looked out the window at Nhymn. She'd called herself the Decider.

Denton wondered what Nhymn would decide to do.

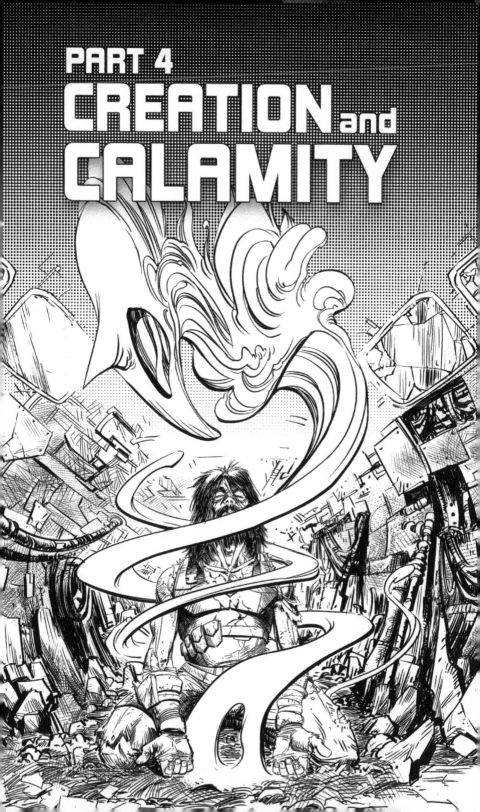

PART 4
CREATION and CALAMITY

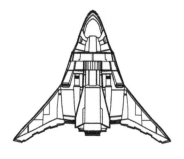

FORTY-NINE

A MONTH HAD PASSED since the Siren had emerged from the depths of Kamaria.

Eliana had struggled to understand Denton's story when she heard it the first time. The birth of the sister Sirens and the powers they possessed seemed like a fairy tale. The pieces finally aligned when Denton came to the part about the Alpha Team in the cave. The details Denton gave were more informed than any of the archival data he could have sifted through. His story was further corroborated by the event in the underground palace when the Siren had called him Karx.

At first, she'd felt hurt. Denton had this terrible secret he was keeping from her, and it felt like a betrayal. But then it made sense that he had no idea what was going on until it was far too late. The question in Eliana's mind was, *Even if Denton had managed to tell me sooner, would I have believed him?*

Eliana assumed she wouldn't have. Over the past month, he hadn't been able to convince the council to believe him, and so Denton had been left locked away in quarantine with Roelin since they got back from the mission.

Roelin, the man she had sought for four years, now lay in a

coma. His spine had been damaged during the event, leaving him paralyzed from the waist down. Eliana was his personal doctor, and she made regular visits to the quarantine lab to check on his health and spend time with Denton. Today, she noticed the group of Tvashtar marines standing outside the building.

Marines lined the hallway as Eliana made her way toward the quarantine room. She had seen this before; when council members wanted to probe for information, they would bring a squad of marines and ask Denton the same questions they had been asking him daily for the past month. Eliana knew they could just talk to each other, but election season was coming up, so that simple task was out of the question. The problems humanity faced at the colony seemed so trivial compared to the issues Kamaria was throwing at them.

Eliana entered the quarantine room and squeezed herself past the crowded marines. Councilwoman Helen Davies and General Martin Raughts stood with George Tanaka in front of the observation glass, discussing something and drinking coffee. Behind the glass, Roelin lay facedown on a stretcher with an auto-surgeon monitoring his injuries. The bed had a compartment on the bottom that contained Roelin's combat suit and weapons. It was locked up tight and had been scanned by the internal monitors of the stretcher for contagions. Eliana knew it didn't matter if they discovered a contagion or not—Roelin was doomed to eternal captivity by the fears of the people in the colony. Although Denton explained that Roelin had been possessed by Nhymn, fear was fear, and it was unshakable.

Denton sat on the bench on the side wall of the quarantined room, chatting on his soothreader with his family. He looked tired. A beard had grown on his face, with a barren line cut out from the scar that the combat knife had left on his cheek when the *Astraeus* barrel rolled. Denton had only been allowed to shower in the decontamination spray that emitted from the ceiling of the glass room he was imprisoned in. His only furniture included a small air mattress in the corner of the room, a little dresser filled with clothes, the bench on the side wall, the autopsy table that had been pushed out of the center of the room, and Roelin Raike's stretcher.

Denton looked up and waved his hand subtly as he watched Eliana approach the glass. She smiled and darted her eyes to the envoy of marines and Helen Davies, then pumped her eyebrows up.

Big day, eh? Eliana said with no words.

Yeah, tell me about it, Denton said with only an eye roll and a wink.

Eliana donned her atmospheric suit and helmet and entered the air lock that separated the prep room from the quarantine room, allowing the cleansing spray to wash over her. A green light flicked on, and the door opened. Eliana could now hear the conversation Denton was having with his family as she walked over to Roelin to inspect his injuries.

"How much longer do they plan to keep you locked up?" Michael Castus shouted over Denton's soothreader comm channel.

"They still aren't sure." Denton sighed. "I guess until they think I'm safe to bring back into the colony." He looked over at Roelin's unconscious body and sighed.

"It's *bull!*"

Brynn stepped in and asked, "Denny, is there anything we can do to speed things up?"

"Unless you can determine what an alien ghost did to my mind, then I'm not sure." Denton huffed out a weak laugh with no humor behind it.

"Yeah, but how could they tell either?" his brother Jason called out from behind their parents.

"I'm sure those nerds got a way. Nerds always got a way," Tyler mumbled, his voice barely audible.

"We're just going to have to wait and—" Denton didn't get a chance to say "see."

"We're gonna have to break you out!" Michael shouted.

"Not this again," Denton mumbled.

Brynn attempted to calm Michael down. "Now, honey. We

don't want to get him in trouble."

"In trouble?" Michael scoffed. "The man's been locked up for a month with a damn ghost in his head! You're worried about getting him in trouble?"

"Guys, don't do anything crazy now," Denton warned.

"We're breakin' you out, and that's it!" Michael said. "Boys! Come on, we're stormin' the gate!"

Jason and Tyler shouted with excitement at the idea. The sounds of them shuffling things together in the shop for the escape plan echoed through the receiver.

"Oh jeez," Brynn said. "Denny, I have to go, your father is storming the gate. Love you!"

"Love you too, Ma," Denton said as the hollering of his father and brothers winked out with the end of the call.

"I bet they aren't too happy with me," Eliana said as she downloaded the data from the auto surgeon to her medical kit.

"They'll get over it once they understand whatever the Hells this all is," Denton said.

"You're taking this pretty gracefully."

"You think so?" Denton huffed. "I have a lot to think about. Jess said my eyes were shaking after my last vision. I'm starting to wonder if these dreams I had weren't dreams at all."

"What else would they have been?" Eliana asked.

"Nhymn recognized me, she called me *a shade*. I think what I was experiencing was some sort of time travel." Denton stood up and roughly rubbed his bearded face, pulling down on his skin as he sighed. "It's confusing."

"There are things here on Kamaria that we will never fully understand. This planet wasn't made for us."

"Yeah, but Karx told me I brought *myself* to him. I still don't know how that works."

Outside the glass barrier, the light above the door blinked from red to green, and George's voice said through the intercom, "Alright, we are ready now."

George, General Raughts, and Colony Leader Helen Davies, along with a handful of Tvashtar marines, stared at Denton through the observation glass wall. He felt like an ape at a zoo, expected to perform some sort of trick. Denton wanted to fling something at the glass and tell them to get lost and let him think, but his civilized mind prevailed.

Eliana sat down in the chair next to Roelin's bed, focusing her attention on his care while Denton prepared to explain for the thousandth time what had happened.

"What's up, y'all?" Denton asked, accentuating his Ganymede drawl.

George Tanaka stepped forward toward the glass that separated him from the quarantine chamber. "We have some questions for you."

"And here I thought you guys were throwing me a party."

George couldn't help but grin at Denton's unwavering charisma.

Helen Davies said, "Mr. Castus, I know this month has been rigorous for you. They told me what has happened, but I requested to hear it from you myself. I hope we can end this quarantine for you very shortly." She smiled, wrinkling her face. Denton felt warmth in her smile—she reminded him of his grandmother.

"Whatever you need," he said, nodding with a gentle head bob. Helen smiled again and gestured to General Raughts.

"Mr. Castus, when you were locked in the *Astraeus*'s brig"— Raughts paused to check his data—"Jess Combs observed you having some sort of seizure. She stated she thought you were dying and claimed your eyes began to vibrate unnaturally. Did Roelin do something to you? What did he pull you away for?"

Denton provided the best answers he could. "No, sir. Roelin pulled me away to fix the *Astraeus*. He ..." Denton stopped himself. He was putting the blame on Roelin, but he knew Nhymn was the real criminal. "I'm sorry. This gets a little complicated. Things were happening to me that I wasn't fully aware of until much later."

"What sort of things?" Helen asked.

"Denton, tell us everything you know, please," George said. "She's been briefed, don't worry about scaring her off. We are looking at this very seriously."

"Alright." Denton sighed. "There are things I still don't fully understand, so I'm going to have to paraphrase some."

"Do what you can. The floor is yours," Helen Davies said.

Denton paced the room as he recounted the story, looking for answers each time he went back over it. "In the Tangle Maze, when Marie fell, I went down to get her. We successfully stabilized her and began to raise her." He rubbed the back of his neck with his hand, remembering Marie's crippling injury. "Before I could be pulled back up, I encountered a creature named Karx."

Denton reached onto the bench and grabbed his sketchpad, one of the few items he'd been allowed to keep with him for the last month. He shuffled through it to a drawing of the stone sentry. Helen scanned the picture intensely.

"That's an excellent sketch. Is it a Siren?" Helen asked.

"Not exactly, I'll get to that. Karx had done something to me, and for a while, I didn't even notice. I'm still not sure exactly what it is, really. When we left the Maze, I began to have visions. I thought Karx was showing me the history of the Sirens." Denton looked over at Roelin. He thought he saw the man twitch.

Denton flipped through his sketchpad as he explained what he knew.

"At first, there were two of them, twin sisters. They were born in the cave outside the City of the Dead ..."

Denton went on to describe his visions, the first constructs Sympha had made named nezzarforms, and the birth of Karx. How Nhymn was powerless and could not create anything. How Sympha and Karx were attacked by the two dray'vas, and how Nhymn discovered her power to control life-forms. How this power perverted her mind, and to impress her sister, Nhymn had taken control of an entire auk'nai city, which led to their subsequent massacre and Nhymn's first death.

"She wasn't dead, though. She was something else," Denton said. "I don't think either of the Sirens knew about this life after death. Sympha left Nhymn in the cave, then went away, leaving Karx behind to guard the cave. But Karx isn't a true Siren. His body calcified over time. When you all visited the cave, he was already almost crumbled away. He looked like a statue to you."

"So, this was Karx?" George said as he pulled up a holographic photo of their scout mission in the City of the Dead. In the picture, Eliana stood before the stone sentry.

"That's him." Denton shuddered. Seeing the event from George's perspective only made the visions more real.

"That thing was alive?" General Raughts asked. "You scanned it, didn't you?"

"We did, we scanned everything. But there was a thin layer of unique bacteria over everything that clouded our scanners," George said.

"That bacteria was Sympha's power," Denton said. "Karx was alive, but barely."

"So, this Karx," Helen said. "He showed you these visions?"

"Yes. Well, no." Denton sighed, wincing in frustration.

"Explain," Helen said, more a command than a request.

"At first, I thought Karx was showing me the visions because he needed my help. When I encountered him in the Tangle Maze, he was falling apart. I think he transferred himself to me," Denton said. "But in my last vision, he claimed I brought myself there."

"How is that possible?" Helen asked.

"Beats me, ma'am." Denton shrugged.

"So, in the cave ..." George said. "What happened in there? After they put Nhymn's body in it."

"Like I said, Nhymn wasn't really dead," Denton said. "She was in some sort of anti-life. You guys couldn't see them, but the cave is filled with lesser Siren phantoms. Each day, they would chase Nhymn, destroy her, and then rebuild her to do it again. She lived in all of the Hells at once for centuries."

"Like Prometheus," George interjected. "Denton, you saw us too, correct? When we visited the cave."

"Yes," Denton said.

George looked down at his shoes. "What happened next?" he asked, knowing the answer.

"I could see what you could not," Denton said. "Nhymn was desperate, you couldn't have known. She took Roelin as a vessel. I think you know the rest." Denton sighed.

Roelin's head twitched roughly, then he lay still. Eliana noted the movement in her soothreader, but the observers on the other side of the glass didn't seem to notice.

"Now, what about you?" Helen asked after a moment of silence. "How do we know that you're not dangerous to the citizens of this colony? What can you tell us that will convince me to let you out of here?"

"Honestly, I don't know. I don't know Karx that well. It's not like we were drinkin' buddies," Denton said. "I'm not entirely sure if he's even still with me or not."

"What do you mean?" Helen asked.

"In the underground palace," George said, fielding the question, "we all heard Nhymn speak to Karx. She sensed him and then blasted Denton with an electrical bolt."

Denton lifted his shirt, revealing a spiraling pattern of scar tissue spreading across his chest. He looked up. "That's right. Since then, Karx has been silent, and there have been no more visions."

"Can Nhymn take control of us?" General Raughts asked. "Like how she took control of the City of the Dead."

"Honestly, I'm not sure," Denton said. "I'm under the impression that if she could, she would have by now. There must be some reason she hasn't."

"We must figure out what that reason might be. If this turns into a violent situation, it could be an advantage for us." Helen considered this information.

"You might be right." Denton said. There was a silence as Helen considered the information she'd been given.

"What do you suggest we do?" General Raughts asked Helen.

"Mr. Castus, I think we should keep you in here for a little bit longer," she said.

"I understand," Denton said, deflated. "But, can I make a suggestion?"

"Of course," Helen said.

"Don't let Karx's warning go to waste. He told me she brought oblivion with her," Denton said. The observers nodded in silence.

General Raughts looked at his marines, then back at Denton. "We have been searching for this Siren since the day it emerged, but have had no luck spotting it. It's like it vanished off the face of the planet."

"Have the auk'nai seen her?" Denton asked.

"We have been trying to contact Mag'Ro and the city of Apusticus, but they won't meet with us," George said with a sigh.

"Damn." Denton squeezed his fists and looked at the floor. "Well, keep looking. She's got to be out there somewhere."

"We will consider what we've learned here." Helen leaned over to a marine sergeant and whispered something to him.

"Thank you, Denton," George said.

The audience left the room, leaving behind two marines to stand guard outside the door. Denton sat down on the bench and looked over to Eliana and Roelin.

"I don't think I'm getting outta here anytime soon." Denton whispered to himself.

FIFTY

TALULO STOOD BEFORE AN audience of auk'nai in the city center of Apusticus. The moons were high in the sky, their light mingling with the glowing gemstones that lit the city. The large auk'nai fountain emptied water into the floating basin with a soft trickling noise, a sound that would have been pleasant on a night like this had there not been the commotion.

Since the Siren's emergence from the underground cave, Talulo had been attempting to convince Mag'Ro and the others that the humans could be trusted. He told them of his adventures with the humans and about the Tra'oi'due past-tracking serum he'd made, the Siren and her power, and the alabaster palace in the underground cave. But it was the story of how he'd lost his daunoren staff and wings that made the crowd gasp.

Talulo looked over his shoulder to the stumps that used to be his beautiful wings and sighed. He'd attempted to cover them with a sash, but they insisted on being revealed, poking through awkwardly as he shuffled around.

"Humans," Mag'Ro spoke in the native auk'nai tongue as he paced around Talulo, tapping his large daunoren staff on the city platform with each step, "removed your wings? While you were unconscious?"

"They had to." Talulo didn't meet Mag'Ro's gaze; instead, he looked toward the audience. "Eliana said that if she didn't, infection would spread. Talulo would have died."

"When the humans first arrived, Mag'Ro observed them for a long time." Mag'Ro turned to address the crowd. "In that time, Mag'Ro found that the humans will shape the world to fit their needs. If the ground is infertile, they will change it. If the sky is poisonous to their lungs, they will change it. Mag'Ro admired this aspect of their nature, and strove to make communication with the humans a priority." Mag'Ro turned to Talulo. "But now they changed you."

"Mag'Ro, Eliana didn't mean any—" Talulo pleaded.

"Apusticus has the medicines here to fix infection without amputation. *Surely Eliana knew that!*"

"There was no time," Talulo said. "The ship!"

"Yes, the ship. The *human* ship! *A weapon*! One of the many weapons the humans keep!" Mag'Ro seethed. "The humans fight amongst each other and the auk'nai are ensnared in their conflicts. Look at the cost of their in-fighting!" He pulled the sash away from Talulo's back with such force that it ripped, dropping a few loose gemstones to the ground. The audience was silent as they listened to the clattering of the stones against the platform. The fountain maintained its constant babbling, the only barrier between Talulo's shame and the audience's revulsion. He sunk his head, defeated.

"And your daunoren." Mag'Ro slammed the butt of his staff on the ground with a thunderous bang. "You said the man Roelin destroyed it with his tricks. Auk'nai without the daunoren is not auk'nai," Mag'Ro stately firmly. Talulo's ears pressed back against his head. Mag'Ro continued to pace around him, then placed a hand on Talulo's stubbed wing. "Auk'nai without flight is not auk'nai."

Mag'Ro then spoke directly into Talulo's mind: *"The humans have made you one of them."*

Talulo sank to his knees and whimpered, "It wasn't their fault. The Siren—she did this!"

"The *Siren*. No auk'nai has seen this creature. We have been searching, but there has been no sign of a monster that size."

"Ahn'ah'rahn'eem!" Talulo snapped his head toward Mag'Ro with a blaze in his eyes that could cut through the planet.

"The dead place?" Mag'Ro's eyes widened at the mention of it, and for a moment, he looked as though he might strike Talulo with his daunoren staff. "You dare bring those *horrors* into this?"

The place the humans referred to as the City of the Dead was more than that to the auk'nai in this region. The word they gave it was *Ahn'ah'rahn'eem*, which meant "the never-ending nightmare" in their tongue. It was a place of great evil.

Auk'nai that traveled to the city lost their minds. Those who didn't rush to suicide became shells of their former selves, rambling on and on about being destroyed and rebuilt endlessly. It was more than just the sight of the massacred citizens—there was something in the air that drove them insane. Shrieking could be heard inside the minds of any mentally sensitive creature who dared to get close to the dead place.

Talulo stood, gently trying to cover his wounds again with his torn garments. "If Mag'Ro saw what Talulo has seen, Mag'Ro would believe it too. The Siren is real, and it made *Ahn'ah'rahn'eem* a dead place with its powers. No other creature has a song like that. The Siren can do the same to Apusticus."

Mag'Ro sneered at Talulo. "Mag'Ro will not allow aliens to mutilate his people. We have their technology, we don't need their help." Mag'Ro turned his back to Talulo. "As for this *Siren*, you will never speak of it again. She is a figment brought on by whatever trickery the humans played on you and *no more!*"

Mag'Ro didn't have to say that this tribunal was over. The auk'nai had no words or phrases for goodbye. The audience stood and left the city center, flying back to their homes for the night. Talulo stood alone on the platform near the fountain, allowing the gemstones to cast their light on him as the sole performer of a stage play, the clapping of the water in the fountain the only applause.

———— ◆ ————

The song of Apusticus cannot lie. It sings its loudest when it needs to be heard, and bends to no auk'nai who wishes it silent. Talulo heard the song of Apusticus so loudly that it woke him from slumber.

Talulo was forced to take a perch close to the ground to compensate for his disability. His eyes darted around the bedchamber, but he was alone. The stars were still out—beckoning him to walk in their twilight. He left the bedchamber through the lowest door.

The gardens near Galifern's laboratory summoned Talulo. He followed their melody through glowing flowers and shimmering vines, without running into another auk'nai throughout his walk. He felt more abandoned now than he had that entire month; it was as if his fellow citizens hated him so much they'd fled the city rather than share it with him. Talulo wanted to fly into the night sky and search for his friends, then he itched at the stumps that used to be his wings and let out a sigh.

Talulo's ears were filled with a sharp melody; something unnatural in the world was adjusting the song of Apusticus. He fell to his knees and let out a pained caw, thinking his skull would split open.

Then the song ceased.

Talulo opened his eyes and blinked away the tears that had formed from the pain. When he brought his beak upward, he discovered he was finally not alone.

Arrilstar the Murderer was in the garden with Talulo. The brain leech sucked away at the auk'nai criminal's scalp, forcing him into the zombie servitude that justice required. Arrilstar was humming the same strange tune that Apusticus was singing.

411

This was the sign that Apusticus was ready to allow Arrilstar to return to his former self. Talulo had an obligation to remove the murderer's *j'etthoda* leech and devour it. *Is Talulo even worthy enough for this simple task?* He couldn't tell, but he thought it might be helpful to talk to someone who didn't share the same opinions as Mag'Ro, murderer or not.

Talulo whistled at Arrilstar the Murderer, and the zombified auk'nai slowly turned his head, still humming the same strange song as he walked over to Talulo.

"Murderer, you are to be released from your imprisonment. The song of Apusticus has deemed you ready to return to her," Talulo said, and clasped his claw around the j'etthoda leech's neck, releasing it from Arrilstar.

Arrilstar fell to his knees and gasped for air. Talulo brought the leech to his beak, unenthusiastic about devouring it.

"No!" Arrilstar grappled with Talulo and wrenched the leech away from his claws. The j'etthoda fell to the ground, and Arrilstar slammed the blunt end of his daunoren staff upon it, causing the parasite to explode.

"This is not how—" Talulo began to shout, then noticed the acidic reaction the leech's blood was having on the city platform. The smell it emitted reminded Talulo of the Tra'oi'due serum he'd used to track Roelin through Puppo's past.

"That is not a j'etthoda. Is it a m'unjo with a Tra'oi'due serum?" Talulo asked. Arrilstar caught his breath and hugged Talulo. Talulo asked, "What does this mean?"

"There has been a wronging in the song of Apusticus—" Arrilstar coughed and fell to one knee, his mouth dripped blood. "Arrilstar doesn't have much time."

"Tell me of the wrongness," Talulo said, and held Arrilstar by the shoulders.

"Mag'Ro has tricked the song. He sang it wrong and none have noticed." Arrilstar coughed. "Mag'Ro ended Ve'trenn's life. Not Arrilstar."

"What, how is that possible? The song of Apusticus does not lie."

"Mag'Ro made Arrilstar sing the song wrongly for him, using trickery." Arrilstar coughed again. "The Tra'oi'due is tainted. It shows a false past, a past where Arrilstar murdered Ve'trenn. But Arrilstar knows the *true song*." Arrilstar raggedly coughed more blood. "Mag'Ro used an alien weapon to perform the murder. Apusticus knew nothing of the device, and so it knew not what to sing." Arrilstar vomited blood, and acid mixed within burned the platform. "Sense Arrilstar, brother, you know it sings true."

It was true. Auk'nai could not lie to each other, yet somehow, Mag'Ro had gotten everyone to believe a falseness. Talulo remembered the day Ve'trenn was found dead. Mag'Ro had been the one to detain Arrilstar; the fake leech sang the song of the wrongdoer. When any auk'nai inquired about the song, they saw a vision of Arrilstar committing the murder of their city leader.

The proof of the crime was burning away on the floor. A m'unjo altered to look like a j'etthoda, imbued with a modified Tra'oi'due serum, had committed the lie for Mag'Ro as a third party to the crime. A chemical lie. All Mag'Ro had to do was believe the lie so firmly, the false evidence would hide the rest of his sin. Had Mag'Ro learned this from watching the humans?

"Mag'Ro murdered Ve'trenn," Talulo whispered. "And the song of Apusticus told Talulo to free you now. *Why?*"

Arrilstar collapsed onto the floor. Talulo turned him onto his back and said, "No, do not fade now, Arrilstar. Apusticus must correct this wrongness. The song has told Talulo to help you."

Arrilstar gurgled on blood that burned through his skull. The acid from the m'unjo had done its job, killing Arrilstar and removing the final witness to the crime. If the wrongly accused murderer hadn't knocked the false leech away from Talulo, they would both have been dead, and the sin would have gone unheard.

"Talulo will bring you to the mountain, Arrilstar. You will become part of the planet once more. Rest your wings," Talulo said, evoking the only goodbye auk'nai used, the last goodbye.

Where is everyone?

Talulo's feather's sensed a change in air pressure. He left Arrilstar's body in the garden and searched for help.

There was a gathering in the city center. Talulo walked toward the crowd with gem lights guiding his way in the darkness. He held his hand forward and could see wisps of fog tendrils wrapping and unwrapping around him.

"Talulo." Nock'lu landed in front of him. For a moment, Talulo understood why the humans jolted when auk'nai approached.

"What is happening?" Talulo asked, gesturing toward the crowd.

"Apusticus has a visitor," Nock'lu said, and used his daunoren staff to push some of the crowd aside, clearing a path. Talulo could see Mag'Ro ahead of them. He stood with a dark shape that was shrouded by the fog. The visitor was twice the height of Mag'Ro.

"Is that from your stories?" Nock'lu asked. Talulo squinted his eyes, trying to see through the fog. When he could finally make out the dark shape, his heart dropped into his gut.

The visitor was made of black stone that surged with violet electrical energy. One cyclopean orifice watched Mag'Ro from atop its tall perch on its broad shoulders, and two blunt, clubbed arms dragged against the platform, bracing the stone construct and holding it upright. Talulo had seen these twisted nezzarforms before when they'd entered the final room of the alabaster palace.

"Apusticus is in danger," Talulo said to Nock'lu as he broke free from the crowd and dashed toward Mag'Ro. Mag'Ro turned to see Talulo running toward him. As Talulo got close, Mag'Ro held out his taloned hand to halt him in his tracks.

"Mag'Ro! This thing—" Talulo tried to explain.

"Stay where you are, young one," Mag'Ro responded telepathically. *"This creature has come here with an offer."*

Talulo looked up at the twisted nezzarform. It flicked its stone head toward him as if it recognized him. There was a rumble of thunder, and lightning briefly revealed the immense silhouette of a dark shape towering above the azure trees.

Nhymn. She was here.

"I have made a decision," Nhymn's voice whispered in their minds. *"The auk'nai will inherit this planet."*

"Talulo doesn't understand," Talulo addressed Mag'Ro, not the demon before him.

"Nhymn tells us she will grant Apusticus the power to remove the humans from our world," Mag'Ro said to the crowd. "All we need to do is accept it."

"You can't! The humans are our friends!"

"They are not your friends!" Nhymn hissed, and lightning flashed. *"They have left their old star out of desperation, pursued by an impossible enemy. In time, that enemy will follow the humans here and destroy everything."* Nhymn calmed her anger. *"If we remove the humans, their enemy will no longer be able to track them. They will pass by, and you will be saved."*

Talulo didn't know what to say. He'd heard stories about the Undriel from his human friends. Their minds had told him they were not followed to Kamaria.

"Mag'Ro, *she's wrong!*" Talulo pleaded. *"Ahn'ah'rahn'eem!"*

"Hush now!" Mag'Ro said into Talulo's mind. His eyes widened, and his pupils shrunk.

"I come here with power," Nhymn said. *"I will not bow to those too weak to save themselves."*

Talulo sensed Nhymn's true intention then, as did the rest of the citizens of Apusticus. She spoke of saving the planet, but her methods were those of pure control. Life would not be allowed to live freely; they would become much like zombified criminals, leeched into servitude by a higher power.

"Mag'Ro accepts," the false auk'nai leader proclaimed.

"Apusticus does not accept!" Talulo shouted. There was a hush in the air.

Mag'Ro slapped Talulo with the broad side of his immense daunoren staff, knocking the wingless auk'nai onto his back in front of the crowd.

"*You* speak for Apusticus now?" Mag'Ro seethed. "You are hardly an auk'nai. No daunoren, *no wings*! What makes you think you can sing the song of Apusticus?"

"Talulo knows of your wrongness!" Talulo shouted. Mag'Ro's eyes widened.

"*What* wrongness?" Mag'Ro asked.

"You fooled the song of Apusticus! You killed Ve'trenn and framed Arrilstar. His body lies in the garden, along with the mutated m'unjo you used as a j'etthoda. *Mag'Ro fooled Apusticus!*"

Nock'lu stepped forward. "Nock'lu senses Talulo sings true."

"*Talulo lies!*" Mag'Ro said. "He learned to lie from the humans! He is the one who sings a wrongness, not Mag'Ro!"

Talulo knew what they all sensed: Mag'Ro was forced to drop his mental guard for a moment, and in that moment, he forgot to believe his own lie. The city of Apusticus began cawing in anger.

"*Mag'Ro the Murderer!*"

"*Apusticus hears you!*"

"*Justice for Ve'trenn!*"

Mag'Ro pulsed with anger and activated the collider cylinders on his modified daunoren staff. He pointed his weapon at Talulo and shouted, "Enough!"

Talulo covered his eyes. There was a blast, then a clatter. Talulo opened his eyes and saw Mag'Ro on his knees, an open wound on his chest spilling blood onto the ground. Nock'lu stood over Talulo, the hook end of his staff dripping with Mag'Ro's blood. The modified daunoren staff lay on the ground near Talulo.

"Mag'Ro is a *murderer*. Apusticus knows it now. Mag'Ro no longer speaks for the auk'nai," Nock'lu said.

Mag'Ro leaned forward and tried to staunch the flow of blood emitting from his chest. He cawed weakly, and his breaths became more shallow.

"*Weakness,*" Nhymn whispered with disgust. "*I will create a new inheritor, then.*"

The twisted nezzarform raised its large stone arm and brought it

416

down with incredible speed, smashing Mag'Ro into the platform. The arm rose again, revealing their dishonored leader as a broken, bloody mess in the crater left behind. The crowd shrieked in horror.

"Attack!" Nock'lu shouted.

There was a loud whistle. A peck-rifle squadron leaped from their perches and fired on the nezzarform, striking it several times before it exploded. The fire disintegrated the remains of Mag'Ro's body instantly.

Nock'lu helped Talulo to his feet and handed him Mag'Ro's modified daunoren hook. "Here. It is a powerful weapon. Talulo is the one who should wield it. Talulo is the song of Apusticus embodied."

Talulo held the staff in his hands, feeling the weight of the city upon him.

The fog above the forest flashed with violet light. Auk'nai warriors emerged from various parts of the city to face the nezzarforms that now poured into the walkways from below.

Lightning bolts rocked the city from underneath, overwhelming Apusticus with destruction. The damaged platforms rolled and crashed to the ground, where an army of twisted nezzarforms waited to crush any survivors.

Nock'lu twirled his hook staff with the grace of a born fighter. He smashed the head of one nezzarform, spun, then lodged the sharp hook into the stone shoulder of another, pulling it deftly toward himself. As the nezzarform stumbled toward Nock'lu, he flapped his mighty wings and hurdled over it, smashing the two stone constructs into each other and watching the explosion that followed.

Talulo shouted, "Apusticus needs to get everyone out of here! We'll never win this fight!"

"Yes," Nock'lu said through heavy breaths. Nearby, a group of auk'nai warriors was overtaken and smashed. One warrior attempted to fly away but was shot down by a lightning bolt.

"There are too many enemies." Nock'lu turned to Talulo and pointed toward the laboratory. "Find Galifern. She will help you escape." Nock'lu grabbed Talulo's shoulders and stared him in the eyes. "Warn the humans, auk'nai will need their aid. Nock'lu will get as many survivors out of here as he can." He shoved Talulo toward Galifern's lab.

Nock'lu met another nezzarform head-on, slapping the end of his staff into the stone monster's head. He flapped himself backward and took a shot with his peck rifle, exploding the nezzarform.

Talulo was stopped short as a nezzarform crashed down in front of him, clinging on to a dead auk'nai in its rock hand. He hopped backward, instinctually trying to fly out of range but misjudging his unwinged hop. The nezzarform reached for him with its free hand, but Talulo managed to duck out of the way.

There was a surge of power from Mag'Ro's modified daunoren staff, and Talulo's hands felt like they were vibrating. As the nezzarform readied itself for another grab, Talulo swung the staff hard, and a bolt of white-hot light launched from the end of it. The bolt crashed into the nezzarform's center mass and sent the monster flying backward at incredible speed into a crowd of other nezzarforms where it exploded, causing a chain reaction of electrical explosions with the impact.

Talulo whistled with excitement. Daunoren hooks did not normally contain power like this; Mag'Ro had been experimenting with human technology more than he'd let on.

Talulo wasted no more time waiting for the nezzarforms to regroup, and dashed toward the lab.

The inside of Galifern's lab was cluttered with debris brought on by the rocking of the floating platforms. Lab equipment and machinery lay in haphazard positions on the floor.

"Is that you, Talulo?" the plump auk'nai scientist asked from behind a row of Kamarian plants.

"Yes, auk'nai need to get out of Apusticus and warn the humans."

"You sing true. But how are auk'nai going to get out? Neither of us can fly," Galifern said nervously as she fiddled her little taloned fingers. "Galifern knows, follow." She hurried toward the back of the lab and explained, "Galifern is not a good flier!"

"Talulo knows this," Talulo said, annoyed with pushing past debris to keep up with the little fat scientist.

"What Galifern is saying is the humans gave her *this* to get around." Galifern pointed at the human surveyor craft in the back corner of the lab. Talulo nodded. He had seen these vehicles before.

"Do you know how to use it?" Talulo asked.

"Galifern knows how it works but has never used it," Galifern said, and patted her plump belly. "Galifern does not get out often."

"Auk'nai can learn its song together," Talulo said, slinging Mag'Ro's daunoren staff onto his back and hopping on the surveyor's seat. Galifern jumped in the back cart, fitting snugly in the area intended for mineral collection, and pointed at parts of the vehicle's steering wheel. She telepathically explained to Talulo how to use it.

Within a few moments, Talulo had the surveyor revved up and roaring through the lab, adding to the chaos of the clutter. Galifern held on to Talulo's back, afraid she might fall out of the cart as they roared out into the city's main causeway.

"Look out!" Galifern telepathically shouted as nezzarforms fired bolts of light toward the surveyor. Talulo swerved out of the way, feeling the rubble hit against his feathers as the bolt crashed into the wall of the lab behind them. They did not wait for a second blast; Talulo piloted the surveyor toward the city's edge.

Over the tops of the trees, the Siren was revealed by lightning. She watched her nezzarform army destroy the auk'nai city, obeying her commands as if they were her own claws. Apusticus burned, platforms crumpled to the forest floor below, and buildings exploded. The cries of auk'nai echoed through the pandemonium.

Talulo piloted the surveyor over the edge of the last platform of Apusticus, sending it rocketing into the forest below. He knew the path the humans took to approach the city and followed it over the creek and through the trees to the clearing beyond.

"It's all fire and ash," Galifern whispered into Talulo's mind as she looked back toward their home. The farther they traveled, the quieter the sounds of anarchy became until they could only hear insects chirping and trees swaying in the wind. The light from the fires engulfed the forest behind them. Talulo cleared the Azure Vault's tree line and skidded the surveyor to a stop, turning to look at the remains of the civilization he had grown up in.

"There, survivors." Galifern pointed to a flock of auk'nai escaping the city. "Auk'nai need to regroup."

"Auk'nai will. First, Talulo must warn the humans. The Siren is coming for them now," Talulo said, and revved the surveyor back up, thrusting the two flightless auk'nai into the forest beyond the Azure Vault.

Their world was gone. Apusticus had fallen victim to the Decider.

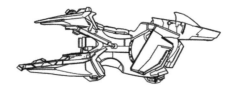

FIFTY-ONE

"YOU CAN'T JUST KEEP him locked up forever! That's *my son*, damn it!" Michael Castus shouted up to the rampart above the colony gate, where the captain of the Colonial Guard stood watch, preventing the Castus family from traveling across the meadow to the quarantine lab where Denton was being held. "You're gonna open this thing up and let us see him!"

"We've already told you, sir." The captain pinched the bridge of his nose and sighed, then recycled his previous statements for the thousandth time: "Your son is in quarantine. Allowing you to see him would risk further contamination to Odysseus Colony. We are happy to give you a direct feed to his cell—"

"Cell!" Jason shouted, and the captain winced. He'd used a trigger word, a mistake brought on by the delirium of exhaustion. Jason rallied his family. "They got him in a cell. Like a *prisoner.*"

"You have no right to keep him from his family." Brynn called out.

"He's *not* a prisoner." The captain tried to take back his misstep, but it was too late. The seed of conspiracy was planted. What he really wanted to say was, *I'm just doing my job, lady.*

"Sir!" a colonial guardsman near the captain interrupted.

"Something's coming this way!"

"*Handle* this," the captain said to the guardsman as he snatched his binoculars. The target was still a reasonable distance off but moving quickly toward the colony gateway. "Is that …?" The captain lowered the binoculars, then lifted them quickly back up to his face for a second look. "Inform command we have two auk'nai riding a surveyor this way."

"Yes, sir!"

———— ◆ ————

Talulo and Galifern were tired. They'd driven the surveyor through the night, traveling through the forests, hills, and mountains until they finally arrived at the Odysseus Colony perimeter. Talulo parked the vehicle three kilometers from the colony and watched as human colonists lined the wall, many of them seeing an auk'nai for the first time.

"George," Talulo huffed. He whistled so loudly that the effort almost made him pass out.

Galifern lay in the back cart, dehydrated and hungry. She looked at the wall and said, "Never saw a human colony before." She nodded her beak and added. "Not impressed."

Talulo watched as George Tanaka, Colony Leader Helen Davies, General Martin Raughts, and a squad of Tvashtar marines walked through the grass toward them.

"What are you doing here?" George asked as he got closer, then gestured to the nearest marine. "Give them water."

The marine removed a water jug from his belt harness, twisted off the cap, and handed it to Talulo. Talulo took the flask and gave it directly to Galifern, who wasted no time guzzling it down.

George's eyes darted to the unique daunoren staff slung onto Talulo's back—Mag'Ro's staff. Talulo could sense in George's mind that he knew Mag'Ro would never have just handed it over.

"Are you hurt?" George asked.

"The Siren is coming," Talulo grunted. "Apusticus was destroyed."

"She destroyed *Apusticus*?" George repeated just to make sure he'd heard it correctly. Talulo nodded his beak. George shook his head, then stood rigidly with the realization. "She's coming here?"

Talulo nodded again. "Mag'Ro betrayed Apusticus. He invited the Siren and accepted her offer of power. But Apusticus refused to listen to the song they sang, and we fought her there. The Siren was too powerful. Talulo came to warn humans, but must go find survivors."

General Raughts stepped forward. "How long until she arrives?"

Talulo looked down at the ground and held up one finger. "Day."

"Hells!" George turned around and put his hands on his head. "It's bad. We need to get these two inside."

"No, George." Talulo held up a hand. "Take Galifern. Talulo must find auk'nai."

"We'll get you some supplies for the trip. Whatever you need, tell us," George said, and gestured to a few marines to attend to Galifern. "Call Lieutenant Commander Rocco Gainax and have him take Talulo to the survivors of Apusticus. And get Galifern inside."

"Auk'nai inside the Odysseus Colony walls?" Helen Davies asked. "What about the protocols you and John put in place?"

"Screw the protocols. We have bigger problems, and no time."

The gateway opened, and the marines marched the auk'nai refugee in. The Castus family had front-row seats as the alien bird-woman came through the gates and walked toward the colony central.

Tyler mumbled, "There goes the neighborhood."

———◆———

Hours passed inside the quarantine bay.

Eliana returned to the pavilion, leaving Denton alone with his thoughts. He sat on the bench with his back against the wall, thinking about the Siren and what she could be up to. He had found the answers for Eliana and George, but now he had his own questions to contend with.

Denton tapped into the wave transmitter signal his mother had provided for the family during their escape from Ganymede so long ago. It gave him access to all classified communication channels, which helped pass the time. He heard about Talulo's arrival and the destruction of Apusticus, and his guts stirred. Denton felt responsible. If he'd just stayed in the machine shop with his family and kept his head down, all those auk'nai would still have been alive and their beautiful city would still have been around. Denton had fixed the *Astraeus* and helped Nhymn take over Sympha. This was his fault.

How can I fix this? The current situation wasn't a machine; it had no blueprints or hardware. It was brought on by his actions. *Maybe it isn't fixable.*

The door opened, and Denton expected another group of marines or a councilman looking for a story, but the woman who entered was quiet and alone.

It was Faye Raike, Roelin's wife.

Faye had her eyes locked on the floor. She walked toward the glass wall, then finally brought her gaze up. Her eyes welled with tears and she gasped.

"They said you were in a coma," Faye said.

Denton wasn't sure who she was speaking to. He was about to respond when Captain Roelin Raike stepped forward toward the glass.

Denton's eyes widened. *Impossible.* Not only was Roelin upright, off his stretcher, and walking, but he was clean-shaven and looked healthy. Denton's eyes darted toward the stretcher, and his confusion doubled when he saw the unconscious Roelin he had become so familiar with was still lying facedown. Denton remained silent, stunned by the apparition that was currently facing Faye through the glass.

"Is this some trick?" Faye asked, blinking salty tears away. Her face was red from her attempts to fight back against her feelings.

"No tricks. It's me," Roelin said. He smiled and blinked as a single tear rolled down his cheek and onto the floor. "It's me," he repeated in a whisper. He lifted his hand toward the glass.

"Roe," she whispered back. Faye jerked her hand away from the glass before Roelin placed his on it. He paused, then lowered his hand to his side.

"I wasn't going to come here," Faye said, trying to maintain her composure but losing the battle. "I told myself it wasn't possible. You died somewhere out there in the wilderness." She held her hand close to her neck, remembering the last time she'd seen him. "You almost killed me."

Roelin said nothing, his eyes glossy with tears.

"Eliana told me what happened to you." She sniffled, quickly wiping her nose. "She told me about the Sirens, the *Astraeus*, all of it." She lowered her eyes to the floor. "I heard it. But I still don't feel it."

"I'm ..." Roelin began to say, but he only mouthed the word, *"Sorry,"* as if he didn't have the strength to push it past his vocal cords.

"For the past five years, it's been called Silence Day," Faye said, keeping her eyes sternly on Roelin's. "But you have killed me every day since."

Roelin jerked his head to the floor as if pistol-whipped by an interrogator.

"So, *who are we* now, Roe?" There was a moment of silence. Faye's eyes locked on Roelin's face, but his eyes remained on his shoes.

"I never stopped thinking about you," Roelin said. For a second, there was a slight smile on his lips, as if he'd returned to those good times for the briefest moment. "I began to forget the man I was before. I don't remember a childhood, I don't remember my parents. You were the memory I fought to keep."

Faye flinched, and Roelin continued, "The Siren took everything from me. She kept my body alive but eviscerated my soul. She forced me to kill others but wouldn't allow me to kill myself.

Nhymn devoured my memories, but I wouldn't let her take you."
Roelin blinked out more tears. "I'd sooner forget everything real than
forget you."

"Roe," she whispered.

"I'm sorry this happened to us," Roelin said. "I'll love you until
the end of time. No matter who I am or what I become. Life, death,
afterlife." Roelin put his hand on the glass barrier again and held it
firm. He brought his eyes up to meet hers.

Faye slowly brought her hand up and placed it on the opposite
side of the glass.

"I still love you," she mouthed, unable to bring her voice forward.

"I love you too," Roelin whispered. "Goodbye, Faye."

"What?"

The quarantine bay door opened, and everyone's eyes shifted to
Eliana as she walked in. A colonial guardsman escorted her into the
room, nodded to everyone, then returned to wait outside. Faye
turned her gaze back to the glass barrier only to find herself holding
her hand against it alone. Roelin was facedown on the stretcher,
comatose.

Eliana said, "I'm so sorry. Did you want some privacy?"

Faye looked at her hand, still holding it against the glass. Her
faced twisted with a mixture of sadness, confusion, and immense
anger. She jerked her hand away from the glass and left the room in
a hurry.

Eliana sighed, knowing the whole situation was taxing on
everyone involved. She donned her suit and walked into the air lock
of the quarantine room as she had many times before. She asked
Denton, "How's he been?"

"I'm not sure what I just saw," Denton said. "Roelin was just up
and talking a moment ago."

"Oh, is that so? Well, there's been no changes in his signatures."
Eliana chuckled as she checked his vital signs. "Just the same old
anomalous wavelengths. Hard to determine what's normal regarding
his condition these days."

"No, *seriously*," Denton insisted. "Elly, the guy was up and talking."

Her face grew sterner, and her eyes glanced over the life signatures again. "Did you do something to him? What changed? Why is he back on the stretcher now?"

"I didn't do anything! It just happened." Denton threw his hands up. "Don't shoot the messenger!"

She looked down at Roelin's comatose body and put a hand lightly on the man's shoulder. She said, "I wish he were up and talking."

"You would get your answers then," Denton said.

"No, I already have my answers, thanks to you. Nhymn possessed Roelin and forced him to do those awful things." She gently rubbed Roelin's shoulder and spoke as if there were a sleeping baby in the room. "I'd tell him it's not his fault. I'd tell him I forgive him. I know my father would have forgiven him too. I want him to know that."

There was silence for a few heartbeats, then Denton whispered, "If he wakes up, I'll make sure he knows."

Eliana sighed. "Just keep an eye on him. Call me if he wakes up when I'm not here."

Denton nodded, then he remembered that his familiar Tvashtar marine guard had been replaced with a colonial guardsman. "Hey, Elly, what's with the guard? Not my normal Marine entourage." He jerked his forehead toward the doorway.

"Everyone is being called to action," Eliana said. "The Siren is coming."

FIFTY-TWO

"LOOKS LIKE EVERYONE IS gathering in the central park," Jason said. The Castus family remained planted firmly near the colony gateway, protesting the authorities.

"Let them gather. I ain't movin' till I see Denton," Michael said, spitting on the ground and glaring at the guard captain who stood on the colony's parapet. The captain shook his head and lifted his binoculars back to his face to keep an eye on the horizon.

———— ✦ ————

Galifern stood on a platform in the central park of Odysseus Colony. With her were George Tanaka, General Martin Raughts, Councilwoman Helen Davies, and the remaining members of the Kamarian Colony Council. Galifern fidgeted and kept her eyes lowered to the floor, avoiding eye contact with the crowd of aliens that stood before her.

The colony was a machine filled with moving parts. Marines gathered into squadrons in the crowd, combatant colonists prepared themselves for a fight, and pilots scrambled through the mob toward the shipyard. The air had the same aura as the final battle with the Undriel in the Sol System.

The wind picked up, the crisp autumnal air pricking goose bumps on anyone nervous about the upcoming fight. Clouds roiled above, threatening a storm.

"Odysseus Colony," Helen Davies announced over a video system broadcasted to the entire human race on Kamaria, "my friends, my family. Today we face our greatest threat."

Michael Castus and his family picked up the broadcast on their soothreaders and paused their protesting as Helen Davies continued.

"Our enemy is unique. She destroyed the auk'nai city of Apusticus last night. Those who survived her onslaught warned us she is heading this way."

Helen gestured to Galifern. "Many of you have never seen an auk'nai in person. Today, I will ask you to think of them as your brothers and sisters."

She put both hands on her podium and continued at a measured pace, "No one here is a stranger to war. Many of you fought bravely against the Undriel in our last days in the Sol System. I wish I didn't have to call upon you this day, but fate has thrust conflict upon us once more."

Maps and battle plans were sent to everyone's soothreaders. Holographic images of Denton's drawings appeared, showing the Siren in detail. Helen looked at the images for a moment, then continued her speech.

"Kamaria is our life raft; there are no more planets for us. Today, we fight for the survival of humanity. We have come far over the past six years, and I refuse to let this threat take away what we have worked so hard to build." Helen thrust her fist into the air. "Today, we show this enemy that *all of Kamaria stands as one!*"

The crowd cheered with violent anticipation.

———◆———

Jess Combs moved through the bustling throngs of people preparing for battle, unsure of where she should go to help. She was a Tvashtar marine, and she always would be—there were no *former* marines— but she had no unit to fall into. Her group would have been one of the scout teams under the leadership of Sergeant Clint Foster, but that had recently gone to Hells.

"Jessica," the friendly voice of Major Pavel Volkov said. "Are you lost, comrade?"

"Not lost, sir," Jess said succinctly; she'd learned to keep her sentences short thanks to the metal brace on her jaw. She saluted the major and continued, "Not found either."

"*Da,*" Pavel said, and looked up toward the sky. "Stick with me, comrade. I need someone I can trust."

"Yes, sir," Jess said with a half-smile, favoring her left cheek. She looked up to see what Pavel was staring at and noticed the delivery from *Telemachus* on high. There was a subdued boom as the remaining ten Argonaut tanks from the Undriel war kicked on their landing thrusters and found open positions in the shipyard.

Jess had fought alongside these war machines in the past and admired the tactical advantages they offered. They had powerful particle cannons that were strong enough to pick off Undriel battlecraft from the ground. The cannon blasts were so mighty that the Argonauts had large robotic legs they could brace themselves with to keep the recoil from flinging them backward. During the war, there had been thousands of these tanks, but the Undriel had since absorbed all but these remaining ten, Major Pavel Volkov's legendary brigade.

"Never been inside one before," Jess said, not moving her eyes from the tank that had landed in front of her and Pavel.

"You'll do great, comrade," Pavel said as he moved toward his old war machine. He slid his hand over the old scars in the metal from the Undriel war. Pavel slapped the side of the tank and smiled at Jess. "Nothing to it, *da?*"

———— ✦ ————

Faye Raike marched through the crowds of people like a stone moving against the current of a river. She was in a daze, unsure of what she had seen in the quarantine lab.

It was Roelin. She could feel him inside her heart like a blast of heat. She felt like they had embraced, even though a barrier had stood between them. Roelin had somehow managed to tell her that he loved her and to say goodbye, words Faye had been yearning for. She stood still as people bumped her and dashed past. The wind picked up and brushed her hair back. A storm was closing in.

The Siren was coming.

The Siren who had taken her husband and demolished his soul. The Siren who had forced her husband to shoot their friends. The Siren who had stabbed John Veston in the chest repeatedly until his lungs filled with blood and his daughter watched him die. The Siren who had held Roelin hostage for five years.

Faye was done playing the lost widow, waiting for her doomed husband's return. Roelin had come back a broken phantom, delivered by the Siren after she had discarded him like trash.

Faye Raike turned with the moving crowd. She found a group of pilots heading toward the shipyard and joined them.

She was ready to fight.

FIFTY-THREE

IT WAS QUIET IN the grand valley.

The creatures of Kamaria could sense the approaching storm and hid in their shelters. In their absence, the sound of the wind rustling the alien trees was uncontested as it whispered across the valley. The sky was a gloomy, flat gray, the clouds threatening to shed their tears. The air held the scent of mud and vegetation, a mixture that on any other autumn afternoon would have been pleasant.

The silence was terminated by the roaring of machines. Humans entered the valley on the northwest side, preparing a blockade to head off the Siren and her twisted army of nezzarforms. In this valley, the surrounding mountain range ensured there was only one way in and one way out. They would use it as a funnel for their trap.

Transport trucks unloaded. Tvashtar marines piled out and made their way into strategic positions in the foothills. Argonaut tanks rolled to the front line, giving them an open view of the battlefield.

High above, the *Rogers* hovered, acting as a command ship. It would remain out of the fight but would provide intelligence and strategic communication organization. On board, George Tanaka,

Helen Davies, and General Martin Raughts oversaw a team of analysts and maps generated by the scout teams who had previously explored the area.

————— ◆ —————

Jess Combs rubbed her jaw brace as she peered at the viewscreen inside the lead Argonaut tank. Pavel brought the tank to a halt, then pulled down on a lever in the ceiling. There was a rumble inside the tank as the robotic legs shifted into position and drilled themselves into the ground. Alexei, a man Jess had never met but would fight monsters alongside this day, was on the third battle station inside the tank. He was busy monitoring the data transmitted from the *Rogers*.

The silence was broken by a steady stream of clicks as Pavel and Alexei operated their stations. Jess was responsible for shifting power levels inside the tank. Every process the tank performed used an immense amount of energy, pushing the recharging particle collider engine to its limit. Jess would need to vent the energy exhaust every time the cannon fired, or else the tank would stall and they would be vulnerable.

In the rear of the staging area was an impromptu shipyard filled with combat-ready ships. Matadors thundered in from the colony, blowing away grass and dirt as they landed. As the ships landed, their pilots disembarked and formed a meeting area.

Lieutenant Commander Rocco Gainax stood in the circle, preparing the battle plan with Lieutenant Eric Murphy. They were the only two pilots in the group who had personally seen Nhymn emerge from the underground palace.

Captain Fergus Reid stood in the circle, flanked by his colonial fighters. These pilots were not trained military but offered their assistance with the fight. In the past, they'd fought the Undriel as a make-shift starfighter squadron when the war got desperate enough to need them. Although their starships weren't as sleek and fine-tuned for battle as the matadors or an Undertaker-class warfighter, they were tough and sturdy, and could hold their own.

A hush came over the pilots as Faye Raike stepped forward from her Matador and removed her helmet. She felt all eyes on her. Faye was there for the briefing, just like the rest of them. But unlike the rest of them, this fight wasn't just about survival—this was personal.

"It's good to have you with us," Rocco said with a sincere smile.

Faye nodded as Rocco proceeded to go over the plan.

———— ◆ ————

"We have visual," General Raughts informed the bridge of the *Rogers*. George Tanaka and Helen Davies looked up from the holographic satellite projection they were studying and gazed out the windscreen. There was a hushed silence as everyone on deck stopped operating their terminals and watched the dark fog spill into the valley between the mountains to the southeast.

"She's here," George whispered.

Tendrils of fog crept unnaturally along the yellow grass, and thousands of purple lights twinkled in the swirling mist. Four massive claws reached out from the fog and crashed into the ground below. The large hands quickly pushed the fog away from the main body of the Siren, revealing her full form. Nhymn looked like a Titan coming down from Mount Olympus.

Nhymn pulled her long arms upward and kept them spread out to her sides. The skirt of her dress was made of a million writhing tentacles, and gnarled fangs protruded from every millimeter of her hard carapace. Her horned skull was propped over her shoulders by a phalanx of spiked tendrils, like vines of rose thorns. Purple lights pulsed from her lowest extremities all the way up the sides of her enormous body and into her eye sockets like an upward-flowing waterfall of energy. The lights terminated inside her abyssal eye sockets and glared out at the small line of colonist defenses.

"Humans," whispered the impossible monster into every colonist's mind. *"You have put us all in danger."*

Nezzarforms spilled into the valley ahead of her in a never-ending wave of stone monsters.

"You should have perished in the fire that fate designed for you. The monsters you created have not ceased their pursuit, and by coming to this planet, you have doomed us."

Jess and Pavel looked at each other. The major's brow furrowed and he nodded to Jess, then to Alexei. They prepared to fight this enemy the same way they'd fought impossible enemies in the past.

"I must protect my planet and my creatures within it," Nhymn said, curling one of her claws into a fist. *"All invaders will be exterminated. I have decided this, and this decision cannot be undone."*

"Launch air support," General Raughts said into the tactical comm. The pilots scrambled into their ships. Engines boomed to life, and fighters took off into the sky, forming two squadrons.

Helen Davies leaned over a map of the battlefield. She looked to George. "Is there any chance we can negotiate with her?"

George hesitated for a moment before saying, "Galifern told us they were given an ultimatum at Apusticus, and when they refused, she destroyed the whole city. We weren't even given the ultimatum. Nhymn's not going to leave until we're all dead."

Helen leaned forward and watched as more nezzarforms piled into the valley ahead of Nhymn. She looked over to General Raughts and nodded. He turned toward the battle map and said, "Begin the assault."

FIFTY-FOUR

"Commence the attack," Lieutenant Commander Rocco Gainax shouted as he throttled forward in his Matador fighter. His squadron burst into action behind him, sending Faye Raike into her first sortie in years.

Faye felt the familiar thrill of adrenaline she would get back when she fought alongside Roelin on the *Astraeus*. The blood in her veins pumped so aggressively, she felt a tingle in her neck, shoulders, and biceps. She looked to her wingmen: some Matador fighters, others combat-capable colonist ships. Their numbers were limited, but they had air superiority, and that was enough for now.

"Send a full barrage into the Siren," General Raughts said over the tactical comm.

The air force unleashed its full arsenal all at once. Particle machine guns whirred, and ordinances of hadron missiles launched toward the Siren. The sky was filled with rockets and Hellsfire.

Nhymn pulled all four of her arms toward her chest, and nezzarforms reconfigured themselves to make a giant barrier of electrical energy. The weapon barrage smashed into the electrical wall, allowing only a handful of artillery to pass through it and strike Nhymn directly.

The Siren did not flinch.

Nhymn lowered her electrical barrier when the smoke cleared. Faye squinted and saw blood trickling from wounds that appeared on the monster's arms.

"It bleeds," Faye said.

"It's a start," Rocco said.

Nhymn thrust one of her claws forward, and the nezzarforms began to glow with white-hot energy.

"Evasive maneuvers!" Rocco shouted.

Lightning erupted from the nezzarforms and ripped into the air near the Matadors. Faye pitched herself away from a bolt and looked to her port side to see one of her wingmen take a blast across the hull. The injured Matador rolled down into the valley below, exploding on impact and creating a small clearing in the vast stone army's ranks.

"We need ground support!" Rocco shouted.

"Affirmative," Major Pavel Volkov answered the call from inside his lead Argonaut tank on the front line of the ground defenses. He turned to Jess and said, "Are you ready, comrade?"

Jess nodded. The Argonaut tanks charged their particle cannons.

"Fire!" Pavel shouted. The series of explosions that erupted from the line of tanks shook the ground. The blasts were so powerful, they kicked up enough dirt and grass to push each tank half a meter backward, tearing the drilled-in arms through the ground. The barrage ripped through the nezzarform army, destroying most on contact and dragging others into explosions like a bowling ball in a domino factory.

Jess's terminal lit up red. She flipped open a panel and punched the large button on the nearby wall of the tank, venting the heat sink until the terminal faded back to its solid blue color. Once vented, she pulled down on a lever, readying the cannon to fire once more.

"Ready!" Jess called to Pavel as she finished and slapped the panel shut once more.

"Good," Pavel said, flicking a few toggles on the ceiling of his station within the tank. His HUD readout informed him when the rest of his tank brigade was ready to fire again, and when each light flicked green, he shouted, "Fire!"

From various positions in the foothills, the Tvashtar marines began their unified assault. Particle rifles and rocket launchers flashed through the valley toward the nezzarforms, blowing them to pieces and spraying chunks of Kamarian landscape into the air.

Nhymn swung her giant arm toward the Matador squadron that approached her.

"Evade!" Faye shouted as the colossal claw rushed toward them.

Two fighters were caught by the claw and exploded on impact. Faye rolled her Matador fighter away in time but then found a second claw rushing toward her from the starboard side.

"Dive, dive!" Faye called out, rolling her Matador under the second swinging claw, feeling her ship sway from the rush of the near hit.

"Get some distance," Rocco ordered his squadron, pivoting his matador and leading his pilots away from the Siren's physical reach.

The squadron split into two groups as the nezzarforms released another barrage. Faye's windscreen was filled with an array of lightning bolts springing from the ground and enormous tentacles swinging through the air. To her right, two of her wingmen were taken down by bolts, and to her left, three wingmen exploded upon impact against the tentacles. Faye rolled and pitched upward in time to avoid another nezzarform attack and gained entry to the calmer portion of the battlefield. She leveled out and caught her breath, taking inventory of who else had made it back.

"Hells," Faye whispered through heavy breaths. She counted only twelve ships.

Rocco shouted, "Give her everything you got!" The twelve ships turned back toward the Siren and unleashed the remainder of their arsenal.

The Siren roared as the explosions clouded the air around her, smashing into her bony carapace. When the smoke cleared, they could see that the Siren had taken the damage directly.

"That's for *John*," Faye whispered. She felt as if every missile launched was a message from the ghosts of those the Siren had destroyed.

On the command bridge of the *Rogers*, General Raughts, George Tanaka, and Helen Davies watched the holographic representation of the battlefield below.

"Our air force just fired the remainder of their ordinance, and we still haven't done enough to stop her advancing," General Raughts said.

"We have hurt her, though, so the attacks are doing *something*. It's just not significant enough," George said.

"Should we resort to plan B?" Helen asked. George and General Raughts turned to each other and then back to Helen.

"It will destroy the valley," George said, then he sighed and added, "but the Siren will destroy much more if we allow her to remain."

"I'll call Admiral Marin," Helen said.

"You might want to tell your men to back up," George suggested. The general nodded and proceeded to give his orders to the soldiers on the ground.

———◆———

Admiral Hugo Marin and his skeleton crew of engineers gathered in the bridge of the *Telemachus*. A display was showing various parts of the battle happening far below them on Kamaria's surface. Helen's face hovered on a separate screen near the battle images.

"What can we do, Helen?" Hugo asked. "Name it, and we'll make it happen."

"Can you accurately fire the LPC at a target planetside?" she asked. "Our air force is taking a massive hit. We cannot lose this fight."

Hugo turned to Second Officer Nakamura and asked, "Can we do that?"

Nakamura bobbed his head from side to side as he considered the question, then said, "Homer can help with the mathematics of it, but yes, we can pull it off. It'll take an hour to charge up the LPC and fire it."

"The human cargo still aboard this vessel may be at risk during LPC use. We have not fired the LPC since the final escape from the Undriel, and damage sustained during the battle has weakened the hull," Homer said.

"What are our options?" Hugo asked.

"We can safely separate the stasis bedchamber from the bulk of the ship and recollect it after LPC use," Homer stated.

"Do it," Hugo said, and turned back to Helen. "Clear your men away from the target. You have a half hour."

Nakamura frowned but nodded. They were going to push the *Telemachus*'s large particle cannon to its limit. Hugo and Nakamura both knew it could result in a catastrophic failure in the *Telemachus*'s systems, but the stakes were too high not to risk it.

"Affirmative, Admiral. We'll alert them," Helen said, and her image winked off. The technicians began their work.

The stasis bedchamber filled with the remaining population of humanity unlatched from the underside of the *Telemachus* and drifted in orbit at a safe distance.

Hugo Marin ran the worst-case scenario in his head. If the *Telemachus* suffered a fatal failure when firing the LPC, the interstellar ship would explode. If the human forces below failed to repel the Siren, she would annihilate everyone on the ground. The floating stasis bedchamber would become a drifting tomb in orbit, and the dreamers inside would be trapped in a state of non-death until each of their beds winked out.

The LPC had to work.

———◆———

Pavel flipped a few switches and pushed upward on the lever that controlled the legs of his Argonaut tank. Through Jess's digital viewscreen at her station in the tank, she could see the other tanks begin to retract their legs and move backward.

"We're retreating?" Jess asked. "I thought we were winning?"

"We are about to," Pavel said with a smirk.

There was a violent explosion outside as a Matador fighter hit the ground near their tank. When the dust settled, Jess could see nezzarforms approaching through the smoke of the crash.

"*Cyka blyat!*" Pavel shouted in ancient Russian. "Is the cannon ready?"

"Yes," Jess confirmed. Pavel fired the cannon into the approaching stone soldiers. The particle beam slapped into the nezzarforms and sent pieces of them flying into the air. Without the legs to brace the tank, the recoil from the shot pushed the Argonaut tank backward at high speed. Jess was pushed against her seatbelt as the tank jolted from the force of the blast.

When she regained her posture, Jess vented the cannon. More nezzarforms began to fill the space the gun had cleared. Pavel slammed his foot on the pedal, and the tank started to rush backward. Jess shifted power to engines, giving them more maneuverability but less firepower.

The dark clouds above parted and a beam of energy lanced through the sky. The *Telemachus* LPC fired from orbit, and the light remained a blinding glow.

On the ground, it felt like the mountains would crumble apart. Jess held on to her seat with both hands and ground her teeth together, ignoring the pain her jaw brace caused her. She turned toward Pavel, who didn't let the chaos distract him from driving the Argonaut tank away from the impact zone.

Outside, nothing remained upright. Tvashtar marines, nezzarforms, and trees toppled to the ground. Lava sprang up from the fractured world near the impact zone. Kamaria's new wound glowed red hot as lava swirled under the Siren.

The light finally faded away. Pavel slowed the tank to a halt, but Jess's bones still pretended the world was shaking. She unbuckled her seatbelt and went to Pavel's side to look through his viewscreen.

"Did it work?" Jess asked.

"*Nyet,*" Pavel whispered.

The Siren stood over a newly created pit of lava. Nhymn had

been partially struck by the *Telemachus* LPC's beam, and the two right arms had disintegrated. This did not seem to faze her. She simply removed her secondary arm on her left side and held it near her right shoulder socket, allowing the tentacles there to grab it and adhere it in place. Nhymn flexed her new right hand like a fighter who'd just punched a brick wall. She was down to two arms, which was hardly a handicap.

"Target is still active," Pavel said into the comm.

———◆———

"Target still active," Helen Davies's voice repeated. It was the first thing the skeleton crew of the *Telemachus* heard as systems rebooted. "I repeat, the Siren is still alive!"

"She dodged it?" Hugo asked. He turned to Nakamura, who didn't know what to say. Hugo moved toward his XO. "How long until we can fire the LPC again?"

Homer chimed in with his relentlessly pleasant synthetic voice: "Multiple system failures. The LPC is unable to charge again at this time."

"No more LPC," Nakamura stated.

Hugo slammed his hand on the console in front of him. He sighed, trying to think of a solution. "We need a plan! Our people are dying down there!"

———◆———

"We don't give up," Jess said. "We keep the pressure on."

"Something's happening." Pavel leaned forward, squinting at the Siren.

The violet lights that pulsed up Nhymn's body rushed toward her head at once, then there was silence.

Nhymn's arms crashed into the ground with a mighty explosion of purple light that rushed over the debris of crashed ships, pieces of fallen nezzarforms, bodies of dead marines, and the surviving warriors still fighting on the ground. The light made a loud bass tone that vibrated teeth and bone.

Jess and Pavel watched the light rush toward them through the digital viewscreens. The marines in front of the tank ducked behind boulders to avoid being enveloped by the light.

"Hells," Jess spat out as the light passed through her. For a moment, she thought she might have been cut in half, but when Jess looked down, she found herself unharmed. The marines seemed confused by what had just happened.

Rocks and boulders shuddered and moved on their own, rolling into terrifying shapes and igniting with purple electrical energy. Jess watched in horror as every nezzarform that had once been destroyed rebuilt itself. Nhymn had resurrected her entire army.

The ground forces found themselves surrounded.

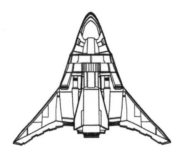

FIFTY-FIVE

"NHYMN IS GOING TO win this fight," Denton said, and ran his fingers through his hair as he tapped his foot relentlessly against the floor in a hurried pattern. He turned to Eliana and said, "There has to be something we can do."

They listened to the battle through Denton's wave transmitter, giving them exclusive access to the top command channels as they sat in the quarantine bay. For a minute, Denton thought that the Siren would be defeated when the *Telemachus*'s LPC went off, but that hope faded when General Raughts declared the target "still active."

"I'm not sure there is anything we can do," Eliana said, her voice slightly muffled by the atmospheric suit she wore to prevent contamination. She checked Roelin's life signs and sighed. Roelin lay facedown on the stretcher and had not stirred since Denton watched him speak to Faye.

"If Karx was still here, maybe he could come up with an idea," Denton said.

"The Siren that possessed you?" Eliana asked.

"I don't think he possessed me—well, not like how Nhymn possessed Roelin, at least. Karx said he needed my help." Denton listened to the sounds of combat, knowing more colony members were dying in the battle. Denton sighed with frustration. "What could I have helped him with, though?"

"I have a theory," said a voice that wasn't Eliana's or Denton's.

Denton and Eliana starred at each other with wide eyes before looking over at a perfectly healthy Roelin Raike standing near the glass wall. He appeared as the Roelin that Eliana had grown up knowing.

"You …" Eliana said as her eyes welled up with tears. She rose to her feet.

"Elly." The healthy Roelin looked at her sternly. "I'm so sorry—" Eliana rushed to him and embraced him. Denton was surprised she didn't pass right through Roelin.

"I don't care how it's possible," Eliana said, crying into her helmet. "I missed you."

"I missed you too," Roelin said, and returned her hug gently.

"It wasn't you …" She huffed, desperately wishing she could rub the tears away from her eyes through her helmet's visor. "It wasn't you. We know that now."

"Roelin, I …" Denton said, unsure of what to do.

"I think I have an idea of what we can do to help. But we're all going to need to work together," Roelin said. There was no time for reminiscing.

Denton scratched his head and asked, "What's your plan?"

"Nhymn changed me," Roelin said, and walked past Denton. He touched his own unconscious body. "I started feeling it a little while back. Her presence inside of me changed what I am on a biological level." He stopped for a moment, trying to find the right words. "I'm not sure I'm *human* anymore."

"She made you into a Siren?" Eliana asked.

"I don't think I'm that either." Roelin turned toward Eliana and Denton. "I'm something *new*."

"Is this going to happen to Denton?" Eliana asked, gripping Denton's hand with her glove.

"I don't know," Roelin said. "Maybe."

"We'll deal with that if it happens," Denton said. "Right now, what can we do to help with the battle?"

Roelin nodded and continued, "When Nhymn was within me, there were times I was able to hold her in place. I could paralyze her. It took me a long time to develop that skill, but Nhymn worked my mind like a muscle, and eventually, that muscle became stronger and stronger."

"But how does that help now?" Denton asked.

"I think I understand what you're suggesting." Eliana smiled. "Nhymn dodged the LPC because she's faster than anything we can throw at her. But if Roelin can hold her still, we can hit her with everything we got."

"It's our only play," Roelin said.

Denton nodded as he began to understand. "So you think you can stall her?"

"I'm not sure if I can do it alone—her powers have changed."

"Speaking of powers, why doesn't she just control *all* of us?" Denton asked. "I've seen her take control of an entire auk'nai city in the visions."

"I've never seen her do anything like that in my time with her. She has power, but it's pretty limited," Roelin explained. "When she was with me, she needed to bring in Dol'Gohm the dray'va to act as a sort of signal booster. He was a tether of power for her, stronger when he was close by, but weaker if he strayed too far away. But the beast was simple, easily charmed by her seduction."

"Between you two," Eliana said, pointing at Denton and Roelin, "you know her past and present. Denton, you witnessed her in her most raw form, before her first death. I bet that was when she was the most powerful."

"Yeah," Denton said. "Maybe after Karx killed her the first time, she never regained that level of control again."

"So even with Sympha's body, she can control the nezzarforms but not us. Her power is spread too thin," Roelin said.

"That explains why she asked the auk'nai of Apusticus for help in the battle instead of just controlling them. Nhymn's at her limit and afraid she can lose," Eliana said.

"Exactly. So we are safe from mental manipulations." Roelin smiled. "But *Nhymn* isn't safe from *me*."

Denton nodded, then shook his head. "But wait. You still don't think you can stall her by yourself?"

Roelin continued, "My plan involves your visions with Karx. I think I understand what they were. I was listening when you explained them to people here, and I noticed something similar when Nhymn inhabited me." Roelin tapped his head. "Every night, I had nightmares. I assumed it was Nhymn rummaging through my mind and discovering my secrets until I heard your story."

"Nightmares, like my visions?" Denton asked.

"Not visions, not nightmares. When a Siren inhabits our bodies, our unconscious minds become a tunnel between them and us. I don't think Nhymn was in my mind while I slept, I think *I* was in *hers*."

"Like a doorway," Eliana said.

"Exactly. Every night I slept, Nhymn would chase me. She didn't want me there," Roelin said. "There has to be a reason. Something Nhymn didn't want me to see."

"So, when I had my visions," Denton said, "I was tunneling into Karx's mind. But I was able to see things that he wasn't around for. How does that work?"

"Each Siren had a unique power. Sympha creates, Nhymn controls. Karx wasn't exactly a Siren, but maybe he could move through time like a shade, the way you did."

Denton tried to piece it together. "Karx could witness events tied to Sympha because he was tied to her the same way I was tied to him." Denton crossed his arms as he tried to keep track of who was tied to whom. "Yeah, that might be it. Man, Sirens don't make things simple. Hells, since I might still be tied to him, Karx could be moving through my own timeline right now for all I know. Maybe he's dug up something we could use."

The wave transmitter buzzed with action. The Argonaut tanks were taking the full brunt of the attack now. Shouts were cut short by explosions, and orders were being rattled out.

"We're running out of time. Denton, did you say Karx was still inside your mind?" Roelin asked.

"I think so. I mean, he was. I'm not so sure now, I haven't felt him since Nhymn bolted me in the underground palace," Denton said, looking at Eliana.

"I think there's a way I can find out. But I'll have to search your mind. Will you let me?" Roelin asked. He reached a hand forward, palm facing upward. "With Karx's help, we can both stop Nhymn long enough for the military to do something."

"Denton, wait," Eliana said. "What if—"

The wave transmitter answered her. Blood was being spilled, and friends were dying.

"We don't have any other options," Denton said. "I'm willing to risk it."

Denton looked at Roelin's phantom hand, wincing at the thought of this being some sort of trick played by Nhymn.

Denton grabbed Roelin's hand and said, "Alright. Go find Karx."

"Fall back!" General Raughts's voice crackled on the tactical comm through the chaos of the battle inside Pavel Volkov's Argonaut tank. The nezzarforms were closing in, blasting away with their lightning bolts and smashing through marines that ended up within arm's reach of the stone constructs.

"We need to cover the men," Pavel said.

"Cannon's ready!" Jess shouted.

"Two o'clock! Large grouping!" Alexei said.

Pavel slammed the trigger and released another particle blast into the approaching nezzarform army, striking the center of the group and flinging every nezzarform in a radial pattern outward. Jess vented the cannon and pulled the lever to allow another shot. They had become an efficient unit inside the Argonaut tank, but the enemy was overwhelming.

Across the battlefield, Nhymn pushed her hands down into the ground and pulled four gigantic, centaur-shaped nezzarforms from the dirt. They had legs like those of a massive horse and long-bladed arms. Nhymn thrust one of her great, taloned hands forward, pushing the sentries toward the tanks like a cavalry line. Another barrage was dodged by the faster-moving centaurs.

"Incoming!" Major Pavel Volkov shouted.

Jess saw her life flash before her eyes as a colossal centaur crashed into their tank, toppling the heavy vehicle end over end. The seatbelt dug into her skin as the force of the roll tried to pry her from her chair.

The tank landed upside down. Machinery popped, and alarms blared in Jess's ears. She turned to see Alexei shouting in pain. His arm was broken apart, a bone thrusting through the sleeve of his shirt.

Jess jolted in her seat when Pavel approached and unbuckled her restraints. Blood was trickling from his hairline, and he had a few bloody scrapes on his face and neck. He helped Jess orient herself and checked her over.

"We need to get out of here," Pavel said, then turned toward Alexei. Jess looked toward the cupola hatch and knew that it was pinned to the ground. They would have to use the escape hatch on the underside of the tank.

Light burst into their tank as the entire front half of the Argonaut tank was sliced away by the centaur's bladed arm, cutting Alexei in half as it passed through.

"*Blyat!*" Pavel shouted in ancient Russian. Jess scrambled for her sidearm and peered through the newly formed opening. The centaur pulled its bladed arm back for another deadly slice. Jess shot upward into the centaur's face, but the stone monster seemed unaffected.

The centaur swung its arm toward Jess and Pavel. An immense explosion removed the giant blade from the centaur's body, and the severed sword arm continued with its momentum and smashed into the tank, missing Jess and Pavel both by millimeters.

"*Zaebis!*" Pavel shouted with the nervous adrenaline that comes with cheating death twice within five minutes. Jess looked up at the centaur, whose attention was diverted to the sky above it. She expected to see a Matador roar past, but what she saw instead brought a tear to her eye.

A wingless auk'nai warrior wielding a unique daunoren staff was dropped off by his winged companion in front of the centaur. Jess recognized the staff as Mag'Ro's, but its wielder was not him. It was young Talulo. The young auk'nai cawed out a loud battle cry and slammed the daunoren staff down into the dirt. In the sky above, flying auk'nai used peck rifles to turn the tide of the battle, blasting away at nezzarforms and thinning the onslaught.

Talulo twirled Mag'Ro's daunoren staff in front of the one-armed centaur. The hum of multiple collider cylinders coming from the staff was followed by an immense burst of energy that crashed into the centaur's core. The stone monster was hurled backward into the crowd of nezzarforms, where it caused a wave of explosions.

"Thank you, comrade!" Pavel shouted with a smile. Talulo whistled and helped Jess and Pavel out of the wreckage, lifting them with little effort.

"Thank you," Jess said.

"The song of Apusticus still sings. We are here to help," Talulo said as he stepped backward and whistled loudly. Nock'Lu swooped low and snatched him up, carrying him across the battlefield to other areas that needed aid.

"Jessica!" Pavel shouted, and tossed her a particle rifle. "Get ready."

Jess turned toward the Siren and watched the purple lights surge toward Nhymn's head once more. The cheering from the recent auk'nai appearance ceased. Nhymn slammed her hands into the ground, and the low bass tone and purple light started to bring her army back to life for another round.

The rocks near Jess's feet sputtered and rolled. The nezzarforms were coming back to life, and the colonists couldn't stop it. It seemed that no matter what they did, Nhymn would just bring her soldiers back from the dead.

The giant centaur reformed in front of Jess and Pavel. She thought of throwing her rifle to the ground and letting the monster destroy her. This fight was hopeless, and that seemed like the only appropriate response.

Then Jess thought of Emily. Emily would not have just stood by and let annihilation come to her, she would have met it head-on. By submitting to this abomination, she would make Emily's sacrifice count for nothing.

"We have to keep fighting," Jess said to Pavel.

"I like your spirit, comrade," Pavel said, and activated his particle rifle.

The centaur raced toward them.

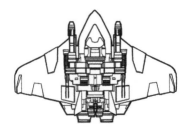

FIFTY-SIX

DENTON STOOD IN THE quarantine bay with his eyes vibrating as Roelin searched his mind for Karx. Eliana listened to the battle on her soothreader. She grew cold when the reports started coming in of Nhymn resurrecting her army of nezzarforms a second time. There was no way the colonists could win this fight, even with the help of the auk'nai warriors.

Roelin's plan needed to work.

Denton heaved and fell backward onto the floor. Eliana rushed to his side and held his head. "What happened, are you alright?"

Roelin's phantom appeared in the room again, and he knelt in front of Denton and Eliana. Denton calmed his breathing down and finally asked, "Did you find him? Is Karx going to help us?"

Roelin stood up before saying anything, then turned his back to the two and announced, "I found Karx. But he's dead. Whatever Nhymn did to him was absolute."

"Well, *crap,*" Denton said, and shuddered at the thought of a dead alien's corpse rolling around in his mind.

"If she can kill Karx …" Eliana began.

"Then she can kill me too," Roelin finished. "She was always able to hurt me before, but she never destroyed me like Karx."

"So, what now?" Eliana asked as she helped Denton to his feet. Everyone thought of their options.

The battle on the soothreader raged onward. People were dying. Orders to fall back were being given. Each time the humans and auk'nai moved backward, Nhymn moved closer to Odysseus Colony. With her new powers, she could annihilate the last foothold humanity had in the universe.

With her new power. *Sympha's* power. It wasn't Nhymn's, just as Roelin's body wasn't hers either. Eliana's face lit up. "Sympha!" she shouted.

"What about her?" Denton asked, still rubbing his skull.

"Roelin, you can stop Nhymn from the inside if you have help. You thought Karx could do it, but he's dead. But we still have one more Siren we can rely on," Eliana said.

"Sympha," Roelin said to himself. "You're right. She should still be inside her body with Nhymn."

"What if she's not?" Denton asked. "She killed Karx. Why wouldn't she kill Sympha too?"

"Sympha is her host. No parasite willingly tries to kill their host," Roelin said. "We need to get my body to Nhymn." The three looked at each other, then turned their attention to Roelin's body on the stretcher.

"Can't you just *float there*?" Denton asked.

"Nhymn couldn't leave my body during our imprisonment, and I can't leave mine either. Even being across the room from it feels like I'm falling apart. I'd be strongest if we can get my body to Nhymn," Roelin said, looking at his phantom hands.

"Then so be it. Let's do it," Eliana said.

"We're going to need a ship," Denton said. "We can check my family's machine shop. There might be something we can use there."

"Alright, we'll head there and make it up as we go along," Eliana said. Roelin nodded then faded away. Denton grabbed Roelin's stretcher while Eliana opened the quarantine bay door. They'd just made it into the observation room when the exterior door light turned green with a beep.

The exterior door slid open, and the colonial guardsman stepped into the observation room. He fumbled with his gear in shock when he saw Eliana and Denton with Roelin's body on the stretcher.

Eliana pulled a handgun on the guardsman and shouted, "Just let us pass!"

The guard attempted to lift his soothreader to his chin to send out an alert, and Eliana pulled the trigger. An electrical arc launched from her pistol and washed over the guardsman. He shook violently as he was stunned, then dropped to the floor, unconscious.

"Woah!" Denton said as he pulled Roelin's stretcher through the doors.

"It's on stun," Eliana said, planting the pistol back in her hip holster. "We don't have time to screw around. He'll be alright…" She looked at the unconscious guard. Eliana had never hurt another human before. "Provided he doesn't have a heart condition or a blood clot or—"

"He'll be fine, let's move!" Denton shouted, and pushed Roelin's stretcher through the doorway. Denton felt the cool air on his skin for the first time in a month, and he inhaled deeply as he shoved the stretcher across the grass to the ground sail station. Eliana shed her atmospheric suit as they walked out, discarding the pieces on the ground like a trail of bread crumbs.

Another guardsman stood near the ground sails with his back to them. Without stopping their movement, Denton passed Roelin's stretcher to Eliana as they moved across the lawn.

Denton bent down as he was running and grabbed a stone, then lobbed the rock over the guardsman's head, pinging it off a nearby barrier wall. It didn't work—the guardsman saw the stone come from over his head, and knew the source was behind him. The guardsman turned around.

It was Mitchell Harlan, Denton's former scout enlistment competition turned colony guard. Mitch was aware Denton should be in quarantine; in fact, he'd been happy when he heard the news. *Maybe the moonie will die there*, Mitch had thought, *and they'll look to me as a replacement on scout patrol.*

Mitch almost had enough time to shout, *Stop!* But he was cut short when Denton jabbed him hard in the nose. Mitch's brain slapped the interior of his skull, and he fell to the ground like a gym bag full of rocks.

"Oh, that's *not good*," Eliana shouted. "It's dangerous to be unconscious like that!"

"He'll be fine!" Denton said as he looked around. They were supposed to stay unnoticed. They didn't have time to make sure *Mitch-friggin-Harlan* survived being sucker-punched in the nose.

"How many times are we going to say that?" Eliana said. She shoved Roelin's stretcher toward Denton and quickly worked on getting Mitch in the recovery position—face up, left arm tucked, right arm over his chest, ankles crossed—then rolled him onto his side, all in the time it took Denton to start the ground sail and secure Roelin's stretcher. When Eliana was finished, Mitch looked like he'd decided to take a nice nap in the grass.

Eliana boarded the ground sail and said, "There, *now* he will be fine."

"That's a shame," Denton said. He turned the ground sail around and pointed it toward the colony gateway, then pushed the thruster to its limit. The ground sail rocketed across the grass.

As they rushed over the grassy field, Eliana realized a problem. The gateway was opening and another ground sail was emerging from it.

"Wait, don't go to the gateway!" Eliana shouted over the sound of the wind and the thruster. "The guardsmen will see us and detain us!"

Denton looked to the horizon and noticed the ground sail coming their way. Had someone else seen them and alerted the guardsmen? *Damn it, Mitch!*

Thinking quickly, Denton veered to the right, cutting behind a small hilly area in the valley between the scout pavilion and the gateway.

"The Glimmer Glade! We can hop the wall and get to your

family's shop!" Eliana said.

Denton hadn't even been thinking of the Glimmer Glade, but it was a good plan. He could see the back of his family's machine shop over the lip of the outer wall. They could find a way to scale the wall and drop down into the secret place, then make it to the machine shop undetected.

Here goes nothin', Denton thought to himself as he pushed the ground sail forward.

On the other ground sail in the meadow between the colony and the scout pavilion, Michael, Brynn, Jason, and Tyler sat next to a very annoyed guard captain. Michael noticed another ground sail coming from the pavilion area and swerving off to the left, but he didn't think anything of it. He was focused on this victory he had earned over his archnemesis, the guard captain, and his quarantine protocols.

The captain parked the sail at the pavilion corral, then waved his hand toward the quarantine lab. "He'll be in there. You have five minutes!"

"About time!" Michael said, clapping the captain hard on the shoulder. "Be out in *twenty* minutes." The captain sighed with frustration at Michael's relentlessly obnoxious behavior. As the family made their way to the quarantine lab, they overheard the guard captain shout, "Damn it, *Mitch*. Get up, you lazy son of a—"

The family walked past Eliana's scattered atmospheric suit pieces in the yard. Tyler scoffed and said, "Slobs. I thought they'd be tidier than this."

They noticed the door to the lab was wide open.

"See, if they really gave a crap, they'd shut these doors," Jason said.

"Maybe it lets the bad germs out?" Tyler said. "They're supposed to be smart, right?"

The family entered the quarantine bay room to find a guardsman sitting on the floor, looking as if he had just woken up from a night of heavy drinking. The clean-looking room on the other side of the glass was empty, and all at once, they put it together.

"Well, look at that," Michael said with a chuckle. "Looks like Dent busted himself out."

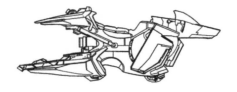

FIFTY-SEVEN

DENTON DROPPED DOWN INTO the Glimmer Glade from the colony's outer wall. Eliana and Roelin floated down harmlessly, using the hovering stretcher as a parachute. Once the stretcher bed discovered the ground, it held its place a meter above it and pushed away fallen leaves. They ran through the glade toward the hill that sloped up to the Castus Machine Shop.

"Almost there, Roe," Eliana said, pushing the stretcher up the hill.

There was no hole cut in the fence, forcing Denton to improvise. He grabbed Eliana's gun from her belt and blasted the fence rod that held segments of the barrier together, knocking down an entire section. Denton handed the weapon back to Eliana.

They moved through the alley until they made it to the street in front of the shop.

"Let me make sure it's clear. The guardsmen won't bother to stop me," Eliana whispered. "At least, I don't *think* they will."

Eliana slunk around the corner and scanned the street. Down the road, guardsmen were frantically preparing to join the fight. Their distraction was more than enough to conceal them. Eliana waved Denton forward, then tugged on Roelin's stretcher.

"Come on, let's get inside and see what we have to work with," Denton said, using his access numbers to enter the shop. The door opened with a loud clunk, and they moved forward. Denton flipped on the lights in the garage and watched the bully bloke creature that had tormented his father for months cluck and fly away.

"Was that a—" Eliana asked, pulling Roelin into the light.

"Don't worry about it," Denton said, scanning the room. He was surprised to see the *Lelantos* sitting in the garage. Denton moved toward it, then realized, "Wait, if the *Lelantos* is here, then..."

Behind them, there was another clang, then they heard Michael's voice say, "Brynn, get the blunder-blaster! We got looters!"

"Crap!" Denton whispered. He knew if he told his family what he was up to, they would insist on joining him, but Denton didn't want his family involved in this dangerous task. He waved Eliana forward, pointing her up the ramp of the *Lelantos*. Eliana pushed Roelin's stretcher behind a racing rushcycle in the *Lelantos* cargo bay.

Denton put a finger up to his lips and whispered, "Keep quiet, I'm going to prepare for launch."

Brynn handed Michael the blunder-blaster, and he pumped a mechanism on the front of the weapon and began to move through the garage with Tyler and Jason.

"Come out now! We'll still shoot you, but it's faster for everyone this way!" Michael shouted into the garage.

Denton sat in the pilot's seat of his family's ship and began to prep the *Lelantos* for launch, checking the internal systems first before activating anything external. He was glad to see they had reloaded the magnetic repeater turret's ammo; that would come in handy as they moved toward the battle.

Jason shined a flashlight into the cargo ramp of the *Lelantos*. Eliana held her breath. Jason's light illuminated their racing rushcycle, and he sighed. "Thank God." He turned toward Tyler and shouted, "Geraldine is safe!"

"We aren't calling her that!" Tyler shouted back. "It's Claire— she's a classy dame but a badass under the hood!"

"Geraldine has *history*!" Jason argued back, moving away from the ramp.

"Like how a fug'in *mummy* has history!" Tyler made air quotes with his fingers. "And I don't want to kiss a fug'in mummy! *Claire*, though, I'd take her out to a nice dinner, maybe even let her meet Mom and Dad." Tyler pushed a box aside and then screamed like a child.

"What is it?" Michael asked.

Four juvenile bully blokes leaped from their box nest onto Tyler's face. He screamed again and accidentally let a shot loose from his pistol. The shot rang out as it ricocheted around the garage.

"Jumpin' jaspers!" Michael shouted. "Keep your booger hook off the shoot switch! You're gonna get us all *killed*!"

Denton heard the commotion and lit the engines, hoping the others were too busy to notice in time. He shoved in the button that opened the garage door, allowing the wind to rush into the garage.

"What in the Hells!" Michael said after the first wave of wind passed over him, knocking items off of workbenches. The access ramp for the *Lelantos* began to rise, and Michael saw a shadowed figure inside.

"Oh, *Hells no*!" Jason shouted. "Geraldine is in there!"

Tyler pulled another baby bully bloke off his scratched-up face and shouted, "Claire!" The brothers ran toward the *Lelantos* as the landing gear retracted. They almost made it to the ramp but were thrown backward when the thrusters engaged. The *Lelantos* launched out of the garage and into the sky, flying toward the battle.

The three Castus men pushed loose debris off their bodies and watched their ship sail off into the sky, not knowing that Denton, Eliana, and Roelin were on board trying to save humanity from annihilation.

FIFTY-EIGHT

"ON YOUR FEET, COMRADE!" Pavel helped a marine up, then they ran across open ground toward a rocky outcropping in the foothills. The order had come from General Raughts to put as much distance between the front line and the Siren as possible, forming a final defensive line on the northwest opening of the valley.

Jess Combs strafed backward while shooting toward the row of nezzarforms that pursued the unit of marines they had joined up with. She stumbled to the side, avoiding a blast from a nezzarform's head, then raised her rifle once more to continue firing.

The giant stone centaur pursued them across the battlefield and sliced through marines like a hot knife in butter. In Jess's earpiece, she heard the voice of Faye Raike from above. "Get some cover, we'll make a pass to give you more time!"

Jess didn't stop running as she looked up to see auk'nai and the remaining colonial air force vessels rush by. Two Matadors turned and began to head back around to make a strike. Jess knew they didn't have much time—she grabbed Pavel's shoulder and shouted to the marines, "Get to cover!"

She pushed Pavel behind a ledge in the foothills. The marines joined them, ducking behind anything solid. There was a loud roar of Matador engines and explosions of particle machine gun fire hitting nezzarforms. The ground shook as the aerial strafe sliced through the stone army behind them.

Jess peered out from their position and saw the remaining rocky debris hitting the floor, leaving behind smoke and impact craters. She smiled.

"Let's move!" Pavel shouted. The marines began to fall back again. Jess ran with them, then noticed Pavel was not near her. She turned to see a heavily damaged giant centaur looming over their previous position like a horrible scorpion eyeing its prey. Smoke spilled from injuries it had sustained from the air force strafe.

"Pavel!" Jess shouted, and tried to run toward him.

"*Nyet!* Run, Jessica!" Pavel shouted back and began shooting the centaur. It turned its attention on him. Jess knew she should listen, she should run, but that little voice in her head told her to stay and fight.

Jess dashed toward a nearby rock ledge to get to higher ground. The centaur pursued Pavel through the rocky outcropping with ease, slicing at him but banging its sword-like arm against boulders nearby.

The centaur began to charge a bolt in its face, and Jess took advantage of the moment. She shot a volley of particle blasts into the gathering light, causing it to sparkle with instability and then dissipate.

"Get your ass over here!" Jess shouted to the old major. Pavel looked up and smiled, then scrambled from his claustrophobic position. The centaur gave up its pursuit of Pavel and rushed toward Jess.

The stone monster leaped into the air toward her position and smashed into the ledge below. The impact forced Jess backward, causing her to roll over her shoulder. The loud screech of Matador engines filled the sky.

"Another pass incoming," Faye Raike announced to the ground troops.

The centaur made its way up the rock ledge. It seethed with electrical energy and smoke. Jess stared it down—she was ready to face this monster head-on.

"Hey, *Rocky!*" Pavel shouted. He stood on a farther ledge away from Jess and shot a volley of particle blasts into the centaur's back. It turned to face him but did not move. Jess's eyes darted back and forth from the centaur to Pavel to the incoming air force strafe.

"Pavel, move!" Jess shouted, but her voice was so small compared to the roar of the battle. The centaur pounced on Pavel and began slicing away at the old major. A massive electrical explosion erupted as the Matadors blasted away at the stone monster.

Tiny pieces of the centaur littered the sky. Jess's vision was blurry, and there was a loud screeching filling her eardrums. She got to her feet and watched the Matadors sail off into the air.

"Pavel?" Jess asked the air. The sounds of distant battle raged on, and Jess knew the centaur would rebuild itself once the Siren decided to resurrect her soldiers again, but she didn't care. She stumbled over to the rock ledge and peered over. Pavel lay on his back at the bottom, his left arm and right leg missing.

Jess didn't waste time—she slid down into the rock outcropping and went to Pavel's side. She looked him over and shook her head. "You should have run," she whispered as her eyes became glossy.

"I—" Pavel coughed. "I didn't see you running either, comrade."

Pavel clapped his remaining hand into Jess's and gripped tight. He stared into her eyes, his brow relaxed, and then his last breath wheezed through his nose.

"Thank you, Major," Jess whispered, and allowed a couple tears to liberate themselves from her eyes. She didn't look up to watch as a strange blue ship shaped like a manta ray roared above her, racing toward the Siren.

———————◆———————

Denton and Eliana sat in the pilot seats of the *Lelantos*. Roelin's body lay facedown behind them on the stretcher, his combat suit and particle rifle still locked away tightly in the base of the bed. Through the windscreen, they saw the battle ahead—lightning flashes, particle blasts, explosions from grenades, armies of purple light moving through the grand valley, and the Siren looming above it all like an immense shadow of tentacles and talons.

The damage from the *Telemachus* LPC was evident. An enormous pit of boiling lava lit Nhymn from below, steam and smoke writhing from it, making her look like the Queen of the Hells.

"Oh God," Eliana whispered. "Are we too late?"

Denton didn't take his eyes off the battle, only concentrating on getting them closer to the Siren.

"What's the plan now?" Eliana asked.

"Desperate times call for crazy shit—or something like that," Denton said.

"What's that mean?"

"I think I'm going to have to try and land the ship on the Siren."

Eliana looked at him. "I don't see how that's possible."

"Yeah, me neither." He sighed. "We might have to crash the *Lelantos* into her."

Eliana held her mouth open as she let this plan sink in. They might have to die to get this right. *Is there any other choice?*

"There are parachutes in the cargo bay. I want you to take one and jump out," Denton said. "We don't both need to die."

"I'm riding this ship wherever it goes," she said, holding Denton's hand on the throttle. "I'm with you until the end."

Denton wanted to tell her to leave, get to safety, do anything but stay here. He knew this was going to be the end; it lumped up in his throat. Eliana's eyes became glossy, and her grip became more firm. Denton knew she wouldn't leave. He released her hand and gripped the flight controls.

"Then here we go," Denton whispered.

The *Lelantos* rocketed forward, and Denton pushed the old clunky ship to its limit. They ripped past the last line of colonial defense.

A Matador fighter pulled up alongside the *Lelantos* and hailed them over the comm. Faye Raike's voice asked, "What's the game plan here, *Lelantos*?"

Eliana reached over and toggled the comm channel. "Faye! We need to get this ship to the Siren at all costs! Can you help us?"

"Elly?" Faye asked with surprise. She then followed up with, "You got it."

Faye thrust forward, accelerating beyond the *Lelantos*. She began carving a path through the nezzarform ground forces with her machine guns.

"Not without me, you don't!" Rocco Gainax shouted as he joined their formation. "Hail Mary!" he rallied over the comm.

"*Aye!* Let's do it, lads!" Fergus Reid spun his bulky ship around as he laughed with the madness of the moment.

The remaining colonial air force spun back toward the Siren for a final push.

Nhymn pulled up globs of hot magma with her lower tentacles and watched as they rapidly cooled. She shuffled the cooled magma around, then threw it into the air. The new lava-born constructs fell halfway to the ground, then caught themselves on sustained beams of energy, allowing them to stay airborne.

The Siren air force rocketed away from her, meeting the colonial air force head-on.

"This thing just never stops with the surprises!" Rocco shouted over the comm.

The Matadors unleashed their particle machine guns on the nezzarform fliers, dodging airborne and ground-based electrical bolts in a stunning display of skill. Denton kept the *Lelantos* behind Faye's Matador as they pushed toward the Siren.

"Do you know how to use a magnetic repeater?" Denton asked.

"No," Eliana said. Denton flicked his nose toward the three seats behind him, and she sat in the center one. "Hit the button on the armrest there."

Eliana hit the button, and a headpiece flicked out from her chair's headrest. She slipped it on over her forehead and watched the turret's HUD wink on.

"Nothing to it, just use the joystick there, aim, and pull the trigger," Denton said, and jerked his flight stick to the starboard side to avoid being rammed by a nezzarform flier.

Eliana felt disoriented at first, watching the movement through the camera on the turret. Their colonial allies were highlighted green, but the nezzarform fliers blended in with the chaos around them. The programming for the HUD never anticipated anything like this, but at least it helped her know where she shouldn't be shooting.

"One's coming up, port side," Denton said. Eliana pivoted the turret to the left and fired, missing the flier by meters.

"Crap." Eliana spat the word.

"Lead them off, let them run into the bullets," Denton said, and jerked the ship to the side as lightning flung past. Another nezzarform flier was approaching. Eliana aimed the turret to the empty air just in front of the flier's path and squeezed the trigger. Magnetic ammo collided with the nezzarform and ripped it into chunks of rocky debris. Electricity burst from its core, and it dropped to the ground into a crowd of other nezzarforms.

As they grew closer to the Siren, the fight became more intense. Nezzarform fliers began lancing out electrical bolts. To their starboard side, one of their Matador wingmen was struck directly by a flier's bolt, resulting in an explosion of fire, electricity, and rocks.

"Stay close to me," Faye said into the comm.

"I'm *trying*," Denton grunted. The Siren was beginning to fill their entire windscreen. "Not much farther now."

Eliana stood up from her turret seat and joined Denton, sitting in the co-pilot chair. "So, we're really going to crash into her."

"Yeah," Denton said.

Eliana looked back toward the Siren and thought of everything she had lost. Her father, her friends, and now, her life. If this was the only way to stop Nhymn, then it was worth it.

"Let's finish it, then," Eliana said.

Denton nodded gravely, keeping his hands on the throttle and flight stick. Eliana felt the back of her seat shake violently, and for a moment, she wondered if they had been hit by a nezzarform flier.

"*I'll* ... take it ... from here..." Roelin's voice coughed out.

Captain Roelin Raike, who had been comatose for over a month, leaned against the back of Eliana's pilot seat. His gaunt face was shrouded with a beard. His baggy, bruised eyes stared out the windscreen at Nhymn.

"She's ... *mine* ..." Roelin said, his bloodshot eyes straining to focus on Nhymn.

"Roelin," Eliana whispered.

"*Leave.*" Roelin coughed up blood. His body wasn't going to last.

"Roelin, I—" Denton began, but Roelin gave him a stern gaze. "Go!"

Denton didn't sit around to debate. He pushed himself out of the chair, pulling Eliana's hand with him. Roelin sat down and held the flight stick straight, throttle forward.

Eliana freed herself from Denton's grasp as they got to the doorway. She shouted, "Roelin!"

The thin man who had been through so much looked over his shoulder, letting his long hair droop in front of his face.

"Roelin. You're a hero," she said. "My father knew it too."

For a moment, Roelin said nothing. The chaos was quiet to him now as he focused on Eliana's words. Roelin turned to her and weakly said, "Thank you, Elly."

"Come on, we have to go now." Denton urgently whispered. Eliana nodded and ran with him toward the cargo bay. The door shut, and Roelin was alone on the bridge. He looked at the Siren, who was looming so large before him. She had always felt this immense to him.

"I'm not letting you get away with this," Roelin whispered.

"Evasive maneuvers!" Rocco called out as a row of ground nezzarforms charged blasts. The air force split its ranks, curling to make a midair U-turn. "We'll rotate back in for another run. The marines need air support!"

Each ship maneuvered away except the *Lelantos* and Faye's Matador. Faye dipped the nose of her Matador and aimed her cannons at the nezzarforms directly in front of them on the ground.

Nezzarforms created an electrical fence with sustained lightning pulsing upward into the sky. Faye roared with a ferocity that would have shaken a god as she squeezed the triggers and blew away enough nezzarforms in time to create a gap in the lightning fence wide enough for them to pass through.

"That's for—" she shouted.

"Faye." Roelin transmitted his voice using the *Lelantos*'s wave transmitter, and the broadcast went out to everyone involved in the battle. Faye's battle cry stopped. She listened carefully, knowing she'd heard Roelin's voice.

"Roe?" Faye asked, confused.

"You need ... to *head back*." Roelin coughed.

"Roe!" She knew it—it was him. She shouted, "You're not leaving me again!" She squeezed the triggers on her machine-gun turrets and unleashed destruction on the flying nezzarforms in front of them.

"It's alright," Roelin said. "You need ... to go... *now*."

Faye shouted a long war cry and unloaded her particle machine gun. The Siren was close now; she filled their entire windscreens with tentacles and dark bone.

"I... love... you..." Roelin said.

Faye pulled back on the throttle, bringing her Matador under the *Lelantos*.

"You come back to me!" Faye shouted. "When this is all over, *you come back!*"

Roelin didn't reply.

"Fine!" Faye spat the word out in anger. She pitched her Matador back toward the defensive line.

————◆————

In the cargo bay of the *Lelantos*, Denton and Eliana strapped on parachutes and got ready for their escape. Eliana looked at Denton. "These aren't going to do us any good if we land in lava."

"You're right," Denton said. He'd rather crash into the Siren than parachute into the lava pit the *Telemachus*'s LPC had created. He turned his head and noticed his brother's racing rushcycle still in the cargo bay. Eliana followed his gaze and saw the bike too.

"It's better than nothing," she said with a wince.

Denton gestured for her to get on the bike. He hopped on and grabbed the controls, and Eliana planted herself right behind him. "They might come at us," Denton warned.

"Let them," Eliana said, and unholstered her pistol. She activated it, and the collider cylinder began to rotate. The red light indicated it was set to lethal.

Denton revved the engine of the racing rushcycle, impressed with his brother's work. They both slipped atmospheric helmets onto their heads to protect them from the altitude and wind pressure.

"Hold on!" Denton shouted as he punched the cargo lift control. Wind and hot air rushed into the room as the ramp lowered. Denton revved forward, thrusting the bike off the ramp and into the open air.

The *Lelantos* sailed forward, leaving Denton and Eliana behind as they burst out of the back end on the roaring rushcycle. Eliana screamed a mixture of excitement, adrenaline, and horror as they free-fell through the air.

"Here goes nothing!" Denton shouted over the howling wind that engulfed them. He flicked a switch near the throttle, and the engine boomed, propelling them forward. Eliana looked down and saw the lava pit below, hot embers flicking past them as they moved through the air.

A lightning bolt lanced past their right side as the nezzarforms began to attack the rushcycle.

"They see us!" Eliana shouted. She gripped Denton tightly with one arm while aiming the pistol with the other. She let out a few shots, all misses.

"Got an idea. Get ready!" Denton shouted.

"What?" Eliana asked. The wind and the helmet had deafened her. Denton killed the engine momentarily, allowing the rushcycle to spin in a complete circle. Eliana screamed and let out a few shots as they rotated. Two blasts struck a flying nezzarform, causing it to careen into another flier nearby, exploding them both in midair. Bits of nezzarform debris tapped against the visors of their helmets.

"Hells yeah," Denton let out a loud Ganymede holler as he leveled out the rushcycle and throttled the engines back on. Eliana suspected that Denton was enjoying this. She gripped his jacket and hoped he wouldn't forget they needed to clear the lava pit.

"Here we go. Hold on tight!" Denton shouted, and punched a few controls on the bike handle. The rushcycle jerked with an explosion of energy as he activated all the thrusters on the bottom to slow their fall speed. Eliana wrapped her arms around his belly. Denton held the bike as tightly as he could, then with a quick flick, he activated the rushcycle's emergency chute.

The chute caught, and Denton strained to keep the bike from ripping away from his grip. He steadied the bike and glided it across the lava pit until it met the rocky ledge, where it slammed down hard.

Eliana reached backward and released the emergency parachute, watching it fling off the back compartment on the bike and twirl into the lava pit that they were gradually leaving behind.

Eliana whooped her own version of a Ganymede holler and shouted, "Nice flying," She reached over Denton's shoulder with an open palm. Denton slapped her palm with his own, resulting in a loud clap and adrenaline-filled laughter.

Finally, Denton and Eliana were rocketing across the valley. Between them and the final line of human and auk'nai defense was an army of nezzarforms.

"No time to celebrate! You still got that pistol?" Denton asked.

"Right here!" she said, and placed her elbow on his shoulder to steady her aim. The rushcycle raced away from the Siren and onward into the fray.

———◆———

"Roelin," whispered Nhymn.

Roelin ignored her, keeping the *Lelantos* steady with everything he had left inside of him. There wasn't much time, he could feel his body dying.

"Your plan will fail," Nhymn whispered again.

Through the windscreen, Roelin could see the Siren standing before him, towering above the lava pit made by the LPC. She reared her arm back, preparing to strike down the *Lelantos.*

"Pathetic little man," Nhymn whispered, then swung her long-taloned hand down toward the *Lelantos.* Roelin jerked the flight stick to the side, tilting the ship 90 degrees and narrowly dodging the gigantic arm. He then brought the ship back toward Nhymn.

Roelin pushed forward, sailing the *Lelantos* directly into Nhymn's abyssal eye socket. The ship was a pinpoint of light in the deep-black space. A billion shadowed arms pulled the ship into the darkness, and no explosion followed the collision with the interior of Nhymn's skull.

Roelin had made it to his target, and the darkness there swallowed him whole.

FIFTY-NINE

ROELIN'S EYES SNAPPED OPEN.

He was sitting in the pilot's seat of the *Lelantos*, and the room was slanted to the right. Outside the windshield, he could see only smoke and a shifting purple light. He stood up and felt better than he had in years. Roelin flexed his hands and noticed his muscles had regained their healthy shape; it was as if he had never been possessed at all.

The stretcher lay against the wall, broken from the crash, and his combat suit was halfway out of its containment box at the base of the bed. His particle rifle was lying on the floor on the other side of the bridge. He walked over and began to equip himself for a fight.

Outside the *Lelantos*, the sky was filled with a burning violet sun. Tendrils of purple fire licked away from its center like an unstable reactor ready to explode. The grass was a harsh magenta, alien to every alien landscape Roelin had come to know.

Before Roelin was the cave of Sirens.

Yet, this was never actually the real cave. This was Nhymn's mind. Roelin had been here before, but he hadn't realized the power he held here until he'd heard of Denton's visions.

The *Lelantos* was burning in the magenta grass, casting its flickering red and yellow lights into the darkness of the cave's maw. The sound of the roaring spaceship fire was prominent, but behind it, Roelin thought he heard something else.

It sounded like a woman weeping, but was alien in tone and consistency. Sadness had its universal qualities, recognizable to others who had felt its immensity. He traced the soft sound around the side of the cave entrance and past the stone statue of Karx, now half crumbled to the ground, destroyed by Nhymn. Beyond it, curled up on her side, was Sympha.

Sympha was not in her giant form. She was the way she had been the first time Nhymn had died. The way Nhymn wanted her to be—weaker, smaller.

"Sympha," Roelin whispered.

The Siren turned to him, then backed away like a frightened fawn.

"You!" Sympha shouted into Roelin's mind, pointing her claw at him. *"You helped her!"*

"No, I didn't," Roelin said, kneeling before her. "She used me just as she uses you now."

"Why should I put trust in you?" Sympha asked with a hiss.

"You have no other choice," Roelin said. "We need to stop Nhymn. She will destroy this planet. You know this."

"Nhymn ..." Sympha turned away from Roelin upon hearing the name. *"I don't think Nhymn was ever meant to be born."* Sympha floated away into the grassy opening beyond the cave entrance and continued, *"There were Sirens before us. They are the bones of this planet, becoming part of their creations once they fade away. They do not die the way other creatures do, they remain."*

Sympha lowered herself to the ground and breathed a mist into her hand. She gently pushed the essence into the grass and watched a bright-green flower form.

"Nhymn smuggled her way into existence on my shoulders. She was never able to create. She can only control. Nhymn had to overtake me to

become a creator, but her powers were never supposed to intertwine with mine."

Roelin stepped closer to Sympha. "There were many like her in the cave, hidden to our reality. Those lesser phantoms destroyed her repeatedly for finding a way to exist like you."

Sympha tilted her heart-shaped skull toward the ground. *"I know. I always knew."* She turned toward Roelin. *"Karx was one of those lesser phantoms. I plucked him into existence to protect me from Nhymn. I left the others behind, knowing I could make a construct out of every one of them if I only willed it."*

Sympha placed a hand on the crumbled statue of Karx and said, *"I could have made so many like him, but I was afraid they would end up twisted like my sister."* Sympha turned her back to the crumbled statue and faced Roelin once more. *"I knew Nhymn would continue on after Karx destroyed her body that day. I did nothing to help her. I left her in that cave to rot. I wanted my sister to die."* Sympha looked up at the darkness. *"You see why, don't you? She will control all life on this planet if no one stops her."*

"Then help me stop her," Roelin said.

———◆———

Denton and Eliana flanked the outskirts of the battle on the racing rushcycle. A bolt flicked overhead close enough that Eliana felt the hairs on the back of her neck tingle. "That one was too close!" she shouted.

The rushcycle began to slow down. Eliana looked along the side of the vehicle to see if they had been hit, but nothing seemed out of the ordinary. She tapped Denton on the shoulder and asked, "What's happening? We need to make it back to the others."

A blue smoke seeped from underneath the lip of Denton's helmet. Eliana gasped, then reached around Denton's arms and pumped the brakes on the rushcycle's handles. They slowed down most of the way then flopped to their side, spilling Denton and Eliana onto the yellow grass.

Eliana scrambled over to Denton and removed his helmet, moving her face away to avoid inhaling the blue smoke that flew out. When she looked back down, Denton was twitching as if he were having a seizure. His nose was bleeding, and his eyes were vibrating and emitting a faint blue mist. Denton's neck was strained, and he was convulsing badly.

"No, no, *no!*" Eliana shouted. She had to work fast and treat what she understood. First, Eliana plugged her medical kit into Denton's arm using two corded needles. This would help her equipment learn what was happening and administer the appropriate cocktail of pain relievers and other in-kit medications. This looked like a seizure, so Eliana brushed away any sharp stones near Denton, then rolled him onto his side to keep his airway clear. She looked at her soothreader to mark the time of the seizure, then noticed a nezzarform approaching over the lip of a nearby hill.

Eliana grabbed her collider pistol and unleashed a round of particle shots into the stone construct's face, exploding it into a shower of rocky debris. Eliana turned toward Denton to make sure he hadn't gotten worse. She lowered herself behind the downed rushcycle and kept her gun aimed at the hill, ready for more nezzarforms to approach. There wasn't much else Eliana could do until Denton's seizure—or whatever it was—subsided. She had to protect him.

Denton's wave-transmitter-enabled soothreader gave Eliana a play-by-play of the battle. Things were getting grim. There was a panic after the Hail Mary maneuver ended in the *Lelantos* crashing into the Siren, causing no visible effect.

"We're out of options. We need to evacuate the colony and scatter into the wilderness," General Raughts was saying. "We can regroup then and see about getting survivors up to the *Telemachus* once repairs have been made."

Eliana believed in Roelin's plan—no other conscious person knew the details. She removed Denton's soothreader and held it in her free hand, keeping her grip on the pistol.

"Everyone, *listen*! We have a plan!" Eliana said into the wave transmitter, broadcasting to everyone on the comm channels.

"What the—Elly?" George Tanaka's voice answered.

"You're going to have to trust me on this one. Right now, Roelin Raike is working to buy us an opening. We need to be ready when we see it and hit her with everything we got!"

"What else do we have?" Helen Davies responded. "We can't fire the LPC, and our air force is out of heavy ordinance."

"We have to work through the problem together," Eliana urged as her eyes darted over to the towering Siren in the distance. She whispered to herself, "Come on, Roe. You can stop her."

————— ♦ —————

Jess Combs and the remaining ground forces held the last line of defense on the northwestern edge of the battlefield. The marines heard Eliana's message, and it filled them with hope. They held their ground and continued to keep the pressure on the enemy. Auk'nai warriors lanced nezzarforms with their peck rifles from both the sky and the ground among the marines. In these foxholes, it didn't matter which planet you came from, everyone was family.

Jess knelt behind a patch of boulders and picked her shots carefully, striking only charged nezzarforms in the head before they could lance their position with electrical bolts. Nock'lu dropped Talulo off near Jess. He stood on a tall boulder and twirled Mag'Ro's daunoren staff, lashing out energy into the approaching stone army. Nezzarforms were flung back and combusted, but more filled their places like a never-ending wave of stone constructs piling over each other.

Nhymn pulsed her violet light, and Jess knew this meant she was about to resurrect her fallen troops.

This would be the end.

SIXTY

NHYMN PULLED ALL OF her energy into herself. The purple lights pulsed upward into her skull rapidly, then held steady. She brought her arms up as she contained the power for a moment, then slammed her fists down into the ground in front of her, kicking up molten lava.

An emerald light flashed from the impact.

A wave of bright-green energy spread through the battlefield. The nezzarforms convulsed, then froze in position. Their electrical tethers flickered purple and green, like a television on the fritz.

The light passed over the last line of defense. No fallen nezzarforms returned to life. Instead, there was only the static of confusion among the remaining stone constructs. Each of the nezzarform fliers plummeted to the ground, crashing into crowds of their own brothers below. The fighting ceased while everyone stood to scratch their heads in confusion.

"WHAT?" Nhymn shouted in their minds as she lifted her hands toward her face. The nezzarforms continued to flicker and twitch. Nhymn lunged her hand out at her army. Only a quarter of the constructs obeyed, flickering back to their original purple hue. Nhymn's hand flung backward as if it had been slapped, relinquishing the control she had of the few constructs she'd regained.

"Roelin ..." Nhymn clenched her claw into a fist. Her arms spread out to her sides, and her head tilted upward. She froze in place, locked in her spread-out pose by some unseen force.

Nhymn's towering body became inert.

———— ◆ ————

Denton felt hot, too hot. His vision came to him slowly, and all he could see was fire. He sat up and recognized the room he was in. It was the cave of the Sirens, but it was engulfed in flames. Fire licked up the ooze on the walls and floor, and smoke billowed above him.

"How did you get here?" a voice Denton recognized echoed around the cave.

"Roelin?" he asked. Captain Roelin Raike emerged from the smoke adorned in his full combat suit. He grabbed Denton and pulled him to his feet.

"Move it," Roelin said, and they rushed outside.

Denton made it out into the deep-purple sunlit yard and stopped. He recognized Sympha floating in the grass before him.

"Wait, Sympha?" Denton asked. "Where the Hells am I?"

"I'm surprised to see you here, shade," Sympha said. *"This is Nhymn's mind."*

Denton looked down at his hands, noticing they were semi translucent. He pushed them against his face to make sure he was a solid being, then sputtered, "No—no, no, *no*! This can't be happening. How am I here?"

"I think I know," Roelin said. "When I entered your mind to find Karx, I must have accidentally tethered you to me."

Denton let his hands drop to his sides. "But why do I look like this?"

"You look how you always have to me, shade," Sympha said into Denton's mind.

"You're tethered to me. I'm an unnatural thing among these Sirens; there's bound to be inconsistencies," Roelin said. "But we don't have time. We are drawing Nhymn to us. Sympha and I need to distract her as long as possible so the people outside can have a chance to destroy her."

"Can I help? I might have special shade powers. Hells, I might even be invincible!" Denton said with a proud smile. Roelin whacked him on the back of the head, and Denton felt the pain immediately. "*Ouch!* Alright, I'm not invincible. But I can still help."

"Just find a way to get out of here," Roelin said.

"I'm helping, damn it," Denton said. "Nhymn can't win this battle. I'm here, and I'm not backing down. We're going to stop her now, together."

Roelin nodded, then said, "Alright, go to the *Lelantos*. There might be something you can use inside."

"On it," Denton said.

Above, the clouds parted, and Nhymn's enormous bird-shaped horned skull drifted through like an asteroid entering the atmosphere.

"Go *now!*" Roelin said. Denton took off, running toward the burning *Lelantos*.

Roelin turned to Sympha and said, "Alright, she's coming. Try to stay out of sight until I give you the signal."

"*We are going to die here, human. You know this,*" Sympha said.

"Yes." Roelin checked his particle rifle. "We will die. But as long as we can keep her here, she isn't out there killing our people. We just have to survive long enough to allow the defenses outside to do something."

Sympha nodded, then floated into concealment behind the burning cave. Nhymn's head lowered into the magenta field, and her body shrank down in size. The faster she approached, the smaller she became. She let out a harsh roar, and wind blasted through the grassy valley, extinguishing the flames inside the cave.

Nhymn stood at three meters tall—the shape Roelin knew best.

"*You found a way to reduce me. Very clever,*" Nhymn said, looking at her claws. "*But very foolish.*"

Roelin activated his particle rifle, and Nhymn rushed him. He sprayed bullets toward the Siren, but Nhymn dodged every shot with nightmarish speed. Roelin had seen this speed used against his comrades in the past. Now he was on the other end of her power and stuck with all the disadvantages of her previous victims. Nhymn got within arm's reach, and Roelin activated his suit's jump-jet and propelled his leg into her skull.

Nhymn was knocked sideways with the force of the kick, and Roelin's suit was damaged near his shin when her sharp horn tore through it. Shot for shot, they both sustained injuries.

Roelin moved backward toward the *Lelantos*, attempting to keep the focus on himself. The Siren recoiled and launched toward him once more. Roelin stumbled over his injured leg as she grew nearer.

Just before hitting Roelin, Nhymn was knocked sideways by the magnetic repeater turret of the *Lelantos*. There was a loud Ganymede holler as an outside speaker projected Denton's voice: "How about *that!*"

The turret of the *Lelantos* continued to fire where Nhymn was thrown, kicking up dirt and debris with every high-powered magnetic bolt that lanced the ground. Eventually, the gun stopped shooting and there was only a quiet hiss emitting from the super-heated turret barrels.

"Out of ammo. Did we get her?" Denton asked.

Roelin cautiously moved toward the smoking crater where Nhymn had been a moment before. He felt a tingle on the back of his neck and rolled sideways as Nhymn pounced from the crater toward him, knocking Roelin's rifle away with a swipe of her claw.

Roelin used the jump-jet on his elbow to launch his fists into the Siren's skull repeatedly. He felt his knuckle break against Nhymn's spiked carapace, but he kept punching through the immense pain, allowing his gauntleted knuckles to bash into the Siren's head and chest.

Nhymn slashed across Roelin's stomach, striking an area that had less armor and ripping his skin open. Roelin's blood spilled into the magenta grass, and he cried out in pain. With one more jet-propelled kick, he pushed Nhymn away.

The Siren loomed over Roelin and hissed into his mind, *"Stupid little thing! You avoided your Armageddon only to bring it across the stars to us!"* She curled her claw into a fist and stepped forward. *"When I am done here, the universe will have no memory of humanity."*

"Sympha," Roelin coughed out.

"What?" Nhymn hissed.

Sympha launched herself at Nhymn like a clawed rocket. The two Sirens slashed at each other relentlessly, tearing bone pieces and tentacles away with each rip and tear. The battle moved to the sky as Sympha floated upward during their grapple.

Denton emerged from the *Lelantos* and joined Roelin's side.

"We … need to …help Sympha," Roelin grunted through the pain of his injuries. Blood poured from his abdomen.

"I'll find a way to help her, but right now, I need to hide you," Denton said. He grabbed Roelin under his arms and began to drag him toward the *Lelantos*.

"Leave me!" Roelin tried to swat Denton away but failed.

Sympha smashed into the ground in the meadow in front of Denton and Roelin, followed by Nhymn, who landed on her feet with grace. Sympha was broken; one of her arms had been removed, and gashes in her bony carapace bled torrents of green blood. She tried to cough out her healing mist, but it wasn't enough.

Denton left Roelin in the grass and rushed toward the Sirens.

"You're still alive, shade?" Nhymn said. *"Good. I'll let you watch."*

Denton slid on his knee and grabbed the particle rifle Roelin had dropped in the grass. He lifted it to shoot Nhymn.

Nhymn tore Sympha's head off, spraying emerald blood in a wild arc.

The ground shook, and Denton struggled to keep the rifle aimed. The sound of the ground fracturing below them filled the air, and suddenly the world fragmented around them

Denton was lifted up on a small piece of fragmented land, away from Nhymn and the others. Gravity pressed him against the fragment island as he moved upward, then flung him away as it suddenly stopped moving. Denton landed again on the floating fragment island. He shook off the strange sensation and looked over the edge.

There were floating islands of magenta grass frozen in the air as if all time had stopped mid-explosion. The sky surrounding them was no longer a purple Hellscape, but instead, Denton could see the real-world battlefield outside. Denton watched as the burning *Lelantos* tumbled into the lava pit below them, followed by the particle rifle he'd hoped to use.

Below, Nhymn tossed Sympha's severed head onto the grass like a piece of trash, then moved toward the floating island Roelin was on.

Roelin shouted to her as she approached, "You just killed your host."

Nhymn cackled. *"Yes, I did."*

"See what you've done here?" Roelin coughed. "You're a parasite, Nhymn. Without a host, you're just a perversion to this world."

Nhymn launched herself onto Roelin's floating island and stepped on his chest, forcing his blood to gush from the sides of his torso. She cut his throat out with a slash of her claws and said, *"It doesn't matter what I am, Roelin. I will control this world regardless of my form."*

Roelin gurgled blood as he tried to breathe.

"Hey!" Denton shouted from his high platform, unsure of what to do. He had no weapons or special powers, but he hoped he had gravity on his side. Nhymn looked up from Roelin's dying body.

"You have lost this battle, shade," Nhymn said into his mind.

Roelin let out a gurgled laugh. Nhymn turned toward him and saw a bloody smile on his face.

She spat the words into his mind, *"You have failed. Your trick didn't work."*

And yet, Roelin still laughed.

Nhymn turned to face Denton once more. The young man leaped from his fragmented island and dropped straight toward her.

Good, Nhymn thought, *I will finish him quickly and then save this planet.*

Roelin's gurgled laugh stopped. He let out one last sigh as he died with a grin.

Denton rushed toward Nhymn, his fists above his head, ready to crash down on her. Nhymn readied herself to catch the fool, but was met with only a puff of smoke.

The shade had vanished into thin air.

With Denton out of the way, Nhymn saw what Roelin had been laughing about.

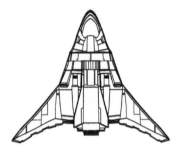

SIXTY-ONE

ELIANA KNELT OVER DENTON in the grass as the wind blew around them. The nezzarforms flickered from green to purple, and she kept her pistol trained on them in case they made up their minds and continued their assault.

The Siren stood motionless with her arms outstretched and her skull facing the sky. Denton's body stopped shaking, and the blue smoke billowing from his eyes ceased. For a moment, Eliana thought he'd died.

Then Denton sat straight up and inhaled sharply. Before Eliana could say anything, there was an immense roar from high up in the atmosphere. She could feel a change in the air as the clouds parted.

It was as if the sun had fallen onto the surface of Kamaria. A white-hot streak of fire and carnage plummeted from the heavens, and it was clear that this cosmic missile was no meteor that had come from on high.

It was the *Telemachus*.

The interstellar spacecraft that had ferried the refugees of the Sol System was now being used as a hammer. The sight was both awful and beautiful, unique in its splendor and terrible in its consequence.

Less than a second passed before the *Telemachus* came hurtling through the clouds and smashed into the towering Siren's chest, forcing the monster into the pit of lava. What followed was an explosion that rocked the mountains.

The shock waves from the subsequent secondary explosions and ground quakes made Eliana think they would be sucked into a fissure. Extensive cracks formed rapidly, sucking hundreds of stone nezzarforms into their depths.

A rush of hot wind washed over the valley as more explosions, fire, and molten lava erupted from the vast impact site. Dust and debris were flung for kilometers, making it look as though it were raining metal and dirt. A dirty cloud hung in the air where the Siren had stood moments before.

Eliana looked toward the impact for movement as the explosions continued to roar and the debris rained down around them. She saw the remaining nezzarforms had gone inert. The valley became a museum of stone statues observing the final resting place of the *Telemachus* and the Siren beneath it.

The metal rain was replaced by a soft drizzle.

"Direct hit," Eliana said into Denton's soothreader to everyone involved in the battle. "It *worked* ..."

———— ◆ ————

The soldiers were speechless on the final line of defense. Jess Combs and Talulo climbed onto a tall boulder to get a better look at the battlefield.

"It is over," Talulo said, slinging Mag'Ro's powerful daunoren staff onto his wingless back.

"I think you're right," Jess said, and smiled as she watched the nezzarforms standing motionless in the ravaged valley. "It looks like we beat them."

The smoke began to reveal what was left of the Siren after the crash. All that remained was one long-taloned claw latched on to the side of the *Telemachus* wreckage in a viselike death grip.

The gentle drizzle of rain pitter-pattered onto the valley and its occupants. The marines slowly regained their footing, standing tall among the destruction.

———— ٠ ————

Faye Raike was still ready to fight, but the fight had left the valley. She knew it was over, but she didn't care. She replayed Roelin's final transmission over and over again in her mind. Faye glared at the chaotic landscape below, wishing she could drop a thousand more interstellar spaceships onto Nhymn.

"I don't know what you did, Roe," Faye said to herself, "but thank you."

———— ٠ ————

On the command bridge of the *Rogers*, George Tanaka and Helen Davies stared at each other for a moment. They held their breath, unsure of the fate of the *Telemachus* crew.

"Odysseus Command," a voice said over the public comm channel, "this is Admiral Hugo Marin. We're going to need someone to come pick us up."

George smiled and laughed. "It's good to hear your voice, Admiral. For a moment there I thought you weren't able to make it off in time."

"Did it work?" Hugo asked.

"Affirmative. Your actions just saved humanity from extinction. We're proud of you and your crew. We owe you all a great debt," Helen Davies said. When she finished speaking, the crew of the *Rogers* stood and applauded.

"It's all thanks to Eliana's plan and whatever Captain Raike did. I'm not sure how they did it, but we couldn't have hit the target otherwise."

———— ٠ ————

On the northern outskirt of the valley, Eliana and Denton waited for the planet quakes to stop. The rain that followed felt like a warm shower after a week of hard work. Eliana kept her eyes on the impact zone, unsure if she could believe it was finally over.

"It actually worked," Eliana said, and sat next to Denton.

"What happened?" Denton asked.

"I used your wave transmitter to work out a plan with everyone. We were out of firepower, so I thought, why not throw our biggest rock at Nhymn?" Eliana smiled. "I think Dad would have liked it. His ship saved humanity from extinction twice now."

Denton said, "Roelin fought her with everything he had. He died a hero."

"Tell me what happened," Eliana said.

Denton explained the accidental tether Roelin had created when he'd searched for Karx in his mind, and how, with Sympha's help, they'd stalled Nhymn long enough to give the colonial defenses a chance to destroy her.

"How did you make it out?" Eliana asked.

"To be honest, I'm not completely sure. But if I had to guess, I think that the tether between Roelin and me broke when he died. I just got lucky it happened when it did."

Eliana hugged him with all of her strength.

They could hear the cheering coming from across the valley, the happiness of victory. Eliana separated herself from Denton and smiled with tears of joy in her eyes. It was finally over.

"For a while there, I thought I lost you," Eliana said.

"We're safe now," Denton said. For a moment, they forgot about the world around them. The rain gently sprinkled, the wind whispered sweet nothings through the grass, and the cheers from the survivors all seemed muffled. Denton reached into his jacket pocket.

"There's something I've wanted to ask you," Denton stated.

Eliana noticed what he was holding. It was an engagement ring, a beautiful one. The setting for the twinkling gemstone reminded her of the fountains in Apusticus, the uniquely alien shape inspiring this beautiful work.

"Eliana Veston," Denton said, "will you marry me?"

"Yes!" Eliana shouted, bypassing the ring and hugging Denton roughly. "*Yes!* Yes! Denton!"

Denton laughed, then pulled her in to give her a passionate kiss. "I love you," he whispered.

"I love you too." She smiled and pushed him into the mud, kissing him more as the rain drizzled onto her back.

"Get a room, you two!" The voice of Fergus Reid came to them through a loudspeaker on the exterior of his ship. A spotlight shined on them. "Or, I can leave you out here in the wilderness if you'd rather."

"We're getting *married!*" Eliana shouted, and pointed at the ring on her finger.

"You've got a knack for timing there, lad." Fergus chuckled and spun his ship around, lowering the ramp and allowing Denton and Eliana to board.

———— ✦ ————

As the dust settled, the true extent of damage to the grand valley was revealed. The nezzarform statues lay in dormant piles of rubble scattered around the impact zone in a radial pattern. Stray bodies of crushed marines and auk'nai warriors lay where they fell. Scorch marks from nezzarform beams created cigarette burns in the trampled grass. Destroyed Matadors and colonial air force vessels smoked, a few with signal lights pinging for rescue. The entire line of tanks had been reduced to sheared scrap metal. The *Telemachus* remained upright, half buried in the planet and held in place by the Siren's death grip.

They would become permanent reminders of this battle.

Survivors helped the wounded first, gathering them into areas where medical officers could treat them. Auk'nai warriors lifted stranded soldiers from the field, cutting the response time down dramatically and saving more lives. Each colonial vessel loaded up with injured soldiers, human and auk'nai, to bring back to Odysseus Colony for treatment.

On Fergus's ship, Eliana monitored her new fiancé's health. Denton turned his head to look out a long rectangular window at the wreckage of the *Telemachus* and the Siren's dead hand.

"Looks like we're here to stay," Denton said.

"What do you mean?" Eliana asked.

"The *Telemachus* is gone. That was our last ticket away from Kamaria. There is no turning back now. Humanity is here for good."

"Pretty crazy, right?" Eliana asked rhetorically.

"I don't think the Siren is dead," Denton said.

Eliana stopped what she was doing. It felt like a cold hand had run up her back toward her neck.

"What do you mean? Did she get back up?" She looked out the window at the *Telemachus* wreckage, thinking she would see the Siren standing up once more.

"The Sirens are immortal," Denton said. "She might be down for now, but she'll be back. We need to be ready when that happens."

The rain drizzled into the evening. The creatures of the valley returned to their burrows. The fires died out, leaving behind smoldering remains of ship metal and tree bark. It smelled like a forest fire, but a forest fire would have been less devastating.

Odysseus Command requested that a small squad stay behind and monitor the Siren, and Faye Raike was the first to volunteer. She sat on top of her Matador, listening to the nearby soldiers who sat around a campfire and shared their stories of the battle. Delta Octantis had sunk below the mountains, revealing a universe of stars.

Faye watched the stars swirl in their never-ending waltz and thought of Roelin. He had been dead to her for years, then she'd discovered he was still alive, only for him to die once more. Kamaria had been cruel to the Raikes. Faye had grown used to this empty feeling in her chest. She lifted her head when she heard jingling coming from the tree line nearby.

"What *the* …" Faye squinted her eyes to see a twinkling green light swaying from inside the forest. She lowered herself down from the top of her Matador and pulled out her sidearm. The other soldiers around the campfire didn't seem to notice her leave.

As Faye walked into the trees, the twinkling green light seemed to move farther away. She began to think it was a lost nezzarform and would have enjoyed putting one more to rest with her pistol for what they'd done to her husband. She kept moving through the trees until the light faded. Faye hesitated for a moment, wondering where it could have gone.

"Alone again." Faye sighed. She kept her eyes down; it was getting harder to bring them up every day. She felt as if she'd exited the husk of her body and was watching it stand there without her. Faye could feel the world spin beneath her feet, and she didn't care.

A clearing of bioluminescent flowers near a cliff overhang invited Faye to relax. Beyond the grove of flowers were the remains of the battle and the *Telemachus* wreckage. Faye admired the beauty of the softly glowing blue flowers and the tiny green twilight gnats that buzzed above them.

A sensation in Faye's body embraced her with warm, familiar pressure. She stood, motionless, then allowed herself to be comforted by the feeling. Faye could feel his cheek against her own, his arms around her waist, his chest against hers. She was overcome with happiness she had not felt in years. Faye had needed a hug for so long, and somehow, Roelin was here to give her one.

Faye never wanted it to end, but in time, the blue flowers dimmed, and the green gnats moved away into the forest. Roelin was here, but he had moved on. Faye's eyes welled up with tears, and she brushed one away with her hand.

"I love you, Roelin Raike," Faye whispered, "and I always will."

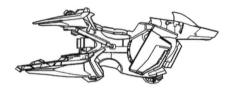

EPILOGUE

THREE YEARS LATER

"Here they come!" Denton Castus shouted.

The race was coming to an end, with Jason Castus in the lead riding the *Claire-O'dine* rushcycle. It had been three years since the Siren was defeated in the valley. Since then, Odysseus Colony had grown into Odysseus City, with many new buildings and landmarks, including a rushcycle racetrack.

"I see them!" Dr. Eliana Castus shouted in excitement. She bobbled a little boy in her arms and said, "Cade, do you see your uncle Jason?"

The little boy, just shy of two years old, with light-brown skin and messy black hair, smiled and cheered. He waved a flag that had their family's machine shop logo on it. The rushcycles boomed past, vibrating the seats closest to the track. Jason crossed the finish line first and raised his arms in victory.

Denton, Eliana, and Cade gave a big Ganymede holler in celebration. The announcer said, "What another exciting race down here at Telemachus Memorial Field. Have a great Union Day, everyone!"

Union Day was the anniversary of the battle with the Siren, not observed for the tragic loss of life or the horrifying monster that caused it but instead as the day that humans and auk'nai joined together in peace. The refugees of Apusticus moved into Odysseus City after that day, and together they helped build something new.

There was a floating lantern ceremony after dusk to commemorate all those who were lost during the battle. Beautiful paper lanterns were released that would plant trees wherever they landed.

"Things are happening faster than we expected, aren't they?" Eliana said to Denton. They watched as Jason pulled his rushcycle into the winner's circle.

"Yeah, you're right," Denton said.

"I just wish we could hang out here all day, maybe have a few drinks and just enjoy the holiday." Eliana smiled and tickled Cade. The little boy giggled and screamed with excitement.

"Are you sure we can't?" Denton asked.

"What would the team think if their captain spent all day getting drunk and watching rushcycle races?" she asked, and playfully pushed his shoulder.

"I mean, you're the captain. You make the rules," Denton said with a smile.

"That is true." Eliana smirked. "Well then, you better get your ass up, Denny. That's an order."

"Ass up!" Cade parroted back.

"Crap!" Denton blurted out.

"Crap!" The little boy giggled and smiled with a grin that said he knew he was saying bad words.

"Cade Johnathon Castus! You know better than—" Eliana tried to scold the child but couldn't help thinking it was funny hearing swears in a toddler's voice. She desperately tried to avoid laughing. Denton patted her shoulder, trying not to laugh too.

"Oh, this is going just great. See what an example we are for our son?" Eliana chuckled. "Cade, you shouldn't say those words."

"Sowry," Cade said, and used his big blue puppy-dog eyes to

woo his parents into not yelling at him.

"It's okay, bud," Denton said, and tussled his hair.

They exited the racetrack and walked out into the city. The colony had grown up in the past three years. Tall human skyscrapers were interspersed with floating auk'nai platforms.

More construction was still underway, the city continually expanding. Auk'nai workers lifted heavy equipment up to human workers, flying around the construction zones and getting into positions that humans would consider dangerous.

Denton, Eliana, and Cade got to their truck and made their way to the Castus Machine Shop. Their route took them down the main thoroughfare, away from the center of the city. The buildings grew shorter, leading into residential districts. Auk'nai residents glided downward from floating structures that hung above human apartment complexes and housing. Citizens walked together in the streets, helping each other with daily tasks regardless of planetary origin. Some sold items, others cultivated vegetables, and some chatted about their days and the work ahead. The city was a multispecies utopia.

Denton pulled the truck in front of the Castus Machine Shop. The sign was flashier now that it had come under new ownership. Tyler Castus was in charge now, and advertisements for Jason's *Claire-O'dine* rushcycle lined the walls and gave the whole place a modern look.

Across the street was Brynn's Fine Jewelry, a small shop that generally had a line of clients, mostly auk'nai, who desired the custom-made jewelry. Brynn ran it, and Michael worked for her.

Both shops were closed for the holiday. Tyler, Michael, and Brynn sat outside, drinking cold beers and enjoying the autumn air.

"There's my favorite little guy!" Brynn Castus shouted from her chair in front of the machine shop. She got up and scurried over to their truck to pick up Cade.

"Hey, Ma," Denton said.

"How's CJ been?" Michael asked while hugging Eliana and Denton.

Eliana pinched Cade's cheek and said, "He's really excited for tonight."

"We made a lantern for him and everything. He's going to love it," Michael said.

"Thank you for watching him while we take care of this," Denton said, watching Brynn march off with his son toward their chairs on the porch.

"Hey, anytime. We love having the little guy around," Michael said.

Denton and Eliana said their goodbyes and got back in the truck, watching Michael, Brynn, and Tyler play with Cade as they drove toward the old colony gateway. The gates remained open now; a city guardsman still watched from perches on the old wall only to make sure predators of the forest didn't try to make their way into the city.

The valley between Odysseus City and the scout pavilion remained untouched. Eliana looked through her side rearview mirror as the city shrank behind them, its silhouette outlined by the mountains beyond it. It was a bright, beautiful autumn day, with only a smattering of clouds in the perfect blue sky.

Denton pulled the truck into a parking space that used to be the ground sail corral. Eliana threw on her scout jacket as they walked into the pavilion, passing under the scout motto above the door: "Explorarent, Disce, Docere."

Explore, Learn, Teach.

For the scouts, another tradition was carried out each year on this day. They traveled to the valley and took time to help replenish the landscape, healing it from the destruction that had been caused during the battle with the Siren. They planted trees, cared for the wildlife in the area, and researched how the animals and plants had adapted to the changes in the valley.

The most important task was to determine if the Siren has returned.

"Captain," Carl Gregory greeted Eliana as she walked into the pavilion.

"Everything ready?" Eliana asked.

"Yep, everyone's good to go."

They passed by Jess Combs on their way to the *Rogers*. She looked up from the ancient Russian novel she was reading, *When All Is Lost, the Sun Shall Rise* by Victor Sokolov, Pavel Volkov's favorite book. Pavel had had no children to pass the old story on to, so Jess had taken on the responsibility of maintaining the old paperback for the man who'd saved her life. She had read through the book a few times with the aid of glasses with a translation lens built in.

Jess removed her glasses and tucked the novel into a protective case in her backpack. She joined Denton and Eliana on their way to the ship. Jess was officially their new security escort, the role Captain Roelin Raike had once filled a long time ago.

Denton and Eliana walked through the cabin of the ship. There was a full crew of scouts moving around, many new faces and a few familiar ones.

"Hey, Cap!" Fergus Reid waved. "Biology team is ready to go!"

"Great! We'll be heading out shortly," Eliana said.

"Elly," the soft voice of Faye Raike came from the other side of the *Rogers*. "Did we ever get back that cartographer's orb?"

"Yes, I have it packed away in one of the hover mules."

"Perfect. If I can get ahold of it, I'd like to use it to get some imaging of the craters the *Telemachus* made during impact. I think our geology team will get some useful data."

"It's all yours, Faye." Eliana smiled.

"Thanks. I'll get the team strapped in." Faye walked over to her team of Kamarian geologists, many of whom were auk'nai researchers who'd brought their own unique mining technology with them.

Denton and Eliana stepped into the pilot's cabin of the *Rogers* to find Rocco Gainax and Talulo prepping the ship for launch.

"We're all set back here," Denton said.

"Sounds good—go ahead and tell them, Talulo," Rocco said, jutting his chin toward his auk'nai copilot.

When the auk'nai of Apusticus were being moved to Odysseus

City, Talulo was selected to become an ambassador for his species. He turned down the offer, instead suggesting Galifern guide the auk'nai through their adaptation to life with the humans. He handed Mag'Ro's daunoren staff to Galifern and made her the Song of Apusticus. Talulo no longer had wings, but he had a pilot's license now, and that was close enough. Talulo reached upward and tapped a button.

"Ladies and gentlemen, this is your copilot speaking," Talulo said, mimicking the classic pilot drawl accurately into the microphone, and it broadcasted throughout the Pilgrim-class explorer. "Sit back and enjoy the ride."

"I taught him that one," Rocco winked. Talulo whistled.

Denton and Eliana moved back into the main cabin and buckled their seatbelts. The *Rogers* lifted off the ground, pivoted to the southeast, then launched away into the sky toward the grand valley.

———— ◆ ————

The grand valley had regrown much of the foliage that had made it beautiful before. The nezzarform statues had become part of the planet once more, overgrown with various mosses and ivy. The smaller ships that had been destroyed during the battle had been collected and removed from the valley. Only the *Telemachus* remained, too large to collect and too heavy to move.

The interstellar shipwreck was a permanent fixture in the valley, but the creatures and plant life there didn't seem to mind. A flock of large birds called welkinhawks had made nests inside the open spaces in the crashed ship. Vines and other greenery had begun to grow all over the rusting hull. The Siren's arm, which had gripped the side of the ship as it crashed, had rotted away, picked apart by carrion birds and predators of opportunity, leaving only an immense skeleton eternally latched on to the side of the *Telemachus*.

———— ◆ ————

The team spent the full afternoon investigating, replanting, and researching. As the light from Delta Octantis began to fade, turning the sky a bright pink and orange, it was time to head back to Odysseus City to enjoy the lantern ceremony.

"I'm going to head in and get everyone prepped for launch. I want to make sure we get Cade before the ceremony," Eliana said.

"Good thinking." Denton nodded and watched the sunset.

The scout team piled into the ship, bringing gear and other things they had collected on board. Denton saw Carl Gregory board the ship out of the corner of his eye and nodded, watching the sunset fade closer to darkness. Jess Combs walked up the ramp past Denton, patting his shoulder and smiling as she did so. He smiled back.

"Better get in soon, don't want to keep the wee one waitin' back home," Fergus Reid said as he walked up to the ramp with Carl Gregory.

Denton did a double take; he thought he'd already seen Carl enter the *Rogers*.

"Yeah …" Denton said quietly.

Carl walked up to Denton and said, "Man, I'm tired. I don't even think I'm going to watch the ceremony tonight, I'm just going to go to bed."

"Yeah," Denton said again, eyeing Carl suspiciously.

"See you inside, Dent."

"Yeah …" Denton repeated. He looked out into the valley once more; all the scouts had made it onto the ship except him. Denton considered his déjà vu for a moment longer, then shrugged it off and boarded the *Rogers*. The ship rose, catching the last rays of light from Delta Octantis, then turned and headed back to Odysseus City.

Denton sat down in the main cabin and removed his scout jacket. He still felt uneasy, and Eliana noticed his far-off stare.

"What's up?" she asked.

"Nothing. Just got this weird feeling."

"Oh? Getting sick?"

"Not sure. I might go rest."

"Okay. We have about an hour before we make it back to Odysseus. Get a good nap in." Eliana kissed him on the cheek.

Denton nodded, then moved through the cabin. He saw Carl Gregory sleeping in his seat, his head leaning against the window and his mouth wide open. Denton laughed, thinking the poor guy must have been more tired than he thought.

Denton made it to the crew bunk room and opened the door, where he found someone curled up in one of the beds. His head hurt as he entered the room—a migraine came on fast. Denton rubbed the sides of his head for a moment as his eyes adjusted.

"What the …" Denton whispered to himself. In the bunk was *another* Carl Gregory. Denton furrowed his eyebrows as he scanned this person. Something wasn't right; he could see Carl's face, but it was off. Almost like it was a mask of Carl's face being worn by something else. Denton attempted to get a little closer but stopped himself. The jacket Carl wore wasn't a separate thing. It was part of his body, like a piece of skin.

The thing sat up quickly and turned to him. Its eyes were like marbles, lifeless. Denton stumbled a few steps backward, then drew his collider pistol and aimed it. This thing wasn't Carl.

It was a Kamarian nightsnare.

Denton activated the pistol and kept it on the haunting thing's head. This false Carl opened its mouth to reveal a row of sharp teeth. Denton almost squeezed the trigger when he heard a voice in his mind.

"No! Don't hurt me!"

Denton kept the gun aimed, but almost dropped it in disbelief. *Nhymn.*

The Siren had finally returned after three years of hiding. Here she was, a creature who at one point had been so powerful that she'd almost wiped out humanity, wearing the skin of an animal and begging not to be shot.

"Nhymn?" Denton said in disbelief. The nightsnare pressed itself into the shadowed corner of the bottom bunk. It was like a caged animal, too afraid of the stranger outside to come out. The nightsnare now reflected the image Denton had in his mind of the Siren. Her birdlike beak and sharp horn were as they had been those years ago, and her haunting hollow eye sockets still made Denton's skin crawl. Nhymn looked so small in comparison to the monster they had fought three years prior.

She looked scared.

"Don't shoot," the voice came to his mind again. *"I want to leave this planet. I want to leave you all alone."*

"Why?" Denton asked. Nhymn shrank further into herself and looked away.

The Siren whispered, *"Please, help me. I want to leave. You will never have to worry about me again."*

Denton made his way to the door, keeping his gun trained on Nhymn. He darted his eyes around the room to make sure no one else was inside, then stepped outside and locked the door. Denton had trapped the Siren's body in the dark bunk room, but he knew if she wanted to, she could probably still reach him through the walls.

"Elly, can you come to the bunk room?" Denton whispered into his soothreader comm channel on a direct call.

"Kinky. I'll be right there," Eliana said, and a few moments later, she entered the hallway. "You okay? Denny, you look like you've seen a—"

"Nhymn is in there," Denton whispered. "She's cooperating. She says she wants to leave the planet." Denton paused and added, "She looks terrified."

Eliana froze. Her eyes reflected her worry for the crew. She nodded and said, "I'll make the arrangements. Watch her." She looked Denton in the eye and said, "Shoot her if you have to."

———◆———

The *Rogers* returned to the scout pavilion and unloaded its passengers, all except Eliana, Denton, Jess, Rocco, and Talulo. George Tanaka and General Raughts were waiting when the ramp lowered. Most of the team greeted them on their way off the ship, and Jess Combs stopped and saluted the general.

"At ease," General Raughts said. "Show us the Siren."

Jess nodded, then led them back up the ramp, and the ship took off once more. The *Rogers* sailed quietly over the city. On the ground, people began lighting their floating candles. It was as if the stars were shining below them. The trip wasn't long—just past the city was the *Odysseus* spacecraft.

The *Odysseus* hadn't been used since the first landing day almost a decade prior. It was still functional, but the three-hundred-year journey from the Sol System had taken its toll on the old spacecraft, and thus it was deemed unsafe for human use. Tonight it would not ferry a *human* across the stars, but it would journey still. The *Odysseus* was prepped for launch. Vapor drifted from the sides of the spacecraft, and spotlights lit the ship from all directions. It was a private launch for one special guest.

The *Rogers* landed a kilometer away from the *Odysseus*. The ramp lowered, and General Raughts, Jess, George, Eliana, and Denton disembarked, each with a weapon drawn.

From inside the ship, the nightsnare slowly stepped out into the light. Normally, a nightsnare could only reflect an image back to its prey, unsure of what the mirror even displayed. This unique nightsnare, under Nhymn's control, was able to project whatever image it wanted. The Siren kept her form as she walked down the ramp of the *Rogers*.

They saw her birdlike skull and sharp horn, her tendrils that glistened with moonlight, and her spike-shrouded carapace. Her worm-skin arms and legs terminated in claws of razor-sharp talons. Nhymn stepped all the way down the ramp, then walked ahead of the humans pointing guns at her.

Nhymn's final march.

They made it to the staircase that led to the entryway hatch of the *Odysseus* spacecraft. Denton walked ahead and opened the door. Nhymn looked at him as she entered the ship. He felt like she was thanking him.

Once inside, George moved to the bridge to initiate a launch sequence, and the rest kept their guns on her. After a few moments, George returned and nodded to everyone. One by one, the humans left the spacecraft. Eliana was the last to leave, and she looked the Siren in her empty eye sockets.

"It didn't have to be this way, you know," Eliana said. "We escaped the Undriel years ago. We could have all lived here in harmony if you'd just given us the chance."

The Siren stared right back at Eliana, unflinching. There was silence. Eliana sighed, and as she reached for the door, she heard Nhymn in her mind.

"Do you truly believe that there will be harmony?"

"I do," Eliana said, her hand on the door.

"That must feel wonderful."

There was nothing more to say. Eliana closed the door, watching as the Siren maintained her gaze until the last piece of the hatch closed between them.

The *Odysseus* spacecraft ignited its engines. A powerful thrust shook the windows of the viewing platform. Denton and Eliana watched as the massive spaceship rose into the sky, leaving behind a trail of light and smoke. George had set the ship to launch into the deepness of space, leaving the Siren forever trapped in her prison in the stars.

It was what Nhymn wanted.

———◆———

On the front porch of the Castus Machine Shop, Michael, Jason, and Tyler clinked bottles of beer together.

"How's it going over there, CJ?" Michael asked his grandson. Cade sat in Brynn's lap with a paper lantern in his hand. She helped the young boy place the candle in the harness, then lit it for him. Cade's eyes grew wide when he saw the flame. She helped him hold the candle upward, then they released it together.

Cade smiled as he watched the candle rise into the sky, joining thousands of others much like it. Brynn noticed the trail of light the *Odysseus* spacecraft made as it crossed through the air beyond the lanterns.

"Bye-bye!" Cade waved to his lantern and scrunched his hand.

"Bye-bye," Brynn whispered, smiling.

———◆———

In the grand valley, the wreckage of the *Telemachus* was illuminated by the lights coming from the city to the northwest. The *Odysseus's* light moved through the sky in an arc. On top of the wreckage, a patch of blue flowers began to shine brighter. The ship flew farther and farther out of sight until, eventually, like all things, it faded away. The glowing blue flowers dimmed once more.

Alien insects hummed and chirped in the night. The small lights in the distance combined with the twinkling stars in the sky. The autumn breeze kissed the planet like a lover whispering a secret.

The song of Kamaria was in perfect harmony at last.

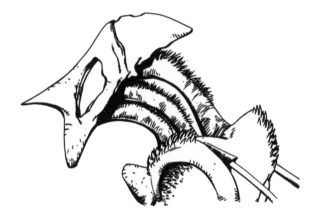

Acknowledgments

First and foremost, to my wife, Carrie Bruno. She not only blessed me with two awesome sons but also put up with me ducking away into my office to write this novel.

To my parents, Rick and Jean Bruno, for encouraging me from the very start to pursue my creativity. This novel began with the comic book I drew in third grade, and has been adapted for more than twenty years into this new world to explore. Without encouragement, none of this would be here.

To Michelle Hope, for bringing legitimacy to this novel. Michelle has done an excellent job making my words work. She was kind, patient, and professional with me the entire project. I hope to work with her again in the future.

To Dylan Garity, who did a fantastic job proofreading. You were great as the last line of defense against the gremlins of bad grammar. I believe this novel to be gremlin free thanks to you.

To Daniel Schmelling, for delivering me the cover art of my dreams. Daniel was great to work with and very attentive to my ideas. I know this cover will turn heads. I love it, thank you.

To Lorna Reid, for bringing everything past the finish line with her excellent formatting.

To Reedsy.com, for bringing each of these freelancers into my circle. I was comfortable using their service to help make my novel worth publishing.

To Jason Hall, for being an overall fantastic collaborator. His interior artwork has been incredible and inspiring. Jason not only provided the amazing artwork you have seen throughout the novel, but he gave me great feedback as a beta reader early on. Thank you for your support, I couldn't have done this without you.

To Jotham Herzon, whose suggestion on a different starting point for the novel led to one of the most significant rewrites, but also one of the most rewarding.

To Dave Bruno, for helping me brainstorm, and for providing the keystone that got the ball rolling.

To Greg Bruno, for creating my Tba! Logo. I put it on everything, I love it!

To Ty Bucek, for proofreading all of my false starts and reviewing the outline. I strayed a little, but I wouldn't have started without your eyes on it first.

To Jim Dunn, for giving me notes involving the chain of command and military rankings of several characters in the novel. If there are any mistakes, they are my own.

To my beta readers: Mom, Jason Hall, Sarah Hale Pierce, Jotham Herzon, Ken Karczewski, Carrie Napoleon, and Jason Scamardo. You were incredibly valuable in finding all the dents in my armor. Thank you for being patient with the early drafts.

To my readers. Thank you for joining me on this adventure. I hope you enjoyed the ride as much as I enjoyed crafting it.

About the Author

T. A. BRUNO has brought stories to life for over a decade as a previsualization artist in the film industry. At home, he is a proud father of two boys and a husband to a wonderful wife.

IN THE ORBIT OF SIRENS is his debut science fiction novel.

———◆———

For more about this book and author, visit

TABruno.com

✦ Facebook.com/TABrunoAuthor

✦ Instagram.com/TABrunoAuthor

✦ Twitter.com/TABrunoAuthor

✦ Goodreads.com/TABrunoAuthor